The Legacy of Lanico: Reclaiming Odana

E Cantu Alegre

To my children Anasofia and Mateo,

Dream big and Do big. Have God-sized aspirations.

You were made in His image. The only *real* limits that exist,

are the ones you place on yourselves.

To Him, in which all of this was possible.

Every breath, every beat, and every step,

thank you, forever,

and ever.

Prologue

King Oetam Cantus Cyntar Loftre ruled over the Odana realm for a great many years. It was a largely successful and peaceful reign. His expansive kingdom had enjoyed much peace, beauty, and prosperity. The citizens enjoyed peace and unity under his sovereignty. Odana was a place where young, carefree WynSprigns could go bounding off, or leap into the towering trees —for fun.

Dividing the landscape, the living and sacred purple-hued Odana Mountains were to the east. They were freckled with deep green trees and flourishing with an array of flora and fauna. Crystal rivers flowed freely throughout, providing abundant life wherever their sparkling waters trickled. His home, the Castle of Odana, was itself a marvel of the ancient's ingenuity.

Carved deeply into a granite mountain and proudly perched upon a cliff, the stone castle's spire defied elevation, demanding in its silence that it remain visible for countless miles. With the exception of its main entrance, the Castle of Odana was almost completely surrounded by a sharp drop-off. Scaling the precipitous walls was almost impossible, *almost*. It was a perfect height and location for a castle, for it discouraged attack. Even those wielding grappling hooks would be dejected at the lack of their effectiveness at finding purchase. An attack would also have proved daunting, for the news had been far-reaching that King Oetam had the most elite armed forces in all the lands as his disposal—the Odana Military.

Beyond the castle, heading west, was the WynSprign village, the hub of their kingdom and frequented by travelers. It held bustling inns, taverns, and various shops – shops that were almost as worthy as those of Prondolin. To the east of the castle and carved further back into the same northern chain of mountains was the Odana Military headquarters, hidden beyond throngs of towering pines.

Overlooking the eastern side sparring area where the Odana Military trained, a high veranda had been sculpted into the castle's side. King Oetam enjoyed languorously, watching his Soldiers and Knights from a throne-like chair whilst they practiced far below. Moving far back, beyond the sparring circle and pines, lay the Odana Military barracks and headquarters. The barracks were a flurry of activity and precise organization.

Not only was their military of highest reputation, but the King purposely surrounded himself with those he held in the highest regard. Several of those nobles included the elders of the present-day Great Mist. The nobles had been the King's trusted friends and advisors for many years and many of them had daughters—daughters who had ambitions to become Queen by way of marriage to General and Prince Lanico Loftre. It had been common knowledge that King Oetam would rule until his own death and never planned to hand over kingship to his only son and heir, Lanico, but rather to Lanico's firstborn son. The King had plans for him to marry a noble born woman, and he felt there were many suitable options.

King Oetam felt himself to be a great ruler and wanted to ensure he reigned over the kingdom for as long as possible and Lanico, however, had always understood he wasn't intended to be King and never questioned his father on this decision. Having the highest position in all their land wasn't enticing to him, especially if it meant that he had to engage with the snobbery that surrounded his father. Therefore, he accepted his positions in the military and in the kingdom, and chose not to ponder it at length. He distanced himself from the royal court and nobility. He remained ever loyal to his father and to the kingdom, and kept Odana as his highest priority, *always*.

In fact, all Lanico's decisions and actions had been consistently for the betterment of the kingdom—he had been trained for this. He was a servant of his father's people and was careful to keep this in mind in all that he did. He was serious and determined to do the will of the kingdom. Though Lanico was years older, the only fun he ever had was with his best friend, Izra.

Izra, sworn brother, was a noble himself and had shown promise at a young age. His father was a high-ranking Odana Knight, therefore he was well trained in weaponry and combat. From the early years-years of which the two appeared around the same in age to anyone, the young men had trained together in almost all things, even in formal dancing.

Though Izra loved the ballroom, especially the waltz, Lanico couldn't quite share that same love. Izra would whirl across the floor with practiced maidens, a charming peacock on display for all the nobility. But Lanico felt himself stumbling and awkward with the same unpretentious patrician girl, not quite as dazzling despite his status and the many eyes that roamed over him.

There were other things as well about his sworn brother that seemed drastically different. Lanico never understood Izra's depthless fascination for magic, either. It was an odd interest that he often balked at himself. They had their differences, but held an undying brotherly love for each other, it so that they became oathed brothers.

In keeping with tradition enforced by his father, when the time was upon him, Lanico entered an arranged marriage. It was a marriage not based on love but rather upon a unity that strengthened his father's ties to other nobility. Lanico was not particularly happy about his betrothal. Complicating matters further, the bride was to be some daughter of his father's Advisor, Trayvor Odmire. Lanico had longed for someone else—for a woman much like himself, ready to spar and full of controlled fury. *A challenge for fire's sake.* Nevertheless, as he accepted many things in his life, Lanico accepted the marriage, for the will of the King for his kingdom, was a greater responsibility.

Lanico met Raya Odmire on their wedding day, as was tradition, at the altar. Her face was unfamiliar, for she had never appeared at any of the royal balls or parties. *Why was this*? Raya was not only beautiful, but had a playful light about her. Lanico was thankful that she looked nothing like her other Odmire family members. Her dark curling tendrils were a stark contrast to the rest of the Odmires' golden manes. She had a bright smile that seemed to appear rather easily and giggled nervously standing next to him, despite the officiator's disapproving glare. Lanico's obedient heart softened for her a little in that moment.

Their single duty was to produce offspring for the throne, and on their wedding night, Lanico found success. His secret Fray bloodline allowed him to know the moment of conception. However, after that night, out of frustration over the arranged marriage, and denying himself the love he secretly longed for, Lanico chose to busy himself with duties that seemed significant but had brought him little satisfaction. He placed himself away from her. He trained the Knights, patrolled, and assisted his father with Kingly decisions. He gave himself to the kingdom fully, and purposely increased his share of responsibility.

Months passed and the time came for Raya to give birth. Lanico had been stationed near the southern Odana Mountains. A rider told him that he was urgently needed back at the castle. Immediately, Lanico rode home, but upon his return to the castle, the somber energy felt like the terrifying cold prison of a tomb. No one had to say it. He already knew.

Racing through the castle and up the stairs, he arrived at Raya's bedchamber. Servants' downcast faces greeted him in the hallway and they wrenched open the door for him. Inside the smell of burning tallow candles greeted his nose. And on the bed - Lanico's breath caught at this. On the bed, Raya lay with a small wrapped bundle in her still arms. The room was dark save for the dim candlelight.

Everything in Lanico's body rejected going further into this room, tensed against it, yet, through cold nerves, he pressed forward. As he neared, he could see Raya's soft face was pale, paler than his own. Blue, almost. In her arms . . . Lanico shuddered . . . a son—Tyren, the nursemaid named him. He was fashioned in Raya's likeness, and his small body was still as well. Lifeless.

Lanico felt his knees give out under him. His heart sank. He collapsed and wept on the stone floor. He had failed in his duty to the kingdom. Failed in his duty as a husband and father, and more. At an unknown hour later, when he emerged from the chambers, he emerged broken, and would remain so.

He dismissed the doled platitudes and blamed himself for her death and the death of their son. With his hidden capabilities, he could have helped her, saved her - saved Tyren even. In the following days, the kingdom quickly handled Raya's death in the traditional way: the funeral, the customary time of recognized bereavement, and then it was back to business. It was all too formal, too quick. His marriage to Raya had endured for less than a year.

Lanico hardened himself. He had learned, it seemed, that her death was a consequence of the royal marriage. She was used to create an heir, and with feigned emotion from those around him and the brevity of it all, it seemed she was not important for much more than that. He was guilty of this as well, in playing the leading part in this betrayal. He was filled with deep regret over his lack of love for Raya and his failing to stand for something more. To honor her, he commissioned a painting of his late Princess to hang above the fireplace in his main chamber, something to remind him when he woke every morning. It was the least that he could do for her. To remember her.

~

Five years had passed and so much had changed. So much had happened in that time, but on *that* day, the black flags of mourning were flying from the castle buttresses to commemorate the fifth anniversary of Raya and Tyren's deaths. On that day Grude, the infamous Mysra leader, requested a visit. It was no secret what he so greatly desired. All who lived in those days had heard of Grude and his love for trillium. When he arrived, he boldly asked King Oetam for access to the Odana Mountains. The Mysra had an insatiable addiction to trillium, and Grude would do everything in his power to keep this purple mineral for his people, for himself. There would be no secret—he told King Oetam that he wanted to mine for precious trillium, furthering his people's addiction. Grude did not waste time mincing his words, or offering over-the-top niceties:

"The operation won't take up much space—perhaps just one mountain?" Grude made the request in a deceivingly humble manner, holding his low, sweeping bow for moments longer than necessary.

King Oetam twirled at his long white-red beard and thought over the unexpected request. He was cautious at such dealings, especially knowing this Mysra as a tyrant.

"We could pay you handsomely with gold," the bowing Grude continued with his nasally voice.

While King Oetam sat thinking over this proposal, Trayvor Odmire approached him and suggested in a whispered voice—that was still loud enough for anyone close enough to hear—that the King consider Grude's generous offer. "Having gold *would* enhance your riches, Sire. It would help the whole kingdom and our armed force, especially since General Prince Lanico will not be producing an heir soon. You'll need to keep the wealth and use your influence to lure another noble family to arrange a marriage with him." *As I've already donated my own daughter to him*, Odmire thought sadly, sliding his eye to the vacant spot where General Prince Lanico should have been standing, but wasn't.

Overhearing Trayvor, Grude let a slight smile spread on his humbly lowered face.

Gold. Gold plundered from neighboring realms and kingdoms by the Mysra these past years, no doubt, the King considered. This was why he himself had increased the number of his own forces over the last several years.

Major Stoutwyn Stoutlet, who at times served as Second Advisor in addition to Trayvor, was also in attendance, along with a number of additional Knights, and winced overhearing the proposal, for Trayvor's words stung his friend the King. It was true that Lanico would have to produce an heir, but King Oetam didn't need to think about ordering his son into another marriage. Not just yet. For they, and only they, knew of the General Prince's lengthy abundance of time.

On the other hand . . . King Oetam leaned forward, considering. He was wise to the effects of trillium on the Mysra. He knew all too well that they'd use up all the trillium and seek to use the other mountains in his kingdom once the western ridge had been decimated—the Mysra always left destruction in their wake. Their desire for the purple mineral was unappeasable; thanks to their leader and the control, it created for him. The Mysra were like locusts swarming over the Odana. Moreover, there was another reason that glimmered at the back of his mind. It was only after that sobering thought that he answered:

"I hear your bid, Grude, leader of the Mysra, and after brief consideration, I have decided not to grant this request. We haven't need of gold, and our purple mountains are most precious to us. We enjoy them unspoiled. The mountains and lands are alive in this part of the world, and they are connected to a host of other creatures that thrive with their well-being." The King's heart beat faster as he considered a specific being that he did not want to enrage. He had, after all, already broken his promise to her.

Grude remained under control, but inside seethed. He managed a small smile that was more like a grimace. He was a small Mysra compared to the others, but his cunning and persona made him an enthusiastic and strategic leader for his violent throngs of Mysra, and his smaller size made him deceptively unthreatening.

"I thank you, King Oetam, for hearing my request," he said simply.

"I thank you Grude, for your understanding," the King replied.

Grude bowed a small short bow and quickly turned to stride out from the castle, his warriors flanking him on the way out. His anger quickly boiled and fed his existing hatred for not only WynSprigns in general, but for King Oetam in particular. He stormed out and did not return—until a few days later.

~

Unknown to the Odana inhabitants, Grude had brought with him a sizable army that remained hidden in the woods beyond the southern ridge. The likes of his army weren't conceivable to General Prince Lanico, Lieutenant

General Izra, the 'Emerald Knight' Second Lieutenant Treva, nor to any of their other Lieutenant ranked Knights and Soldiers in arms.

These past years, by the hundreds, the Odana Military had slaughtered the Mysra forces in battles throughout the lands, and were confident the Mysra had little manpower remaining. There long persisted a mystery how so many countless droves of Mysra warriors came that day. The way they had descended upon the kingdom at precisely the perfect time was unimaginable.

The seizure of the Odana Kingdom seemed too perfect to have been coincidence. It was too well planned for even the wily Grude to have been the mastermind. Something more had been at work. Something far darker.

Chapter One

Present Day

None of them realized it was going to be this severe, this intense. *Oh fires . . .* and he was furious!

Lanico clenched his fists beneath his cloak, hiding them from judging view. He hated having to leash the near-boiling anger that coursed from his gut. He could almost feel the heat of it, licking his neck and brow with every throbbing heartbeat.

The council met once every full moon. For the past one hundred years, that had always been the way. But not a single elder, including Lanico himself, had ever considered they must deal with the type of issue raised this evening. It was, by far, the most concerning they had ever had.

The four leaders sat about the fire. There was not a careless gaze, not a hint of a smile made. The intensity was dense enough to cut through.

It was bound to happen—this meeting, this *topic*.

Trayvor, the former Advisor to King Oetam, glared at Lanico, a blazing furnace in his eye, "If you don't tell him to straighten-up, he WILL be banished from the Great Mist," Trayvor barked. He looked to the other two elders, who remained silent, uncomfortable, then continued: "Unlike *others*, I don't care if he is your ward, Lanico!" His teeth glinted in the firelight. "*I'm* the one that spotted him beyond the boundary, and *I'm* the one honest enough to say he'll bring danger to us ALL!" His antipathy against the General Prince was palpable and always had been. His resentment against Lanico for not caring enough for Raya, his deceased daughter, intensified into hatred after she and their infant son, Tyren died They were Trayvor's would-be royal kin, and they would have paved him a way further into the castle.

The brief moment following Trayvor's tirade was silent but for crackling wood and a few distant owls at their nightly calls. Fenner, the former Odana Military Chief, exhaled sharply, and the former Major and Second Advisor Stoutwyn shuffled his feet. They all were quite uncomfortable with this, with all of it.

Lanico's jaw clamped, his features now more angled in his tension. *Marin isn't my 'ward', he is my own adopted son. My son! It has been years!* He controlled the rising urge to jolt forward and hammer a fist into Trayvor's lifted chin. *I'll get him, too . . . get him to kiss the ground.*

But no.

Fiery ash flurried toward the sky as a charred log rolled in the fire and brightened it. The next seconds seemed an eternity. Remembering himself, his position, his training, Lanico straightened on the stump he sat on and restrained the roaring inside. He had over a hundred years' experience challenging Trayvor, and, consequently, snuffing out the anger he summoned. One hundred years. That thought alone was enough to set a weight in his stomach and stun him. Glaring at the flames, he understood he himself was the better man, and he had long held greater responsibility.

Lanico broke focus from the flames and steadied his gaze into Trayvor's fire-glossed eyes. The slight creases around Lanico's eyes deepened, the anger stilled. "You banish my son, ANY of you, and you'll have to answer to me." His voice resonated deep and confident: "I don't take easy to talk of banishment. Only we are old enough to remember what's out there and what we recall . . . is a death sentence." He shook his head slowly. "No. There are other ways to deal with his misdeeds—not banishment."

"Banishment has been a rule since we settled here," Trayvor said, closing his eyes smugly with a slow blink. Hearing only silence, he opened his eyes to view Lanico's seasoned warrior's glare upon him and considered the horrific possibilities behind that glare. The seemingly ageless half-breed General was visibly controlling his fury. Suddenly, wisely, Trayvor felt uneasy. "Hmpf!" he retorted simply. There was no contest with Lanico, not with that—that death stare still piercing into him.

Trayvor glanced at everyone, his scouring expression flared by the fire. "Right." He grumbled. He wasn't going to lower himself, to reason with the half-breed—too wild to tame. *Fires to him and his heathen ward!* He whirled from them, swinging his cloak around him, grabbed his walking stick, and without delay stomped off through the earthen path and brush heading back to the village. His thick legs and feet kicked up dirt at his stride.

He glowered back briefly with his WynSprign glowing eyes. "You'll regret it, not choosing banishment." His voice faded in their minds as he stomped off. From over his shoulder he yelled out, "Wisdom over brawn!"—getting in the last word in his defeat.

Stoutwyn and Fenner held their gazes uncomfortably at the fire in front of them. It was a mutual instinct to avoid eye contact. They shifted their weight uneasily on their designated wooden tree stumps. Lanico's anger could be frightening, more than most, and the three of them including Trayvor, were the only ones who knew why. Though they all had long been considered equals, it was difficult to watch Lanico being blasted at and so disrespectfully by Trayvor, and over such a delicate matter.

"Well!" said Fenner suddenly, hoping to end his share of discomfort, "I guess we accomplished a lot this even'." He smirked. "Oh, we'll sort this all out in the morn'n'." There was silence. He nodded after the lack of response, and then stood to stretch his thin body, his dark brass-toned skin accentuated by the blazing flames.

It was late. Certainly too late for this level of debate.

Still stretching, Fenner raised his thin arms high. "Oh, Lan . . . don't go glomering on so. Ya know that Trayvor has always been a bit . . . well, hasty." He paused and stifled a yawn. "I'm treading on home now. Good even' to you both." He bowed, slightly, a forgotten sign of respect for Lanico, their General Prince—if indeed those titles still applied. He turned to march toward his home quite a stroll away, his mane of hair bouncing with his strong strides.

Lanico turned his glance away from Fenner and gave the seated Stoutwyn a forlorn look, his Fray face only paler in the night. It was just the two of them now. Stoutwyn and Lanico had been friends since before the seizure of the Odana Kingdom. Lanico had always had good sense and taken Stoutwyn's advice, just as his deceased father Oetam had.

Stoutwyn looked reassuringly at Lanico. "Now, c'mon now, Lan, Marin was caught not following the rules . . . again. Why must he wander outside of our Great Mist realm?" It was more of a statement than a question. Their realm had been kept secret, protected, all these years. Stoutwyn scratched his head. "We know that he's not a bad young WynSprign, but he must be dealt with in a way that teaches the others . . . He is not above our rules, you know?" He held his floog out on his knee.

Lanico leaned toward Stoutwyn, stretching his long body. His elbows rested on his knees and he cradled his forehead with one hand, as the other hung low. He turned through his curtained hair, grimacing at Stoutwyn. "But banishment?" he asked, his teeth glinting from the blaze.

"I know, that was a bit extreme," Stoutwyn puffed around his pipe stem. "We all know that Trayvor is a bit quick to speak."

"—And slow to think," finished Lanico, a slight smile lifting the corners of his mouth.

"Aye!"—Stoutwyn blew out smoke quickly— "And it's not as though we can contain the young lad. But," he rationalized, "something must be done, Lan." His stare was uncommonly serious. "Something . . ."

"Stout, you and I both know that if Trayvor weren't here, this conversation of banishing Marin wouldn't be taking place . . ." He raised his voice. "It's been over a hundred years since he was advising at my father's side, and he *still* holds my heritage against me. He *still* seethes that I chose to adopt Marin—claiming him as my heir. He still blames me for . . ." Lanico felt his pulse quicken and throb. *No, I blame himself for that too.*

"Aye. Trayvor blames you for *everything*." Stoutwyn knowingly interjected.

Lanico swallowed against the truth in that statement, but he continued, "It has been obvious that—that swine still secretly wishes he could be King." *Damn him!* A rumble of distant thunder growled over some far-off place. Stoutwyn remained silent, giving short nods as response.

In the silence, Lanico Loftre, the General and Prince of Odana, sighed pensively. Marin himself only complicated the matter and Lanico was allowing his temper to get the better of him. They were past the days when Marin would come to him after falling and seek a kiss on an elbow to heal the scrapes. No, Marin was old enough to rebel and try to escape from their secret forest realm.

"I'll talk to Marin about this in the morning," Lanico breathed, looking back to the fire, glowing ash still lifting toward the sky. "He's probably asleep by now." He paused. "I'll let him know that if he is caught again, he will face banishment. It seems the options are limited and we are *well* over the limit on his attempts."

"That's the way, Lan." Stoutwyn nodded again through smoke. "He'll listen this time."

Lanico reasoned with himself. It hadn't been easy, being the only guardian for Marin all these years. He tried his best, always. *Tomorrow's talk will go all right,* he reassured himself. He would convince Marin to stay in their territory, or so he hoped. He felt a sense of calm return and slid his gaze and his infectious smile to a weary Stoutwyn seated next to him. "Your turn!" he called out suddenly.

In one quick streak, Lanico leapt straight onto the high tree branch above them. Though years older than all of them, he remained youthful with his Fray heritage and still seemed young enough to be the son of any of them. Some had begun to have their suspicions about Lanico's heritage—there had always been rumors. He shrugged them off, as all his fellow elders did—it was their sworn duty of course, one of the last ones. Even Trayvor upheld the trust. They would take to their death the identity of Lanico's holy Fray mother.

Lanico quickly began to climb off into the dark night toward his section of the Great Mist.

Stoutwyn could hear him laughing as his voice faded into the darkness above and stood looking up at the branches. He grumbled, "Pfft. That show-off"—he waved his thick hand in the air with annoyance— "leaping about like a crazed squirrel . . ." He picked his way to a nearby pool of water for the fire bucket and doused the fire. Their glowing meeting site immediately blackened in the night.

Stoutwyn's eyes flickered with a dim glow in the newfound dark.

~

Lanico approached the heavy wooden door to his home, a simple house carved into the side of a tall hill covered with living trees. Ancient tree roots supported the interior walls to the home he shared with Marin. The door gave a low moan as it opened, revealing the still and quiet that lay within. Without the aid of moonlight, the interior was dark. Lanico's eyes were glowing lightning blue in the enveloping darkness. He left the door open for only a moment so the bright moonlight could show him the candle on the thick wooden table by the door. Once lit, the candle illuminated the small kitchen and eating area. He removed his green cloak, hung it on a small hook, and closed the door.

The candlelight hinted at the sitting room hidden beyond, and faint light gleamed on his sword that hung on the wall there. He ran his fingers through his long, silver hair, whispering, "What to do with Marin, what to do with Marin . . ." He moved with caution, for the young WynSprign would be asleep in his den.

Lanico's boots thudded softly against the wooden floor planks as he entered the sitting room and cleared a small stool from his path with his foot. The scrolls resting on the stool rolled and bounced onto the floor mat below.

Lanico sank into troubled thought on his favorite chair, his arms along the armrests. The wall behind him displayed his sizable collection of weapons around the sword, all well used in practice and in combat. The staffs had scuffs and dents and the swords were dull, with thousands of tiny scratches from countless strikes. Reluctant Leader, as Lanico called it, was the sword he wielded as the Odana General Prince. He was *still* the crowned Prince of the WynSprings. The sword was truly the most prized item in their simple earthen home, recalling his rank in days long past. Constructed from the finest steel in all the world and Lanico kept the Reluctant Leader razor-sharp. Despite the countless strikes it had endured, not a blemish or mark marred it. It was perfect, made of a rare steel available only to royalty, cryntanium.

Lanico had become accustomed to the silence of his home these years. Marin was often wandering outdoors and leaping into trees—and lately, leaping into trouble. He had tried to raise Marin as best as he could, but the circumstances were quite different from when he lived in the castle. There, they would have had ample assistance; cooks, maids, tutors, trainers, and of course his own Fray mother, who would stop by occasionally. Here in the wilds, there had been none of this.

The responsibility of raising Marin had also come to Lanico for the sake of his friends Lieutenant General Izra and Second Lieutenant, "Emerald Knight" Treva, Marin's late parents.

"Treva," he breathed. Closing his eyes and seeing details of her lovely face now etched in memory. *What would she have thought about all of this?* He had no living offspring, but having raised Marin as his own since the boy's birth; he would see to it that Marin was next in his line for the throne. He whispered to the lost love who wasn't there, "I could get it back for him—the people of Odana will need a respectable King, after all." He took another slow breath and continued, "And unlike my mother, I—I won't be around forever."

He felt a lump rising in his throat. Open, his eyes glowed cyan again. He thought about the staggering odds of returning and claiming the throne, and immediately brushed this dream aside. *Who am I kidding? General Prince Lanico died during the Battle of Odana, as well as did any chance of reclaiming the throne.* It was a nice dream, however pointless.

He glanced down to spot a scroll just at his foot. "But, that's a thought for another day . . ." he muttered quietly. The past hurt too much to deal with, every memory a sharp blade. Without an army, or even a sizable group of trained warriors, any plans to take back the throne would be a fool's dream.

He quieted his painful thoughts and swallowed hard against the stone in his throat. His face hardened and he moved onward, inscribing on the scroll the events of the night's elder meeting, as if it were somehow more important.

Chapter Two

The breeze filled and stirred the trees, the soft blast sending tens of thousands of leaves in a mighty rush upward. They clambered against their unseen, but genuinely felt, foe—the wind. The expansive branches of the great oaks gave low groans in response to the surrounding power. High and away from the everyday repetitive life below Marin perched where he often sought refuge in this great tree. He called this particular tree Girtha for her formidable size and menacing height. Girtha's large trunk gave way to thick roots below, roots so large they supported walls for the tavern beneath—the tavern that would supply his dinner tonight.

It was here, up in the air, up in the trees, where he felt truly free. Up here there was enough room and open space to let his mind go. He smiled. Tendrils of sweet smelling, sap-scented air and filled his lungs. Mornings following the mysterious meetings, Lanico slept in—sparing Marin from practice. Since he could remember, Lanico had made sure that Marin practiced at sword sparring several times a week. They practiced for hours, wielding swords and wooden staffs and leaping into trees. His own skills paled in comparison. Lanico's skills had been honed over the many years he served the Odana Kingdom and moved himself up in ranks to General. He had served many more years than Marin had been alive.

It was common knowledge that Lanico was not Marin's father by blood, even though Lanico had been the only father the youth had known. His guardian, Lanico, had encouraged Marin to call him by his preferred name, Lanico. He made it clear he did not intend to take Izra's place as a father, but in training, he *did* voice expectation that he would teach Marin as well as he had trained Izra. He often encouraged Marin that with hard work and training, perhaps he too could develop into a great warrior. Lanico and Izra had trained for many years together. Izra, before his death, was his second in command - his Lieutenant General. Though Lanico had mentioned that Marin's skill was improving, Marin still wasn't convinced that he could gain that prowess.

Therefore, he preferred inactivity and to daydream, when given the opportunity.

Today especially, Marin wanted to stay clear of home to avoid a lecture from Lanico, since Trayvor had spotted him outside the realm . . . again. Until he could escape from the Great Mist, even if only a few hours, Marin's heart would yearn and pull for something else . . . but for *what*? He did not know. He felt this deep yearning and pleading rise from his very soul. He needed something else outside this life in the Great Mist. He knew that there was something more beyond their borders. He couldn't figure out what it was and that pull, that yearning—it was beginning to make him feel anxious.

There wasn't much else to bid his time. Marin hadn't worked on a trade yet. He had no interest in woodworking with the Stoutlet clan, nor hunting with Fenner Bricklebury's prized sporting grandsons, especially Freck who always seemed to make him the butt of one odd joke or another. Marin's hands clenched the branches tightly as he thought over this. "Freck can't even leap . . . none of them can," he mumbled low. Marin was beginning to feel trapped at his prospects.

He straightened; suddenly he noticed a deep blue figure bumbling into view below. *Trayvor*, he thought, making a wry expression—*a pain in the rump for both Lanico and me.*

Trayvor hobbled over the uneven ground to the tavern far beneath Marin. He wore his usual weathered dark blue cloak, holding a portion of it draped over his arm to avoid getting it muddied. His other hand clutched tightly his trusted cane, and of course, he wore his customary smug face. *Always.*

Trayvor graced the humble tavern with his presence frequently, finding contentment only at the bottom of a large wooden mug of ale. He had been mighty in his day, strong and a noble, but those days were gone, and his painfully hobbling knees showed everyone he was no longer robust.

Watching that cantankerous man below made it difficult for Marin to believe the old stories.

Before the overthrow, Trayvor had worked at King Oetam's side, as his trusted Advisor, Lanico had once told Marin. Trayvor ever wanted more responsibility and power and had always been envious of Lanico as King Oetam's son and only living heir. Marin once heard him grumble about Lanico, "Such a privilege and power shouldn't have been wasted on a quiet, introverted WynSprign like him." Even now, Trayvor remained bitter. The Great Mist that he had secretly hoped extraordinary things for, was not the Great Mist it had turned out to be.

Trayvor selected one of many vacant tables outside, all equally well visited and weatherworn, so the selection wasn't difficult. He leaned his trusty walking stick against the chosen table, and his great heft made the thick chair creak beneath him as he lowered his weight onto it. He looked around with a sour face, signaling his impatience. Maybell, the tavern's bubbly serving maid, hurried out and greeted him by promptly setting a large wooden mug of ale in front of his waiting hands. The routine had been practiced countless times, and he handed her a small coin. She smiled, showing her dimples, and quickly made a small bow that jiggled the mop of her dark, curly hair. She hurried away without a sound.

Trayvor's expression remained unchanged, but Marin found himself smiling down at her even from his great elevation in the tree. It seemed only Trayvor was resistant to Maybell's charm.

Marin took a sharp breath—startled—as he spotted a figure almost out of view. It was a thin wafer of a shadow near a tree across from the tavern, at Ms. Bre Bricklebury's home. The person was not hidden but almost invisible in the shade, and still. It wasn't clear whether the dark-hooded figure was looking up at him, or across the way, at the tavern. *Who is this?*

As if sensing the presence himself, Trayvor looked over, then beckoned the shadowed figure over to the table. Marin watched intently. Without sound, or notice from the few in the area, the man drifted over, then he and Trayvor talked in hushed voices. Normally Marin wasn't a fan of eavesdropping, but he had unusually good hearing, and though his guardian would disapprove, this *was* a mysterious situation unfolding below. He leaned in a little . . .

Trayvor looked nervous and glanced around a bit. He took back a big slug of ale and whispered loudly, wetness on his breath, "Okay . . . tell me, what news comes from Odana?" He leaned forward, wiping his mouth with his forearm, setting the heavy mug down with a thud.

The hooded man replied, in a thinner voice, "Well, it seems Odana continues to be occupied by Mysra. Grude has plundered the trillium from the purple mountains for his own power. Taking advantage of the WynSprigns' natural resistance to the effects of trillium, he continues to use the remaining ones to slave in his mining works and forces them to toil endlessly."

Trayvor seemed oddly unmoved by this horrific news, as if he had heard it before. In a thick whisper he replied, "Okay, thank you, trustworthy friend." Looking around, then back at the informant, he said, "Now's not the time to go into too much detail about plans. At sunup tomorrow, let's meet at Horse's Clearing, just outside the boundary, where there's more . . . privacy."

His companion nodded in silent answer. He looked around before slipping away into the trees from where he had come. The unassuming Maybell returned to the table with another mug. Curiously, no one else had been around to spot Trayvor's mysterious friend.

Marin thought this was most interesting. Horse's Clearing was just outside of the Great Mist boundaries, and it was where secret, a trusted outside Prondolin merchant would meet with a clan leader—usually Trayvor—to exchange money or goods for things that weren't available in the Great Mist. It was a rare occurrence that he'd venture this way, but Trayvor monitored the clearing daily nonetheless.

Though it was against the rules, Marin was one of the very few WynSprigs that had seen Horse's Clearing before, though he had never witnessed the surreptitious trading that took place there. He was dazzled at the expanse of golden grass that grew there and wondered what mysteries lay beyond it.

Marin sat in his tree, in awe at this conversation, at the mysteriousness of it all, and at the horrendous thought of *slavery*. Those few spoken sentences were much to absorb.

Chapter Three

Lanico sat in his study, documenting events of the day, and of the details of the meeting, and . . . he still needed to talk to Marin. His hands went still, holding the quill, his eyes fixed, deep in thought, the top of the scroll curled over his ink-stained fingertips. His life here had been so different from what he would have imagined for himself all those years ago when he lived as a General Prince. It never would have occurred to him that he would have this life, here, in the wilderness of the Great Mist.

His thoughts swirled, placing him back in time, back with Marin's father, Izra. Those last moments together, still raw.

Lanico fought with his whole soul—with everything he had. He always did. The sounds of shouts and the high-pitched twang of swords still rang in his ear. He could still feel the tingling within, *still*, after all these years. Reluctant Leader sang, clashing steel to steel with Izra's own sword at practice. The now-wall-mounted Reluctant Leader flashed a reflection of candle flame from the desk.

Together they had witnessed the great battle, this fight to keep their kingdom, and had themselves, taken many Mysra lives. Lanico's throat knotted at the thought of his father, King Oetam of the Odana, dying in their castle home. He trembled recalling the image of Treva's unmoving body. Of the arrow that extended from her side. Lanico's eyes welled as he recalled the lifeless weight of Izra in his arms. He was Izra's oathed brother, and Izra his Lieutenant General, his most trusted. Devastation gripped him.

Lanico held Izra firm against his own armored chest as his friend's warm blood rushed from the back of his head, making Lanico's hand slippery under the wet tangles. Time was short, and Izra's wounds beyond healing, and there it was, his friend took his last breath on the battlefield that day.

Lanico still felt the slick black tangled hair between his fingers, the warmth of his ragged breath as he held him close. The smell of grass and coppery blood were *still* real. In those final moments, Izra had made Lanico swear to take the infant Marin in as his own.

Countless of years of training turned against Lanico in that moment. He had never actually considered his friend, *dying*. He never considered the way he'd handle this type of blow.

His eyebrows raised, Lanico felt his heart sink when Izra told him from pale blood-splattered lips that Treva had fallen. Lanico's thoughts spun and he felt a crack deep inside his chest. His eyes darted, searching surrounding the chaos for emerald green, and failing. *Too many bodies lying about. Too many . . .* His stomach lurched and his mouth quivered, denying him a scream at this revelation. Though forbidden by all standards, he had always secretly loved her.

Time is short, the voice whispered again into his mind.

He managed a sharp inhale and regained his focus onto Izra. "I promise my brother," he said through stiffened lips. The sob at the back of his throat threatened to escape. He hated these words. *Hated*. Dreaded what was taking place.

Izra responded in a rasping voice, almost too faint, "Thank y . . ." And, after one slow blink when time itself stilled, he allowed himself loose from his body and became limp. A long, misty exhale rose between them. Izra's lips slackened.

Lanico shook his head. The reality of the moment struck him, a thunderbolt to the heart. Izra, his friend, his brother, died.

He felt his stomach churn, and his lips stretched in a grimace. *No.*

He inhaled hard.

"NO!" A bellow loosed, fire rushing in his veins.

His heart pounded, even now, all these years later. He remembered the brief moments following, the panic he had felt. His racing heart. He had to find Treva. Because Marin was newly born, she would have him somewhere close to her. And by then, Lanico already knew . . . the castle had been breached.

Time is running out! The voice was now shouting.

"Close. He has to be close. He has to be close."—chanting under his breath. Numbing panic engrossed him.

With squelching steps through the blood of the battlefield, he moved over lifeless bodies, searching, Reluctant Leader drawn. Within seconds his eyes landed on her, on Treva, the Knighted, the Second Lieutenant, slain only steps away from her husband but almost hidden behind another. Her arm and hand, outstretched, reaching – for him. She was near, just as Izra had said.

Lanico had to step back a few paces. He recognized her emerald hair flowing over the trampled grass, her lifeless body still glorious in her shiny armor. It was too late to help her. From a distance, she looked merely asleep, save for the arrow in her side. Lanico noticed her trademark tooth necklace loosely hanging around her neck, gleaming in the sun. Going closer to her, he couldn't bring himself to look at her face, avoiding the paralyzing stare that he wouldn't be able to break himself free from. He knelt and yanked the necklace from her—for Marin.

Time is running out! The voice screamed.

Lanico stood and whirled, looking. His best soldiers were dwindling in number, by the second. There! The bushes—she would have found a nearby hiding place amongst the brambles. Just then the purple glint of Marin's tiny eyes sparkled, as if in confirmation, from within the bushy cover. Lanico sighed in relief. Marin was only just newly borne, days old. It was only by the grace of Odan that Marin wasn't loosing a newborn's wail at that moment and betraying himself.

Holding Marin against his chest, Lanico looked at the atrocities taking place in every direction as the Mysra slaughtered the WynSprign warriors by the dozens. So many of his Soldiers trying to aid the subjects were made vulnerable, and taken down. He was panic-stricken. In shock. So many of his people had been captured, and their screams of terror echoed a nightmare that made him blink feverishly, as if to wake. The surrounding grounds were littered with the bodies of dead WynSprigns and some Mysra. *I need to go, to help, but . . .* He glanced at the baby cradled against him.

Major Stoutwyn had proved himself levelheaded through this disaster. After spotting him, he advanced to Lanico, breaking his bewilderment with shouts that roared in the General Prince's ear. They needed to move quickly, to gather the nearby remaining WynSprigns to flee—to leave Odana.

Leave Odana?

He knew they had to find safe ground, fast—away from their trillium-filled mountains. Away from the promise of death. He had to move quickly before he and the baby, were discovered and claimed by the Mysra - to whatever fate.

Stoutwyn demanded they head northeast, into the cover of an ancient wilderness. The Great Mist.

Lanico was beside himself with grief at the loss of his father, Izra, and Treva, but all he could muster was a nodded response. He stiffened his countenance and moved quickly, joining Stoutwyn in gathering the remaining, nearby WynSprigns. He fled.

Lanico lost a great deal that day. He lost his family legacy, the throne, his subjects, land, titles, his desire to lead, his beloved Treva, and his soul friend, Izra. He had only Marin now to care for, and the saved WynSprigns.

With a pounding heart, Lanico found himself suddenly whirled back to his present. His candle flickered. He heard something . . .

Chapter Four

Marin slowly opened the thick, weatherworn door of their home. It opened hesitantly with a loud, deep creak, releasing the warmth inside. He grimaced— he was caught now.

"Marin! Is that you?" Lanico called from the other room. "Listen, I'd like to have a word with you . . . Please come over and sit for a moment." Lanico sniffed and righted himself in his chair as he cleared through the lump in his throat. Regality and stoicism—his way. He wouldn't acknowledge the trembling of his fingers and instead, focused on the wall that Marin was hidden beyond.

"Yes, Lanico." Marin already knew what this was about. He had this talk before. Suddenly his legs felt heavy and his shoulders drooped at the prospect of having to meet with his guardian in the sitting room.

He leaned back to close the heavy door, then slowly made his way to where Lanico waited. The welcoming walls held sketches of a Fray rendered in yellow dandelion pigment. Other sketches showed galloping horses that seemed to glide over yellowed grasses. These were all things that Lanico claimed to have seen in his years. Though as dull as the older man had seemed, other than on the sword-training ground, Marin didn't quite believe it.

Lanico sat in the large cedar chair, the largest in their home. His long silver hair faintly reflected the flickering candles in the room. It was dim, and the glow of his azure eyes, fixed on the scroll upon his lap. He had been writing. In this place, Lanico diligently wrote about the rules and daily occurrences of the Great Mist, to keep track of them.

As disciplined and wise as Lanico was, his home was not quite a reflection of this inner orderliness. It wasn't that the home was dirty, but rather disorganized. When he wasn't practicing at weapons with Marin, or on patrol, Lanico was usually numbed and preoccupied in thought. All his effort didn't leave time for housekeeping. Honestly, it was not his priority. He'd place tables and chairs in various places as the notion came to him to stop and write down notes. Because Lanico was ever lost in his writing and in his thoughts, it seemed the countless wandering scrolls, writing quills, and furniture never had a permanent placement in their home.

Marin slowly approached, minding the small table and chairs that blocked his way. He chose a stool across from Lanico and looked down at the woven mat beneath as he sat. It was a tired and well-used mat, familiar to his feet and to the multitude of random scattered scrolls. It was a comfort, being home after having spent the day roaming about their village. The stew from the tavern he had filled himself on earlier still weighed in his gut. He was ready to turn in. *Hopefully, Lanico will make this lecture a quick one.*

Marin's eyes strayed to the one item in the home that dismissed age and dust—Reluctant Leader. Lanico's large silver sword was never dull or tired-looking and gleamed as usual this evening, in the firelight; placed on its proper mounting on the wall. Marin often felt the sword was watching him. He didn't like to hold it, practice with it, or actually touch it at all. Every attempt sent a tingling sensation that made the hair on his arms prickle.

Lanico began in his usual calm and proper tone after first clearing away the recent sadness from his throat. "Marin, you have been spotted again outside our realm." He wanted to avoid appearing angry—in fact, more than angry he was fearful. He needed to convey the importance of this message but Lanico had difficulty disciplining Marin and he knew it, and Marin knew it . . . everyone knew it. Of course, Marin was the perfect combination of Lanico's two most-loved comrades. With unspoken command, Lanico moved with authority wherever he went and with whomever he encountered—Marin was his only true weakness.

"Now . . . I know that we've had this talk before, Marin. I know this is far from your first time sneaking out—I am not *that* dull." Lanico gave him a sly but knowing look.

"But—" Marin started.

"No, please," Lanico interjected, raising a weary hand. "Please listen carefully to me."

He drew a calming breath and paused. "Alright"—he slapped his thighs— "I have fought to protect you at our meetings—several times now. The rule has *always* been banishment if one is caught wandering outside the Great Mist. I have rejected this form of punishment for others, and especially for you—*my* son. Others who were caught wandering close to the border took heed and obeyed, so fortunately we've never had to enforce this rule. They seemed to understand the great danger outside our boundaries and the seriousness of banishment. You, on the other hand, have not obeyed. You cannot be above the rules, even if you are my adopted son. Last night," he breathed, "I agreed, reluctantly, that if caught again, you would be banished."

Lanico sat straight, looking at Marin eye-to-eye. He was serious, more serious than Marin could remember.

The tavern stew that Marin had eaten suddenly threatened to resurface. Pushing his queasiness aside, the boy broke the intensity and looked down at the mat. A section of long curling black hair had managed to escape the tie at the nape of his neck, and he tucked it behind his ear. That subtle move reminded Lanico of her—of Treva.

He blinked that image away. "Please know, Marin, you have been mine. I feel that I know your soul and the longing that pulls at you—I know how you feel. Please know that I cannot bear to separate myself from you. That's why it's so important that you busy yourself with other things and not venture out from our boundary"—he paused and thought for a moment. His mind quickly danced around ideas. He knew he was asking in vain but figured he might as well try.

"Why don't you join the hunting team? Fenner's grandson Freck would probably welcome you on. *And*, you'd learn how to use a bow and arrow." He smiled weakly. "O—or, perhaps take solace having a small garden to sell turnips and carrots like Joso Stoutlet? He seems content." He paused.

"-Or, what about a girl? Marin, you're a good-looking young WynSprign—why not try to be friendly with a nice girl, perhaps—uh—Maybell?" Lanico raised his eyebrows, hopeful.

But, *silence* greeted him.

He could tell instantly by Marin's uninterested expression that none of these suggestions had been enticing. Lanico caved. "All right. Look, all I ask is that you stop this adventuring and grow some roots before you land in real trouble." He studied Marin's face.

Marin sighed, feeling defeated. "Lanico"—he paused in search of his words— "What you ask of me tears at my very heart, at my spirit . . . to keep me from adventuring is like . . . like taking my wings away. I *cannot* stay here, I *cannot* become like the others, pretending to be content living this boring life amid the mist, feeling trapped without any dreams. I feel a pull, a longing, a *need* to leave. Something out there is calling for me."

Lanico understood very well; he shared this same longing and felt its calling at all times. He, however, chose to deny it. Marin, like Lanico, was of a long line of warriors for Odana. Marin's mother was a Knighted Odana Second Lieutenant, his father a Lieutenant General. Adventuring ran through Marin's veins. He didn't have to be told of his heritage—he *felt* it.

Lanico reminded himself, *Longing or not, Marin mustn't put us all at risk.*

"Marin, there is great danger outside the Great Mist realm . . . There are some who want to profit from our misery." Lanico put this lightly, of course understanding his people in Odana, were likely in misery. "Please know that if we are found, we will all be in grave danger . . . danger beyond your own understanding." As protector, he never intended Marin to know the full truth – a truth that he himself, still wasn't fully aware of.

Marin remembered Trayvor and the hooded man. He considered telling Lanico about them, but if he did, Lanico would only be upset at his snooping about in the trees again. Perhaps once more he'd venture out to Horse's Clearing—just to hear the conversation. It would be a shame to sit idly by while secret plans were made - plans that might be ill intentioned. He heard the mysterious man mention enslaved WynSprigs. The very thought of this stirred a fire in Marin. He looked up steadily at Lanico and then stood. Without a word, he walked toward the hall. He wasn't going to give an answer to Lanico yet. Silence was the only answer he could give, for now. Lanico gave a slow blink and nodded at him, in understanding. The conversation was indeed over, for now.

~

At his sleeping den, Marin opened his curtain divider and closed it well behind him, mindful of his candle. He took off his boots and tunic quietly, fighting back the silent sobs that had erupted from deep inside. His tooth necklace bounced on his bare chest over his quiet heaves. Warm tears trailed down his face. He gathered his bedding in a feeble attempt to make it more comfortable and lay down sprawled out. He held the tooth on his necklace in his hand as he always did in times of great sadness. He liked the way the pointy end felt when he pressed his thumb into it. He stared into the dancing candle flame for a long while before blowing it out.

~

Still in the sitting room in silence, Lanico was unable to write about the day's events. He despised the talk he had just given to Marin, but he knew his point was made. He knew the youth understood the severity of the circumstances. Nevertheless, he remained unsettled. Lanico had been denying himself, all these long years, the freedom to ponder the past. Freedom to answer the call to his *own* spirit. Like Marin, he also felt the pleading for him to return to his home Odana.

As he did with many other things in life, he shoved the yearning – the thoughts of the past to the back of his mind, in an effort to have forward movement, normalcy.

Lanico had long known about the detained WynSprigns. He *was* supposed to be their leader since King Oetam had died. He grappled with the thought that he had abandoned them at their greatest time of need. When he and the others fled the Odana after the seizure, they lost so much.

Lanico conceded he wasn't capable of being a leader—he wasn't fit for it. His mind was not willing or able to take on this great responsibility. Now, all these years later, and in this quiet, this responsibility was starting to weigh on him. Visions of the suffering raked through his mind increasingly as of late, and Marin's desire to leave only enhanced his own *pull* to the beloved Odana.

Chapter Five

Before the mist-veiled sun rose, Marin sat up in his bed. Though his small room had no windows, with the blanket weary over his limbs, he could sense it was still dark outside. *Good.* He felt he had slept only a few hours. In the dark of his den, his eyes glowed a soft purple hue. He carefully and quietly pulled on his tunic, which had grown tight around his shoulders—it wasn't the best to climb in, either. He wasn't quite fully grown yet, and he'd need new clothes soon, but for now this would have to do. He carried his boots, opened his doorway curtain, and inched out past the sitting room. Lanico had once again fallen asleep leaning back in the tall chair, a curled-up scroll on his lap. Marin looked at him affectionately but warily before continuing down the hall.

He made his way quietly to the pantry and grabbed two carrots and a roll from the table. *These will do for now*. He shoved these into Lanico's satchel and slipped over to the entrance. *Okay, now the tricky part*, he thought. He slowly and quietly lifted the bolt and pulled open the door, which tried to make a creak but gave only a low groan at Marin's slow touch. He quickly put himself on the other side of the door to slip through and just as slowly, he closed it.

The world was still dark and sleeping. His eyes glowed dimly as he glanced around. He then leaned over and pulled on his weathered boots. Getting to Horse's Clearing was not challenging—there were many trees to leap up and climb into, and they all seemed connected. Their branches were always so close—as if they wanted to touch one another. The tall, ancient interconnected trees were his familiar friends throughout the Great Mist. He leapt into the branches and after some time spent climbing and swaying among the boughs, he got his reward. He could see the clearing ahead as the trees began to thin out in the distance. This bit of travel was not new to him—he had been adventuring quite a bit. Every step placed on a branch and every swing around a tree's trunk had been a well-coordinated dance that only he knew the moves to.

As he approached the open space, Marin's spirit lifted and a heaviness in him diminished. There was nothing quite like the open sky and the yellow glowing sun to warm one's cool skin. The orange glow of the dawning sun peeked through the trees, and the bright hues of pink, orange, and yellow chased away the misty fog in the clearing beyond. It was marvelous. The sun brightened the huge expanse of golden grass just over the tree line.

How could anyone want to keep themselves from this magnificence? He sat on a thick sturdy branch, staring into that other world. Then his eyes roamed to the forest floor far below and he noticed some large cages. *That's odd.* At the sudden grumble from beneath his tunic, he realized he was hungry. The cages were now a fleeting thought. He opened Lanico's small satchel and decided to eat the roll—the quieter choice of his hastily chosen options. After all, he didn't want to give away his position. It would be too far costly.

The breeze stirred the leaves gently and Marin heard distant movement, approaching—heavy footsteps on dead crunchy leaves and small breaking twigs. "Ah, yes. There is Travyor," Marin murmured under his breath. Travyor's blue cape swung, appearing purple in the rising sun as he emerged from the forest. At almost at the same time, from along the tree line, the hooded man from the day before appeared. He seemed thin under that cloak, with bony shoulders. Marin still could not view his downcast face.

The two came closer to one another and resumed their conversation. Marin desperately wanted to hear what they were saying about the Odana Kingdom, but at this height, he wouldn't be able to. Lanico had taught him the history of the Odana but the accounts had seemed quite ancient—now it seemed different, and Travyor wanted to keep it secret. If Marin was to learn about the bad doings he suspected, and tell his guardian, he'd have to have a clear understanding of what exactly was being said.

He started to move slowly, carefully climbing a little lower, to a hanging branch of the neighboring tree. He did not want to descend too low and be discovered, so his movements were slow, calculated. Then, another figured approached from the expanse of Horse's Clearing, large, gray, and looming, and on a horse! Marin felt the hair behind his neck rise, and he avoided letting out a gasp. The gray figure, Marin knew from Lanico's written descriptions, was a Mysra—there was no mistaking it. Lanico had warned him of the Mysra giants, enemies of the WynSprigns, but without much detail. This one was really quite massive, the description unable to capture the reality of his size. His biceps alone were the size of Marin's head. Marin had never actually seen a horse before, either, but knew about them from Lanico's writings and drawings.

Lanico had been accurate—perhaps he *had* actually seen these things himself! Marin's mind raced.

Trayvor called over to the massive figure, gesturing for him to come closer: "Gish! Is that you, boy? Please come in closer."

Marin's eyes widened. *Trayvor is familiar with this Mysra?!* The branch beneath his footing groaned slightly.

The Mysra dismounted from his tan horse that almost blended into the surrounding grasses. His booming voice sounded his response: "I have been waiting in the grasses for you." He jerked his head back toward the clearing.

"Did you have to wait long?" Trayvor asked pleasantly.

"No, only just *all* last night!" The Mysra's voice was gruff, rumbling seemingly octaves lower than any voice Marin had ever heard. And irritated. He sounded most irritated.

"I hadn't quite expected you, yet." Trayvor added.

Marin sat amazed, and blood began to heat in his veins. He'd have quite a lot to report to Lanico—proof that Trayvor himself was talking to the Mysra! *Just wait until I get home. Lanico, Stoutwyn, and Fenner will be raging at this.* Thoughts swirled in his head—Trayvor wanted very badly to catch Marin and banish him. *And to think, now he's the one actually putting us all in danger, talking to a Mysra—and so close to the Great Mist!* His hands squeezed the branch.

His thoughts went to Lanico and his response to anger, and Marin drew a deep, calming breath. He had to remain focused—he must avoid being seen or heard. He loosened his grip a little. The voices were a little clearer now. He leaned ever so slowly and carefully to hear more. He was intensely focused when suddenly—

CRACK!

The branch snapped under him. He plummeted. Hurling down, whizzing past dozens of other high branches that whipped past his head and forcefully thrashed against his limbs as he tumbled.

His small beaten body landed with a THUD that quaked the before surprised men's feet. Marin's arms and legs jolting up with the force of the impact. He lay motionless, his hair spread out like a wavy black river over the ground. He weakly opened his eyes and looked up, only to meet the surprised gaze of Fenner under the darkened gray hood. Marin took a sharp breath in to speak, or scream, but instead he blacked out.

"Well now, it seems our little plan worked better than I thought," said Trayvor with a prideful smile. He sent a look to Fenner, who stood surprised and motionless over the boy. "Banishment will now ensue."

Trayvor had found good fortune. He had kept a daily patrol in this area to check on Prondolin business that might arrive from a lone merchant, or clandestine Mysra business – like the present. The Prondolin merchant, however, who only appeared at irregular intervals of time with his wares, understood well that his own Prondolin home would never accept the displaced WynSprigns. For the merchant himself, in all his wanderings, was also considered an outsider and out of their favor. He chose to keep the WynSprign's business and the unusual location to himself.

"Luckily," Trayvlor resumed, "we have already summoned Gish here from Odana." He paused considering, "Well, damn! You can take the boy back now—we don't have to wait. We just caught him in the act." Trayvor paused and looked over at Fenner again—and saw he looked worried. Trayvor stiffened at the perceived weakness and pointed at him. "You're my witness to this banishment, Fenner Bricklebury!" It was a command for the former Odana Military Chief from the former Advisor to the King.

Trayvor then turned to the Mysra. "Gish! Tell your father that we have our first trade installment. Things will now change in our secret realm, and your father can expect more misbehaving WynSprigns for his trillium endeavors, following this one"—he tossed a glance at the cages behind them, only just visible in the undergrowth—"Those can be used for caging a few at a time and can be taken back on your wagons at planned intervals."

Also, under the cloak of secrecy, Trayvor commissioned the Stoutlet clan to construct the wooden cages presently stored beyond the clearing. He lied, telling the crafters their intent was for animal trappings. Only he and Fenner knew of the cages true purpose. Yes, Trayvor felt himself very forward thinking indeed.

Gish lowered his gaze to the small, motionless WynSprign at his feet. He remembered his task and lacked the social tact required for dealing with the troublesome Trayvor. The Mysra didn't attempt niceties, rather they took or demanded what they wanted, but Gish tried, "Are there many more misbehaving WynSprigns? For our business efforts, *we* need more transparency from you. My father demands to know. Where are they—in your secret realm?"

"Tsk, tsk!" said Trayvor with a smile that tempted Gish's large fists. "No, Gish, I know what your father wants. I will not show you to the WynSprign village, nor will I tell you the location. It is to remain *secret*. I *will*, however, expect a reward from your father for this first, installment"—he pointed to Marin— "and for the others to follow. We'll share in a civilized trade deal—your father's kingdom . . . and us."

With all the tracks likely beyond the woods behind Horse's Clearing, the village should not be difficult to locate, Gish knew, but he wouldn't mention that, taking advantage of Trayvor's obvious dimness. Instead, he shifted his gaze to assess the surroundings. The distant snapped twigs and trodden grasses were an easy giveaway, to even a newly trained tracker.

To cover his new knowledge, Gish gave a sour face and tossed the reward to Trayvor. The small bag of coins jiggled as it landed heavily in Trayvor's hand. Gish bent down to heft the unconscious boy over his massive shoulder, walked with ease to his waiting horse, and draped the boy behind the saddle. Once Marin was tied and secured, Gish mounted the sturdy horse. He then turned to glance at the two WynSprign elders' faces before he galloped away.

Fenner looked on, noting that they rode off in the direction of the Yellow Vast brook, a small channel that diminished over the many miles from its main source, the Odana River.

~

Marin's head throbbed from slamming up and down against the rump of a galloping horse. His eyes peeled open to the burning bright white sun he'd never felt so close. He blinked, trying to regain sight through the bright, the sting of it, and tried to move, but his wrists and ankles were bound with rope. He realized he had been rolled and tied into a faded red blanket, like a netted sausage

In front of him on the horse was the massive Mysra he had seen earlier, his immense back a solid, impenetrable wall. Next to him were tied saddlebags, and Lanico's satchel, all bouncing in unison at the horse's strides. Adrenaline pumped. Panicked, he started to wiggle, hastily trying to untie his itching wrists with numbed fingertips. He wanted to first free his hands. Then, while scrabbling, pulling at the rope, his elbow jabbed the Mysra's back and he slid. Falling again. His body slammed to the ground racing beneath them.

~

Slowly. Painfully. Marin started to move his limbs. He felt the grumpiness of sore, tugging at every muscle. His eyes opened barely, to make out a boulder face before him, glowing orange from a fire behind him heating his back. Becoming more alert, Marin sorted out that his head throbbed and his body ached, but the earth was still. He was lying on the ground and could hear crackling wood of the fire. A delicious aroma danced in the air, something roasting. His thoughts came back to the pain that radiated everywhere. He had fallen hard, twice now. At least he thought it was twice. *The Mysra must be sitting nearby.* Marin felt his rope bonds, again, with subtle movements despite his racing mind, and knew that his odds of escaping now were low. His heart beat hard.

Too fearful to turn to face the monster behind him, he lay still, with no idea where he was.

Chapter Six

Trayvor and Fenner made their way back into the Great Mist village. Trayvor was not an agile or limber WynSprign anymore, and his days on patrol were numbered, which is why he wanted to secure another role in the Great Mist. He had long sought noteworthiness amongst his people and his plans would allow him the physical relief and the status he so desired.

Fenner traveled with him, his mind elsewhere. Lanico would not take the news of Marin's banishment well. *If Marin is gone* . . . Fenner gulped at the thought. He wrung his hands nervously. Trayvor didn't seem to care in the least; in fact, he seemed quite proud of their current circumstances.

After their long, slow walk back to the Great Mist, they stopped at the tavern for ale—for Trayvor. Fenner avoided drinking, and he sat and shuffled his feet in great anxiety. Trayvor threw back ale, mug after mug, and he seemed a bottomless pit. It was baffling that one could hold so much liquid.

Fenner slowly sipped at the tavern's stew for lunch and it had grown cold when he tasted it hours later for dinner. His appetite had disappeared entirely.

After countless rounds of ale, Trayvor belching and wiping his mouth with his forearm, and through a breathy fog of brew he suddenly announced, "I'm calling for an emergency meeting." Those seated nearby and amongst them paused, and glanced quickly at him before resuming their business. Trayvor had been generous to them all tonight and the crowd there didn't care about the elder meetings they had.

Fenner dropped his spoon and nodded in agreement but remained silent. His mind was still spinning over Lanico's imagined response. He felt himself quivering, anticipating Lanico's reaction. He remembered how threatening Lanico could become, and having spent the majority of the day at the tavern hadn't dulled that fear.

Trayvor didn't seem nervous at all about having this emergency meeting. He quite looked forward to telling the former Prince exactly what was on his mind.

"Things will start changing around here"—Trayvor pushed his emptied mug to the center of the table, signaling he was finished— "We'll see what Lanico has to say to that." Trayvor had once told King Oetam that if a person was too weak to lead, then someone else would gladly step in and do it for them—whether that leader wanted that or not. To him, Lanico had been the weakest leader.

~

Their first stop was Stoutwyn's home at the base of a large oak tree. It had a wide door that conveniently accommodated his size, and small windows scaling up the tree in various places. It was a simple home, common, and unremarkable to most.

It was starting to get late in the day, and the windows were already glowing soft yellow when they arrived at his door. To the disapproval of Fenner, much of the day had been wasted at the tavern. Trayvor loosed a cat-like grin at Fenner, and rapped at the door with his walking stick. The sound was small in their space.

After a few moments, they could hear shuffling and movement inside. The ground trembled slightly at his heavy-footed approach. Stoutwyn fussed with the small door window curtain and squinted out at them, trying to see who had come to call. Trayvor's and Fenner's eyes started glowing in the dim light. Stoutwyn closed the small curtain and unlocked the door, opening it slowly to reveal that he was ready for bed. He fingered for his looking glasses in his deep chest pocket and placed them on the bridge of his pronounced nose.

"Good evening, gentlemen," Stoutwyn greeted the pair. "Wh—what has you calling at this late hour?"

Ignoring the insinuation of intrusion, Trayvor narrowed his gaze and smugly announced, "Due to some recent concerns, I am calling an emergency elder meeting. It's to be held at Lanico's." He fumbled at his cloak ties and tossed a glance back at Fenner from over his shoulder. Fenner remained expressionless behind him.

How in the fires is he not drunk? Fenner marveled in silence at the well-spoken Trayvor. His mouth gaped slightly in disbelief at his composure.

"I see, I see," said Stoutwyn quickly. He nervously fumbled for his robe on a hook near the door.

Trayvor, clearing his throat, said, "Yes, please follow us there once you're . . . *decent.*" He scowled, flicking his gaze down at Stoutwyn's nightclothes, and wore a sour expression as he turned to walk away. Fenner paused his steps to light a small lantern on the path toward Lanico's.

Stoutwyn stood alone in the doorway, still a little befuddled. They hadn't held an emergency meeting in years. Then, with a robe quickly wrapped around him, Stoutwyn scrambled to close his door behind him. He carried his own lantern, which swung greatly at his uneven strides. The dense trees that surrounded their homes and paths came to life as night insects and owls started their dusk melodies.

After a time walking through the darkening haze, they approached Lanico's quiet earthen home. Tufts of grass and moss covered the house and gave it a green allure still visible in the fading light.

Trayvor rapped on the thick door with his walking stick. After a few moments, a loud clank broke the silence and the door cracked open. Lanico peered around the door and sighed at the sight of them, and not Marin returning home for the evening. He looked at their serious faces. *Probably yet another complaint about Marin*, he determined.

Like Stoutwyn, he had also been getting settled for the evening but still wore his clothing. Lanico appreciated bedding early and rising early. Despite his discontent with this unexpected nighttime visit, he remained gentlemanly. He flashed a feigned smile. "Good evening, fellow elders. Please, please come in." He held the door open for them.

The elders came in and gathered in the quiet sitting room, choosing their spots. Lanico sat in a small chair against the wall adorned with weapons, for Trayvor had taken the larger cedar one. They didn't speak right away and Lanico waited for one of them to begin. *They are the ones who came here, after all.* After a moment of shuffling, Trayvor spoke up, stiffening into official business: "Well, gentlemen, I am moved to call this emergency meeting because of a serious development. As we all know, young Marin has been caught in the past outside the boundaries of the Great Mist. Just earlier this day, we—Fenner and I"—he shot a glance at Fenner— "we caught the boy at Horse's Clearing, just at the tree line. We made the decision to banish him at that very instant." He paused. "We made that choice because we knew *you* wouldn't, Lanico."

There was a brief silence.

Lanico looked stunned in disbelief. A nervous laugh escaped him. "Did I just hear this accurately?" He paused to gauge Fenner's expression. Fenner looked down in shame.

The smile faded and a cold sweat claimed him. Lanico casted a look of incredulity. *No.*

"No," his voice whispered.

Travyor gave a single slow nod.

Lanico's heart fluttered as he drew a sharp breath. He shook his head with a feeling of great rage, confusion, and . . . *fear.* A wave of fear washed over him. He felt as if a blow just had slammed into his gut. His face flushed and his heart thumped quickly. *No!*

Trayvor held onto his smug smile. He looked around at the others, proud to be in that large chair, certain that he had accomplished something great.

More silence.

Lanico, breaking the stunned moment, brought himself back into the room. There was no time for arguing and anger—action was needed. He needed to move. Panicked, he fumbled asking questions: "Wh—wh—where will his lodgings be?" He blinked nervously, trying to get basic information. "Wh—what"—he inhaled deeply— "what town or village was he sent to? Prond-?"

He struggled to keep composure as his throat knotted, his heart now racing. "Did he have enough rations for his journey there, to the vill—to—to where he was sent?"

Trayvor looked around nervously and said with caution, "Well, no. Ah"—he paused to glance at Fenner's lowered face— "No. We had no arranged lodgings in any location." He started to feel uneasy and that smart smirk he wore vanished.

The wood floor creaked as Stoutwyn shifted in his chair. The room became darker instantly, a response to Lanico's very emotion. Outside, a distant rumble of thunder trembled. Stoutwyn immediately recognized Odan's gift in him, a Fray gift rarely seen.

Lanico stood slowly. His Fray heritage, revealed in his uncommonly tall height for a WynSprign, grew so that he loomed over them. Only they knew of his Fray blood, and up until now, they had somewhat forgotten it. As he had been trained, Lanico maintained his regal nature and spoke clearly. His bewildered thoughts and emotions did not show outwardly, even if nature's elements *did* hint at the storm raging within him.

"You banished my son . . . hours ago, without any prior arrangements?" His voice echoed of rumbling thunder. "He's wandering the wilderness alone?! No provisions, no planning, you just set him up for . . . for doom!" He swept at a random table, and it flew to the side. The table cracked, the wood splintering at the solid strike. Ink spattered and pooled from the broken inkwell. "Is that it? I know my Marin is different from the others, but THIS! . . . Such betrayal!" he hissed. Keeping his anger at bay, he clenched his fists so tight they grew numb.

Elders Stoutwyn and Fenner, were fear-struck, unsettled, they wriggled in discomfort. Stoutwyn was learning for the first time that Marin was alone, and Fenner knew that *no*, Marin wasn't wandering alone in the Yellow Vast—he was in the custody of a Mysra. It was ever so much worse than Lanico yet knew. Countless years had passed since they had seen Lanico's fury. The wood floor creaked slightly with their shifting movements. Trayvor sat still in the big chair, his arms crossed over his large belly in defiance.

Lanico released them from his fiery gaze, and it was as if the trio could breathe again. He spun on his heel and started riffling through various woven baskets and wood boxes that had been buried under blankets and scrolls behind his desk for years. He bent over, searching, his long silver hair hiding his pained face. "I cannot believe the irresponsibility—the foolhardiness! —of this whole thing!"

He tossed baskets and blankets aside until he came upon a large box and pulled open the lid. His eyes widened at seeing his forgotten gilded armor inside. He blinked back, focusing. *Where is it? Where is . . .?* His tingling fingers felt it at the bottom. A tinderbox, a few small traveling necessities . . . He then pulled up his brown leather sword sheath. He stood straight and quickly fastened it around his narrow waist, hidden beneath his white tunic. The well-worn belt fastened in its well-worn notch, but Lanico adjusted the belt one hole looser to accommodate his slightly larger girth after all these years.

He turned to the wall and grabbed Reluctant Leader from its mount. Holding it sent a tingling to his hand. The weight was familiar to his strong arms, an extension of his own wrist. He sheathed the sword immediately and turned to the group, his silver hair swinging.

"You leave me no choice"—he pointed accusingly with his free hand and grit his teeth— "I am setting out to find Marin. My share of the Great Mist is under your protection until my return. I'd prefer not to leave, but you must understand that you have placed me in a vastly difficult situation . . ." Stopping himself short, he inhaled, fighting hard to keep his resolve. No. He would say no more.

Trayvor's face remained unchanged.

Lanico's worn leather boots thudded as he walked quickly over to the eating area and searched for his satchel. He grunted, rolling his eyes in annoyance—*Marin took it. Of course.* He grabbed a brown sack lying close by, and a canteen. The others could hear him rustling around in the food den. Along with his traveling items and tinderbox, he tossed bread rolls, rabbit jerky, and carrots into the satchel.

The others were silent, looking around at one another. Stoutwyn, still in shock himself, quickly stood and walked over to Lanico, who paid him no mind as he finished rummaging for food. Lanico grabbed his green cloak from the hook just beside the door. He stole one last daggered glance at everyone— Fenner and Traylor calm, just sitting there, Stoutwyn fretting. Lanico grunted in anger as he opened the door, which moaned loudly. He pulled hard and the door slammed behind him, the metal bolt rocking. He stormed furiously away, leaving everyone behind in his home. His mind and his focus were elsewhere.

Inside, Stoutwyn anxiously looked at the others. There was only silence.

With a last look at the other two Stoutwyn advanced. The door moaned again as Stoutwyn passed through, looking for Lanico, who had stopped and occupied himself fumbling with his cloak, awkward with his sword. Lanico's breath fogged around him just as plainly as his glowing eyes shone, and the sounds of chirping tree frogs, thousands of them, reverberated in the night air.

"Listen, Lan, I can accompany you," Stoutwyn offered. His eyes were now glowing dimly in the newfound darkness "L—look, I knew nothing of this till just now." His face was concerned as he looked up at Lanico.

Lanico stopped fussing with his cloak and straightened himself, turning his gaze down at his old friend and seeing plainly that Stoutwyn was just as surprised as he was at the news of Marin. He studied his tone and measured his words: "I knew as much, Stout. I'd never assume you'd give in to this, this . . . ridiculousness."

"I will accompany you on this journey," Stoutwyn declared. "I can be an additional set of eyes and legs—as you're looking for Marin, those would come in handy." Stoutwyn offered a small smile.

This was an honest and selfless gesture, especially since Stoutwyn was now limited physically. His days of being an Odana Major were far-gone. Lanico felt his gaze soften as he looked down at him. "My friend"—Lanico paused— "I need you here, to assist in watching over the WynSprigns." It was understood between them that Fenner was not capable of standing up to Trayvor without some assistance. Lanico sighed. "I don't plan on being gone long." He sighed again. "Oh, fires. And, even then—when we're back—I'm uncertain of what to do . . . I'll have to figure out where to place Marin, or if I should bring him back here temporarily until other arrangements could be made or . . ." His voice and thoughts trailed away.

Noticing his overwhelmed state, Stoutwyn loosed another feeble smile. "All right, Lan, it's all right . . . One thing at a time, hmm? First, find the boy."

Lanico gave a small sad smile. They patted each other on the shoulder heartily, and then Lanico turned, and started into the dark mist of the woods.

Chapter Seven

Marin first heard himself moan as he started to wake. He wiggled against his restraints, forgetting until that horrific realization came back. He had been captured. He was tied. He was immobile—something that he had never been in his entire life. A deep and dark dread swept over him . . . doom. He was doomed. His heart resumed hammering within his chest. He moved ever so slightly to avoid attention from the monster while he tested the bindings.

Still completely tied.

Still on the ground.

Still captured.

Still . . .

He hoped. He hoped to avoid blacking out again and measured his breathing to calm himself. Then the pain returned as reality set in. His body was stiff and wracked with agony from the falls he had endured. He was still facing a big wall of boulders, a monolith. He blinked and looked as far as he could. This was like the base of a small mountain. He *had* to do something. The menacing Mysra put him at a physical disadvantage, but he could try to communicate with the Mysra and *act* confident. While he had the nerve, he decided to roll over quickly and demand to know where they were.

He took a breath and rolled—but the small campfire was out, though smoke still lingered over the charred remains. He must have fallen asleep for several hours. Marin's eyes darted around quickly, searching for the Mysra. *He's not here!*

He had to act fast.

He wiggled, like a caterpillar trying to free itself from its chrysalis. He managed to push with his feet and sit up against the boulder, facing the fire pit. His curly hair was matted like a black nest and his face dusty. Blinking slowly, he focused. The sky was a beautiful blend of fuchsia and lavender and at every passing moment, brightening. From this point, the land was wide and golden . . . with no trees. Only yesterday, he was staring at this same sky, but under very different circumstances.

Marin didn't have much time. He couldn't see any knives or sharp objects lying about but he decided to use the sharp edges of the rock before him. He sawed the rope back and forth until bit by bit the strands broke and swirled free around his wrists. It seemed only moments until he managed to free his hands and then his body. He sat up, working on the ropes that secured his feet. Suddenly, he heard something—pebbles grinding and muffled thuds from footsteps approaching. Marin startled, inhaling sharply.

The Mysra rounded the small mountain and glared at Marin, who felt the hair on his arms prickle in terror. He held his breath.

The Mysra had several dead rabbits flung over his broad shoulders, tied together with a bit of twine – the same that Marin had just freed himself from. The look of him and the kills only heightened the fear that Marin felt pounding within. The Mysra wound through the boulders with heavy thudding steps toward the fire pit. He added new wood to the smoldering black remains and promptly got the fire restarted using a small flint and twine.

Marin sat staring at him intently, forgetting to be brave and bold. He had never encountered a Mysra before . . . or any other race beyond his familiar WynSprign. The Mysra, feeling the weight of Marin's stare, glanced up from the kill he now was quickly skinning on a flat rock. He scowled. The glow from the fire enhanced the Mysra's own boulder-like appearance, the gray rippling muscles.

The Mysra could plainly see that the boy was loose from his ropes, but he had no concern at this. *The boy hasn't had food or water in over a day. Out here, if he tried to escape, he wouldn't get far.* It wasn't worth the small effort of retying him. He resumed cutting.

Marin, trying to steady his trembling body, dug deep within himself to summon courage. "Wh—what's your name?" The sound of his own voice was small in the open air. His throat bobbed. He caught the glow of the Mysra's bloodied knife.

The scowling Mysra remained at his task. He pierced the sliced rabbit meat on skewers, and then responded, His voice low and gravelly: "It would do you good not to ask questions." The familiar basso of his voice sounded again.

Marin sat up a little straighter. He was weak. Dizzy. "Well . . . I"—he paused to choose words carefully, leaning back on the boulder. He had to be smart at this. He acted casual— "I just figured that you and I will probably be together for some time, and I figured I might as well know your name, instead of only knowing of you as a Mysra . . . and that's all."

Silence.

The Myrsa looked up. The look on his face read as if he were offended, but he considered for a moment. He looked back down at his completed work. "Gish," he muttered, low.

"Gish." Marin nodded slightly. "Gish, my name is Marin."

Silence.

Gish was not talkative and honestly . . . he couldn't give a shit.

The flames crackled when Gish set the meat over the fire. They both sat in silence. The shade from the great rocks behind them was a comfort as the rising sun was quickly beginning to warm the earth.

Marin sat still while the rabbits cooked. He didn't want to anger Gish by asking too many questions. Gish was strong, short-tempered, and had a knife—a big, jagged knife. Marin was curious about his own feelings in this moment. He should be terrified, and he was a bit scared, but not to the extent he would have imagined. The initial doom he'd felt, had diminished some. He was thankful for Lanico's training.

Lanico. He started feeling things again. *What am I going to do without Lanico?* He would have awakened by now and Marin would be nowhere in sight. He imagined Lanico looking all over their realm and up into the trees, fetching food for both of them only to realize that he had forgotten Marin was gone. His heart sank.

In his state of fear, he wasn't hungry, but he realized that he hadn't eaten or drunk in well over a day. The savory rabbit meat was sizzling now on the open fire. Marin licked his parched lips. He took a deep breath in and his throat and lungs felt dry. He *needed* water. He *needed* to eat. His body needed nourishment if he was to survive . . . whatever lay ahead of him.

"Gish," Marin began with a raspy voice. Gish returned an unpromising glance, waiting. "I don't suppose "—he tried to manage a nice tone— "I could have some water and some of your meat? I haven't eaten in quite some time."

Without saying a word, Gish slowly leaned closer to the fire and pulled out a small rabbit flank. It was charred and hot. In that moment, Marin couldn't imagine anything more beautiful. Gish bent over toward Marin and handed him the skewer.

Gish stared at Marin's untied wrists, as if to say, "I noticed you freed yourself," and he then quickly looked Marin in the eye.

"Th—thank you, Gish." Marin nervously stuttered.

Gish then turned and poured water from a canteen into a small cup. He placed this closer to Marin.

Marin quickly took a small bite of the hot sizzling meat. It was too hot to chew properly so, he simply swallowed it. The hot meat burned at his throat as it slid down. His eyes watered. It didn't matter—in that moment—it was perfect. He turned and quenched his burning throat with the water Gish had supplied.

"This tastes really great . . . thank you," Marin said, adding another mouthful of hot meat.

The scowl lessened.

Marin looked around at the endless expanse before them and noticed something missing. "Gish," he asked, with another small bite of rabbit rolling about in his mouth, "What happened to your horse?"

Gish swallowed hard. The corners of his mouth turned down. The scowl returned.

Oh, shit, Marin thought-fear resuming.

"The horse is dead," Gish grunted.

Marin gulped. He was taken aback. *Did Gish kill the horse? Did it run away? Did it get injured and left behind? Did he leave it somewhere on purpose?* Marin knew better than to ask questions—he wanted to avoid ending up like the rabbits on the skewers—or whatever had happened to the horse.

Marin reached for his tooth necklace, to hold it in his hand for comfort. His hand patted his chest, and then feverishly felt around his neck. No. It was gone! He suddenly knelt, scrambling. He looked around next to him, on the ground.

Gish glanced up curiously. His small aqua-colored eyes focused on Marin's sudden odd behavior. Marin patted the ground and ran his fingers over the loose dirt around the rocks, picking up bits of charred wood and tufts of fur. He looked over the boulder and near the rock he had used as a pillow. Nothing. He had lost it. Plain and simple. He'd lost it. His most valued possession . . . gone.

He felt a stone growing at the back of his throat. It was the one and only thing he had from his mother.

Gish turned his curious gaze from Marin and glanced at the horizon. He commanded unexpectedly, "Up, boy."

Marin obediently stood. His feet and legs were sore. His head, still spinning. He patted his chest and neck again in vain. Lanico had spent hours telling young Marin about the great adventures of his mother and father—how his mother had taken this tooth from an enemy she had defeated. Even though the thought of keeping a tooth from a slain enemy was a little . . . savage to Marin, he deeply appreciated having it. It was so familiar on his chest. He often grabbed it to feel the point pressed into his thumb. A defeated feeling swept over him.

Gish rolled up mats and loaded items into various satchels, including Marin's. He seemed to be in a hurry.

"Where are we going?" Marin asked, regretting the question as soon as the words left his lips.

Gish grunted.

"I guess we'll be walking," continued Marin, "since there is no horse. I imagine we have far to walk."

"Yes!" Gish snapped, and Marin inhaled sharply.

As they walked from the small mountain in the middle of the Yellow Vast, Marin felt growing despair and every muscle in his body groaned painfully. It was with great acquiescence that he ambled onward. He was alone with this threatening monster. He was worried for his guardian, and he had lost his tooth necklace. He would not dare asking Gish about it. Because it was a Mysra tooth on the necklace, he'd—well, Marin didn't even want to think about his reaction. Marin gulped hard. He looked back as the mountain slowly shrank into the distance, every step becoming increasingly regrettable.

Chapter Eight

Lanico, wrapped tightly in his green cloak, was cold and damp with dew. His bones ached. Lying on the hard, bare ground all night was not ideal for an elder no matter how fit he might be, and he was by far the fittest. He stood slowly, his bones creaking as he straightened and groaned. With annoyance, he shook small twigs and pine needles from his hair and cloak.

He had slept just at the edge of Horse's Clearing, sheltered by the tree line but with a view he seldom saw in the Great Mist. The morning sky was painted with brilliant fuchsia hues. Looking out over this expanse, he sighed. *How beautiful. Wherever Marin is this moment, I pray he's enjoying this painted sight.* He swallowed dryly. There was an ache in his chest.

The twinkling song from nearby morning sparrows reminded him that time was not on his side. Lanico started tracking as the morning brightened. Even though WynSprigns had great vision, it was not perfect. In order to track well, he depended on the sunlight. Marin had last been seen at the edge of this clearing.

Lanico looked thoroughly near his camping site, kept purposely small to leave little trace and to aid his tracking. He noticed several footprints in the moist ground. The growing light highlighted an area of impact, of something large that had landed here. Then his attention was drawn to the tracks that led past the boundary.

No.

Marin prefers the company of trees. Perhaps he stayed here, on the border. The more Lanico looked at the untouched foliage, the more it became clear that Marin was not in this area. At the tree line there were recent hoof prints. He studied the tracks. The horse had approached at a walk from the clearing and turned galloping away. He wondered, wrestling with his thoughts. He did not want to leave the border—*What if Marin is close?* He glanced back at the area of impact, then at the branches above it. He couldn't help shake the thought that Marin had been in a struggle there.

It was a decision not easily made. However, Lanico decided to follow the feeling in his gut. He'd follow the horse tracks that headed beyond the clearing. If Marin was on a horse, he'd be farther away and it would take more time to reach him on foot. Lanico needed to move. He stepped out from Horse's Clearing and into the brilliance of the Yellow Vast. Immediately the expanse, the growing brightness, was overwhelming. His eyes were shocked with the adjustment. His heart pounded. He hadn't seen *expanse* in many years and was used to everything being in close proximity in the woods—for far too long.

Determined, he followed the horse tracks, shading his eyes against the almost-blinding sun. Lanico sighed hard in frustration and wiped his brow. He actually felt himself *sweating*. He loathed direct sunlight. Even when he and Marin sparred and trained, they were exercised well, but he did not recall sweating as he did immediately upon stepping into this new environment . . . It was hot. He drank minimally from his canteen, an effort to preserve his strength and the supply.

Gray Rock was the only destination for a great distance. Legend claimed the collection of large boulders and monoliths had been thrust into the earth, into the middle of the Yellow Vast. There was only one other area like it on the other side of the Odana kingdom—the Jaspirian ruins. Both locations were believed to have been made by Fray Jaspia herself in a fit of wrath. She was first created daughter of Odan, the most beautiful of them all. Aside from her believed fury, she was known for being the Fray of rock and song. It was said that she hurled the monoliths in a torrent of anger against her father, the god of all. Why had her fury been so great? No one quite knew the answer, and Lanico had never met this elder Fray aunt to ask her.

Lanico thought over his memory of Gray Rock. There should be a brook before the formation—the direction the horse seemed to have headed. He'd fill his canteen there. It could take days . . . But something tugged at him. He remembered from his past that there was something to be cautious of once at the brook. A danger lurked there. Nothing specific came to mind—only a faint whisper of caution. It *had* been many years after all . . .

Well, if it was that important, I'm certain I would have remembered.

He continued to track the horse's strides through thigh-high golden grass. Luckily, this made tracking the horse easier—and would hide Lanico from others if need be. The horse seemed to have galloped a long distance before slowing down. Lanico was hoping to find more clues. *Anything . . .*

How did he find himself here, now, after all this long life?

Chapter Nine

Gish held strong solid strides, while the smaller Marin worked to keep up with his pace through the burn of aching muscles.

"I sure miss your horse," breathed Marin.

"Me too," grumbled Gish.

Marin was delighted to hear a response from his captor. It made him feel somewhat more valued.

After a brief silence, Gish stated abruptly, "I had to kill him."

Marin turned to look up at him. "Who? . . . The horse?" He was startled that the Mysra was suddenly engaging in conversation.

"Yes." Gish paused. "After you fell from his backside, I turned Gladin around too hard." Gish breathed out a big sigh. "He snapped two legs and fell. The horse—he had to be killed after that."

Marin was astonished at this revelation—mostly that the Mysra seemed to regret the killing. Marin also noticed the dirt and yellow grass stains that trailed along Gish's side and covered his scraped forearm. They evidenced the force of the fall.

"So, that must have been . . . very difficult to do," Marin said, trying to *feel* empathy, but with his menacing captor?

"Yes," Gish answered shortly.

There was another moment of silence. Gish seemed to be deeply upset. "I'm sorry that you had to do that," Marin said, squinting up at the Mysra.

Gish had his focus ahead. He glanced down at Marin briefly, though they were both struggling to talk and walk fast at the same time.

After a moment of thought, Marin asked, "So you carried me and all these things we're lugging around, all by yourself? How long did you have to walk like that?"

Gish answered, "Long."

They walked on for what seemed like hours, in silence. Through the sound of the rustling golden grass and Gish's heavy footsteps, Marin could hear something rumbling in the distance. On the horizon, two wavy figures were on the move, fast.

"Gish—"

"—SHH!" Gish ordered. "Down, boy!"

They both hit the ground and lay flat in the tall grass.

The rumbling grew louder. As the sound of the thundering gallops flew near, there was no question—they had been spotted.

Marin's breath quickened. He stared into the forest of yellow grass around him.

Gish fumbled in his pocket and took out a small pouch that contained a light purple powder. He quickly held this to his mouth and swallowed its contents. The smell of brass filled the air. He pulled the strings to close it up again and pushed it back into his pocket. He felt for the handle of the long sack Marin had been carrying on their journey.

Gish's voice was low. "Stay down. Stay quiet. Stay still." He took the sack and grabbed the rolled sleeping mat from Marin's fingers as well, then popped up to start his approach toward the riders closing in.

Marin obeyed. Without moving, he looked up and through the grasses could barely make out the sight of two scowling Mysra riders. Gish seemed smaller as he approached them—or perhaps it was because he was not mounted on a horse. They looked even more menacing than Gish.

"Why were you hiding and where is your travel companion?" greeted one.

"I wasn't hiding—I tripped—and I haven't a need for a travel companion." Gish responded smugly.

"We seen two of you walking," the second Mysra added.

"You're mistaken. See, I was only carrying this roll and bag. You only saw these at my side—which is why I tripped." Gish held up his rolled mat and the long sack in one arm. These, when held together, were about the length of Marin. "My horse snapped legs and had to be slaughtered . . ."

Marin was terrified. Why was Gish trying to hide him from the other Mysra? *Shouldn't they all get along?* He wondered if this would be a good time for him to escape—but if Gish was hiding him, he might be valuable and they'd all chase him down. He weighed his options. There were three Mysra—two on horseback and Gish. They were in an endless sea of yellow grass, the *Yellow Vast*, Gish had called it. There was nowhere to hide.

After a few long seconds, he decided against escape—at least for now. Marin felt around for a possible weapon. He couldn't move much, for fear of disturbing the tall grass.

"I'm traveling back to Odana," Gish continued.

Marin's ears perked up. *Odana!*

"Yes, but *where* have you come from?" the second rider demanded; annoyance set in his tone.

Gish stood silent for a moment.

While Gish hesitated, the first rider curiously started off toward Marin's hiding spot, closing in on the small space of grass that had a visible hole in it. Marin could hear his horse breathing, and the hoof beats on the padded grassy ground grew nearer.

Droplets of sweat gathered on Marin's brow, and a fly landed on his neck and was tickling him with tiny legs. Despite the fevered urge to swat the fly and wipe his brow, he remained still. Breathing. Slowly. His hand was still nervously riffling deep inside the Mysra bag that lay at his side—his fingers were growing numb.

Gish strained for an answer, then suddenly, with a trillium-induced burst of speed, he grabbed the rider near him by his tunic. With raw force, he pulled him down from his saddle, and his boulder-like body pounded into the ground.

Gish turned and ran from him toward Marin, toward the other rider, who grabbed for a hatchet fastened at his side. Gish quickly flashed to grab him with his left hand, just as he had with the first rider. This time, Gish produced his large knife and stabbed the rider in the side with a quick, smooth thrust. The Myrsa roared before slumping to fall off his horse.

Marin gasped aloud.

The first rider—now on foot—ran toward Gish from behind, his face bloodied from his landing. He grabbed Gish's massive shoulder and delivered a hook-blow to his face. His enormous knuckles landed squarely on Gish's mouth and nose. Gish, eyes wide, slightly stumbled at the impact, and black blood gushed down his ash-gray chin. Then he took another blow, this one to the gut. Gish licked the blood and grinned wide at the fight-ready rider, his teeth painted gray in dark blood. The rider, proud of his punch, smiled with delight right back at Gish.

Marin could see the rider fumbling for something. Unable to lie still any longer, he sprang up by reflex just as the rider produced a small folding knife. In a flash, the rider jabbed this into Gish's thick left thigh while he was still bent from the gut-punch.

Marin didn't know why, but in this very second, he leapt to tackle the rider with all his strength and agility. Gish yelled in pain at the stab, and Marin and the rider both tumbled hard to Gish's left side, Marin's small legs flying into the air. Turning toward the rider, Gish quickly threw Marin like a child's doll further off to the side and grabbed the rider by his tunic. Glaring into the other Mysra's eyes, Gish unexpectedly jolted upwards, stabbing the rider deep in his chest. The knife drove in so deeply that it stopped only when the grip was flush with the victim's chest. Satisfied, he dropped the rider's body to the ground.

Dying, the rider rasped and with a bloodied smile said, "He'll never want you now, Gish . . . even . . . with the captured WynSprign sl—" A gurgle emitted from his throat where the words had ended. His eyes stared sightless at the sky.

Gish grunted and with strength pulled his large bloodied knife out from the mound of the rider's chest, jolting back slightly at the effort. Dark, thick blood gushed from the Mysra's gaping chest wound. The buzz of trillium still tingled in Gish's veins.

Marin was stunned. In trying to stand, he stumbled a little, but once he gained bearings, he bent over and dusted off his thighs. He and Gish both panted, their hearts racing. Gish, still bent over, wiped at his gushing nose as thick swaths of blood drained to the ground below him. Marin suddenly felt hot and dizzy. Without warning, he collapsed onto all fours and vomited the coveted rabbit meat into the yellow grass. His black hair hung wild about his bent head, and Marin's thin limbs shook with his heaves.

Gish's face softened. He then suddenly belted a laugh at Marin's unexpected response to this confrontation. His big toothy grin was still stained with blood.

Hearing his hearty laugh, Marin, in between heaves, glared at Gish accusingly, and then, seeing his bloodied grin, felt the urge again. He quickly jolted away to resume his loud retching.

Gish made a louder robust laugh. Though horrific, especially coming from his bloody mouth, his laugh was booming and enjoyable as he found some hilarity at Marin's expense. *It is as if the boy has never seen a fight.*

Of course, Marin hadn't seen a fight like that, nor had he seen death.

Once Marin had finished vomiting, Gish offered him water no longer cool, but nonetheless most welcome to his acid-burned throat.

Gish collapsed to sit on the yellow grass. His thigh was throbbing and continued to ooze thick blood. Laboring with all the load he carried would be more of a challenge and would extend their travel time. Gish was examining the wound when suddenly they heard a horse whinny. The smile returned to Gish's hardened face as he remembered—*Yes!*

"We have horses!" he exclaimed joyfully. The stretch of his grin displayed the range of his large pointed teeth.

Gish was confident that Marin wouldn't try to escape, even on horseback—*where would he go?* They were in the middle of nowhere and the boy would have no way of knowing what direction to take. *And, in this blistering heat and with other potential threats . . . no way would he try to escape.* It was almost laughable. Gish smiled easily.

Marin stood, but then crouched, creeping closely to the horse as if he were afraid it might attack him. Gish grinned at the youth's inexperience, and, forgetting about his injury, slapped his large hands down on his thighs, then loosed a string of colorful curse words at his self-inflicted pain.

The horses remained standing as they grazed on the nourishing yellow grass. They were saddled and ready to ride and ignored Marin's close proximity.

Gish grunted as he rose to stand again. "Marin, when you're done over there . . . uh"—Marin had started to cautiously pet a horse— "just, get over here. We are going to ride these. I'll show you how."

Marin stood straight. He dusted his hands and knees off and wiped his mouth with his forearm. He looked worse than he ever had before, but somehow, oddly, his spirit felt great. He slowly approached Gish, who was now walking toward the brown horse, then slowly stroked its face and began whispering to it.

It was astonishing. *Gish can be peaceful . . . with horses at least,* Marin thought to himself. He glanced down at Gish's leg. He, which was still bleeding profusely.

"You okay?" Marin asked, staring at his leg.

"Yeah," Gish answered in his gruff manner, still focused on the horse. He could feel his rage seeping away at every downward stroke of his hand against the horse's velvet face.

After a moment, Gish was ready. "Let's get you trained to ride a horse and then we can ride out. We'll stop at a river on the way and rest there for the night." He squinted at Marin.

Marin hesitated. It was the most that Gish had yet said, and his voice was almost certainly more pleasant.

Gish assured him, "They're harmless animals. This one"—he stroked the dark chocolate snout close to his shoulder— "this one is Criox." He shot a glance to the tan one nearby, still nibbling at the grass. "That one there is Aspirim." He approached Marin. "I'll teach you all the basics . . . just like I trained *them*"—he pointed to the lifeless riders on the bloodied ground. Grasses hissed in the breeze.

Gish trained them. He didn't like them, but he still trained them. The truth was that he didn't like anyone who served his father. They were all the same: power-hungry, untrustworthy, and cruel. All of them, content to create affliction in others for personal gain. Gish wanted to avoid any other encounters, as he didn't know what horrors other Mysra would inflict on the boy. He wasn't eager to return home with an innocent. This, bringing a WynSprign home, it hadn't been a part of the plan, but perhaps given his status he could keep the boy from any major harm.

Marin looked back up at him. He didn't find total comfort in Gish's response. He didn't find comfort in any of it.

~

Never before these days would Marin have expected to see a horse, let alone ride one! Yet that afternoon Gish helped Marin learn how to mount the horse and use basic commands. The horses ran under Gish's order. He was a master. Marin was in awe at the beauty and grace Gish displayed while working with the beasts. His blood-soaked leg was almost forgotten in magnificence as he worked in tune with the peaceful creatures. It was hard to believe this was the same Mysra that had stolen Marin and killed two of his own kind. *Who in the fires was he?!*

Gish made Marin learn how to pull himself up, mounting the horse, how to sit, how to hold the reigns, and how to give the basic commands. He made Marin learn because he didn't want to have to share a mount and cause undo physical stress for the animal. He also preferred his space. Soon it seemed Marin would be able to move the horse freely, under his own will. Gish was silently satisfied of his work.

Marin was feeling a bit proud of himself—confident, even. He had considered taking a horse and running off with it to escape. But that thought quickly fizzled. He had barely learned how to track in the Great Mist. He had no idea which way to head in these yellow grasses—it seemed they were in the middle of nowhere. Their steps that would have been easy to track in the forest had already long disappeared in waves of swaying golden grass and only an expert could determine the direction from them. He could never find his way back home in enough time to elude his captor. Somewhat defeated, he decided that he would continue to ride along with Gish . . . at least for now.

They strolled a bit on horseback for practice before Gish decided to have them pack up and actually leave. They didn't have much to carry, thanks to the horses. Gish pilfered the contents of the dead Mysra horsemen's pockets and bags and took several items including a canteen, so now Marin could have one of his own. Other items included a piece of meat jerky, a knife, and the hatchet of the dead rider—of course, Gish took this item. The meat jerky wasn't meant to last long. The riders were likely going to hunt for more food, given what little they had.

The two relaxed in the grassy spot to allow Gish time to gain strength. Since they were also unable to hunt, for Gish's obvious fear of being caught by other patrolling Mysra, they'd have to eat the sparse food available and go hungry otherwise. With a rumbling gut, Gish fumbled ineffectively through the satchel.

Is Gish a fugitive himself? Marin's thoughts spun as he watched his abductor.

"Unless . . ." started Marin, almost reading the Mysra's thoughts. His mind flicked to the healthy grass shoots that surrounded them. When hungry, the WynSprigns could always dig for grubs in the small grassy spots of the Great Mist. This was a giant, endless grassy spot. Without explanation, Marin started to dig around him, gently uprooting the thick mats of yellow grass.

Gish looked at him with a confused expression—a stark contrast to the stony demeanor he usually displayed.

Marin looked up to meet his gaze and said simply, "Grubs."

"*Grubs?*" asked Gish.

"Yeah, you know, foraging for grubs."

Gish had never actually eaten a grub, nor had he ever foraged—this was not common for the Mysra to do, for they were talented natural hunters.

"What about grubs?" Gish asked.

Marin was puzzled. "Don't you eat grubs? You know, when food is low?"

"*No*. I never ate grubs," he answered in disgust.

Marin explained the WynSprign practice and resumed digging. After a few moments he squealed, "Success!" He produced a few plump and wriggling peach-colored grubs with black faces and small pincers.

Gish was repulsed. "Baaah! You eat *those*?"

"Well, sure. Really, they're not so bad if you swallow them whole." Marin held his hand out quickly to Gish. The grubs jiggled with the friendly offer.

Gish made a twisted face. This fierce Mysra, with a body that looked to be made of carved stone, was afraid to try a tiny grub. Marin thought this was hilarious but didn't dare laugh, and he worked to maintain just an amused face.

"Okay, look—watch me now," Marin said. He opened his mouth wide, leaned his head back slightly, and popped a grub in. He then swallowed. The grub felt fat and bouncy as it squished against the back of his throat before it went down. He grinned. "See? Now I won't be quite as hungry. Okay, your turn."

Gish grunted and took a grub from Marin's opened hand. He opened his mouth wide and tossed the grub in. He proceeded to swallow it whole while squinting one eye tightly. He then took a moment, remaining expressionless. It was hard to tell if he approved or not. Then, he thought he'd try the last one that Marin had foraged for. He reached forward and took it.

It wasn't long before they had a grub feast. It wasn't the best—they were tasteless, but the grubs satisfied their hunger. In fact, with the carrots, the small bits of jerky, and the many grubs, the hunger that had stabbed at them both was now satisfied.

Marin, after eating, turned over onto his belly and started replanting the uprooted grass stalks.

"What are you doing that for?" Gish asked, his voice graveled and low.

"Well, I'd hate for this small circle we uprooted to die. I'd like more grubs to grow here in this very spot in the future. The only way to make sure that happens is to return the grassy stalk roots to their original condition . . . and this is easy to do, of course."

Gish grunted with a thoughtful nod.

It wasn't long after their feast that they mounted. Gish grimaced with pain but said nothing about his injured thigh. He managed to sit properly on top of his horse and was able to avoid telling Marin of his true intent.

Chapter Ten

Gish and Marin journeyed. Marin hadn't noticed the land had slowly inclined over the last few miles and was now a plateau, still covered with the annoying yellow grass. Marin felt an ache that slowly began to crawl up through his thighs and bottom. Saddle sore. It seemed the more they journeyed, the more the pain barked. Knowing Gish would not welcome comment; Marin remained tight-lipped about this detail and secretly hoped for a rest soon.

They championed their way to the top, and it was there, at the edge of their yellow world, they could see the layout. It was there, on the shelf, that the majesty of Odana finally revealed herself. A swirl of breeze lifted his spirits and Marin's heart pumped a response.

"Odana," Gish announced, pointing toward a line of miniscule light purple mountains in the distance. They were only just visible against the expansive horizon. Though the journey had been lengthy already, Gish clearly wasn't happy about having reached this point. He didn't show any sign of joy at the gorgeous sight of the mountains sleeping in the distance, the color, the beauty, the teaming life before them.

Marin, however, sat on Criox awestruck at the colorful landscape that lay in front of him. He took in the expanse, the up-swelling air that scented of something . . . different. Different from the smell of hot grass. A blue ribbon in the middle distance—a rushing river—was likely the one Gish had mentioned earlier. Then, after the river was a dark blanket of forest that covered the foothills before giving way to the purple veiled mountains whispering in the distance far beyond—and their secret Lanico had taught him: The Castle of Odana.

It was astounding that while Marin had never been here before, he could feel the land pulling him into an invisible embrace. He knew in his soul that this was where he was meant to be. He was a part of this land. The blood that coursed through his veins was once nourished through his mother from the earth here—the vegetation, the water, and the trillium-laced air. He could never leave it again. There were no words that could have allowed Marin to explain it exactly, but this was *his* land. His mind cast back to Lanico's stories as he felt them ever coming true.

Marin studied himself and realized in that moment that this was the yearning; this was what his soul had been pleading for all this time, all these years since childhood. For the first time, he felt as if he were in the exact place, he needed to be . . . with a sense of purpose. There, on that edge overlooking the world beyond, Marin felt his spirit soar.

They began their steep descent down the switchback terrain. The tall yellow grass that he had become accustomed to, thinned out in the distance and gave way to spots of brush, small trees, and other greenery. Marin could see that beyond the river and rolling hills the land appeared greener, but the forest and mountains slowly disappeared from view as they reached the plain below. The greenery, though, this was a welcome change. Marin longed for the color and the comfort of trees again.

Gish made a clicking sound with his tongue and encouraged Aspirim onward. Marin's chocolate mare, Criox, followed closely behind.

It didn't seem long before they arrived at the river- the same one that had appeared as a mere ribbon before. They dismounted, tying the horses to small trees near enough to the edge that the horses were able to walk on the wet pebbles and freely drink the clear-flowing water.

Gish apparently decided it was all right to relax a little, for the horses' sake. A few sparse trees and bushes grew near the riverside, and Marin concluded they would be helpful to provide them cover while letting them see possible dangers.

It was somewhat embarrassing to Marin that the Mysra had to help him off the horse. Gish had seemed a bit friendlier since Marin had helped him with the Mysra attack-or at least, attempted to help. He took out his weathered canteen and the new one and filled them with the fresh, cool river water as Marin hobbled across the ground, stretching his aching muscles and rubbing his backside. Then they both sat in silence on rocks, listening to the nearby rush of the current.

Feeling only slightly more comfortable with Gish, trusting that he might not kill him, Marin bravely decided to ask questions. He straightened, "Gish— what's Odana like?"

Gish took a drink from the canteen, careful of his swollen lips. "Odana has many mountains"—Gish gave a wet sigh—" and the mountains are filled with trillium."

It was obvious to Marin that mountains were not all that the Odana had. From the height of the plateau, Marin had clearly seen forests and hills—the land was vast and lovely, with places that he could perhaps run to and hide in under the cover of night. Gish mentioned "trillium," a word that he had heard before. "What's trillium?"

"Hasn't anyone told you about trillium?" Gish sat up with a look of disbelief.

Marin shook his head slowly in confusion. "Ah . . . no."

Gish sighed in annoyance, and Marin felt like a small child he had to tend to, had to teach.

"Well," Marin continued, "no one ever told *you* about foraging for grubs." He gave a weak smile—he had been bold just then.

The Mysra didn't seem to mind, though. Gish took another big swig of water. "Well," he breathed, "trillium is only the best fighting aid that we Mysra have. And those purple mountains"—he jerked his chin toward the horizon, toward the mountains that were now invisible from this lower elevation. "They're filled with it. It's what gives them that purple shade." He took another swig. "We've been mining the trillium reserves in those mountains since after the Great Divide—the seizure of the castle."

Marin knew that, too, about the seizure—he wasn't that dim. He thought back to the small pouch of powder that Gish had. "What's trillium do?" he asked slowly, trying to read his captor. The Mysra shifted to make himself comfortable.

Chapter Eleven

"When we Mysra take trillium powder," Gish said, wondering what the already boy knew, "it gives us incredible strength and speed." He paused. "It gives us the ability to be effective warriors. We *always* use it in battle." *We always use it . . . Always.* Gish chose to leave out their reliance on the substance. The way his father punished the Mysra by withholding it . . . the contemptuous effects of this discipline.

"Do the Mysra battle often?" Marin asked.

Gish was thankful the WynSprign had changed the topic. He considered the question and realized that he'd find out soon enough, as he soon would be living amongst them. "Yes, we do . . . well, not as we used to. We battle among ourselves." He smiled, thinking of past battles. He loved the surge of energy in a good fight. They all did.

"What was all the battling for?" Marin continued.

"Well . . ." Gish chose his words carefully. "WynSprigns are no longer fighting us. We claimed and took the Odana from them, so we could have access to the trillium in the mountains." He tried to smile but saw alarm in the boy's eyes and went grim again. "Now," he continued, "we fight to prove our strength amongst ourselves."

Gish remembered the dying words of the Mysra: "He'll never accept you now, Gish, even with the WynSprign sl—" Had the boy caught that? Did he know what they were traveling toward?

Marin looked up at him with a question: "Gish . . . Why are you taking me to Odana?"

Gish swallowed hard and narrowed his eyes at Marin, and his voice became lower, somber. "I made a promise." He shot a quick glance toward the hidden mountains, many miles off, and then back at Marin. "I need to take you back."

The boy furrowed his brow and looked down with a frown. He had a spirit about him that suggested he would not go along so meekly, especially if he knew what awaited him. If Gish just remained friendly . . .

The Mysra thought back to the events that had brought him here as he continued to wrestle with himself about his place in the Mysra order. The dying rider's words echoed in his mind. As ludicrous as is seemed, he *still* didn't know what he was going to do with the boy.

Gish had been a constant disappointment to his father, the Mysra leader Grude. Since their creation under Fray Jaspia, the Mysra had been a strong brutish race unapologetic in all their conquests and as mighty as the boulders they had been formed from, black blood running in their veins. It had been Jaspia's intention to design them in this way. As the next ranking leader of the Mysra under Grude, Gish had duties and expectations to adhere to. He had long been viewed as soft, easily bent to care for the slaves and the horses he kept. His most recent disappointment before Grude and the occasion for this task of capturing a taken WynSprign from the Great Mist, was that Gish had prevented a Mysra guard, Fuemer, from punishing a WynSprign slave. That alone made him a shame to the race.

But then, Gish committed the most disdainful act, one that should have been punishable by death.

Gish did not stop with protecting the slave but, in a blind rage, killed Fuemer. It was only because he was Grude's son that Gish was spared execution. To prove his love and loyalty to Grude, he was to retrieve information about the hidden WynSprign village. This would prove to Grude Gish's worthiness to continue as his son and heir.

He hadn't *exactly* discovered the hidden village, but he was very close to it, and he had retrieved a WynSprign. Perhaps that would be good enough.

Gish thought this over while sitting near the calm river. Something about the boy made him think of the slave he'd spared that day. He dug his feet into the gravel below his boulder as he heard again the crack of the whip and Fuemer's fury. He narrowed his eyes in thought.

The slave was one Gish knew well—she had an old wound that tore at her side and hindered her work at times. Gish purposefully looked away, ignoring her feeble work. When he looked at her, she'd slide a soft glance at him, adding a subtle grateful nod. She was a stoic one. There was something about her. Something about the strength in her expression . . .

That day the guards had brought her out from her hut. She kicked and screamed against them, her bonnet-covered head twisting and lolling as they jolted her. They were too strong, pulling her to the center post of the encampment.

They tore her tunic from her with one easy pull and she collapsed in defeat. She knelt exposed, save for the bonnet still secured to her head. Her panting visible at her expanding, visible ribcage. She knelt, waiting. Today they wouldn't secure her to the post. No, instead the guards at her sides held her wrists. The scars on her back were long, white diagonals that ran parallel to one another, testifying to her earlier punishments. The worst scar, on her side, was a deep hole that drew a shadow in the midday sun. Gish didn't know the origin of that particular scar, but whatever inflicted it must have been horrendous. There was the sound of a soft, hot breeze before the familiar *CRACK*!

Gish grunted out loud, just thinking of the way she had jerked upward. A jolt against the piercing sting. The skin on her bare back split instantly. The wail-like moan of her voice remained clear. Her thin, quivering arms were held firmly by two Mysra guards. He clenched his fists as he remembered Fuemer's pleasure-laden smile, now etched in his mind.

Fuemer was most pleased with his work. The new crimson line that ran diagonally matched the white ones he had placed there before. He fondled the familiar grip in his hand, curling his fingers around it. He coiled back, ready again for another strike. It would be three in total for today's disobedience—ignoring the call to work.

Before he could strike for the second time, Gish ran toward him, determined to stop the next whip. It was unbearable. Every pounding step took him nearer. He heard his voice as he shouted, "Fuemer! Stop!"

Fuemer paused, his eye twitching. Waiting . . .

Gish closed in, panting, "Stop. Stop punishing the slaves in this way—it's not going to cause them to work harder, just slower . . . from pain."

Fuemer's flush of pleasure turned to rage with every second that Gish spoke, and Gish could see contempt on Fuermer's face. He read the message: *You weak son of Grude. The ONLY thing that makes you remotely significant is your place as Grude's son. That. Is. All.*

Fuemer's fist tightened around the grip and the leather groaned, and he sneered at Gish.

"We need to get more production from them—not pain," Gish added quickly, his breathing ragged. "We'll get more out of them without . . . this"—he gestured between the slave and the whip.

Fuemer glowered at Gish, and Gish saw his whip hand twitch—*He'd love nothing more than to whip me, too.*

Gish looked around to see other Mysra guards and a few slaves watching this dishonoring confrontation.

Then Fuemer tilted his head back to swallow a pouch of trillium, and a growl crawled from his throat: "It would do you well to keep to yourself and pay this no mind. Just because you're Grude's son, you think you can order me around." He swallowed the grit down and tossed his pouch to the ground. "There is no room here for weakness, Gish, nor is there room for belittling me in this moment of discipline." As he spoke, all could see the trillium dance in him, surging. His flush of pleasure from the whipping had been fully replaced by anger.

The bloodthirsty crowd were writhing in anticipation to see how Fuemer was going to teach this spoiled brat son of their leader a lesson. Nobody liked the interruption of a painful punishment of a slave but a Mysra scuffle—that was even better.

Fuemer pushed up his sleeves to settle the score.

Gish read him.

They locked eyes.

There was a pause and Gish stood silently. His fingers twitched at his sides. He felt years of his own anger bubbling inside, convulsing, twisting, and boiling. This gruesome guard, his judgment—everyone's judgment—his damned wicked father. Their twisted, sick punishments for minor disobedience—even from a wounded slave. His own father was the overseer of all of this cruelty.

Gish was disgusted. Appalled at this ugliness.

Even now—in the stillness, sitting near the river, near the WynSprign that reminded him of that poor slave—Gish recalled his fury.

Gish recalled the wild look, the flash in Fuemer's eyes when he suddenly drove his knife into his chest—and ended him.

News of Gish's "outburst" reached his father when Nizen, the second-in-command under Fuemer at the WynSprign encampment, hurried off, delighted to bear the news that would unleash Grude's fury. Grude, mortified at his son's actions, demanded Gish's presence in the throne room immediately.

There was no fight, no brawl. If they'd had a traditional Mysra grappling, one that would satisfy the bloodlust of all gathered, and if Gish had triumphed through his own strength, Grude could have taken some satisfaction in that, brushing aside the disrespect of challenging Fuemer's administration of Grude's rule. But Gish had simply stabbed him.

It was not a good image for Gish, nor for Grude. It placed Grude in a precarious position.

As Gish made his way, under guard, to his father's place in the old WynSprign castle, he knew what the audience would be like. The old Mysra leader sat on a throne intended for legendary WynSprign rulers who had ruled there over the WynSprign for many generations. Now Grude sat there, not with dignity, but in decadence. In his immense love of trillium and wine, Grude had a small table beside him with a decanter of his private selection of yellowberry wine, taken from the west. Next to it sat a covered silver bowl of trillium. The glittery purple surface of the trillium had the letter "G" pressed into its center, at every daily refill.

Once in the throne room Gish had noticed Neen in attendance, the one who served as Grude's assistant and advisor at times and had no doubt been whispering ideas into Grude's head about what to do with Gish. He stood beside the throne on the dais steps, waiting on Grude like an opportunistic spider. He longed to be Grude's favorite and had been jealous of Gish for being Grude's actual son.

As Gish slowly approached his father, he held a downward gaze and made a small, humble bow.

Grude scowled and inhaled sharply. He wasted no time telling Gish exactly what was in his mind about this atrocious behavior. His thin gray lips pulled back before he hissed, "You are supposed to be next in line to lead the Mysra!" He leaned forward, clutching the armrests of the throne. "We don't apologize to the mountains for taking the trillium—we took it because they stood silent! We don't apologize to the WynSprign—they lost at the battle! It's OUR time to rule this damn kingdom and I cannot rely on you, Gish! All these years I've been trying to groom you . . . I—I cannot!" His higher-pitched shouts reverberated in the expanse of the throne room, and he did not finish his sentence.

Grude sat uncomfortably on the throne, shifting his weight in tense thought, then relaxed a little in disappointment—Gish saw his shoulders slump. "It's almost as if you prefer to spend time with the horses than your own folk, your own people. I don't understand you, Gish. Perhaps it comes from your mother's side . . ." *Yes. Perhaps.*

Neen, standing near the throne, had a slight smile at Grude's railing.

"How is it that I have YOU for a son?" Grude continued. "You've been weak. An embarrass—" Grude withheld the end of the word, pausing as a Mysra servant boy ran to approach the throne.

The boy made a small bow and handed a scroll to Grude. Gish stood silent in front of his father, waiting for more of his verbal lashing, his head bowed. Grude fumbled to open the scroll and read, mumbling the words to himself. His mood changed at whatever news this document held. His gray lumpy body looked as if it were melting into the throne with his intense focus on the scroll. He was losing the menacing muscular form of just about every other of his kind.

Once finished he sat thoughtfully. "Huuuh" rebounded on the walls.

Gish looked up questioningly; waiting for whatever came next from his father's disapproving spirit.

Grude stared at him for a moment, then he spoke: "Gish, I have one last quest for you . . . a task. It is a chance for you to live up to your family legacy. I need you to meet with an old WynSprign ally for me, northeast, at Horse's Clearing. This is to discuss arrangements for adding to our WynSprign collection."

Gish felt a deadly hollow grow in his gut.

Grude looked around. "Everyone!"—he barked—"out!" The few Mysra present in the throne room quickly cleared out, except for Neen. Grude clutched the armrests of the throne and inched closer to Gish, almost standing up from the throne. His neck jutted outward, and he beckoned his son closer. The white tufts of his eyebrows caught stray light from the window. Grude whispered. His warm breath puffed against Gish's ear—"In truth, I need you to visit Horse's Clearing to get him to talk about their hidden realm. Tell me all that you find out. Tell me every word. The ally already knows who you are and may be comfortable with you. In secret, I have been baiting him deliberately over the years and, now is the time." Gish was well aware of the castle menagerie of black starling messenger pigeons.

Gish backed away, his face as solemn as stone. "Yes, Father." Then he looked down and started to turn to descend the few throne stairs.

Gish knew why he wanted to find their hidden realm: he wanted to expand the trade in slaves and the southern range had yet to be mined.

"Here!"—Grude erupted, pulling at something from under the red velvet cushion. He produced a small brown coin bag and tossed it to Gish, who caught it in one hand. "This particular WynSprign will want an award of some kind," Grude said. "Give that to him. It should make him happy . . . for now." Grude rolled his eyes.

Gish looked down, nodded, and turned to walk out.

"Gish, my son!" Grude shouted down the length of the room and Gish paused in place. "This is your last chance to prove your devotion to me, to our cause. Listen!"—spittle flew as he yelled —"if you fail, you will no longer be given the seat of this throne upon my death!" The piercing words echoed through the chamber.

Gish had closed his eyes for a moment, and Neen patted Grude on the shoulder and whispered some poisonous thing into the ruler's ear, Gish resumed his march out of the castle.

Chapter Twelve

Excitement and then relief came over Lanico as he could view trees appearing from beside the distant brook ahead. A smile slid across his face and he loosed a low laugh of thunder. The timing was perfect, as the sun was going to set soon. The trees in the distance gave him newfound energy and he sprinted toward the brook. If he continued to follow the tracks from here, the next stop might very well be Gray Rock.

The tall grasses nicked at his calves in defiance of his every stride. As he approached the brook, he was welcomed by sparse swaying trees and the song of their clamoring leaves. He sighed in pleasure. "The sound—oh—it's like home." He had longed after the color *green* that had kept him partly content in the Great Mist all these years, because it was like his home. To him green signaled life, a promise of more . . . it was his favorite color, after all.

The thick yellow grasses thinned and gave way to sandy and then rocky ground, the closer he came to the water source. There he knelt to fill his nearly empty canteen. The cool water was most welcome to his parched lips and burning throat. He sat on the ground and allowed the heaviness that plagued him to melt into the boulder he leaned back on at the edge of the stream. He was nearly to Gray Rock. His bones were tired. His muscle-corded calves and thighs throbbed from the hours he'd spent walking. He allowed himself to relax, but only briefly, though the few minutes stretched in his mind. He stirred himself and quickly worked to set up a small camp a slight distance away, hidden amongst the trees.

He remained mindful and stayed close to the large footprints and hooves that he had been tracking. The person he tracked seemed to know the terrain and the best way to get here—Lanico was thankful for that. While there was still light in the sky, he eagerly gathered fallen twigs and started a small fire. He then prepared for battle . . . intending to catch fish by spearing them with the Reluctant Leader, straining his awakening triceps with the unaccustomed downward thrusts. After several failed attempts, he finally speared a fish, cutting it almost in half.

It wasn't long before the fish was sizzling over the open fire. Lanico leaned back against a small tree as the cool breeze and the tree songs brought him back home. As the fish roasted, he felt himself drift into sleep. Suddenly, his eyes flew open at the sound of giggling. The sky was dark, the fire was out, and the fish was . . . *well* overcooked. Without a sound, he clenched Reluctant Leader at his thigh.

Silence. Save for the chirping of insects.

The azure of his glowing eyes shot quick glances into the dark. A full-circle moon blanketed all the surroundings in its gentle glow. A side-glance caught movement near the river and, focusing, he could see three figures sitting on river rocks. Women.

Seeing his attention on them, they resumed giggling and pointed at him. He felt it odd but remembered his manners. He could very well be trespassing on their land. It *had* been many years since he'd traveled here after all.

"Hello!" he called, pushing himself off the ground. "I apologize if I am intruding. I was in need of water and a place for the night." He walked over to them, slowly. Reluctant Leader was still sheathed in its scabbard, but at the ready. He brushed his palm against the pommel for good measure. "I do hope it's okay if I stay, just this night . . ." He led with a flashed smile to feign friendliness through the caution he felt prickling up his spine.

He saw that the women were more beautiful than any he'd ever seen—except for *her,* of course. These women were not of WynSprign blood—he knew this instantly. He didn't know what they were, exactly, but their beauty was beyond description. Each had long, full hair in a brilliant color. One had deep purple hair like amethyst, another sapphire blue, and the third—he gulped—*of brilliant emerald.* He hadn't seen emerald hair since Treva. The very sight of her, the emerald-haired one—*Oh, Fires! This must be a trick!* She was *enchantingly* beautiful.

They wore very little clothing. In fact, the diaphanous material they wore was so thin that he briefly wondered what was the purpose of wearing anything at all. *They are practically naked!* Lanico, maintaining his manners and respectability, focused his gaze on their star-filled eyes and translucent, dew-kissed cheeks. He continued ambling forward, saying warmly but with caution, "I mean you no harm." His smile was stiff.

The woman with purple hair started talking, her voice as smooth as silver: "Welcome to our river, most handsome stranger. We'd like you to stay for the night . . . *or longer*." She turned to the others, and they erupted in bashful giggles.

That sound. *It's wrong. Off somehow.*

"Well, thank you, this is most appreciated," he said graciously, "but I'll be heading back now." He made small bows and turned slowly to start back to his camp.

"Don't you want to dine with us?" asked the woman with sapphire hair. Her slow, sensuous voice again sent subtle tingles down the length of his spine. Lanico stopped mid-stride, hesitant to turn to look back at them. He didn't want any part of whatever these women were up to. He looked back at their excited eyes and worked to find words to neither offend nor anger them. "I really would be honored; however, I've already made my meal for the evening." He glanced back at the pitiful blackened fish at his small camp. He frowned at the fish, but turned a smile back to them.

The women started to saunter toward him. As they came closer Lanico palmed the hilt of his sword, but in a swift, surprising move, they shoved him down on the pebbled ground, where the cool grit scrubbed his back beneath him. The women playfully stumbled down next to him on either side, blue and green hair whipping against him. More giggling. He noticed the woman with the purple hair was walking away—she moved along the river.

Taking effort to not harm them, Lanico fought to free himself—to sit up and focus on where she was headed. The remaining two women began massaging his shoulders and back. Their hands met his hidden sore muscles. They cuddled closely, moving into his space, squirming against his sides and arms. He fought, ignoring the temptation of identifying which of their body parts were pressed against him.

"Ooo! So meaty and strong!" one excitedly giggled as they looked at each other with knowing grins. They started pulling at his tunic, rubbing their hands along the lean planes of his chest beneath.

"Ladies, p—please," Lanico tried protesting through the shirt as they lifted it over his head. Still unaware of their actual intentions, he wanted to avoid confrontation. When his bare chest was exposed the one with green hair leaned in front of him, her eyes now fixed on his. They called him in. *Closer. Closer.* A voiceless demand.

His pulse quickened. He felt himself growing tense with excitement. He didn't want to lose his better judgement. He breathed in deep. Focus. *Focus.* He pushed their grasping hands off as he sensed movement ahead. The purple-haired woman came ambling back and smiling a fox's smile. In her dainty hands was a goblet. The green-haired woman grabbed his face forcefully, to refocus his gaze on her. *Emerald hair,* he thought longingly.

"Evelena, don't grab him too hard!" cautioned the beauty with the amethyst-colored tresses, now closing her distance.

"But Neldra, why should you have all the fun?" Evelena answered.

Neldra came close with the goblet she tipped near his lips. Lanico nervously laughed, saying he wasn't thirsty, and fought to stand and free himself from these women, but they forcefully pulled him down again and insisted. Evelena playfully pinched his nose. The women sat close to him, leaning into him while holding down his arms. He focused on the contents of the goblet—a thick pink beverage. He unwillingly drank and smiled at them while swallowing only a very little down. It tasted sweet, but he recognized this wasn't any juice or nectar he'd ever tasted.

And there it was. Instantly he felt his limbs grow heavy. His body became warm and tingly with every following pump of his heart. He played along and made himself seem to playfully bump the goblet, sending its pink liquid pouring out and the cup rolling away. The women couldn't see how much had been wasted in the darkness.

He felt for the grip of Reluctant Leader and grasped it forcefully, only to realize his grasp was only mere pawing. Quickly. He was being overcame quickly. Panicked, he realized he should have acted sooner. He had felt it was wrong to trust them and now, *Damn it!*

Against his own will, he lost control. He leaned back on the grass and felt himself succumb and drift asleep. His head felt heavy just before it landed backward with a thump on the ground and his vision grew dim and hazy. The three beautiful women were sprawled on him and looking down on his fair, slumbering face. The one with emerald locks smiled dreamily down at him, her long hair draped around his face. His heavy lids closed as he found himself dreaming of her again. Of *her*. Of Treva.

~

A metallic clanking sound rang in his ears as Lanico awoke suddenly with a jolt. He was lying on the ground inside a large shack. The reek alone sobered him. A putrid stench of mildew and rot hung heavy in the air. He shot glances around at the walls filled with hanging herbs and other plants and shelves with jars full of black muck, or various animal parts. The place was filthy. He didn't dare make a further move or sound. His head pounded and his ears rang at that damn metallic clang from their spoon, still stirring away.

With caution, he turned his head toward the source of the noise to find three monstrous hags bickering. They hovered over a cauldron like thin, twisted trees, their bony backs to him. They all had long, thin gray hair hanging from their mostly bald heads. From his angle, he could see the large nose jutting out from the face of the one he saw in profile. Their skin hung off their bodies like gray melting candle wax.

"No, no, Nildra! Eel moss will overpower his WynSprign flavor," one hag lectured, her voice shrill. "It has been far too long since we enjoyed the taste of WynSprign—especially a *meaty* one."

"Oh? And what do *you* know about eel moss? You have no idea of its properties." The one called Nildra punctuated her words with jabs of her large spoon.

"Evelena, you confuse the taste of Prondolins with the taste of WynSprigns," the third offered.

"But he's more than WynSprign—*isn't he*? He has an ancient blood in him, far older than the WynSprign." Evelena purred in delight imagining his rich, rare taste.

Lanico was bewildered but in summoning rational thoughts, he realized his need to get out of there. These women planned to eat him! As they bickered, Lanico felt for his sword. *Please, Odan on High.* He slowly moved his hand down toward his side to meet the hilt. Relief swept over him—*The sword is still here!* He was grateful that he hadn't drunk all the liquid in the goblet. The small amount ingested hadn't kept him asleep as long as they had planned, he was sure. They obviously hadn't felt the need to remove his weapon.

Lanico pulled himself up to stand. *Whoa!* The world around him swirled that instant, and he struggled to find his footing. He curled his hand around his sword's grip. The smooth drag of Reluctant Leader sang as he freed it from the sheath. Eyeing the hags, he stumbled as he moved forward, beginning to swing the sword wildly. He wasn't fighting with measured grace, but rather haphazardly, for survival. His careless swipes swooshed through the thick air. The hags didn't hear and remained focused on the cauldron, bickering.

Lanico neared with wild swings and slashed through a hag's arm. She screamed in sudden horror as black blood shot violently from her stump and the arm flopped to the floor. The other two, completely off guard, hissed at him through thick saliva and thin gray teeth. One was trying to conjure a chant. Nildra held up her spoon defiantly, ready to either strike him or chuck it at him. Either way, he didn't want to find out. His heavy footing hinted that he wasn't entirely able to walk at full capacity. He swung his blade at the other hag reciting chants, swiftly taking off her head. It rolled from her shoulders and fell with a heavy thud on the ground as her body followed. Long gray strands of hair coiled around the head through black, trailing blood.

Next came Nildra: he grabbed that damned spoon from her bony clutches, hurling it away. Before she could respond, he ran the sword through her chest in a smooth glide, then pulled it out with the aid of his foot against the trunk of her body, and her thin bones landed on the ground, softly. More black blood oozed out. Black blood . . . creations of Fray Jaspia.

The hag that was now missing an arm was curled up, cradling her new stump in her lap. She stopped screaming and hissed at him. Black splattered blood covered her face and doused her twisted body.

Lanico looked around, dazed, still blinking himself awake from this atrocious nightmare. He needed to leave this hovel of evil. He stumbled to the curtain door and flung it open to inhale fresh, cold air in the early blue of day. The single remaining hag screamed in searing pain inside the death shack. Lanico, who was usually merciful, would have put her out of her misery any other day. However, in his urgency, he didn't care if she lived; he *needed* to find Marin. That was his biggest priority, and too much time had been wasted on the hags already.

As Lanico walked into the dawn of a new day, he *now* recalled why he was supposed to be wary of this river. The subtle alarm he felt before was now understood. He had never encountered these three witches, but had heard stories about them in past years. The legend was that they were once three enchanting goddesses crafted by Fray Jaspia. Creations that Father Odan punished for some reason now long forgotten. Now, they craved flesh, always. At night, they lured and seduced those wandering in the area, with plans to later dine on them.

Once a safe distance away from the shack, he rinsed his face in the river and cleaned the Reluctant Leader before housing it in its sheath.

He needed to get back to his small camp, find the tracks, and get on his way before much more time was wasted. He could just barely see that the tracks going to the shack came from his left. He decided to follow these along the river to his camp. It wasn't long before the howls from the lone surviving hag quieted in the receding distance behind.

Lanico spotted the boulders where he had sat near the river, and his heart lightened. He blinked, feeling the weariness leave his eyes, body, and mind. He hurried to his blackened fish, cold on the long-dead campfire. He gratefully devoured it. He had slept well, *too well*. He found his tunic lying on the dusty ground and quickly pulled it over his shoulders. He wrapped his green cloak around himself, added cool water to his canteen, and grabbed the satchel. He then found the footsteps he had been tracking before and started on his way, aided by a walking stick he fashioned from a fallen limb.

Pushing himself onward, he thought of his time with Izra and Treva so long ago—mostly Treva, his emerald knight. He raked his mind over what could have been had he not turned her away. Had he not denied returning that kiss she planted on him. Had he *not* upheld the integrity of his higher rank – unlike Izra. Yes. He identified he was still bitter over that.

Lanico still felt her lips brushing against his even now. Those lips held that slight yet seductive scar that had been inflicted by only-Odan-knew-what. The scar curving the bow of her mouth more, making a permanent pout.

He breathed out.

Treva had been a far better warrior than Izra, perhaps even better than himself. Her death still hung over him, heavy and dark as a shroud.

He had always loved her, had never stopped loving her. Not even in her marriage to Izra, or even at her death.

Defenses up, he hardened his heart.

She was gone and there was nothing left to cling to, except that part of her that still lived. Except for Marin.

~

The sun had been up for hours, highlighting the Yellow Vast, and was once again showing noon. Lanico had been diligently following the horse tracks after Marin. While deep in thought about Treva, he returned to the present and noticed what seemed to be a clearing ahead. Picking up his pace, he followed the horse's tracks to the spot.

The pace of the horse didn't seem to slow, its hoof prints regular. Then it seemed that suddenly the horse had taken a deep turn and—and . . . there it was. Lanico could see the furry-mounded sides and depressions outlining the horse's ribcage beyond the grasses. After a slightly warm mounting breeze, he realized that he didn't need to see it—he smelled its hot decaying body. Lanico approached the dead animal, covering his mouth and nose with his green cloak and nervously inspecting the area. His silver hair swayed as he looked around.

Whew! Marin is not here, he thought to himself in relief. Before standing, Lanico noticed that the horse had two twisted legs, but had not died from these injuries. The amount of blood that stained the ground showed that this stallion had been slaughtered. Flies had already gathered on its dried unseeing eyes.

It was a most gruesome sight, the end of this stunning animal. However, the rider of this horse had cared enough to allow him to die quickly and end the suffering. He could see in the trampled wave of grasses that items had fallen off the horse, but were all taken, *and . . . a body imprint*? His mind roiled. Based on the small size, he had a feeling that it was—*He fell . . . again?* Lanico was only partially surprised at this revelation. For as stealthy as Marin could be, he had his share of missteps.

From the ground, a small flash shimmered at the edge of his vision. Lanico paused. Down in the grasses, there was a glint of light reflecting— something. Lanico bent to get a better look, his fingers dancing over the warmed earth and grass stalks. He gasped. *It can't be.*

But it was.

Marin's tooth necklace!

The necklace fell into a neat pile in his palm, the white tooth shiny and bright. The weight of it was familiar in his own hands.

A wave of relief swept over him. He was on the right track. Any doubts he harbored about his decision to leave the Great Mist in the pursuit of Marin now fell. He felt a surge of renewed energy and drive to press on quickly. He hastily clasped the necklace around his neck, and the tooth rested snugly between his clavicles, hanging higher for him than on Marin. With a sigh and a smile, he looked out into the Yellow Vast and started to march with long strides forward. Based on the direction of the heavy tracks, a Mysra—possibly carrying Marin? —was headed to Gray Rock. The tooth jiggled on his pale translucent skin at the rhythm of his long strides. He lifted a prayer to Odan. *Please, don't let Marin be captured by a Mysra. If I arrive too late . . . No.* He wouldn't finish the worried thoughts.

Chapter Thirteen

At the Castle of Odana, Grude sat on the throne of his almost-empty throne room. Being one of the select few to practice, he had considered taking to the sword again today, to train. But . . . he had already done that.

He sighed. The sound of even that sigh caused him an eye roll.

Every movement he made echoed against the stone floors, pillars, and walls. So much space. He was annoyed by the constant echoes, or rather it was the boredom. This only enhanced his annoyance with Gish, since he had nothing else to ponder. Grude was impatient—Gish hadn't returned yet from his vital task and the Mysra leader began to wonder, *Is he taking seriously his position as my son?* Other warriors, countless loyal others, would have loved to be in Gish's position. *Why does he have to be such a useless pain in the ass, especially at this time of our great need?*

Grude felt his goal hindered—he wanted to make this kingdom great for himself and for his Mysra. The allotted quantities of trillium for his people had begun to rattle them over time. They *needed* more. Craved more—the temptation, the taste. Even he wouldn't dare go without it.

Yet they couldn't get more trillium unless they could start mining in the southern Odana Mountains range, and they couldn't mine there without the aid of more able-bodied WynSprigns. He loathed the thought of managing the throngs of them, but the ones he currently kept had already been pushed to their limits and many had since died off from old age and poor conditions. He clutched his hands on the armrests. The gray skin over his knuckles stretched white.

He looked over to Neen, a constant accessory at his side. As always, Neen was on alert and expressionless. Grude knew he could trust this servant, certainly more than he trusted Gish. He needed the most trustworthy with him right now. Neen had more interest in acting a like son to him than did Gish. After all, Grude had taken in Neen and his younger brother Gax when they were young, when their parents were killed by WynSprign warriors years ago.

"I'm tired of waiting, Neen," Grude hissed. The shrill reverberation of his voice bounded against the walls. "Gish has not returned and I want news, *good news*." He leaned over and took a long sip from his goblet of chilled yellowberry wine. His eyes roamed over the glistening purple powder on the tray nearby. "I have a task for you, Neen," Grude whispered wetly. "Bring me back Gish. Find him." He paused to swirl his wine, still considering. "Or, if you cannot find him . . . find the WynSprigns' hidden village, at *least*. That's likely a better proposition anyway. Yes. Go to Horse's Clearing and seek out any possible evidence there. We need more hands to mine the trillium and I *know* we can find them."

Neen looked at Grude and nodded without answer. Grude knew Neen was ambitious—pleased to have additional responsibilities that would put him in the right place with his ruler. At this point, he'd do anything that Grude demanded. It was the perfect time. This most trustful and worthy servant was better than Gish, and he'd be willing to prove it.

Chapter Fourteen

Though it hung lower in the afternoon sky, the sun continued its relentless scorching attack on the grasslands. Lanico continued tracking with careful strides. He paused to remove his thick green cloak from his shoulders and back. He draped it over his head and around his neck, using it as a thick shield against the sun. He loathed direct sunlight on his tender skin, but he couldn't take the heat much longer.

After a few more hours, he was filled with gratitude at a most welcome sight. The outline of Gray Rock loomed in the distance. He hoped this small mountain still teemed with rabbits, as it had many years prior. The scarce rations had left him ravenous and he wasn't fond of grubs at the thought of roasting rabbit flanks instead. He stopped focusing on the tracks, for they plainly led straight there.

Once at the abandoned camp, Lanico dropped his belongings and immediately searched for evidence of Marin. There were both the large footprints and a smaller set, a rope that had been cut through, bare spots where things had been placed on the ground, recently charred wood. Tufts of rabbit fur still billowed around. A body imprint suggested someone small had been lying near the small fire. *Marin.* He noticed handprints on the ground. "Marin's hands," he said quietly to himself. When he saw the trailing of fingers through the dirt, he knew: *He was looking for the necklace. He realized it was missing.*

Lanico looked up and around at the high stiff peaks of gray rock, the wrathful work of his Fray aunt. He would not stay the night here. Though he desired pressing on after the tracks, he also rationalized that he needed rest to restore himself for more hours in the lingering, punishing sun. He lowered himself to sit in the narrow shadow of boulders and drank deeply from his canteen. He leaned back on the flat boulder that his Marin had leaned against not very long ago. He wanted to *feel* him there. Being in that same spot brought small comfort. He imagined the warmth of his son's body still lingering upon it.

Never a fan of idle time, Lanico would make good use of the fire pit. He'd dine on rabbit, too, to keep up his strength. Using his supplies, he prepared the small campfire—this was relatively easy since the person who set it up before him didn't douse the fire—everything was dry and ready to ignite. He opened his tinderbox and went to work striking steel and flint. After a few moments of sparks, a flicker of fire started on bits of the abandoned rope. Then he set out on a hunt. It wasn't long before Lanico was eating sizzling rabbit meat. Once he finished, it was time to leave this temporary shelter—there was little time to waste. He dusted himself off, gathered his bag, and bundled-up cloak. He also obscured his footprints, just in case someone was tracking him. Before heading out, he viewed the space that he had just occupied. He pursed his lips, gave a stiff nod in approval, and promptly started heading off. He would once again delve into the Yellow Vast.

He followed the two sets of tracks this time—the large gait, and a smaller one . . . Marin's. The tracks were headed southwest, toward Odana.

~

It seemed like hours had passed when Lanico noticed clearings among the yellow grasses ahead. He could hear buzzing flies as he came near. With a familiar panic, he ran, closing the distance between himself and the clearing. Again, the stench of rot greeted him and his heart raced in fear. Thoughts swirled in a torrent of nightmarish images, waiting to be realized.

He found the bodies of two dead Mysra—but where was Marin? The two appeared to have been stabbed, and their black blood was everywhere. As before, he held his cloak over his mouth and nose to stifle the smell, a smell that would only grow worse as the hours passed. His eyes darted around, searching frantically near the bodies. *Marin?* Lanico's heart pounded wildly. *Did Marin see all this? Who is he traveling with? Is one of these his captor?* His mind roiled over horrific possibilities.

Lanico reviewed the death scene. Then he noticed horse tracks . . . from two horses.

On horseback again, he thought in mounting frustration. He'd have to press harder, picking up his pace. "Perhaps I can catch them at rest, once they've stopped for the beasts," he mumbled aloud.

He looked up to the sky. The sun was hanging at the horizon with hints of orange and rose. Lanico knew that he couldn't track in the night, but he also didn't want to wait any longer to intercept Marin. He'd press on, trying to track as well as he could in the fading light. There was no sense in investigating these two dead Mysra—Marin wasn't here, thankfully.

He resumed his trek in the direction the horses had taken. He could feel the slight incline that indicated he was nearing the end of this long plateau, and his strides were long to match the urgency of his mission—no good was going to come to Marin without his interception. Lanico was a Loftre. A royal, for Odan's sake. He'd sooner die than have Marin, an Odana heir under him, experience a life of misery.

Chapter Fifteen

Slaves, with their hair and clothes covered in purple dust, emerged from the many mines that dotted the eastern Odana Mountains range. They could no longer smell trillium after many years of the fine dust landing in their mouths, inhaled into their nostrils and lungs, ground into their hair and skin and clothes. Trillium had no effect on WynSprigns, which made them the perfect miners for the addictive mineral. The quick flare in temper and in strength seemed to come only to the Mysra, the ones who drove the slaves.

The sun had begun to set, signaling the approaching time for WynSprign mining slaves to return to their huts under the watchtower to the west. It bordered the encampment menacingly.

The small huts were once used near the castle for Odana Soldiers, and many of the huts were relocated to just outside the mine entrances, though some huts remained near the castle for the WynSprign castle slaves. The huts were weathered and in dire need of restoration, but the Mysra had no interest in replacing or repairing them, and the slaves had done what little they could to keep them functional over the many years. The Mysra *did*, however, repair and reinforce the barbed-wire fences and the trenches that surrounded the slave encampments, and maintained other security features as well. There were areas though- areas that they had neglected to update over the years.

Trillium-addicted Mysra warriors patrolled the small hut villages with customary large knives and scowls. The Mysra would start their guard shift with a heavy serving of trillium to pump them up, ready for punishing. The WynSprigns feared the severity of punishment and few challenged the system, but for those that dared, punishment was inevitable. Death was a possibility, but rare. The value of the slaves kept them alive, but only just barely.

The long line of WynSprigns leaving the Purple Halls mine resembled from a distance slightly swaying purple flowers dotting the sides of the mountain. WynSprigns young and old lined up to leave their work for the next day, returning to the small hut village at the base of the mountain. Then they would promptly go into their huts, clean the purple dust from themselves, and gather outside for their final meal of the day.

One WynSprign, small but strong, stood at the fire pit. Like all of them, she had hands stained the characteristic purple from years of mining, concealing the battle scars that laced up from her fingers to her wrists, and even higher.

She stood, leaning slightly forward, holding a large spoon. It was her turn today, after her long shift at the mine, to hand out rolls and stir the large cauldron of stew. She was to ladle out the thick contents to waiting WynSprigns in line. Her long tunic and leggings hid her thin body. A faded bonnet, barely secured by the tie at the nape of her neck, was in need of attention, for a section of emerald hair had loosed and curved around her face. She stopped to discreetly tuck it behind her ear and tug the bonnet lower before anyone noticed, noticed the brazen color.

One by one, they held out their wooden bowls, waiting to receive the brown stew she ladled, and the hard, brown roll she would place atop the stew. Sweat on her brow glistened from the flames beneath the cauldron. While no one was watching, she quickly palmed several brown rolls and shoved them in her pocket. She had never considered that she'd be palming rolls away instead of daggers one day. But those glorious days were long, long gone.

A small boy approached next from the line and held up his bowl. She carefully bent low to dole out the stew and prevent him from getting too close to the boiling pot.

A stab of pain made her suddenly grunt and wince. She recoiled and quickly grabbed at her side, pressing at the thick scar that served as her constant insult, a reminder of captivity. It delivered stabbing pain that limited her movements and reminded her daily of all that she had lost. Or, *perhaps*, she had often considered, *it was a gift from Odan himself, for failing my family, for having failed at my highest duty*. She supposed she deserved this—the pain, even the slavery.

After her former years of rebellion in this shithole, she now embraced it, all of it. Slowly, the dainty veil of complacency had, over the years, turned into a reality. She was broken and atoning. Her days of skull bashing, combat missions, brothel visits, and tavern brawls were faded into the recesses of her memory. The role of *Emerald Knight* had left her.

Even her silent defender, Gish, had left now.

She huffed a defeated sigh and lifted another ladle full of the brown stew, pouring it into another countless bowl. The slight scar on her lip was barely visible with the weak feigned smile she aimed at the next slave.

Chapter Sixteen

The sky was dark but full of brilliant stars when Lanico made it to the edge of the plateau. His moon-glowing silhouette cast a shadow across the landscape behind him. The brass of trillium laced the air. His eyes sparkled as he gazed at his reward.

Odana.

Resting in the distance, she was beautiful in her slumber. At first sight, at the thrumming of his heart, he was in love again with the land, the country, Odana. He belonged here. A wave of emotion swept over him as he fought back the bitter sting of regret. *How could I have denied myself returning all this time?* His throat knotted at the thought of the years that had flown by.

"Moving down this slope will bring battle again," he whispered to the wind, understanding. But there was no way back. He inhaled deeply. It was time. Time to find Marin. Time to return to them, to lead the WynSprigns—to free them from Grude's corruption. Time to reclaim the throne. After lowering himself to kneel, he sent a silent prayer, lifted to Father Odan, for the guidance of every step he would plant moving forward.

Crickets chirped in the grasses and there was a faint rustling from the far-off trees. He pulled in a deep breath and hoisted himself up from the ground.

He took a knowing step. There'd be no going back from this-this choice, this descent.

The bright moon glowed over the amazing world ahead. There, in the distance, was the silver ribbon, the beloved Odana River. "Ama," he whispered the Fray word for mother. For she was a Fray, a wielder of light, the second created daughter of Odan. Until he arrived in her home, he would stay near the river that led to her. It had been far too long to remember any other path. With a rippling snap, he flung out his cloak and swung it about his shoulders. The night was growing cool and he wouldn't find warmth until he arrived to her.

As Lanico marched down the switchback slope, he was mindful of his movements, aware of his glowing eyes in the dark. It took some time before he came near the familiar rushing of the river, the smell of the dancing water.

Nearing the river, he detected the faint sound of voices. In his long habit that came with an increase in his pulse, he felt the hilt of Reluctant Leader against his thigh. He concentrated intensely to make out the voices, searching for Marin's. His heart pounded as he listened. Picking up fine details of the sounds, his eyes darted about as he momentarily forgot about their glow. Hope. There was hope.

Inching closer, he could see two horses tied to a tree near the water. "Two," he breathed under the hush of the river. With his mind swirling, he stayed hunched, carefully setting one foot before the other toward the trees. Then he paused, hiding behind a few small trees. He grew cold at the sight of a large Mysra sitting in the moonlight. *Who is he talking to?* He moved slightly for a better view around the tree and spotted purple glowing eyes focused upward toward the Mysra. *There!*

A sob threatened to burst from his throat. *Marin!* His heart went wild, his breath visible in the cool of the night. He choked back a mixed burst of laughter and a wail. "Where?" he breathed and placed a hand over his mouth. He needed to stay rational. *Survive.* He was trained to do that. Setting his emotions aside, he watched to gauge the situation.

Marin sat near the Mysra and seemed fine, unharmed. The Mysra, however, had the dark stain covering his leg. *Blood, perhaps?* Lanico considered. *They have no campfire, probably to avoid being seen by unwelcome company.* The Mysra had been smart with that decision.

They appeared to be in the midst of a serious conversation, for Marin was at full attention, reaching for his tooth necklace, forgetting it was missing. Lanico smiled a little at this. Marin nodded and continued listening to the Mysra, seemingly spell bounded.

Lanico, remembering his eyes, avoided looking directly at them, even from his cover. He used the slight breeze that, thankfully, came from their direction. Lanico gaped, lifting his tongue to the roof of his mouth, and scented the air. He felt for the familiar feeling, the feeling of threat, danger. There wasn't any that he could pick up with this Fray ability—his mother, his Ama, being a full Fray, had a stronger ability to scent out others. Harmless, his senses told him—it was an odd result but he continued to wait, the breeze carrying their voices to him.

The Mysra was telling Marin about his father, about the constant pressure to prove himself and his loyalty. "In truth," he said, "even though I am a trained Mysra guard and have spent countless hours training others for horseback, my father doesn't approve of me." He hesitated, "Even my ease on the over-worked WynSprign slaves enrages him."

Lanico's heart skipped. He nearly stumbled from his hidden place, and Marin's breath caught at that admission.

WynSprign Slaves?

Gish continued, almost embarrassed. "My father . . . he is important in Odana. He expects much from me." The Mysra looked down.

Who is his father? Lanico wondered, squinting at the back of the Mysra's head.

"I can understand how that might feel, Gish." Marin responded.

Gish? As Marin said the familiar name aloud, Lanico's heart dropped. The father was . . . Grude. Word had spread, even to the Great Mist leaders, about Grude's son, Gish-the next in his succession.

Grude.

Lanico fumed at the name called up from his mind with a flurry of memories about the tyrant. *Grude, who preyed on my father and led the siege of the Castle of Odana. Grude, who ordered his guards to launch a surprise attack and kill vast numbers of WynSprigns, including Izra and Treva, while now enslaving the survivors. Grude, the monster . . . who killed my father.* Lanico's fists coiled. His nails dug into his palms. A spark of rage had now begun to course fiery through his veins.

What life must be like in Odana now? For our people, for the . . . the slaves? He had long denied himself this thought when he was powerless to remedy it. He had known about the torment against his remaining subjects, but not about the slavery. Not about *that.*

Why have I not been angry about this? How could I let my people down? He hastily ran his fingers through his hair and grimaced. *For too long I have lived in a fog, simply raising a child.*

Lanico had been lost and grieving for too long—he now needed to move forward. He shifted his thoughts quickly and knew, without a doubt, that he was back. This quest to retrieve Marin was the beginning, the only way to make things right.

He waited for several moments longer in silence as Gish confided in Marin about the pressures, he felt.

"Actually, Gish," began Marin, "my . . . father was important in Odana at one time, long ago. I always wished that I could have had the responsibilities that I was meant to have." He paused. "But I guess, after listening to you, that it seems being a royal can be overwhelming."

Stilling his anger, Lanico listened closely to the enhancement of the youth's voice, one of the strategies of his training. Marin *sounded* trustworthy. Perhaps Gish would let his guard down, allowing Marin to escape into the nearby woods. *Well played, my boy. Well played.*

~

Gish found himself warming up to the boy as they sat in conversation by the river. He and his captive had more in common than he had considered.

Gish had felt relief in baring his feelings. For too long he had had no one to confide in, save for his horses. They were a true comfort but did not take him as far as this conversation had. He would share one more detail with Marin, trusting that he might understand this one, too. It was an opportunity to have a . . . *friend.* He nervously tugged at the bottom of his tunic, thinking over his words.

"Marin," Gish continued with a softer voice, "there is something else." He wasn't sure how to tell the boy without making him want to tear off toward the woods. After the long ride the boy was exhausted and likely knew he couldn't escape, so, Gish took a gamble and said more to the trustworthy youth, much more than he had imagined.

"Your leader, Trayvor, wants to set up an exchange, selling misbehaving WynSprigns to us for our mining endeavors—that means you, Marin."

Marin took in a breath. *Trayvor? Our leader? Well, that had certainly been a lie from the old drunkard.* His thoughts were engrossed on the second part of that sentence. *Me . . . an installment of slave trade?*

Gish noticed the widening of Marin's glowing eyes and looked down in shame. "To him you were the first installment, a teaser for more that would follow." Gish made a heavy sigh. "Trayvor, well, he didn't realize the ulterior motive behind this agreement. The mission from my father wasn't only to collect a few delinquent WynSprigns for slaves. He wanted an excuse to get closer," The Mysra raked at the back of his neck, "to find the lost WynSprign village." Gish couldn't bring himself to look at Marin. "My father wants to bring *all* the WynSprigns back to the Odana to work as slaves, mining for trillium in the southern range. WynSprigns are the only ones immune to the stuff, and able to do it."

"No," Marin whispered. He slowly shook his head and held it low, in dejection. However, he also seemed to gain energy that Gish watched warily, and the boy sat up a little straighter despite his fatigue.

Gish continued quickly, to deflect the tension: "This was a test for me, to prove to my father whether he could allow me to inherit the throne in Odana, and eventually take leadership over the Mysra." Gish finally looked up to meet Marin's bewildered gaze. "He has wanted to find your hidden realm for years." Gish gulped and then said, "This is why I have to bring you back." *Would the boy wait for more?*

Marin staring at Gish with intensity, digging his feet into the ground a little, fear in his eyes.

~

Lanico listened intently from his hiding place. All the worst, it was true. It had to be. He would put an end to it. He would find a way.

He was bewildered at Trayvor's level of stupidity. *Just when I thought he couldn't become any more senseless.* Nevertheless, Lanico refocused on the current situation. *Perhaps Marin isn't in any great danger—yet. Since this Mysra, Gish, will have Grude searching for him soon . . . to know the outcome of the test.*

Lanico noticed the wild gaze on Marin's face. He knew that look - that poised position. Marin was going to run. His odds were not good—Gish would catch up with him in a flash with one of the horses. It wouldn't take much to bring him down. *Now.* Now was a good time to approach them and make his whereabouts known, before Marin made a witless mistake.

Lanico came from behind the tree and did not want to seem as if he'd been sneaking up on them, so he announced himself right away: "Marin!" Lanico shouted happily from a small distance, squinting his eyes in a look of pleasure that hid his intent.

Marin stood quickly. "Lanico!" His face brightening in the moonlight, and he tore off toward his father, who raised an arm in greeting to the Mysra to ease his mind.

The two WynSprigns had never been more than a few hours apart, let alone days. Lanico embraced Marin, who still felt small in his arms—and would likely always be a babe to him.

"I was so worried about you, Marin. I have been following you both all this time." Still aware of Reluctant Leader on his thigh, Lanico glanced over at an uncertain Gish.

"I'm so sorry, for getting into trouble—" Marin started, angling his head to look up at him. His tangled nest of hair shifted at the movement, and he tucked it behind an ear.

"It's all right, Marin," Lanico said. "We're here together, and you're safe." Lanico pulled him in closer, to hold him; keeping an eye on the Mysra to be certain all was secure.

"Lanico," Marin said as he backed up from their embrace and looked up. A somber expression slashed across his face. "I have to tell you what happened . . . at Horse's Clearing." He increased the small distance between them.

Lanico looked at him with warmth but prepared himself for a feeling of anger. "All right, Marin . . . go ahead," he breathed. *I can take it.*

"Well," Marin started, initially hesitant to tell Lanico everything. Then he let it out in a rush: "I heard Trayvor and someone hidden under a cloak with a hood, talking about how they were waiting on news from Odana, at Horse's Clearing"—Marin touched his chest, forgetting the tooth necklace was not there, and he wrung his hands instead—"So I thought I'd follow them, hiding in the trees. But then I fell, just in front of them."

Lanico's face did not reveal his thoughts. He had already known about Marin's falling but didn't quite know the reason behind it—now he could picture the scene. "Yes, Marin, please continue."

"I remember . . .," Marin thought carefully. He touched his matted head and grimaced at a tender spot. "I remember after I fell, Fenner was hidden under a gray hood looking down over me. After that, everything went black. Then I remember being in an area that was like a small gray mountain—with Gish." He jerked his head toward the Mysra.

"Gray Rock?" Lanico looked over at Gish, who made a slow nod in confirmed response. "So Fenner and Trayvor were at Horse's Clearing, meeting with Gish?"

"Yes," Marin said simply.

Gish stood slowly and approached them hesitantly. Lanico discreetly grabbed the grip of Reluctant Leader concealed under his cloak, awaiting a possible attack. The air betrayed no evil intent. *The Mysra don't plot*, Lanico thought. *If they mean to attack, you know it right off.*

The hulking Mysra announced as he neared the pair, "I am Gish, the son of Grude the Mysra leader." His gray skin glowed in the moonlight, which enhanced the curves of his massive, boulder-like muscles.

Lanico looked at him with a calm gaze and released the handle of the sword slightly. "Gish, I am called Lanico." He looked up at the Mysra with a charming smile and noticed how their heights matched. Gish was small for a Mysra and Lanico tall for a WynSprign. No gleam of recognition showed in the Mysra's eyes.

So, he hasn't heard of me—this was good.

"Lanico," Gish repeated, shifting his massive weight with a look of unease, "I took the boy at my father's bidding. I have not been in my father's good graces for . . . well, perhaps ever. It seems I have a soft spot for WynSprigns. Conversation with this one"—he gestured toward Marin—"has put me over even further." He hinted at a smile. "The boy is in your charge"—he held out his hands in surrender. "My troubles with my father, are my own."

"Indeed," Lanico started, not entirely believing his own words as they came out, "we are truly grateful to have you on our side. Knowing a bit about your father, I know he would expect quick obedience, and your journey has been hindered, my tracking indicates. He may have already sent Mysra riders out in search of you."

"Yes, you are probably right about that," Gish said. "Other riders will be on the move by now."

Marin turned wild-eyed to Lanico. "What . . . what do we do?" His voice was high, panic-laced. "Will you return to the Great Mist, to tell them? I—I can't return."

"All right, be still." Lanico said calmly, setting a hand on the boy's shoulder, gathering his thoughts about their new reality and what might yet come.

"Marin," Lanico began slowly, "it's true that *we* cannot return to the Great Mist. You have been banished. The Great Mist may not be a safe home for us again in any case—who knows what Trayvor has done?" Lanico leaned down to look at him directly. "However, it's important to realize that we have information that is most critical, and we must act on it. We now understand that the lives of all in the Great Mist are in jeopardy." Lanico paused. "I will go to them, to alert them." Having set his eyes on the Odana, knowing the

WynSprigns had in their leadership agreed to banish his son, it was agonizing to consider returning. If it meant saving even a single innocent WynSprign . . . And perhaps there were more than a few: Stoutwyn, Murah, Joso, and others . . . his thoughts became pliable.

Lanico continued: "But before I make the trip back, I will make sure that your safety is secured." He glanced at Gish and swallowed. He didn't want to part from Marin, but he rationalized that it would only be temporary.

Lanico looked off in the direction of the forest. He knew of the helper he had been longing to see for a great many years, who wasn't too far off from this point on the river—perhaps a day's walk. His Fray mother, his Ama, Greta. He would find lodging and safety with her before setting out to warn the WynSprigns of this new information. *Perhaps we can persuade Gish to ally further with us. I will let Greta aid in that decision.*

Lanico lowered himself to sit. "We'll stay here tonight, then we'll make for the Odana woods tomorrow." The forest in the distance seemed a dark looming wall that gave a natural feeling of resistance even from where they were.

Gish began, "If I may, I would like t-to . . . join you. You seem to have the force needed to make a change"—he nodded as if taking in Lanico's strength and bearing, though he didn't linger his gaze on the remarkable sword.

Lanico made a slight smile and nodded in response. "You may." He was confident that Gish was harmless, and even if his present senses betrayed him, he knew he could take out the Mysra if necessary—or if not himself, then the Fray he planned for them to visit could easily manage. "We will awaken before dawn tomorrow to start a small fire and cook any fish we can catch. We'll head southward into the forest, following this river along the foothills of the southeastern section of the mountain range." Well aware of his former kingdom, Lanico knew this side of the mountain range would not have much Mysra traffic, for the veins of trillium ran rich on the other side. "We will walk the horses and ourselves in the river and continue this course until we enter the wooded foothills."

There wasn't much else to add after that plan. The small group then quietly ate, settled in for the night, and two of them soon found sleep beneath the moon's soft blanket of light. The day would start early enough. Lanico's azure gaze glowed, flickering to the slumbering Mysra, watching.

Chapter Seventeen

Trayvor was happy to have the familiar weight of gold coins jingling in his pockets again. It had been far too long. In rare good will, he ordered a round of ale for his tavern friends, for they were all his best friends this evening. A few curious souls wondered how he had come by the gold, but only Fenner knew.

Fenner sat alone by the tavern wall tugging slowly at his pint of ale, looking guilty. No need for his company anymore. Trayvor preferred Fenner's impressionable grandson Freck, who had a quick temper and a thirst for action—all things most pleasing to him.

Trayvor caught a glance of Fenner leaving the tavern and remained unmoved. He had a business proposition for Fenner's sturdy grandson and little remaining use for Fenner. He was also most willing to pay Freck handsomely. He could tell the ambitious young WynSprign would be more determined to do his bidding than was Fenner. Trayvor did not approve of Fenner's sulking around and his downtrodden mood, especially since he was on the brink of a fabulous opportunity for the Great Mist. No. He chose to let Fenner walk out alone.

~

Fenner didn't know what to do that night, who to talk to. He didn't want to be alone. He decided to visit Stoutwyn, who wouldn't be pleased with him, but he was also a forgiving soul.

He walked in a shuffling stride to Stoutwyn's large tree home and rapped at the door. It took a moment before Fenner heard rustling from inside. The curious gaze of Stoutwyn peered from behind his fumbling fingers at the small curtain. When he saw it was Fenner, his gaze soured. He opened the door without a word and glared disapprovingly at him.

Fenner twittled at his black beard, searching for words. Stoutwyn rolled his eyes and opened his door wider, stepping aside to let Fenner in. Fenner bowed a little in unspoken thanks. They went into the eating room and sat. The well-used table was laden with cheese and bread crumbs from Stoutwyn's recent dinner. The delicious aroma of Murah's cooking still teased in the air. Stoutwyn, remaining silent, pulled out a chair for himself, and Fenner also sat, following his host's lead. This was the signal for him to start his confession.

Fenner sighed as he started. "Well," he said, looking down at the bread crumbs, "Trayvor is over at the tavern buying everyone drinks, and blurting on . . . about disciplining Marin and cleaning up the Great Mist—you know, being an enforcer of the rules and all. I—I really didn't want to listen to it anymore, so I thought I'd leave." He took a big breath. "I didn't know where to go or who to talk to, so I came here." Fenner looked up from the small pile of crumbs he had scooped together and studied Stoutwyn with a pleading gaze.

The angry face of Stoutwyn had softened a little. "I'm still mad about what happened, and I'm not going to hide that, Fen."

Fenner had no argument against this reaction and nodded humbly. "I-I know Stout." He said quietly.

Stoutwyn eased in his chair and Fenner relaxed, seeing him softening, and felt comfortable enough to confide his secret. He told Stoutwyn about the plan to lure Marin to Horse's Clearing, explaining it was meant to catch Marin in the act of breaking the rules, leaving their realm – making Lanico dispondent- perhaps to enough to relinquish his control, or even causing him to leave altogether.

Stoutwyn sat and puffed away quickly at his floog, visibly infuriated. He listened while nodding to urge Fenner on. Fenner explained how their luring happened at just the time a Mysra patrol warrior called Gish, had arrived at Horse's Clearing to discuss business with Trayvor.

More quick puffs of smoke lifted from Stoutwyn's floog.

Trayvor, Fenner explained, was making a partnership with Grude to take the WynSprigns away that had broken the rules and needed to be banished. He had already designed wooden holding cages that he could use for this purpose. In return for WynSprigns, Trayvor would be paid in gold coins. Marin being taken was an unexpected bonus.

Fenner, now sensing Stoutwyn's anger, paused.

"Well . . . go on!" demanded Stoutwyn, his face growing red through clouds of smoke.

Fenner blinked and continued. He explained that banishing Marin had become paramount to Trayvor, for it meant that Lanico would leave the Great Mist to follow after him, leaving the Great Mist under Trayvor's control. That plan was now a reality.

Stoutwyn's mouth hung slack at these revelations and Fenner flinched as Stoutwyn's hand clenched at his side. He seemed the devil himself, smoldering red and glaring, and a wreath of smoke now engulfed him.

"Do you have any idea what this means?!" Stoutwyn challenged. "One"—he held up the floog in a threatening gesture— "the Mysra now know our general location! Two"—he leaned over and growled into Fenner's face— "Trayvor, once trustworthy, has proven himself a liar and a scoundrel. Three"— he spoke quietly, going pale— "he is selling WynSprigs as slaves and trying to take over the Great Mist." Then Stoutwyn rose up quickly, shouting, "How DARE HE! So Odan help him!"

Fenner froze in his chair, gaping. His eyes went glassy as he looked up at Stoutwyn looming over the table.

Footsteps came bounding from down the hall and Fenner whipped his head around. It was Stoutwyn's wife, Murah.

"Stout! What's happened?" she called, holding her long knitting needle like a weapon. A look of bewilderment washed over her round face.

Stoutwyn looked over at her, blinking as he collected himself. He picked up his floog and began puffing again. His voice was lower. "Nothing, Murah. I was a bit upset over"—he stumbled for words and shot a glance at Fenner—"a bit of nothing." She stayed, looking at them both with concern and a little suspicion.

He measured his tone. "Murah, please return to your knitting. Everything is fine, dear—it's old battle talk, you know." He managed a small smile.

She was winded and a stray section of gray hair left her bun and swayed beside her face. Her concerned look was replaced with one of extreme annoyance. "Oh, pwhh! Scare the breath from me, will you . . . Bah!" She waved her hand dismissively at them and rounded the corner again, muttering as she walked off down the hall.

Stoutwyn sat back down quickly, stroking at his gray beard. His chair creaked as he leaned forward, whispering to Fenner: "Listen, we need to figure something out here. C'mon, Fen, I know it's been a while since we dealt with the Mysra ourselves, but do you ever recall them being . . . trustworthy? That Mysra guard now knows our general location. What's to stop him, or other Mysra, for that matter, from returning?"

"Trayvor set up a plan to give them only the WynSprigs that were misbehaving. They'll take only those," Fenner assured.

Taking a sarcastic tone Stoutwyn said, "Oooh, sure, Fen . . . sure," and leaned back again. "When was the last time you remember the Mysra being content taking a little bit of anything? Soon they'll want more WynSprigns for their plundering of the purple mountains. It's only a matter of time." Stoutwyn looked worriedly out the small window next to their table, parting the curtain slightly.

Fenner knew deep down he was right.

The greatest of the WynSprigns was gone from the Great Mist, and already the cold feeling of unwelcome change lingered in the air. The forces of power had shifted. Trayvor was a dominating personality, manipulative, and calculating. Now that Lanico was gone, it was up to Stoutwyn and Fenner to handle him and keep him in place, and Fenner knew that meant he must just follow Stoutwyn. Neither of them ever had to be in that position before. Lanico had wanted Stoutwyn to keep Trayvor in check, but he never imagined he'd have to. Fenner had come to his senses, and was glad he'd come to Stoutwyn. Now—now they could be in this together.

"I appreciate you coming here to tell me, Fen. We'll figure this out." Smoke rose from Stoutwyn's mouth as he spoke. "We have to."

Chapter Eighteen

The WynSprign slaves had an unspoken understanding that Gish was an easier Mysra guard. It wasn't that Gish was overtly kind, no—but he didn't actually harm them and there was never a hint of threat from him. News of his recent defense of the slave woman was making the rounds in the encampments. Now that he was gone, WynSprigns were fearful, understanding they had no protectors at all.

Times had been incessantly terrible in the lost decades since the seizure of Odana, but lately, the demand for more trillium was higher then anyone, including the Myrsa guards, could have ever imagined. It wasn't entirely a surprise, though. The Mysra used trillium increasingly not only for battles and fights, but for their daily duties, training, and even before disciplining the slaves. The guards, feeling pressure to push the mining WynSprigns harder and harder for more work, were themselves under great stress and turned to trillium to help feel energized.

WynSprigns caught disobeying the rules were placed in large metal cages inside the mines, or for larger penalty, they were whipped near the center post of the hut village. The caged WynSprigns, mostly youths, were prevented from going home to their huts and therefore from eating their final meal of the day. They would be unlocked early in the morning only to return right to work.

The sun was starting to peek over the horizon on another routine morning for the slaves. The sky, a brilliant pink, gave way to the line of WynSprigns slowly ascending the mountain into the Purple Hall mine. The night before, the cage had housed one young WynSprign known to cause trouble. She was lively and daring, with an escape plan always on her mind. Escape—not for herself only, but for all the WynSprigns.

Anah was young like the majority here that hadn't yet died from illness, injury, toil, or old age – not that the life expectancy was lengthy. They and even most of their parents had not been alive to experience the seizure of Odana. To Anah, life in the Odana before that battle was an old, unimaginable, dead dream. It was a nice thought, a lie told to make them feel soft and warm with the far-off hope that there was another sort of existence possible—but it was only a story and no more than that. She didn't know truth of the life beyond these confines, but determined it had to be better out there—outside the Odana Kingdom.

Due to her constant conflicts with the Mysra guards, Anah had missed the final meal of the day again. She was no stranger to this form of punishment and she was almost old enough to be taken to be whipped, like Treva. That was her future. She accepted it with a cunning smile that enraged Nizen, the head guard. She knew he couldn't wait . . . perhaps for her birthday. She could feel the way he stared at her back, imagining the slashes he'd decorate it with.

Anah shuddered a little at the memory of his eyes roaming over her.

The mine door opened with a loud clank and pink sunlight pierced the dark and transformed it into dazzling brilliance within. Countless purple trillium crystals became illuminated by the sun. If it weren't associated with so much pain and misery, this place might have been astonishingly beautiful.

The light emanating from the mine entrance began to pulse off and on as slaves started entering the cave and cast shadows against the pink light. The walls of the cave returned the soft glow of the entering slaves' rusty lanterns that squeaked as they swayed with the bearers' jumbled strides. The first to enter the cave was always a hefty Mysra guard, a large gray silhouette. He strode toward her. He looked down sourly, fumbling keys on a large ring with his thick gray fingers. Anah had stared often at those keys—it seemed there was an ever-increasing number of keys added to the large ring over the years. Her stomach turned at that thought.

"All right, Anah, out." The Mysra guard unlocked the cage with a CLANK and the familiar high-pitched creak raised the hair on her arms as he swung open the metal door.

A whiff of rust.

Anah straightened as she sat herself up from the hay bedding. Aside from the bedding, there was a jug of water in the cage, but no pot to pee in. Her wild flaming hair was matted to one side of her head but billowed out on the opposite side. She stretched, stood up slowly, and moaned with the ache. Her body was always sore. She didn't pay much attention to that anymore, and at this moment she was grateful to be freed from the cage. She always played the part of the wild animal amongst them.

Without needed command, Anah dutifully marched in the direction of her usual station in the mine. She wandered down between the deep purple rocky walls, leaning carefully in known tight spots as she stepped down the narrow, crudely constructed stairs. Her deft hands against the walls and smoothed stalagmites knew where to cling, from years of habit. She minded her steps carefully and passed other hard-working WynSprigns along the way. Her area was well lit with dozens of lanterns that were spread out for all the miners. She glanced at her hands and arms and wondered if there'd ever be a day when the purple stain would fade away . . . *A silly thought.*

Once back at her area of work, near Treva, Anah found her personal treasure waiting for her, as it did every day. It was locked away with the other tools every night and set out by the guard for her work each morning. She picked up what almost seemed like the missing part of her arm, the pick-axe. She had been welding this particular axe since she was able to carry it, and it had been her mother's. Usually little WynSprign children were given duties to pick off loosened pieces of trillium, sweep up trillium rocks and debris, or push the small carts of trillium to designated areas of the mine for processing. To be handed a tool like a pick-axe, hammer, or chisel was a rite of passage. In Anah's mind—and in her hand—this was a deadly weapon. She smiled wickedly and slightly stuck her tongue out between her teeth at sight of this weapon.

Anah's parents had died when a mine they were working in collapsed. She was still very small when this happened, and their bodies had been laid to rest in the small graveyard that the Mysra created for such disasters. They were placed amongst all the other deceased WynSprign, something her parents wouldn't have thought could have *ever* happened to WynSprigns of their patrician heritage. *Their* graveyard was located closer to the castle grounds and included others of nobility and royal bloodlines. But, no one, noble nor commoner, had been buried there since before the siege. It was lucky that the Mysra allowed a graveyard at all, for they didn't even bury their dead.

At night, she could still feel the axe vibrating through her hand bones, arm, and elbow as she thought of what she'd lost and what she wanted to gain. Lying on her bed, she imagined it was her mother shaking her playfully. It was a way to make comfort where there wasn't any.

All areas of the mine had a designated number of WynSprigns assigned and there was always a Mysra guard at watch with his trillium and scowl at the ready.

"Anah!" Treva whispered, her hideous bonnet quivering at her movements, "stop staring at the axe like that, and get to work!"

Anah, coming back to reality, blinked and smirked at Treva. She reluctantly held up her axe, then started chiseling away at the purple rock. Next to her, Treva watched the patrolling Mysra guard wander away toward another mining group at the other end of their hall.

"You're lucky he didn't notice you staring again," Treva whispered.

As the guard continued away, Treva quickly handed Anah the brown roll that she had stolen from last night's dinner. Anah looked surprised and without a word squirreled this away in her pocket. She was mindful to continue the patterned sounds of her chiseling and not draw attention to her intermittent nibbles.

At every available moment throughout the day, Anah would pull a small piece of bread off and savor it in her mouth, letting it sit on her tongue to grow moist, tasting the wheat. It would be just enough to keep dizziness away. She was ever grateful to Treva and slid a glance to her—the older woman's face was very beautiful, and why she constantly wore that horrendous bonnet was baffling. *Okay, so she has a scalp condition, she said, but does she always have to wear that thing?* Anah sighed and resumed her chiseling. *So vain.*

Ahe understood, without Treva, she'd be in a much worse state. Treva looked after her like an older sister, or perhaps a kind of mother. Treva had once told her she'd been a mother at one time, but she lost her son during the seizure. Anah never asked about this, as she didn't want to pry, or to bring up sad memories. After all, their lives seemed bleak enough. Together they chiseled away with their pickaxes and continued their patterned song.

Dreams of escape would come later.

Chapter Nineteen

Early the next day, before most had had breakfast, a piercing reverberation of ringing sounded, breaking dawn's silence. It was Trayvor. He strolled about ringing a large bell that belonged to the tavern. They used it there on occasion for various drinking contests. He, however, found a different purpose for it.

He belted out from the top of his lungs through the clanging, "Notice! Notice! New rules to protect the WynSprign folk! Go to the tavern to see the new rules posted! —Notice! Notice! New rules posted at the tavern!"

The sound, twanged in his ear and Stoutwyn's eyes flew open. "What in the name of Father Odan?" he grumbled. He tossed off his blankets and darted from bed. He pulled his nightcap off his head and marched outside quickly to address this disturbance. His sleepy, bloodshot eyes widened at the sight. "Trayvor—Trayvor Odmire! What is the meaning of this?!"

Trayvor smiled smugly at the approaching Stoutwyn, and he raised his white eyebrows and closed his eyes lightly with the assurance of authority. His voice was slow as he explained: "I decided that since Marin and Lanico are both gone from the Great Mist, our chances of being found by enemies have increased. I decided to call for additional precautions for all to adhere to."

He was very matter-of-fact about this. Stoutwyn didn't reply right away, thinking it over. Trayvor turned from Stoutwyn to continue ringing his bell, but no, Stoutwyn hastily grabbed his arm holding him back.

"Wait! Why didn't you alert me about this decision, Trayvor?" Stoutwyn allowed the fury to sound in his voice. "We're supposed to discuss these things together."

"I fail to see the point in alerting *you*," Trayvor said, jerking his arm from Stoutwyn's pudgy grip. He studied the other elder accusingly. "You are not nearly as important as Lanico and I, and since Lanico has left, I will be taking the reigns here. Your assistance at this capacity, is not needed, nor wanted."

Stoutwyn bristled and scoffed.

Trayvor sneered, "You seem to think yourself above the rules, Stoutwyn."

"Wh—what rules?!" Stoutwyn railed. His body still stiff with anger, he felt his face grow red with vehemence until he resembled the red-crested owl of that region, with his gray beard and puffed chest.

Trayvor managed a frown before blasting, "OUR RULES! You may see the rules posted at the tavern, like everyone else. And now . . ." Trayvor straightened his sleeve with a tug, before he tore his gaze away from Stoutwyn. He calmly turned and resumed ringing his bell and striding slowly through the village. "Notice! Notice! New rules posted at the tavern!"

Stoutwyn was confused but well sobered from his sleep. He stood still for a moment absorbing this turn of events. He suddenly realized his dot-covered pajamas were on display for all to see, and as the shouts and ringing from Trayvor faded into the distance, Stoutwyn quickly went back into his house to dress.

At the tavern in the next hour, curious WynSprigns gathered to view a large scroll with a list of rules. Before Stoutwyn went through the tavern gate, he studied the reactions from the sleepy crowd that had already gathered and was worried at their concerned reactions. He shoved lightly and apologetically as he tried to make his way through to read the rules himself. As he drew near, he removed his reading spectacles from his chest pocket and quickly polished them on his shirt before placing them on the bridge of his nose.

Until recently, the rules had been very simple: "No stealing," "No leaving the Great Mist realm," and "No fighting." Those were the rules they all lived by. Even before he read the rules, Stoutwyn was most unsettled that Trayvor had posted them without consulting him.

NOTICE

New Rules
1. No elder meetings in the forest clearing.
   To avoid exposure to any undesirables seeking to find us
2. No drinking ale and leaving the tavern alone—for fear of a WynSprign being drunk and leaving the boundary
3. No staying out after the new curfew
   VIOLATORS: Subject to Immediate Banishment

Stoutwyn stood aghast, blinking, his breath foggy in the cool air. He felt hot but was in a cold sweat as well. The WynSprigns clamored around him for answers. "Curfew? I-I had no idea," he said quietly to their questioning faces. "I didn't make *these* rules."

He turned quickly, veering through the crowd, his heart beating rapidly. He needed to get air. He needed to think about this. After a moment of regaining himself, he made haste to Fenner's home.

"Surely Fen didn't know about this either. He would have told me last night," Stoutwyn mumbled worriedly.

Fenner lived alone in a tree home—much like Stoutwyn's. His children were all grown now, having homes of their own. His wife, Ferna, had died long ago. Stoutwyn rapped at his door. There was no answer. He waited and waited. After moments of silence, growing fear crept around his heart. *Why isn't he answering?* He wondered. He pressed his ear to the door, listening for movement inside. Nothing. With reluctance, he left—something was amiss. He felt it stirring in his gut.

Chapter Twenty

After the last meal of the day, Treva hurried to visit Anah's hut. The Mysra guards didn't allow much time for leisurely chats—they monitored all the WynSprign movements and enforced curfew to keep them in check.

Though time was limited, Treva was determined to visit Anah, for she was concerned. This day it had seemed Anah's energy had faded. It was highly unusual, because Anah was always full of ideas and life. She was a spark of light in the bleakness. Treva enjoyed listening to her plans of escape and watching the wonder and excitement that gleamed from her hopeful green eyes. To see Anah down made her feel dejected herself.

Treva entered the weathered hut and Anah looked up quickly and jerked with surprise from where she was crouched on the floor rolling up her sleeping mat. Her wild red hair spilling over her small body.

"Anah, what are you doing?" Treva asked, trying to hide the hint of amusement that had started to curl the corner of her mouth. *I am not the only one with secrets beneath the floor of my hut.* Anah shushed Treva in annoyance and gestured to the curtain.

Treva quickly turned and closed the curtain door, shutting out the world behind her.

Anah then continued to secure the rolled-up sleeping mat. Whispering, she replied, "I'm going to leave—I—I've decided that I'm not a slave anymore. I have tried to think of ways, over and over again, to get all the WynSprigns free from this place, free from the Mysra. But"—the movements of her hands were rough and fast, rolling the mat— "I fail every time." She sighed hard. "No one believes me that the area behind our huts here"—she jerked her head toward the back of the hut— "have harmless ancient landmines that hadn't been replaced—I'm certain they wouldn't explode. Or that, of the whole area, *this* area is actually the best way out. I've memorized every turn in the trench, every mine, every barb in the wire—Treva, we can do it."

She added, "The watchtower, they have a schedule, and I know it. I told you, I've watched them for years."

Treva remained silent but leaned lower toward Anah, her bonnet hiding her face.

"I know the guards' schedules, their rotations—I know it all," Anah continued. "I know exactly when we can slip away." Anah looked deep into Treva's lowered eyes before continuing.

"And, to make matters worse, no one seems to care. I care more about leaving here than anyone else. It's like they all just gave up." She finished tying the mat. "I was born after the battle, and yet even *I* believe that there is another life beyond these mountains. Maybe not like the stories you talk about, but there's more to th—*this*"—she held her arms out wide.

Treva knelt next to Anah and spoke quietly: "I think this is a brave thing, to decide to leave here . . . but you have never left this camp. How will you survive? If you're caught—"

"If I'm caught, then maybe they'll kill me—er, put me out of my misery," Anah grumbled interrupting.

Treva's eyes widened at the words that stabbed and twisted like a knife. The very thought of Anah, dead—it was unimaginable.

Anah changed her tone with a sigh: "Treva, I won't get caught. I was born here. I know the guards' schedules, the mining hours, the whole operation of this place. I know when I can leave." She paused. "And . . . I *will* leave, tonight."

Tonight? Treva measured herself. She wasn't sure what to think about this. *Am I, myself, one of these content slaves that Anah is complaining about?* Treva had a past that was fiery and defiant, too. Her own boldness and determination had made her the "Knight" when it was supposed to have been impossible. *Did I somehow give into this idea that I am nothing more than a slave? Have the Mysra broken me?* She was fearful of her own answer, fearful of her idea of . . . atonement.

She quickly thought back to her first memory after the seizure of Odana. She was lying on a floor mat inside a small hut, in excruciating pain. Her nursemaid Greta dabbed at her injured side by the light of a small candle. She remembered the kind old face; they had shared so much. Greta had insisted that she wear the bonnet constantly, to conceal her identity. If they knew she was the emerald-haired Knight-a famed Odana Military official, no good would come of it. Thankfully, no one was aware of the name, Treva.

"If you want to join me"—Anah's voice broke Treva's memory—"you can, though I realize you may not want to take this risk. I'll be starting behind this hut after midnight, where the trees start to thicken up the hill beyond the trench." She jerked her chin up. "Their rotation will be underway at that point and the moonlight will highlight the steps that need to be taken to avoid injury, or explo—"

"—I'll think about it," Treva said in a small, quick whisper, her eyes still fixed on the floor.

"Pffff," Anah puffed in frustration.

In the distance, a Mysra guard blew a loud and low note on the horn, calling the WynSprigns to their huts for the night. The time for socializing had ended. The horn—the first time Treva heard it, it was for a military exercise. The next, it was blaring to signal alarm for the arrival of Mysra troops. Since then, it had been used for the slave's curfew.

Treva blinked hard and looked around the hut. She slowly stood up and ducked out through the curtain door, leaving Anah to her preparations. If she wasn't going to join Anah, then leaving this way was for the better.

~

Hours later, the shift change was taking place high above in the watchtower, and the ground patrol had finished their final checks for the evening, making sure no one was walking about. The guards gathered by the central fire pit to keep warm and talk amongst themselves. They still kept a watchful eye until the shift changed with new rested and fed guards. The guards were supposed to walk around the encampment all night, but they had gotten lazy over the years. Occasionally a WynSprign might get in trouble for breaking the schedule, or curfew, but this was a rare occurrence.

Anah slowly opened her curtain and peered out with her eyes lowered, knowing they would be aglow in the darkness. Once she saw that the guards were not around, as expected, she strapped her sleeping mat to her back and held a small bag of belongings. She slowly rounded the corner of the hut and then quickly headed to the wooded area just behind it. She repeated a series of steps and pivots that she had practiced in secret for weeks, a dance to avoid the landmines and poison barbs whose location she had memorized. She placed soft steps on the grassy ground until she arrived on the hill above. She didn't keep track of her time, but it seemed to take only seconds.

Anah kept her green gaze at the trees, her target. She ambled into the leafy cover when suddenly, she gasped. She caught herself and held her purple-stained hand over her mouth in surprise. She was looking into a set of golden glowing eyes within the leafy brush. Treva.

Or was it?

It seemed Anah wasn't the only one who had memorized the placement of traps through the trenches.

Treva squatted low under the overhanging branches, wearing something gleaming that blended into the silvery leaves of the tree under which she crouched. Her bonnet was gone and the moon's glow shone over her hair, icy emerald in the night. Dazzling. The light outlined the chiseled sharp edges and details of her ornate attire. This wasn't some cheap metal lashed together for fights. This was . . . *regal* . . . *glorious.*

"What?"—Anah started, forgetting her tone.

"Sshhh," warned Treva, waving a hand at Ana.

Anah's hut was still in view. They *had* to remain silent.

Anah had turned to stone but managed to gulp. Treva was a stunning vision. Something about the armor had *changed* her. The emerald hair—there had been only one woman, warrior with emerald hair. A true WynSprign warrior. No, not just a warrior, a Knight! She was something Anah had only heard of in old tales, the tales she thought were only happy lies.

"Let's go!" Treva whispered dryly, her gaze sharp at Anah.

Anah nodded, still in shock. Anah's thoughts tumbled through her mind with excitement.

They turned and quietly bounded into the woods and away from the encampment. Every pounding step promised a life closer to freedom. They just needed to get far enough away.

They walked for hours in silence, passing though grassy plains of purple flowers Anah knew would be stunning in sunlight. At one point, Anah was about to turn to check the distance behind them when Treva spotted her sideling, and stopped her.

In a stern voice she ordered, "Don't look behind—we're not headed in that direction." Treva explained quietly that if a captive looks back to her place of imprisonment, she'd likely return. It was not only the physical return Treva had meant. They were starting over again. Independent and free. The lives of slavery, subservience, and objectification were to be left behind.

Returning to any of these - it was too horrific to consider.

Anah nodded and resumed, setting her sights on the land in front of them—and unflinchingly keeping them there.

Together, they made their way southeast, toward the wooded foothills of the Odana Mountains. Their once-quick pace over the passing hours became increasingly slow. Their bodies had been broken over the years while their stomachs had always remained empty. With this new and long exertion, their fingers tingled in weakness, and their vision swirled.

"Treva. I'm dizzy." Anah panted.

"Okay. I know. Me too" She breathed. She glanced down at the girl who was now fumbling with her canteen. "Yes, take a drink of water. That'll help a bit." She took a swig of water herself. "I'd like us to get on the other side of these mountains before daybreak," Treva said, breaking the brief silence. She angled her head to the majestic mountain tops just overhead, outlined against the promising deep blue of the pre-dawn sky. "This mountain pass is a little lower and the climb should not be as challenging and it thins out, here, in this spot," she jerked her head toward the mountain "it's only just this one mountain at this location." It had been long since she had traversed these lands, but she knew this area. She glanced over at Anah, who was exhausted but smiled to show her spirits had not flagged.

"Okay, we're both tired," Treva said with deep gasps. "And, I'd forgotten about the weight of this armor—I was much stronger when I last wore it." She stiffened her lips. "Let's . . . let's stop to rest . . . there"—she pointed to a small ledge that jutted out near the summit of the lower mountain. "I remember a cave there, that can hide us. We can stay there and hidden from the sun while we rest."

Anah only nodded—she felt too breathless to respond.

They started their ascent right then, Treva in the lead, walking at an angle up the side of the mountain. The mountain brush and crags dragged against their legs as they climbed, and they had to dig their toes into the side of the mountain as they climbed.

As they stopped a moment to rest, Treva explained that once they were over these peaks, they would be headed back down the other side of the mountain and she knew the dense Odana forest well—it would be hard for a Mysra guard or warrior to find them there.

Anah felt the panic of their pursuers in her imagination, and she kept thinking she heard them shouting or scrambling up behind them. Despite her fatigue, she was spooked to make it up and over quickly. The weathered, ancient mountain didn't have enough vegetation hide their tracks, and some instinct in her knew speed was their best hope.

As they inched up beneath the ledge and drew near the cavern, Anah mistakenly peered over to the land below. "Whoa!" she exclaimed wildly, almost losing her grip.

"C'mon, up we go—no looking down!" Treva ordered. "I need you to keep your footing!" Treva growled an additional command: "Keep your eyes fixed on the goal and you'll make it there." Treva clenched her jaw and Anah saw her pain as the older woman's face became more angular to match her determination. Anah remembered Treva's injury and marveled—she was tough.

"All right," Anah panted, feeling dizzy, not wanting Treva to fear for her. Sweat soaked through her dirtied tunic.

First Treva entered and turned to lie flat and extend her arms down to Anah to assist in pulling her in with an agonizing groan. She trembled under the strain, still persevering, and Anah knew her life depended on her friend's strength.

Feeling guilty at making Treva's pain greater, Anah worked to force herself up with all her might and aid in Treva's effort. With one last push of remaining energy, they hauled themselves up and into the cavern. Anah's slight body came up and over the edge of the cavern with one swift heave. She bowled into Treva. Elbows, legs, and backs collided.

"Whew! We made it . . . we made it," Treva panted with relief, still trembling.

The young Anah recovered almost immediately, stood quickly in her excitement, and forgot the command from Treva not to look down from the cave. Her dizziness renewed at the sight of the great distance beneath them. She felt her arms and legs grow numb and her body begin to sway, and only Treva's quickly outstretched arm kept her from tumbling over the precipice.

Treva shoved her back from the cave's overhang, and Anah finally collapsed at the back of the shallow cave, crumpling to sit.

"Whew!" Treva panted.

Anah hung her head between her knees and massaged the back of her neck, grateful for Treva. *I would not have made it this far without her.*

The cave was just wide enough to cover them and allowed them to lie down and stretch their legs and arms. It was also the perfect overlook to watch for guards.

Treva explained they must soon press on from there, but it wasn't urgent. What *was* urgent was their barking need for rest and food. "Now with the daylight," Treva explained, "the Mysra guards are likely just noticing us missing, but they don't know in which direction. But then again, they are good at tracking and if they use horses, well, they'll find us sooner rather than later."

Anah gulped.

Treva sat up and started rummaging around in her bag. Anah, collapsed on the floor of the cave, couldn't imagine what Treva was rummaging for, but when Treva held a brown roll before her half-shut eyes, Anah looked at it in amazement.

"I've been stocking these up for a while," Treva explained. "I didn't plan on leaving, but I was always saving a few in case I—or you—needed them." She chuckled softly. "Uh—especially for you—with all your stays in the cage."

Anah shot Treva a quick sour glance and sat up to snatch the roll, unloosing Treva's hearty chuckle.

The rolls were hard and several days old. With the great hunger rumbling in her insides, Anah found them more than adequate for now. Both of them had thought to bring flasks of water, and they tried to take as little as they could manage, drinking through the dryness of the bread. They had to make every drop last as long as possible.

They nibbled on the rolls, tearing off small bits, as they peered over the land below, on the other side. Trees dotted the landscape, and there was much green beauty. Anah had never known such beauty existed. There was much she did not know about the land of Odana, the Odana forest, and perhaps even about Treva. At this thought, the splendor below quickly left Anah's mind.

"So, where'd you get that armor?" she asked, chewing noisily.

"Well"—Treva swallowed the dry bread with difficulty—"this armor is mine." She smiled with pride. "I had carried it in this sack to the hill and pieced it on while hiding in the trees, waiting for you."

Anah looked up at her questioningly, trying to read her gaze. That did not answer her question.

Treva studied the torn bread in her dirty, purple fingers and sighed. "Alright. Before the battle, I was an Odana Second Lieutenant, a Knight. To be Knighted formally, one would have made the Lieutenant ranking." She looked up shyly at Anah. "So, I made Second Lieutenant." Treva huffed a faint laugh. "I was the first female Knight."

Really?! Treva? Always meek and quiet . . . this is the first, the only female Odana Knight? Really?

Treva continued: "Well, as I understand it, I was unconscious for the first days after the Seizure of Odana, and when I came to, I was in a hut—it became my hut, the same one you know. I was lying on a floor mat with my wound bandaged. My nursemaid Greta—from before—was there at my side. She was quite great with healing and had bandaged all around my middle." Her mouth lifted a quick slight smile. "She quickly let me know that she had dragged me secretly into the hut. I'm still amazed that her small body was capable of dragging . . . well, *anything*." Treva tore off a small piece of bread and sighed. Her eyes sparkled. Tears.

"She also told me that she had buried my armor in the dirt floor of my hut. I remember looking down at the ground, which had obviously been disturbed. She left me clothes—rags, really, and my bonnet." She chewed on the bread a bit more. "She convinced me to claim I had a skin ailment that affected my scalp and that I needed to wear my bonnet always." She swallowed it down. "Of course, no one questioned that, and no one wanted to come near me." Another swallow. "She left my hut saying that she would see me again, but I haven't seen her since." She focused in thought. "I was always careful to leave the dirt loose on the ground in my hut, keeping the floor covered with a large rug—an old blanket, really."

She looked at Anah steadily. "You're not the only one who thought of rebelling, or who memorized the guard's rotations."

Anah noticed Treva's dirty, jagged fingernails and filthy hands and arms. She must have spent the entire evening digging up the armor, before the midnight escape.

"Greta—she was the only one who knew my true identity," Treva continued. "I was secretly married to an Odana Lieutenant General, Irza . . . the right hand of General Prince Lanico." Treva lowered her gaze, and her voice grew thick with emotion: "We were at battle with the Mysra. They were strong. They used trillium. It was all a sudden shock, the attack. They had left us on neutral terms days before."

She looked at Anah. "We learned the true effect of trillium on the Mysra that day." She paused. "My Izra, he fought so valiantly. I was weak, for I had only just borne my baby." She breathed in pain and a damning tear managed to twinkle down her cheek—the first ever that Anah had seen from her. "I never told you about that . . . but I still had a duty for the crown. That duty came before my physical pain. Despite my efforts, I was struck by an archer's arrow, mid-battle. Izra turned to my aid and in his own duress; he took a sword for me . . ."

She paused with a faraway look. "I cannot remember much after that. My memory then takes me to the hut."

Anah sat in silence absorbing all this news. It was a struggle to digest, imagining Treva in such horror. It brought chills to her whole being.

"I had a son . . . his name was Marin," Treva continued and more tears continued to well. "His hair was dark and curly, like his father's." She blinked and the hot tears streamed freely down her dirt-streaked cheeks. She remembered stroking his tiny ear with her thumb as he suckled. His small body cradled in her arms.

Anah, seeing the pain in her friend, came close to her side and wrapped her arm around her back in warm support, but lightly, to avoid causing her pain. It was clear to Anah that Treva had put her memories aside for a long, long while in order to survive. Perhaps this was what the other slaves did as well. It was most likely what her own parents did. Perhaps this was why Treva had always seemed quiet and meek.

Treva sniffed hard and wiped her face with the back of her wrist. "I don't know what happened to Marin. I had hoped he was with someone in safety. He wasn't among the dead after the battle, Greta assured me. When I look out over this vast land, I wonder—could he be out there? . . . Hiding?" Treva stopped and looked at Anah. "Would he know me? . . . Would I know *him*?"

Anah leaned her head against Treva's. She felt a pit of grief in her own stomach in sympathy for her friend, and she swallowed against the ache to cry along with her. No. Strong—she would be strong for Treva here, at least.

There they sat, side by side.

Chapter Twenty-One

The Mysra guards Gax and Neen had ridden throughout the night, and in all that time found no signs of Gish, nor any travelers headed into the Odana. Continuing on their journey and following their superior's orders, they finally came to the winding Odana River. The last water supply for many miles before the steppes of the Yellow Vast. It was hot, and the cool water seemed pleasant to the horses as they drank. The Mysra riders were most unhappy, and this task only enhanced their disdain for Gish. Experienced at patrolling on horseback, they knew that this would have been the most reasonable stop for Grude's pampered heir before he headed out into the Yellow Vast. It was a bend in the river that had large boulders to sit upon and a few logs lying about. There was no sign of him.

Neen specifically felt himself in constant competition with Gish and resorted to often-ruthless tactics to get his way. This time, he had brought his own "right-hand man" Gax to assist in his search efforts. He could trust Gax. If Neen couldn't complete this mission, Gax would.

"It's possible Gish hasn't made it quite this far yet," Gax growled to Neen. "You know how he spoils the horses." It was more of a question than a statement. He squinted, holding his hand up to shade his view.

Neen nodded in agreement and took a long tug from his newly filled canteen. "Gish is spoiled, so he then spoils the horses—I swear, nothing good comes of him and his doing."

They walked around, inspecting the site. Gax wiped at his thick neck with his purple rag. Twins, Gax and Neen often had to have a way to distinguish between their often-identical belongings. Gax had chosen purple and Neen chose red. The purple rag was from the tattered tunic of their dead older brother.

Gax sat on a log and looked up at the complaining Neen, nodding his head in agreement. He was the smaller of the two and Neen considered his slowness to get angry a defect—Gax was the duller of the two, according to Neen, certainly not as talkative.

Neen decided to lumber up and down this section of the river to see if he could notice any signs of others, and Gax sighed, sinking further into his resting pose and wiping his brow with his purple rag.

Neen walked slowly for a while before pausing. It was odd. "The ground has indentations," he announced quietly. *Someone had been here—but when?* He noticed charred wood and debris, but these were not together in one spot. Someone had been trying to conceal their stay here. He did not want to abandon the spot, *but, there aren't any sure signs, either, no tracks that lead beyond this point*, he thought. Although he was an experienced tracker, he was perplexed. That was rare for him. He knew well that someone could have traveled through the river, but even then, they only had a half chance of getting it right.

~

Lanico continued to walk alongside Criox, holding the reins and guiding him through the flowing water. The horse's brown face brushed against Lanico's shoulder from time to time, as if he wanted comforting. Gish guided Aspirim, holding his reins firm. The men's booted feet were soaked through, but at least the water was only cool and not freezing. It could have been worse. Marin, riding though his stretches in the saddle showed his legs must burn with the ache of it, made no complaints, and his countenance revealed he looked to the promise of safety ahead. He was determined.

Eventually the Odana River led them to the rolling hills and woods, where there was safety in multitudes of leaves and in the height of trees—if needed. Beyond that, there was special safety in *these* woods, with Lanico's mother. Judging from their having entered the wooded hills, he thought they had made good timing. They had only made it as far as the camp that divided the Yellow Vast and Odana as of early that morning, but they had walked for one whole day, as Lanico had requested.

Lanico was pleased to feel the cool of the thickening trees. *Thank Odan—woods.* The dark of shade washed over them, making Lanico's and Marin's eyes glow brighter.

The sky was starting to turn a shade of purple again, and after a bit more walking, feeling the horse's gait, hearing them grunt increasingly, Lanico decided to make camp. He suddenly announced, "Here! We'll stop here." He slowed Criox. "I think this is enough distance that we have trekked."

Not perfect, but it was good enough. They had the shelter of the dense trees, and these woods were plentiful with small game. They just had to hunt them now, before they ventured too far into the woods and too close to his mother, Greta. Most importantly, they needed to be just far enough into the Odana woods to create a stir, for Lanico *wanted* his presence to be known. The distance here, he could *feel* it was right. He didn't know exactly where his mother's home was, only that this was her territory, and being Fray of light and guardian over the expansive Odana woods, she lingered here. She'd come to him.

In preparation for the evening, they dropped their bundles and worked to make camp.

"Lanico, what are the plans for tomorrow?" Marin asked while unrolling a blanket.

Besides his aching for a real bed by this time tomorrow, Lanico didn't know the answer yet. His first goal was to get Marin alive to this forest, to safety. Now that this mission was almost achieved, the next steps would have to be thought through carefully.

"I don't quite know yet, Marin," Lanico answered truthfully, casting his glowing sights over the ground in search of sticks and small fallen branches for a fire.

Marin was a little unsettled by this. "So, there's no plan?"

"Not all things have an easy or quick plan. Some things require thought and time." Lanico controlled a grunt as he picked up a larger branch. "We're safe here for the night, perhaps the next night as well. That's all that matters at this moment, at least." Lanico wasn't quite certain how to tell Marin, or Gish, the identity of his mother—and, thereby, reveal who *he* was. *What* he was. *No, her appearance will be explanation enough.*

It took some time, but eventually they found enough forest wood to start a small fire. But once it was going well, Lanico still couldn't find the rest he longed for. He was feeling a bit overwhelmed by his memories. These woods were enchanting. The land—it was his, and Marin's. So many WynSprigs had lost their lives for the sake of this land . . .

Withdrawing from his haunting memories and emotions, Lanico determined to try to sleep. He wrapped himself tightly in his green cloak and carefully lowered himself to his knees. He wasn't graceful, lying down on the ground, stumbling a bit on his way down and catching Marin fighting a smile. Lanico looked quickly at Gish, whose fixed gaze on Lanico seemed puzzled. Once down, wrapped up tight in a cocoon, Lanico tossed his head back to try to get his long hair from his face. He forcefully blew at strands that landed near his mouth and nose. This was a time when having short hair, or tied hair, would have been a better choice.

Once settled, he listened through the crackling fire for anything to be alarmed about. Gish and Marin would be okay. They were both close enough that he could swiftly intervene if needed. He knew he was overly protective of Marin but couldn't help it—there were only a few people alive in all of Odana that he loved as much. He was responsible for Marin.

These woods, so enchanting . . . Lanico, seeking sleep as he did every night, thought about the day that Treva had come to him all those years ago, after a day of practice. As expected, he was putting away the sparring swords, following yet another training. Treva lingered behind after everyone had left. This was most unusual since she hadn't stayed after since . . . since he had rejected her kiss. He could see right away that she looked nervous. He was intrigued, for Treva never seemed scared of anything. That was one of her great qualities—she was never fearful and desired challenge.

Lanico looked at her in wonder as she approached him. Her thick emerald hair was tied back in restraint except for one loose section that encircled her small, angular face. She was looking down and fumbling with the tooth necklace that hung loosely around her neck. Lanico fought back the urge to tuck the loose hair behind her ear. Almost as if she read his mind, she quickly tucked the hair back. She straightened and looked back up at him . . .

It was a scene played out in his mind, repeatedly every night. A scene that he chose to end precisely there. The memories that followed those moments, when he was lost in her brown-golden flecked eyes, were just too painful. For it was just afterwards that she confided that she was pregnant . . . by his oathed brother Izra. The pregnancy and the secret marriage were the things of rumors amongst the various ranks. With pride and determination however, the couple and Lanico, continued onward with duty.

Tonight, Lanico dared himself to remember how just as Treva's womb grew, the tensions throughout the kingdom grew as well. Not long after it was clear that a war was upon them, Treva labored and bore her son, Marin. It was if Odan himself sought for Marin's early arrival. Had he arrived any later, neither he nor Treva might have survived.

Treva, ever the committed Odana warrior, came to fight for Odana only a few days of rest after the birth. No one would have expected her to do that. He surely would have rejected this. She kept a swaddled Marin hidden close by, and her comrades raised eyebrows at seeing her there in battle so soon after childbirth.

Lying there, in the dark quiet of the woods, and thinking honestly to himself, Lanico knew that he had loved her and wished that he could have had a life companion like her. But there was none. There wouldn't be.

But still.

Still . . . he remembered her. One hundred years after her death, he still loved her. Still mourned her. Her face had warmed the visions of his dreams every night since. Every curve, the faint scar on her mouth—still so perfect in his memory.

He wasn't sure if this was a blessing or a curse. *Why? Why has she remained so fresh in my mind for so long?* He was frustrated that he somehow, could not let her go . . . even in death.

He breathed in the cold night air.

As Lanico toiled in thought and long-held emotion near the fire of their Odana campsite, a loud thunderclap crackled above. The electric blue of his eyes sparked open in response. Rain started falling in heavy sheets. It was good fortune that they were camped under thick cover of the trees, preventing an outright soaking, for only scarce trickles managed to get through. Feeling the damp, Lanico wrapped himself a little tighter. "When will she come?" he muttered under the drowning sound of rain. It was a bit rattling to him that his mother wasn't as timely as he himself. His father had graced his own punctuality to him.

~

The Mysra guards didn't find any trace of Gish, nor of anyone else, at the Odana River, but they did find horse tracks and footsteps that came from the direction of the Yellow Vast and perhaps Gray Rock beyond. They knew that these could be linked to Gish, but no matter. They decided to track the steps from whence they came—to explore where they had been before. Grude *did* say that he had interest in gathering more WynSprigns and of learning the precise location of their realm. If they were lucky, they'd find the long-hidden

Great Mist and get the true credit they deserved. Perhaps these tracks would lead them.

With determination, they once again set out. They headed toward the high hill plateau in the distance, the Yellow Vast shelf that overlooked Odana before them; this was to be the entrance to their destination. They rode the horses quickly up the great switchback hill, determining they needed a running start for this feat.

Chapter Twenty-Two

The golden glow of Treva's eyes flashed open. Her chest vibrating at the powerful resonating that expanded outward for miles at the clap of the thunder. Remembering where she was, she felt the area around her frantically and could feel but barely view with relief the sleeping silhouette of Anah, just next to her. She hadn't intended to sleep this late. Fat raindrops angled into the cave and thumped down upon her head, trickling through her thick hair and over her scalp. She sat up quickly to shield herself in the shallow cave and looked out at the dark below. It was after dawn—but the storm had restored a semblance of night to the landscape. The rain had started to fall in white sheets and created a wet haze in the dim below.

She glanced over at Anah, who gave no physical response to the rain nor the thunderclap. "Well, you're a heavy sleeper," she said quietly, then lightly shook her shoulder and spoke, but to no avail. Concerned at Anah's position so near the ledge, she grabbed the girl with both hands, hauled her to an upright sitting position, and further away from the drop-off. She leaned her back against the shallow cave wall, placing Anah just next to her. Anah's head drooped to the side, and her mouth hung open, then she muttered something inaudible. Treva rolled her eyes and smirked: "Correction—you're a *very* heavy sleeper, indeed." She let her companion slump down into sleep. At least here, in this position, the raindrops couldn't find them.

They would wait until the rain lightened, or better yet, stopped completely, and then leave the cave. Before that, they wouldn't be able to see, and the rain could create dangerous climbing conditions. It would be hazardous even afterward, but there wasn't any choice. They needed to move on.

Now wide-awake and free to let her mind wander beyond toil and fear, Treva needed to keep from thinking about the dull pulsing pain in her back. She decided to muse about things that she hadn't allowed herself to dwell on in years. She thought about the days of old, the wonderful times. She thought about her Knighted companions, her friends, and even her servants, also friends

Greta and Lika. Her mind drifted over what might have been had the Seizure of Odana not taken place. And him. The azure eyes of her General Prince . . .

Chapter Twenty-Three

It was well before the sun came up when something startled Lanico. He could see plainly that the sky was still the deep blue of ending night, and the rain had stopped, leaving the air wet and hazy. Marin and Gish were asleep by the dead campfire—the elements did not hinder their repose. Marin resembled a log and Gish a great boulder. *Oh, to be young and sleeping like that*, Lanico thought, turning his head back and forth to ease the stiffness that had settled in his neck.

He felt a growing warm presence behind him. Was the sun coming up from behind the thick woods? *Which direction am I facing?* He rolled over to view the woods behind him, and the brightness intensified. He winced against it.

In that moment, he knew he had found safety, for *this* brightness did not sting like that of sunlight in the Yellow Vast. And there she was—the second created daughter of Odan, the "Appointed One." A tall and brilliant presence glided toward him. His Ama. Fray Greta's path brightened even the bark on the trees, revealing details of the leaves as she moved gracefully through the woods. She was beautiful—no, exquisitely radiant. Fray over light and nature, she was a handmaiden fashioned by Odan himself, but to Lanico she was—

"Ama!" His voice sounded the Fray word for Mother.

Holding him with her warm smile, she looked down at her grown, sleepy boy. He had in fact grown beyond what she perceived as his middle age, while she had not. She was to him unchanged. As warm and as familiar as the sunrise itself. Lanico sat up quickly.

"Oh, I am so pleased to see you! Thank Father Odan! I had hoped you would find me in these woods—it has been so long. I—I wasn't sure—" He tumbled out the words, awestruck.

"Lanico," she said. Her voice a soft breeze, waving off his rambling explanation. "I have longed to see you for . . ." She didn't finish. "You look so well and are still a handsome WynSprign man. I had wondered if you'd look the same and how the course of time would affect you"—her smile faded—"especially since the ravaging of my mountains. You know that I cannot freely leave the Odana to gaze upon you in places beyond."

Lanico felt ashamed. She was right. He concealed the sorrow and fear that had kept him from making the journey to see her. He had taken for granted that she would never die a natural death, so she'd always be there for him to visit—still, it was no excuse.

"I'm sorry, Ama," he said, coming to stand, bits of leaves and grass falling from his damp cloak. Even though Lanico was the tallest WynSprign—or Fray-WynSprign half-breed—she was a whole head taller than he. "We left the Great Mist," he explained with a sigh, looking back at the sleeping Marin. "He was banished, and I have now learned of the true fate of the WynSprigns I left behind after the Seizure of Odana."

He looked back up at her, his eyes pleading. "We have decided to come home, to the Odana. We know that things here have not been good, for the WynSprigns here in these lands are enslaved. The time has come for us to reclaim our position in this land. It is late for me to act, but now I understand that the safety of even the WynSprigns in the Great Mist, is in jeopardy."

Despite the dire news, Greta's tone remained soft. "We will fix this. Odan is on our side." She quietly explained, in language that reassured Lanico even as he felt alarm at the revelation, that her strength had diminished increasingly over these years as the Odana Mountains in her realm had been subject to constant mining. Though miles away, she felt every twang, every scrape within her of the pick-axe. Her energy was directly tied to these lands, living mountains, and the years, and these past years had been grueling. "I feel almost as hollow as these purple mountains, now mined of their trillium," she confided.

Switching the subject, she inhaled and pursed her lips, remembering. "You mentioned 'we?'" She glanced over to the fire behind Lanico, to the two sleeping figures that lay beyond. Without sound, nor waiting for Lanico's response, she glided toward them.

She bent over Gish and her smile immediately turned to a gape at the Mysra. Her tongue pressed to the roof of her open mouth, and she inhaled loudly to scent him, her eyes turned upward behind her fluttering lids as she breathed in deeply, loudly.

Lanico waited for her response, knowing her more-refined ability of scenting would confirm his judgment of the Mysra—or give him a chance to dispatch him as he slept.

Finished, she smiled but also raised her brows with curiosity. "He doesn't *smell* of Mysra . . . He's'—she inhaled again—"He's different, not a danger, I don't think. However, his scent is familiar, *very* familiar and even . . . safe? It is most peculiar. It's as if . . . no." She dismissed the thought with a wave. *No, not possible.*

Caught in the moment, Lanico didn't press her to continue the rest of her unspoken conclusion. Her verdict of 'not a danger' was answer enough.

She glided toward Marin and angled herself over his face, which was covered by the thin traveling blanket. She waved her hand slightly and the blanket moved at command to reveal his handsome young face and curly hair. She smiled widely and looked up at Lanico. "Marin still looks just like Izra, a little Izra."

Yes. She had said those very words in the past. *Little Izra.*

"I know," Lanico said. "I think of him always, especially now as I see him in Marin's maturing face."

"Not only Izra . . ." she led with a small smile.

To this, Lanico did not respond. He didn't have to. He ran his fingers through his rain-dampened silver hair.

"I wanted her for you, too, my son. I loved her for you, also," said Greta, smiling sadly. Her thoughts reviewed the past. *The wound had been enough, but even if she had survived it, Treva could not have survived enslavement all these long years with the heartache she had endured. If only I hadn't been weakened by the war, unable to assist her then, or to seek her out later—the mining has kept me confined to the woods. I promised I would return to her aid.* She regretted that she hadn't been able to, but didn't share that detail with her son. There was no need after all.

Lanico, feeling his emotions run deep, whispered, "It's all in the past."

Greta gave a tight-lipped nod and looked back down at the handsome young Marin. "Come, Lanico, introduce us and let's gather at my home and remove ourselves from this dark, wet wood."

Lanico nodded in agreement. He knelt and shook Marin to rouse him and the young man sat up sleepily, his curls in wild disarray, adorned with blades of grass and leaves. He stretched his arms out far and slowly opened his eyes. Suddenly he gasped at the unexpected sight of the statuesque, glowing woman smiling down at him. Gish, alerted by the loud gasp, sat up prepared for battle, his knife in his hand.

The woman's beneficent presence warmed them both and the tension melted instantly.

"Marin and Gish," Lanico started uneasily—he wasn't sure how Marin was going to respond to this introduction—"I think it's far past time for this. I'd like you to meet my mother, my Ama, Fray Greta." He gestured toward the ethereal woman who loomed tall over them all, even Gish.

Gish, now standing, bowed a little; he was always sparse with words. "Pleased to meet you, uh—milady, uh—Fray," he managed. If he was shocked, it did not show other than the sputtering of his greeting.

"Wow!" Marin's eyes were wide and glowing purple in the dimness. "You're a Fray? You're Lanico's mother?!" He was elated and could barely get his words out. "So Lanico's part . . . uh, part Fray *and* WynSprign . . . a half-breed?"

"Yes," Lanico replied with a slight smile.

"But I didn't know the Fray were *real*!" Marin said with astonishment. "But then, until recently I didn't think horses were real, either—just bedtime stori-."

"Yes, Marin," Greta continued, "your Lanico is part Fray." She looked with playful accusation over at Lanico and said low, "You never told him?"

Lanico shrugged. "I felt it wasn't information that he needed."

Greta smiled and scolded Lanico with lowered brows.

Once they broke camp, they followed Greta though the dark woods hardly lightened with the dawn, but her presence was a beacon along the way. Marin and Gish looked at each other, as they trailed behind Lanico, Marin calling ahead a flurry of questions about the Fray, about powers, and more. Greta was most accommodating and indulged the young man with answers. It had been a long while since she'd had anyone to converse with.

They trudged with their bags, guiding the horses through these mysterious, dense woods. Once at a clearing near the river, Gish tied both the horses to nibble on the tall grasses that grew wildly around them, the beasts snorting in relief. Lanico and Marin went ahead with the bags to the house that reminded Lanico of all the magic of his childhood.

His Fray mother's home was a vast collection of thin birch trees that had been enchanted. Bent and pulled into the shape of a large house, illuminated from within the trees themselves. Their green canopies sheltered the top of the home with a green blanket that kept out the rain. The tall door was most unusual, woven of tiny filaments that allowed the inside of the home to be visible and circulating fresh breezes.

At Lanico's demonstration that gave him permission, Marin gently ran his fingertips along the door surface in curiosity.

"Oh, I made it using spider silk," Greta explained, noting his curious expression. "I like seeing outdoors and always welcome the fresh air. This door allows these things, without admitting the invasion of bugs. And it trembles at the least disturbance, so I always know who is about."

"It's such a great invention, Fray Greta," Marin marveled, feeling the minute strands with his fingertips.

"Thank you, my dear. Oh, and please call me Greta—you are a grandson to me." Greta smiled at Marin and opened the door widely for them all to enter.

Inside, the home was light, much of it white, and the pleasant smell of moss hung in the air. The ceiling was high. There were no candles—Lanico explained to Marin that Greta had put an enchantment on the large, immaculate home so that it illuminated at her will. He stayed by the door a moment, looking outside to make sure they were not followed, then ushered in Gish while Greta showed them all where to set down their things.

Greta assisted them all to get settled in the sleeping quarters she'd shown them. Marin paused from pulling out his traveling blanket and looked up to meet Greta's gaze.

"I—I have much to learn about Lanico, and you," he said. "And I thank you for your patience with me as I ask questions. I admit that I am still stunned—that Lanico is half Fray. It explains a lot, really."

"Oh? How so?" Greta smiled a cat's smile, and Lanico echoed that smile, glad to have his mother answer Marin's questions for once. After all these years, the adoptive father had been constantly under interrogation at his differences from the others.

"Uh, well . . ." Marin began. "His mannerisms are different from those of the other WynSprigns. And while the others have gotten weaker over the years, Lanico hasn't. His height, his youthfulness, his fairness . . . his frightening moods." Marin slid a glance to Lanico, who now glowered back from where he was unpacking a bag.

Marin gulped and directed his attention back to her. "Please tell me, Greta, what's it like being a Fray? Are there any special skills that Fray have— besides this light that shines from you?"

Greta huffed a slight laugh. "Well, Fray are immortal. We have a few magic properties that allow us to protect the forests and people we love—with limits, of course."

"They can help repair nature," Lanico interjected to explain, choosing not to reveal the weakness she had confided to him. "Some can shape-shift to take on another appearance while others use nature's elements to their advantage. The Fray dwell all over the land, in the thickest forests." He paused. "I was born to Greta, but as you know, I was raised by my father, King Oetam, in the castle."

There were limits to Lanico's own knowledge about the Fray, and therefore limits to his understanding of his own abilities.

Gish listened carefully to the explanations while sorting out the rations they had left.

"I've known you since the beginning, Marin," continued Greta. "I was there to help bring you into this world. I recall the moment I first laid eyes on you, when I helped your mother deliver you." Her gaze now seemed far off. "I still recall when you took your first breath . . . You looked the same as your natural father, Izra—and still do."

Marin's eyes shone with delight.

Later, after they'd cleaned up and eaten, Lanico remained at the doorway, looking out over the narrow clearing of towering pines. Greta drifted over to join her son and gently laid a glowing hand on his shoulder. He placed his hand on top of hers and saw the tears well in her eyes.

"Lanico," she started softly, "I know that you have been through quite a journey, but I wanted to talk to you."

"Well, it's true. We *have* been traveling for some time," Lanico said wearily, not realizing she had started crying.

"Not that journey," she said. "I know that you have been living away from Odana, for I felt your absence in my being for so long . . . Far too long." She sniffed and her aura dulled for that instant.

Lanico made a sad sigh. He opened the screened door and took a few steps outside, Greta gliding beside him.

Outside, Lanico explained that he was weary of not only the journey from the Great Mist, but of his memories and his past actions. He told his mother about the increasing vivid visions that overpowered him, explaining his role in the Great Mist and how the four elders led the WynSprigns.

"I realized only recently, Ama, that I have been dead—dead to my emotions, to my memories, and in my spirit." He was dead to the world and the needs outside the Great Mist. He had left his people behind in Odana. His guilt incapacitated him. He was most ashamed.

Greta came near and embraced him tightly. Lanico's heart melted at the radiating warmth and familiar love of her super-maternal embrace—much like warm honey that melted to cover him body and soul. He was always stoic, but in this moment, in the security of his mother's presence, he was overwhelmed and wept freely.

Lanico wept for his losses—for Izra, Treva, his own father, and for having been so numb for all these past years. He wept for the pain of the enslaved WynSprign subjects. *In denial*—he admitted to himself. He had failed.

Greta continued to hold him tight until his feelings had expelled.

The truth, he explained, was that he was in no position to lead after the Great Divide. He was beyond grief-stricken at that.

Greta, with a tone of compassion, said, "You did not fail, for now you have come back."

Lanico had come back to the Odana and back from the death slumber; he had dwelled in for so long. It was better to come back even now, she explained, than not to come back at all.

Her words were encouragement—nourishment. He sniffed and nodded. "Thank you, Ama. I needed to hear that."

"I know, my son"—she gave a lengthy sigh—"I know." *A mother always knows.*

Chapter Twenty-Four

The rain had only just lifted, and the black morning sky had lightened to a dim blue. Treva knew that this was the time to act. They needed to move quickly. She shook Anah awake. Anah jerked in alarm and yelled out, her voice cascading down the mountain.

"Shhh!" Treva demanded, grabbing Anah's thin arms securely. "It's only me. Listen, we have to get moving. We need to keep distance between ourselves and the Mysra, who are no doubt on our trail by now." Treva was hopeful that the downpour had diminished their tracks somewhat.

Anah nodded and her eyes began to close again.

"No," Treva growled low through her teeth. "*Up*! We need to move out."

"Okay, okay. I'm with you." Anah's voice was weary and weak despite the Emerald Knight's demands.

Their bodies were exhausted from nearly continuous work over the years and sleep was most welcome, but not yet. Not until they reached safety. They rolled up the sleeping mats and grabbed their bags, then very slowly and carefully rounded the corner of the cave to continue down the mountainside they could see through a break in the crags they could not fit through. They were only a few steps from the summit. First Treva went, and then Anah followed. A moment later, they were both straddling the top of the narrow mountain with the sides falling away on either side of them.

"Okay," Treva said, breathing hard. "Understand that this mountain has had a lot of rain. Even though this side of the mountain has trees and some plant life, it can all give very easily with the loosened, wet soil. We must lean ourselves into the mountainside while we trek downwards." She paused for an annoyed sigh. "Expect to get filthy." A section of her hair escaped the emerald mass tied back at the nape of her neck and Treva quickly tucked this behind her ear, as was her habit.

Anah gave a nodded response, though she still looked drowsy. *The next stage will wake her up.*

Treva started downward, grabbing onto small trees and rocky grooves in the rock. Her prized armor made this complicated task even harder, its edges digging into the mud and getting caught on the rocks. She had to wiggle slightly to free herself from these slight catches.

Anah followed a close distance behind, and it was only a few moments later when a rock she had loosened tumbled down the mountain, nearly crushing Treva's head! Treva ducked while Anah gasped and grabbed for another rock, but that tumbled, too, and caused the loose, wet soil to give way! The climbers remained somewhat steady, but Treva herself didn't feel steady and knew Anah could not feel secure, either. A small mudslide formed alongside them and rocks tumbled and bushes were torn up by the force moving downhill.

"Hold on tight and stay still!" Treva yelled over the tumult. "Lean into the mountain—hug it close to yourself!" It sounded lame, but she continued: "Become a part of the mountain itself!"

Treva clung to the mountainside with her body, adhering her face, her whole body into the soil, and hoping Anah was doing the same. She could feel the wet, muddy gravel scrape her face, ear, and head. At last, Treva found purchase balancing on a small tree and holding onto grooves in the rock with clutching fingers, her nails digging into any available fissure.

After a few moments, things had quieted.

Anah, started sobbing quietly above her. "I'm so sorry, Tre," she blubbered, trembling.

It was not Anah's fault. The girl had never climbed a mountain and Treva knew she could have made the same mistake just as easily.

"It's okay, Anah," she called up to her friend. "You didn't know. No harm done. Look!"—Treva laughed a little—"It's okay. We're still okay." She feigned a smile to encourage Anah to stay calm even though her own heart was hammering.

"Tr-Tre, I can't move," Anah called. The smooth cinnamon of Treva's voice did not calm in this urgency. "I'm scared," she whimpered.

"Anah, continue down." It was an order spoken smoothly despite Treva's searing pain that settled in once the panic had passed. "Reposition yourself. We must move in order to avoid capture. We slept far too long and the Mysra guards could be tracking us this very moment and now that the rain has let up . . ." She paused and looked around, squinting, panting loudly. "For us to survive, we need to press forward." *This armor—oh, fires it's too heavy, for my side!*

They both started to move downward carefully, and after a little, the ground below was less distant. They were descending into a lush, green forest that seemed to greet them as a breeze swept through the treetops. It was beautifully tranquil, and the cool air smelled of herbs and pine, without the brassy smell of trillium to taint it.

"Have you ever seen such green," Treva called out in encouragement.

Anah smiled down at her, and Treva completed their common thought: "It's so full of life!"

Suddenly, "HEY!"—a gruff male voice yelled out from the distance above.

Treva darted her gaze toward the sound. Her eyes flashed along the summit, scanning for the source.

Shit!

Two Mysra. Her heart stopped.

They were trying to lumber down the same path the women had used. It was hard to see them at first, for they almost blended into the mountain scape like boulders themselves.

Treva's face twisted into a pained scowl as she looked to Anah just above her. Her lips peeled back from her teeth: "Move! Move! Move!"

In a bold move, Anah leapt down past Treva and they both tumbled hard from the steep slope of the mountain's base and onto the foothills below. They stood quickly, staring up at the Mysra.

They could maintain the distance between them, Treva judged. They could do it. They *had* to.

For only a moment, Treva watched the Mysra move on the mountain and said with a smile, "They don't seem to know how to climb—they may actually injure themselves."

No matter—they needed to lose Mysra however they could. "C'mon!" Treva shouted to Anah, grabbing her arm.

They ran with bags swinging, into the dark, thick woods.

They didn't dare look back.

Chapter Twenty-Five

Greta had just finished giving her guests fluffy white blankets to carry to their rooms. She'd already warmed their spirits up with bilberry tea and honey. The next plan was to discuss the steps needed to reclaim control over the Odana. They had settled in the white wood chairs and began thinking over the facts. Gish was most helpful here. He knew very well his father's intentions as well as other countless details about the security and systems they had in place.

Greta, who was listening intently, paused to focus on something. She felt another stirring in the forest, a familiar tingling in her bones. Without a word and without interrupting the others, she stood slowly and glided away. She looked out a nearby window, then left the men alone in the sitting room and went outside.

Lanico looked up as she left, and Gish's voice slowed to a stop. Greta's glow was visible as she moved outside, along the side of the house and deeper into the woods behind. Lanico stood.

"Stay here," he said calmly to Marin and Gish as he kept his gaze on what he could glimpse through the window. He then walked toward the front of the house, where he had placed Reluctant Leader, and went outside, sword in hand. He followed to where he could see her glow receding into the woods, beyond the other side of her cabin.

He was tempted to follow Greta, but she had not summoned him to follow and he knew better than to go against his mother, or to get ahead of her wishes. She could be far more deadly than even he could, and she could take care of herself. He would keep senses alert, though, just in case. He returned to his companions in the house.

~

Greta illuminated her path and the surrounding trees as she headed straight towards something quickly, with purpose. She felt it like a magnet, a familiar pull toward something—perhaps someone—that she needed and had missed. She grew anxious with every step. *What-Who is this?*

She conjured her gifts from Odan by closing her eyes, tilting back her head, and planting her feet to the earth, murmuring in an ancient tongue—the language of the Father himself. Feeling the surge, she began to run and became a flash that shot past the rush of the hidden falls. The obedience of the trees and brush bent them away from her approaching charge. As she zoomed forward, the forest terrain became hilly and she could feel a change in the air—it was here. She heard thundering footsteps through the forest ground and moved toward the sound, a sound heightened to her.

There! She caught sight of two WynSprign women—a small one struggling to keep up with a taller one that had . . . *emerald hair and a Knight's armor!*

"Oh!" she breathed. Her heart danced.

It's her!

It's really, really her!

"Ha! She made it out!" Greta laughed to the sky.

She watched them bounding in her direction as fast as they could, with terror on their faces. *What are they running from?* Greta wondered through the quickening of her own heart. She slowed herself to stop, positioned herself behind a tree, and transformed with a bright flash so that she could engage them.

Anah and Treva almost slammed into what seemed just a small elder WynSprign woman bent over, picking bilberries from a bush. Her form was fragile and small.

"Whoa! Whoa there!" Greta said kindly through the missing teeth of her new form. She caught Treva by the arm and gripped her muscles with raised eyebrows.

"Ooo! Are you all right?" Treva panted. "I'm so sorry, we—" Her eyes widened.

Greta slowly looked up to meet Treva's gaze and reached up to tuck strands of loosened green hair behind the younger woman's ear.

Treva took a moment, and then stammered, "G-Greta? Is that—is that *you*?" Then her face softened to a smiling, breathy laugh. She bent over and hugged the old woman, lifting her off the ground in excitement.

"Yes! My dear, it's me"—she struggled as Treva squeezed her and then set her down—"Oh my, you're still a strong one, aren't you?"

"Well, you're still as light as a sparrow," Treva responded with delight.

If she only knew, thought Greta playfully.

Treva turned to begin explaining things to Anah, but Greta quickly grew serious:

"You looked panicked, my dear—why are you running?"

Treva stepped back. Her eyes bright. "Oh! We are in danger! Mysra guards are chasing us—I think two of them. Back there somewhere. We *all* need to hide, quickly!"

"Oh, my dears run that way!"—Greta pointed a wrinkled finger in the direction of her tree home. Treva grabbed her by the wrist, to urge her on. The elder woman jerked her hand free and Treva gave her an incredulous look. As Treva and Anah turned to place running steps, Greta raised her hand with authority and conjured a small gust of wind thundering like dashing feet—and she sent it away from them, toward their pursuers. The Mysra guards would hear the thundering footsteps and be diverted away from them, running in the opposite direction.

In the next instant, Greta turned to run with Treva and Anah, now steps away. The fugitives didn't notice her spell, nor the one she was about to cast. The old woman quickly outpaced them while summoning her power again, leading the way to her home.

It wasn't more than a few moments until they came to her tree-covered house, and Treva and Anah stopped in awe, with no idea that they had just been traveling at impossible speeds. The enchanted cottage seemed very close to the mountain pass they had left only moments before.

"Quick—in here, dears," the old woman gestured to them kindly.

They listened but heard no pursuers from the wood behind them, then followed her, looking in awe at the glowing bent trees that formed the large structure that seemingly could hold many rooms. Treva and Anah quickly forgot about the chase and were overcome with awe at this most peculiar home. Greta opened the door slowly. Treva paused behind the elder and the younger, protectively looking out while they entered.

Three surprised males stood just inside. Lanico had kept watch, holding the Reluctant Leader tight. His eyes caught the first glimpse of the mud-caked Anah, who shied from him and his sword and entered slowly. Marin saw her next. She gazed up at him through mud-caked features and stroked back her muddy red hair. She walked quickly and shyly past him, stopping short at the fearsome but familiar spectacle of Gish.

Greta, still in the form of an old WynSprign woman, wore a large smile as she came into the doorway behind Anah, who looked back at her for reassurance. Then, at Greta's encouragement, she lowered her few, muddied belongings to the floor.

Lanico was startled at this girl and at his mother's familiar old WynSprign form. "Ama—" he started, but stopped. Treva entered.

He drew a sharp breath.

No. It can't be.

His heart stopped.

It's impossible.

He stood like a stone, as she looked about, moving into the house in her muddied silver armor.

The familiar name that had nourished his tongue daily for all these years came too softly: "Tre-" *No. It couldn't be. But . . .*

"Treva?!" This time his call edged with joy and confusion. Disbelief. Forgetting all sense of himself or of security—forgetting everything, he dropped Reluctant Leader with a crash to the floor. The world around, the people in it – it all became a blur. All, except her.

Her eyes darted toward the sound. Toward her Prince. Her General.

He was on his knees, his mouth gaping open for a silent scream.

Treva's eyes flickered over to meet his. She inhaled. "L—Lan?!" she whispered; her eyes wide. Her voice cried, "Oh! Odan on High! I thought you *dea*-!" She dropped her bundle and flung herself to her knees before him. Her face flushed and her eyes blurred.

He half-rose and caught her with open arms, but the force sent them both back onto the floor. He clutched her with all his strength, embracing the armor he had given her. He inhaled a soft sob mixed with laughter.

"I missed you so . . ." Her muffled cries were buried in his firm shoulder, and he nodded, too emotional to speak.

It is she! Thank Odan on High it is Treva! My Treva! It was a dream. His mind scrambled as he felt her in his arms, saw the emerald locks of her hair. Heard that voice of *dusty cinnamon.* He swallowed, stifling the urge to completely break down.

Treva breathed deeply in his arms, and Lanico was hardly aware of those who stood around them, witnessing their heaving breaths, hot tears, and trembling hands.

"I thought you dead as well," he barely whispered into her ear. "You were shot. I saw the arrow. Your motionless body, y—you . . ." Then Lanico recalled he had not seen her face on that day. He could not bring himself look upon it at the time. "I felt I had died, seeing you dead . . . I had to live for Izra, for the promise I gave him." He breathed out and his voice was thick, "I've missed you deeply, Tre. There hasn't been a day, nor an hour, that I haven't thought of you." His tears streamed freely. "We're together. Together again." He could feel her nodding against him, her ragged breathing pulsing against his neck, her tears pattering onto him.

He pulled back from her slightly. Tears burned in his eyes, and he stilled, gazing at her—taking in her face, her brown-gold eyes. Then he slowly pulled himself upright and she edged back to sit up. Without care, they wiped at each other's familiar faces and sniffed through soft laughs. He blinked in the silence.

Remembering, Lanico glanced at Marin, who was standing off to the side, misty-eyed with Greta and even Gish. Lanico, still holding Treva's small shoulders between his hands, prepared for what was next. Another dream.

Living, for the promise, Lanico thought. *We are together again.* His words lingered a moment in his mind, then Lanico caught Marin's wild stare.

Marin was confused, his heart still racing at hearing *her* name.

"Treva," Lanico said once more, lifting her to stand with him. He then turned to Marin. He extended his arm toward the young man. "There's someone I'd like you to meet. Until now, it was only in my dreams that I witnessed you meeting."

Marin's eyes were wide with astonishment, and Treva now looked just as dazzled.

Her misty gaze traveled over Marin, then held his gaze in hers. His black, curly hair, his young-man's frame. She knew the soft curve of his jaw-line. Lanico didn't have to say more—her legs trembled beneath her.

"Treva . . . I'd like to introduce you to . . . your son . . . Marin." Lanico's voice remained calm. He blinked through the hot sting of tears, working for maintained composure.

Marin, his face astounded, stepped in closer. He put out a tentative hand to touch her arm.

Treva's mouth opened behind her hand, and she let out a silent shout and reached her arms around the width of Marin's shoulders, pulling him to her. The curled tangles of his hair caught in her fingers. She held him tight and cried, from her gut, managing only his name in a breath. "Marin."

She cradled the back of his head in her hand, as she had the last time, when she had held him as a baby. Now he was larger than she. She breathed him in, moved her face along his, feeling skin she had missed all these years, the firm developing muscles of a young man. He was the very image of his late father, a dream forbidden for all these years.

"My ba . . . is it *really* you?" Treva sobbed through her words. "You were only just . . ." She looked up at Lanico with wide, watery eyes. He looked down at them both, smiling through the lump in his throat. No words would come easily. To sum up Marin's entire lifetime, there were no words.

They cried together, both overjoyed and sad at so many missed memories. She had never been able to warm him with a motherly embrace. She had never witnessed his first strides, heard his first words, was never there to bandage a scraped knee, nor to sing him to sleep during a storm . . . But Lanico was.

Lanico watched the pair with a loving, protector's gaze. Knowing the need for privacy at their reunion, he quietly turned and ushered the rest of the silent group further into the house.

In the dining room, the group followed Lanico's lead and quickly found chairs at the white wood table. They were all silent and shaken at the events they had just witnessed. Lanico smiled with gladness as he looked around at the group. He cleared his throat and took this time to introduce himself and the others to Anah. Gish and Anah were already familiar with one another and were each pleased at each other's presence here. To Gish, it meant that she was safe, and to Anah, it meant that he was increasingly on their side—a helpful ally.

Lanico glanced around at everyone and asked, "Ama, were you planning on tending to WynSprign babes again?" He gave a clever smile.

"Ooo!" Greta laughed at herself. "I had quite forgotten about my appearance. We were all just so moved by Treva and Marin . . ." She paused to clear her elderly voice and considered. "No. I prefer to take this appearance for a bit longer." She looked for understanding from Gish.

Gish had looked confused over who this old woman was, and where she came from, but at Lanico's first sight of her and his indication that she was friend, not foe, he had relaxed and his face how cleared as he learned this was

Greta, his mother. He quietly leaned over to Anah, who was sitting at his side at the table. "This is Marin's grandmother. She is a Fray."

Anah's eyes grew, and she remained in her chair, looking too overwhelmed to move or even speak.

~

After their long, soulful embrace, Treva and Marin stood. Treva smiled and wiped at Marin's puffy eyes and sniffled herself. They laughed a little. The resulting sound: very similar.

Nodding toward the subtle conversation emanating from the eating room, Treva asked in a whisper, "You ready to go in there?"

Marin sighed, "Guess so," his voice deeper than a boy's voice. Save for Gish, they all had tear-stained faces anyway.

"First I want to remove all this armor. I'm not going to war." She smiled, pulling at a clasp. "I couldn't bear to part from it." Her hands made deft movements to remove it all. "It took everything for me to earn it."

Marin watched, impressed, then remembering himself, began to assist her in taking the armor off, carefully laying the pieces down. What honor and responsibility she must have worked for, to receive this armor! It was as Lanico had said of her. After she had put all the pieces in a small, muddy pile on the immaculate floor, Treva pulled him in for one last big soft embrace with her thin form. A *real* embrace. Then she smiled.

"Shall we?"

Marin nodded.

Together they turned to the room where everyone awaited their return.

Chapter Twenty-Six

"Come on then, Gramps! Take these carrots and grubs!" The metal bumped against the rails of the cage as Fenner's own grandson Freck shoved a small spade full of carrots and grubs into his cage. "You'll need to start eating!"

Fenner was boiling with fury and humiliation. All he could do was cower in the corner. He was made to feel like a wild animal, and for what? For Freck to earn a few gold coins? *It's an outrage! An unspeakable and unimaginable outrage for the youth to betray him!*

Despite the hurt that ached within him, he said nothing. He kept his back to Freck, holding onto any scrap of pride and rejecting his offers with sealed eyes.

He was at the edge of the Great Mist, at Horse's Clearing, waiting to be collected as part of Trayvor's banishment plan for WynSprigns who disobeyed the new rules. Fenner sighed a deep, sad sigh and hunched his shoulders forward.

"Urgggg!" his grandson grunted in anger and slammed the spade down. His thin muscles gleamed beneath his brassy-toned skin as grubs wriggled from the bowl of the spade and nestled back into the ground. Freck glowered at Fenner and stomped through the brush and back off into the distance toward the Great Mist.

How could my own grandson do this? Fenner wondered in disbelief. The betrayal would only grow from here, because this banishment plan now involved the Mysra and their forceful removal of caged WynSprigns back to their own territory. *Has he any idea what he is a part of? No.* Fenner swallowed hard. It was a horrible plan. His and Trayvor's own plan. Now it was going to doom him and his most favored grandson. Freck would learn soon enough and it was to be a hard, unfortunate lesson. Fenner was remorseful.

As Freck's footsteps faded, Fenner heard rustling from another location. Heavy steps thudded, twigs snapped, and more leaves rustled. Fenner whirled around, hoping to catch a glimpse of whatever large beast this could be.

"Hey, Fenner," was the familiar voice that came from the sound. Kindly and Sad.

Fenner's fear instantly gave way to relief. "Aw, Stout, it's you," he sighed. "Whew! I will admit to a strange fact—I'm actually happy that it's you." He smiled widely.

Stoutwyn's gray hair greeted Fenner's eyes through the leafy foliage before he could see his face clearly. Stoutwyn was greatly concerned as he looked up and down the length of the cage. "This was made by my folk," he said. With effort, he knelt down next to the cage to be level with Fenner. "I'm certain they had no idea of the true purpose for it."

"Stout, Trayvor has lost his mind," Fenner interjected.

"Aye, and we'll have to figure out what to do to stop the banishment and selling of WynSprigs to the Mysra. The future—our future—depends on it," Stoutwyn said frowning, looking over the well-crafted contraption.

Fenner nodded his black mane in response. "That it does, Stout."

Footsteps were approaching again and Fenner shouted in a whisper, "Stout! Hide!"

Stoutwyn nodded and hobbled back into the brush cover. His blundering movements sent leaves and small branches swaying, and Fenner winced at his clumsiness.

Trayvor was talking to someone as he approached. Fenner narrowed his sights on the approaching group. *This time, they brought Joso!* Fenner pleaded silently to the Father Odan that Stoutwyn would remain calm at this and not give himself away at the sight of his boy. With his timid nature, Joso was an easy target for Trayvor—he wouldn't have made much of a fuss or created a scene.

The young man's yellow hair hung with his bowed head to cover his face—a face washed red in emotion.

They intend to sell him off too—for a ridiculous crime, no doubt. Fenner could imagine Stoutwyn's fury, and thought he might spy his friend's face glaring red in the bushes, which trembled where he hid.

"Here we are," Trayvor said with his smug smile as he they came to the large cage next to Fenner's. Trayvor looked down to dust a few stray leaves off his blue cloak. The capture had left only slight traces of the struggle on his pristine appearance.

Freck opened the cage door and gently pushed the big, trembling Joso in.

"This is your new home, for now," Trayvor continued. "This is what happens when you break curfew."

"But, I—I—I was only trying to deliver cabbages to Ms. Bre Bricklebury—she forgot them after she paid—I—I wanted to get them to her earlier, but—" Joso nervously stumbled over his words.

"*And*, you are still guilty of disobeying the rules!" Trayvor interrupted with a shout.

Fenner twisted his mouth in disgust but remained silent. Trayvor had long had his eye on Bre Bricklebury, one of Fenner's kin, who lived across from the tavern. He must have felt threatened by the unassuming Joso and his alleged 'late night delivery'.

Joso remained quiet. He looked down, sad and pathetic.

"We'll come back soon enough," Trayvor said as he tapped on the locked cage with his walking stick. He then ushered Freck away with him. Freck avoided eye contact with his grandfather. Together they left on the winding path back to the Great Mist.

Once out of view and earshot, Fenner glanced over to the nervous Joso, who was still trembling like a leaf in the corner of his cage. 'Hey! Stout!' Fenner sent a whispered shout out to the still-hidden Stoutwyn. "It's clear—you can come out."

Stoutwyn emerged slowly from his brushy cover. He had a defeated, heart-heavy look about him, his gaze fixed on Joso.

"Joso," Stoutwyn said softly, who looked up with red cheeks and puffy eyes.

"Grandfather?" Joso whispered.

"There, now"—Stoutwyn tried a light tone—"we'll figure this contraption out, my boy." Stoutwyn fumbled for the small saw knife he carried in his pocket. His thick fingers found their way around the grip and he pulled it out. "Ha! *There* now!" he said with a note of triumph and began to saw at the twined ropes that held the cage together.

Fenner felt anxious watching helplessly, wishing there was something he could do.

Suddenly a noise in the brush caused Stoutwyn to freeze.

Chapter Twenty-Seven

A noticeable change had fluttered throughout the Great Mist. Lanico's sound presence and availability for good counsel were sorely missed. Some wondered at the rumors, worried that they'd find themselves with the same leaderless fate as had befallen those left in their old homeland following the Seizure of Odana.

WynSprigns also wanted to know, asking in a roundabout manner, what Fenner had done wrong, so they would not make the same mistake—he was a leader, an elder. Others wanted to know why Joso Stoutlet was not selling his vegetables. "This is peak season—is he now missing, too?" With the lack of their traditional leader's presence, questions surfaced about his disappearance. Their questions led many folks to turn to Trayvor for answers.

The clamoring was all too much for Trayvor, and the questions had become overwhelming. It was no surprise that he hadn't thought this whole thing through. Brash and bombastic, he clearly lacked any real plan for the WynSprigns, nor did he know how to be an effective leader to them all, without the support of his fellow leaders whom he had now parted from. His hope rested in the newfound riches he'd gain for the WynSprigns would be enough to satisfy them.

For now, until those riches materialized, he sought his usual refuge at the bottom of one of the tavern's thick wooden mugs. When it all became too much, he decided to ask the tavern maid, Maybell, to assist in answering questions on his behalf—he didn't like being bothered by all that. He had just managed to imprison Joso, after all, and he was weary.

Trayvor spotted Maybell leaving a table and immediately summoned her over to him. She dutifully set down a large mug of ale for him and held an empty jug in her other hand.

Trayvor summoned her closer, for something secret, he indicated. She leaned down, but her bubbly demeanor straightened as he spoke. Her smile turned into a serious line as Trayvor began to propose an "opportunity" for her to assist him in answering the townsfolk's questions. He tried making this role sound appealing, offering her a role as his assistant. She wiped dry the empty jug while listening intently to Trayvor. After he explained the alleged grandeur of this proposed new role, she looked as if she were considering the prospect. Trayvor eyed her intently.

"No thanks, Mr. Trayvor Odmire," she said simply, failing to keep disdain from sounding in her voice.

Trayvor was aghast, offended by her lack of loyalty to him. "Maybell, I have been coming here and paying you handsome tips daily for many, many years."

"You threaten'n to stop?" she asked with a smart tone. He bristled. Even if she didn't like him, she wouldn't want to threaten her tips. His frequent visits *did* keep her well paid.

Trayvor measured her for a moment. *She dons the same few dresses as always too. What is she saving up for? Whatever.*

He opened his mouth to answer her but she continued, "Mr. Odmire, I wouldn't have any way of knowin'n how to answer *those* questions—just the same as you don't." The clever young woman knew she could get away with talking to him in that manner.

After the initial shock, Trayvor leaned back. "Fine. How about this, Maybell?" he met her glare. "I could tell you the answers, and write them down for you"—he pulled out a coin and showed it to her in his plump, opened hand—"Then you could explain the answers for me, you know, on my behalf." The corner of his straight mouth curved in a mild smile. He felt like a cat watching a mouse.

She considered this for a moment. "It feels like I'm helpin'n you hide, but I'll do it"—then murmured under her breath—"put up with you for now." She straightened up from their conference.

She set the jug down on the table and wiped her wet hands on a rag tied to her side. She smoothly pulled out the thick wooden chair next to Trayvor and leaned over with a sigh to begin examining his scroll. Trayvor raised his head and grabbed for his cane to stand as he noticed a small group of WynSprigns making their way toward the tavern. They shot glances at him as they neared.

Trayvor whispered to Maybell, "I'll be in the back drinkin' my ale. Out of view," and struggled to his feet.

Maybell rolled her eyes and puffed out a sigh. "Don't have any other plans, anyway," she murmured. "Besides, how hard could it be?" She stood up and gathered her pints for the arriving guests, wearing her customary warm, rosy smile.

Despite his physical limitations, he deftly shuffled out of sight as the WynSprigns gathered in the tavern courtyard.

Chapter Twenty-Eight

Once the tree line to Horse's Clearing was in sight, Gax and Neen urged the horses to a full gallop. As usual, they rode the horses hard and arrived quickly at the clearing, leaving all the horridness of the one-armed hag encounter behind them.

Neen slide Gax a scowl. He was still angry about the episode back at the creek. He'd make sure to remind his brother regularly about this. They were only supposed to stop at the creek for a brief rest and he had told Gax not to go to venture off—he had warned him. Now, a lesson had been learned. Gax wouldn't go off to investigate mysterious smelly huts again. No. His curious nature was suppressed.

After hearing a scuffle at the shack, Neen had stormed in and had to save Gax from the wounded one-armed hag who raved incessantly about her dead sisters.

To Gax's credit, at least before they had killed her, she had provided useful information about the mysterious WynSprign warrior that she had encountered days before—who'd killed her sisters. It was further confirmation of whom they might be engaging—a WynSprign. And now, they had been able to track him here—Horse's Clearing. The Mysra fumbled for their trillium pouches to take some crystals before engaging with whatever they might find.

With renewed energy, the brothers dismounted at the tree line. Their panting horses found relief from their exhaustion in the shade of the trees they were tied to. Their coats were frothy with sweat and their tails twitched in defiance of the buzzing flies. Their treatment had been terrible.

With only a few heavy footsteps on the yellow grass, the Mysra were captivated by a new world. They crunched on pine needles and twigs, and the cooler air brushed against their sweaty, gray skin.

They ignored the desire to look around and focused on their task, walking cautiously, looking for tracks, and soon found a well-used path before them. They followed it, passing trees and bushes that became denser with every stride, and after a few moments, they spotted wooden cages in a glade, in the distance. Then, a nice surprise.

Neen's eyes settled on the nearest cage.

The brothers smiled delightedly at each other. For they saw that these cages held WynSprigns—yes! They were *very* close to the hidden village, indeed.

The cage closest to the Mysra held a large young Mysra who whimpered and cowered in a corner. The Mysra eyes roamed from this nearest cage to the next, which held an older WynSprign that looked wild and angry enough to inflict some damage—he glared at them with palpable hatred.

Neen focused on the WynSprigns and wasted no time beginning his interrogation: "Where's your village?" he demanded from the obviously weaker choice. *Surely, he'd talk.*

Joso could not even look at the Mysra. He only whimpered and shook. This was exasperating—a waste of time.

Neen sighed hard in an effort to control his rage. He closed the slight distance between himself and the older one, and he bent to look at him. His voice was slow, graveled, as he threatened, "Okay . . . your turn, tough-Sprign. Where's the village?"

Trembling in fury, the WynSprign erupted, "I would *NEVER* tell a Mysra like you!" With a jerk of his head, he spat on Neen's cheek.

Neen nodded slowly. The spit glistened against his skin but he ignored it and pulled a large jagged knife from the sheath against his hip. He slowly dragged it along the bars of the cage as he eyed the WynSprign, who carefully stayed in the middle of the cage to avoid getting stabbed from any side.

Holding his own knife, Gax stood near the young one's cage but addressed the older one: "Listen, tell us how to get to the village, or else this plump boy is going to get stuck by the pointy end." He waved his knife and bent over to eye the shivering WynSprign inside. "And I *reeeally* want to hear him squeal." Almost playful, he thrust the edge of his knife at the terrified creature, who was too large to avoid a stabbing even if he pressed against the other side of the cage, exposing himself to the other's blade.

"Ow! *Stop!*" the young one yelled, more in fear than in pain. The tip of Gax's knife had jabbed into him slightly, making tiny cuts.

"C'mon! Squeal for me!" Gax yelled and laughed cruelly. Then he paused. He lifted his head at a sound in the brush nearby, waiting . . . No, nothing more over the sound of the terrified WynSprign's breathing.

"Don't tell 'em *anything*, Joso!" the older one yelled, breaking the brief silence. He jolted forward in his cage to grab at the bars in urgency. "Be strong in your spirit!"

Another cruel cackle burst from Gax.

"LOOK!" demanded Neen, whose attention was already elsewhere. "Let's just follow this path. Enough with the interrogation."

Neen's eyes roamed over the forest floor, and he held his knife out, pointing over the disturbed ground. He said low, "We've wasted enough time with these two."

"No!" the old one yelled, desperate. "I'll tell you where the village is!" He clutched the bars of his cage, his face wedged between two. "Y—You're going the wrong way!" He watched in horror, his expression wild as the Mysra laughed and continued toward the village. Fenner's shouting and excitement only meant that they were on the right path.

"Easyyy . . ." Gax said and smiled at his serious brother. The Mysra wasted no time, quickly making long strides along the path without acknowledging the captives further, without even another wasted glance.

It wasn't a long walk before they could hear distant voices and see that the trees thinned out slightly ahead. It was a revelation to see how the WynSprign lived amongst the trees. They hadn't felled them but rather had built around them, and into them. This made the brothers' mission somewhat easier—offering more opportunity to hide. They agreed with whispers to get off the path, walk through the denser trees, and brush until they could see more of the village.

Among dusty paths, the relaxed, fearless, and free WynSprigns lived their lives with no sense of the danger, lurking just beyond their sight.

Is it to be this easy? Neen wondered. *It's almost ridiculous. Grude will be pleasantly surprised.* He made a contented sigh.

~

"We must conjure a plan, and quickly," Stoutwyn said, quietly emerging from the brush to stand between the cages. The leafy cover behind him swayed at his movement. "I've cut loose their horses—can you hear them? A nice surprise for their return journey," he chuckled. "A shame to free them when we could use them ourselves, but"—he neared Fenner— "we need to stall their return and not draw attention." He resumed sawing at the ropes that held the

147

cage together. He handed his lucky paring knife to Fenner to start sawing from the inside of his cage. "I forgotten I had that," he said.

"It figures," Fenner said with an equally sour glance and tone. He then began to cut the rope. How Stoutwyn had outranked him *and* had been the Second Advisor of the King was beyond his understanding. *Then again, the kingdom was overtaken, so . . .*

Bits of twine spiraled as they were cut loose. "Finally!" Stoutwyn declared as one rope gave way.

Fenner and Stoutwyn were able to free one end of the bar from the cage, and Fenner was very thin and could wiggle through. Together they hurried over to start working on Joso's cage. Joso was still nervous, trembling and bleeding a little from the small cuts Gax's knife had given him.

Fenner was beginning to feel the prickle of annoyance at Joso. *I would never have allowed him to be raised in such a weak and fearful fashion,* he thought. The grimace on his face seemed to be for the efforts at sawing the ropes, but was a look actually reserved for Joso's family – *the weak lot of them. Save for Stoutwyn. For at least he had been an Advisor and a Major.*

Together they sawed with fervor to free him.

"We will need to gather everyone—we'll avoid the tavern, of course, to steer clear from Trayvor. He's the one that started all this mess," Stoutwyn said breathlessly.

Once Joso was free, they trotted to the Great Mist, keeping an eye out for the Mysra.

"We'll—gather—everyone," Stoutwyn said, panting between strides.

"Yeah, but we'll need to make a plan to defend ourselves, too," Fenner added.

Stoutwyn managed a nod. Joso jogged behind them and remained silent—the Mysra might still be close.

Stoutwyn said low, "First we'll go and get that bell Trayvor was using to announce his 'rules.' Then we'll gather everyone to start to learn how to fight."

"Fight?" Joso asked from behind them.

Stoutwyn and Fenner paused and looked back briefly at Joso with raised eyebrows—they paid him no mind and resumed their forward strides.

"Right!" Stoutwyn replied, immediately forgetting his voice volume.

"Between Lanico's house, yours, and mine, we have only a few swords," Fenner said. "We have some training staffs, though. We'll have to focus on training the more able-bodied folk to use the swords—since they require more heft and skill." He was a natural runner and was not winded by their trek through the woods.

"Right"—Stoutwyn stopped to catch his breath and raised a hand to stop the others— "But still we don't have enough weapons—nor staffs."

"Well, we will just have to make do. In truth, we cannot just flee the Great Mist without another plan in place. They'll track us," Fenner said, waiting to resume the walk. "And they'll be faster than we are." He shot a quick glance to Stoutwyn's legs.

"But wait!" Fenner added, his finger in the air. "Aren't your kin some of the finest woodworkers ever—can't they make staffs for us—not swords, granted, but weapons nonetheless?"

"No, not swords" Joso piped in unexpectedly, "but every kid knows how to swing a staff."

"Yes!" Stoutwyn grunted, "Staffs will do—if we have enough wielding them." He straightened up to continue through the woods.

They continued into the Great Mist, stirring the brush with their urgent steps.

Chapter Twenty-Nine

The force of their crashing swords ignited sparks that flashed through the dense forest like low lighting. Their battle sounds could be heard in the distance around them, but they didn't care, for the dense Odana woods provided seclusion and neither warrior had heard that illuminating, delicious clash for many years. The twang, the song of steal. The sound resounded in their bones and fingertips—it exhilarated them.

The long sword Treva had borrowed from Greta's treasure trove was no match for the pristine steel of Lanico's blade, but with skill . . . she was just as deadly.

Lanico felt a fabulous surge of well-being sparring with her. It was reminiscent of the precious times before the Battle of Odana. He grunted against Treva as their sword hilts came in close together, forming a V with their blades. He released a burst of breath against her cheek. With a jolt of force, she thrust against his sword to make space between them and was forced back, grinning. She was not up to her old training level after these many years, and was losing, but she dug her heel into the ground. Determined. She was determined and relentless.

Treva smiled wickedly and waited for Lanico to make a strike. Her mouth hung wide open. Lanico knew she had learned this effective-yet-annoying gaping-grin habit from Izra. Normally he'd find this sadistic gaping disturbing, but somehow it reconnected him with a bit of his friend. *A strange comfort,* he reasoned in the face of her maddening grimace.

"Looks like that sword is working well enough," Lanico gulped, breathing hard.

"Well, that falchion sword your mother saved would have been better for me." It was a tired and old argument that stemmed from their early days training together. He didn't prefer that she has been used to one type of sword.

Lanico had revealed Greta's identity as not only his mother, but also a Fray! She had taken it well, already stunned with the revelation of Marin's growing up Lanico's adopted son. "That does explain a lot," she'd said—not only Lanico's ability to rescue Marin after the siege and carry him to safety in the Great Mist, but also the nurse who'd "magically" appeared to care for Treva's wounds. "Greta hid her identity well," she'd said. "Very well."

"C'mon, Tre," Lanico taunted with another strike, "you need the challenge—you know it."

As he expected, she raised an eyebrow, gave a sly smile, and launched toward him in forceful return.

Together, they danced in fluid movement, the weaving and flowing of their articulate strikes the epitome of beauty and precision in motion.

Lanico was taking it easy with her, knowing she was weakened, having been malnourished for many years, and had an injury. The taste of freedom and old muscle memory had them both swinging and giving everything they had.

Before the practice, Greta had given Treva a concoction that dulled the deep pain in her side. "This will work for now", Greta had explained to Lanico "I believe you should intervene with Treva's wound, son, in your own time and at your own will - as a Fray."

And, he knew what she'd meant.

~

Greta and Anah had remained indoors, where Greta riffled through her large chest of collected weapons, blankets, and clothes. It seemed she had every sort of weapon, armor, and clothing, except, to Anah's slight disappointment, a pickaxe.

Despite wearing larger clothing items herself, Greta was determined to find something small enough for Anah. Then she remembered Marin's tunic— she had already given him a new tunic from her collection, for his had become too small for his growing frame. She had already cleaned and mended it. She would give that one to Anah.

When they'd first arrived Anah had been so spent that she'd fallen asleep after tea and a meal, without having the opportunity to clean herself. Now Greta had filled a hot bath in the small pool in her home's bathing room and waited at the door but held her gaze away from Anah. The girl was anxious to clean herself up, sorely conscious of her muddied appearance. She stripped off her dirt-laden clothes and entered the pool, then Greta quickly gathered the clothes and decided to clean and mend them as well as she could, given that, they were more rags than clothes. She left Anah alone to bathe.

Anah peered around at the small room that was still larger than the only hut-home she had ever known. As it was with all of Greta's rooms, this one was ethereal glowing white with a thick matting of trees for walls. Anah cautiously peered between the thickly entwined branches and was relieved that there was no way to see outside—or in—through the tightly woven branches and trunks.

The pool was a small white circle in the center of the room. Anah had never taken a warm bath before but had imagined it after Treva's descriptions. This hot, steamy water looked like thinned milk and smelled of a wonderful flowery fragrance. As a slave, she had only ever cleansed herself with a bucket and rag or in a pond—but it was never warm and certainly never smelled of flowers.

The hot prickling water had taken her foot, then her leg, then the other leg, and then the rest of her. It was the most satisfying feeling she had ever experienced. Once the water reached her shoulders, she leaned back slowly, dunking her head. Her muscles relaxed and melted to become hot liquid, too. As soon as she'd settled her whole body into the bath, she felt herself calmed and enjoyed the warmth enveloping her body. The mud loosened and fell away to reveal the waves of her gorgeous deep-red hair.

"Ooo . . . feeling clean like this is an absolute blessing," she quietly moaned to herself. She let the water still around her as she soaked and relaxed. Steam rose and delicately danced in swirls above her, and at that, she thought she might never come out.

Greta left the clean and mended clothes—including Marin's old tunic—just inside the door.

~

Gish and Marin paused their own sparring in awe to watch Treva and Lanico spar in the distance. Marin was no stranger to training with Lanico, but he'd never seem him move quite like this, with an equal. Treva was a challenge and brought out Lanico's hidden energy and strength that Marin didn't know existed. He was amazed by them. Stunned.

"All right, Gish. Let's get back at it again," Marin challenged, his flushed face turned back to the lumbering Mysra. They were practicing near the ethereal home.

152

Gish was reluctant and knew only about fighting with his trusted knife, but Lanico had urged him to learn a bit about the sword. Mysra were not used to using swords in their battles or in personal fighting—not since before the Battle of Odana, and that had been before he was even born, Gish had explained. During the old time, the Mysra fought with swords, knives, bows and arrows, and more. Only a few Mysra were trained in sword fighting these days, and those were the castle guards and Grude.

Gish was clumsy and awkward with the long sword, as Lanico instructed him on his stance. They continued to practice back and forth slowly, and Lanico was most pleased to see Gish taking on the basics so well. He was also proud of Marin's instruction.

They paused at the sound of Greta's door moaning open. The practicing pair slide their eyes toward the sound. Anah emerged—and Marin's heart skipped.

Anah nervously fumbled a crimson section of hair with her wrinkled fingertips, turning her eyes to his. She was clothed in a radiant white tunic—Marin's own tunic, he recognized. For Anah it was a bit too large, but to Marin, she looked gorgeous. He didn't know why, but for some reason something about seeing her in *his* tunic, made him feel . . . he didn't know. Her flaming red hair, still damp, was brilliant against the white fabric. She looked . . . new.

Marin forgot himself and dropped his sword.

Lanico yelled from somewhere in the background, "Marin, focus!"

Marin blinked at the sound of Lanico's voice in the distance. *Fires he notices everything!*

A rush of warmth rose to his cheeks.

And Anah smiled at him.

Chapter Thirty

Night covered the Odana forest and Gish, drained from all the training, went to bed early. His bulky muscles weren't used to training in this intense way. He retired to the sleeping den he would share with Marin and Lanico, now in one room since the women had arrived, and in an instant, they could all hear the snores of his deep slumber.

Lanico, Marin, and Treva sat in the eating room with Greta, who set down a teakettle and cups for her dew tea. She had fruit, cheeses, and biscuits set out as well for them to snack on. She poured the tea into two cups for Treva and Lanico and served Marin fresh water instead.

"Water for the boy—it's better for him than tea," she said with finality.

No one questioned that decision. At this point, drinking anything liquid was most welcome.

Greta presided at the table and smiled in contentment as Lanico drank the tea and discussed with them all the old days they'd shared, before the battle.

Lanico sat enthralled by just the sound of Treva's voice. Sultry. How could he have forgotten it? He had memorized every detail about her, but somehow had forgotten that. The dusty cinnamon of it.

She caught him watching her and gave a slow half smile, the kind that made him breathe in deep. That was short-lived because the next glance he cast at her, reminded him of the complex creature that she had always been. True to the nature of Treva, in one moment she was glowing, gorgeous, enchanting, and then, in another moment, the crude, feral, gritty warrior he remembered.

Treva palmed a small paring knife and dug at something stuck between her teeth, and then, without noticing the raised eyebrows of the others around her, resumed at her tea as normal—pinky raised and graceful. Lanico huffed a silent laugh at this—the wild, untamed Treva.

~

The recounting of days gone by was stretching far into the evening, and before long, Marin wandered away from the table and strolled outside. He looked up to gaze out at the black sky, covered with an endless array of twinkling silver and white stars. The moon was now a thin sliver that brought sparse light to the world below. The Odana River rushed quietly beside the house, its streaming waves reflecting the dim light from above. Fireflies danced just over the water's black surface. Not just any fireflies—these were of many colors. They danced and each reflected against the others' mirrored bodies, while silky black fish came from within the inky water and plucked them into their mouths and into impending doom.

Marin then noticed movement near the water.

His eyes adjusted to the dim outline of Anah. He had thought her asleep in the den that she was to share with his mother. But, no. She was sitting on a large boulder at the edge of the river. She, too, was studying the dancing fireflies, her back to him. The white tunic was long for her shorter, smaller frame. It hung over the rock as she languidly traced patterns on the water's surface with a long stick.

Marin marveled at her. She was beautiful beyond anything he understood, more beautiful than anyone he had ever encountered. Wild. Free. An adventure unto herself. Yet she had gone through her entire life in such an unimaginable way—as a slave. He studied her. Treva had known her since she was a child and told him that Anah was likely near the same age as Marin. *She may be the same age as me, but we're worlds apart in life itself.*

He carefully and slowly opened the door, to begin a quiet approach toward her, striding smoothly through the thin grass. He did not want to alarm her and take from the enjoyment she was having. She seemed wild and he didn't know how she would react if he just charged right up to her. He drew closer, uncertain of what he'd say. He felt as if the dancing fireflies were now flitting around in his stomach.

He quickly clenched his fists and loosened them, unsure what to do with his hands. With every step, his heart thumped that much faster. Anah wouldn't be able to hear the whisper of his footsteps this close to the river, and he came close, right behind her. The gentle breeze carried to him the fragrant scent from her recent bath. He wanted to touch a tendril of her wine-crimson hair, or the smoothness of her hand that rested on the rock, just there. He dared to come in closer, his breath cool.

Anah turned quickly to see Marin's glowing eyes directly before her, nose to nose. Surprised, she swung her stick to whip across his face, and the force of that lightning strike sent him backward with a thud.

"Ah!"—she winced—"I—Oh, I'm so sorry, Marin!" She dropped the stick and scrambled off the rock to kneel beside a stunned Marin. He held his cheek and jaw in radiating pain and opened his glowing eyes wide in disbelief, moaning. She came close to him and touched his cheek with a soft hand. "Are you okay? I am so sorry, Marin. I didn't expect . . . well, anyone." Her hand was soft and gentle against the throbbing of his face. Her green eyes were large with concern, glowing down at him. Emerald lit fires.

She said my name. Spellbound, through the sting of pain he managed a clenched mutter: "No, Anah, I'm so sorry. I swear, I—I didn't want to scare you." His eyes met hers, and the pain instantly forgotten. He rose to his feet and smiled down at her.

~

"Ha! She got him good," Lanico chuckled under his breath, watching from inside the screened door. He could see that his boy was largely unharmed. After determining the two were safe outside, he turned with his steaming cup of dew tea to walk back into the eating room. There Greta was taking plates and used cups into the kitchen. Treva went in after her carrying the kettle and a tray. *Everything seems fine in here,* he thought. He turned and walked back toward the front of the house to relax in the sitting room, only steps from the door. *I'll just stay here, near—to make sure they're fine.*

~

Treva wanted to help put away the dirtied dishes, and Greta was thankful for the offer but rejected assistance. She conjured a quick spell, using delicate hand movements, and the dishes responded. They miraculously cleaned themselves in the sink full of hot, soapy water. After submersion and bubbling, they floated briefly, sparkling with cleanliness, and laid themselves flat to dry. They gleamed as they lay on the counter, now still. Greta turned to an impressed Treva and smiled.

"Well, I guess you *didn't* need my assistance," Treva said with a laugh.

"No, dear. It's my pleasure, really, to do the work by hand sometimes. It makes me feel like this house is more like a home." Greta turned from her.

Treva noticed it wasn't really 'by hand' that the Fray had washed their dishes, but nonetheless, she missed all the old times with Greta. She was a lovely being, full of kindness and life. She had hidden her powers so well in the old days that Treva was still amazed. She had never quite noticed the Fray qualities in Lanico in all that time they had spent together, either. The signs now seemed so apparent.

Greta looked down at Treva warmly, and as if reading her mind, she sighed, "I missed you, too."

Treva reached out and squeezed her hand.

"Well," Greta sighed with content, "I'm heading in to bed now, my dear. Don't stay up too late . . ." She shifted her gaze toward the sitting room. "Oh!"— she picked up the cup from the table and handed it to Treva—"Please finish the rest of your dew tea."

"Oh. Oh yes, I shall," Treva smiled, lifting the cup of bitter brew to her mouth. "It's . . . uh," she looked into the cup of swirling red liquid, "nice," she managed through the small lie.

Greta pursed her lips, closed her eyes lightly, and nodded. She then turned and glided down the hall toward her sleeping room, and the yellow glowing aura went with her. When she entered her room to sleep, all the rooms of the house grew dim. It seemed that night came when Greta slept.

Treva dutifully drank the bitter tea, throwing it back with a tilt of the cup. "Glahhh," she said, twisting her face at the taste. Then she walked into the sitting room where Lanico sat on a chair, drinking his own tea, watching the steam rise. It was hot this evening, but drinking this hot dew tea was a way to get needed nutrients—or so his mother had told them.

Treva was silent as she glanced out through the door into the inky black of night. She was thoughtful over Marin out there, beyond where she could see him. He seemed to be a happy, healthy young WynSprign man. She didn't know quite how to say 'Thank you' to Lanico. *Thank you for raising my son as your own. Thank you for every meal, every stitch of clothing, for every lesson, for—* She bit her lip as she looked out. Aware of Lanico's stare on her, she turned to engage him. It was almost silent in the room between them—unlike the afternoon's clash of swords and swoosh of blades slicing the air – their common language. His blue eyes met hers, as if he were inviting her to come over to him. She accepted, and then knelt down next to him.

"Lanico"—her voice was soft with seriousness—"I wanted to give you my deepest thanks and gratitude." She exhaled, "Thank you for raising Marin all these years and making him into such a wonderful young man. It's all gratitude to *you* that he turned out . . . so amazing." She looked at him, but his blue gaze revealed nothing. It *was* the best she could say in that moment.

The corners of his mouth slowly turned up. "Well, Treva, I don't know," he said almost mischievously. Holding her stare, he jerked his chin to the door. She stood slowly, and her stiff tunic fell in flat folds as she crossed to take a better glance through the door. She could just make out Anah and Marin sitting together on top of the gray boulder at the river, looking out over the dancing fireflies. Marin was trying to snuggle in closer to Anah. She hadn't noticed *them*, together, a moment ago.

"Ah . . . I see, they're getting to know one another." Her voice was tender.

"Yes"—Lanico shifted in the chair—"He never held an interest in anyone back at the Great Mist. It warms me to see him searching his heart for another."

Treva stood in the doorway watching young friendship blossom near the riverbank. Her long, light brown tunic hung loosely on her, and she was aware that the shapely, muscular build she once had was now thin. Her rich green hair now lay against the tan of her skin she'd regained from the days of her escape, not the paleness of her years toiling in the mines. She was tough, though, perhaps even tougher than before . . . if that were possible.

~

To Lanico, somehow Treva was even more beautiful than he could ever remember. She was a strong, striking beauty, bold as war shouts. The thin scar that ran from the left side of her nose to the top of her lip was a visual reminder of her grit. Though time had changed some things about her, she was now the *woman* he loved—had always loved.

Lanico set his cup of tea down on the table near him. He straightened in his chair and began to take off his white tunic. The air was still hot inside the house. Marin was going to be outside for a bit with Anah, and he wanted to get comfortable and relax before bedding. He shrugged out of his tunic to reveal the large, toned arm muscles of a WynSprign man of half his age. The tooth necklace bounced down between his clavicles as he lifted the long-sleeved shirt over his head. His straight silver hair cascaded around him in perfect smooth order.

Lanico reclined a bit in the chair, closing his eyes lightly, resting his arms on the arm rests of the chair, exhaling. It had been a long, hot day, and he hadn't trained that hard in years. The chair creaked slightly with his movement. Then, silence. In his moment of serenity, he felt the gaze of Treva upon him. He sat up quickly, remembering himself. He was too casual, and quickly blinked the sleepiness away.

~

Treva turned and looked back at him where he sat with his eyes closed. He was a gorgeous sight, the most beautiful thing she could remember having seen. *He kept up his training and ate well over the years—and his body . . . Oh fires . . . No.* She couldn't and shouldn't have any affection for him on *that* level. After all, he had rejected her all those years ago due to his status—her status.

Lanico's angular jaw clenched a moment, feathering his muscles. *But then again, that was a hundred years ago . . . No. There's Marin. I've only just now found him.* She stayed grounded and quickly pushed any thoughts of romance away.

Treva then noticed the tooth necklace pulsing at the base of his neck. "That necklace. That . . ." Treva rushed over to kneel at his side again, taking the tooth in her hand to study it closely. "This—this necklace was mine. Where did—?" She looked up to meet his eyes. His lips, too near. Dangerously near.

A moment passed and her heart pounded.

He leaned in and kissed the scar on her soft, pink lips. Gently. She felt her warm breath escaping her. A kiss.

The kiss.

A kiss imagined for a century was now a reality.

Odan on High. She pulled back, slightly. Her hand, growing hot, still rested on his chest, holding the tooth. She felt the pulsing of his heartbeat between the two firm planes of muscle there. She looked into his eyes, making a careful, stealthy move towards him to return the kiss. It was an impassioned kiss, filled with love, with maturity, after years of sorrow and loneliness. A kiss that had long taunted both of them in their dreams.

~

Lanico felt desire blazing from within himself and leaned forward, grabbing around her back to pull her in closer and hold her tight against him, until she was straddling him. This inexplicable feeling—he wanted more of it. The closeness. Oneness. Pressed against her, he could feel her ribs through her thin tunic. He remembered, in disappointment, that she hadn't eaten her fill in years. The armor and oversized tunic—they had made her seem fuller than she actually was.

Lanico held her tight, moving his grasp lower, squeezing her firmly. She gasped sharply.

Her injury.

He pulled away, breathing, "I'm so sorry, Tre . . . I forgot—"

"No, it's all right," she breathed a whisper, still staring into his eyes.

Once again, remembering himself and his sense of duty, and never breaking his gaze, he slowly peeled back from her, embarrassed and sorry. He didn't know what had come over him. Why would he have given in like this?

His keen ears detected faint conversation outside.

With the inferno roaring inside him, he made the difficult decision to pull away from her. He remembered where they were and felt obligated to make sure Marin and Anah did not see them this way.

"Treva," he whispered, as she followed his slight movement backward, landing her kisses on his neck—, which he loved—*oh fires, but,* "Treva . . . Marin," he whispered.

Treva stopped her flurry of kisses along his jawline and opened her eyes to gaze up at his. She slowly pushed off his warm chest, returning to kneel at his side on the floor.

They could not have Marin, or Anah, catching them like this.

Lanico, while working himself back into his shirt and tunic, explained, "I need to make sure he comes in . . ." He made a small, impish smile at Treva. "It's getting late."

Treva shot a roguish smile at him before he pushed his head through the tunic and lifted himself out of the creaky chair. It was quite difficult to leave in that moment. However difficult, he stood and walked briskly to the door. "Marin! Anah! It's time to come in!" he shouted to the moonlit silhouettes just beyond.

In a quick response, the two young WynSprigns climbed off the large river boulder to leave the dancing river fireflies. Their glowing eyes were visible approaching the house and bouncing with their quick strides, Marin's eyes purple and Anah's green.

"*THERE!*" a graveled voice suddenly belted from the blackness.

Both Anah and Marin froze in alarm.

Chapter Thirty-One

"There's the WynSprign slave!" the horrid voice boomed.

Glowing eyes flashed side to side in panic, Marin and Anah desperate to find the source of the voice.

"*I SEE EM!*" another voice shouted from a different direction in the dark.

Lanico, wasting no time, grabbed the Reluctant Leader from beside the door, the hilt of the sword reverberating against his palm. He tore from the house, and his glaring blue eyes searching for the kill. Treva rushed behind with a long sword she'd found lying near where Lanico's had been. It was not her preferred weapon, but . . . she ran, following Lanico.

Unarmed, Marin and Anah were frozen, Marin's eyes darting up to the trees where Anah could not go as easily as he.

Without a sound, Lanico rushed at the closest of the two-towering moonlit Mysra who were coming in fast toward the young WynSprigns from either side. The Mysra each wielded a large knife and wafted the scent of the brassy trillium they had just ingested.

"HA!" Treva yelled as she thrust her sword from behind at one of the Mysra in a sneak attack. She sent the blade swiftly through the middle of the attacker's back until the sharp tip jutted from his chest. He looked down at the blade and rolled his eyes, collapsing to his knees with a muffled thud and falling forward. Treva landed her foot on the Mysra's back and, with effort, pulled the long sword free. She winced as the effort pulled at the wound in her side.

It was not the WynSprign Knight's way to kill from behind in such a way, but in that instant protecting the young WynSprigns called for immediacy. Treva wiped her blade on the lifeless body, keeping a watchful eye on Lanico as he dealt with the other Mysra guard.

The Mysra had not expected to encounter WynSprign Knights this evening and the remaining one was ill equipped to handle Lanico. His expression made clear he was a poor fighter and got by on bulk and strength. Lanico paced toward him, holding a confident but fiery blue glare. It had been a long while since he had taken a Mysra down. And this one, Lanico scowled, this one was trying to catch the two for a most repulsive reason, slavery. Lanico decided he would enjoy ending him.

The Mysra tried to face his opponent as Lanico slashed a torrent of swipes toward him, the warrior dodging and swinging from Lanico's unyielding blade. He proved nimble, avoiding a direct hit from the onslaught of flashing metal. Lanico did not pursue this useless game of chase and paced back, creating distance between himself and the Mysra. He held the Reluctant Leader by the grip, as if it were a dagger, lifting it into the air and launching the sword forward, arcing it downward like lightning towards the Mysra. A flash. It landed with a smooth thrust, entering through the lower neck and exiting mid-back, the blade buried so deeply into the hulking Mysra that only the sparkling hilt could be seen.

The Mysra's last steamy breath rose from his mouth where he lay in the grass. He loosed a gaping grumble, his eyes staring sightless into the still night.

Marin broke the moment of cold silence: "Lanico, Mother! Are you all right?" He sprinted to them. "That was outstanding! Absolutely amazing!"

Anah appeared next to him, her emerald eyes wide and wild, like her untamed red hair.

Lanico panted a little. "Yes . . . Yes, Marin . . . We're fine." Lanico looked back over at Treva, who was also panting, holding onto her sword. Both of them smiled wolfishly, intoxicated with the fight and the dew tea.

"These were the two Mysra guards we saw earlier today," said Treva, "the ones that were chasing us." Treva's once-neat and obedient green hair was now even wilder than Anah's.

Lanico thought it strange, but the mess of her hair excited him. He exhaled, shook his head, and fought to regain focus on the matters at hand. "Well, our chances of being found are now back to being very low, since this is a remote area of the Odana woodlands." He grimaced and twisted to release the tight muscles on his sides. "This is a lesson learned—you're to carry weapons when outdoors," he said to the young ones. They nodded. "It was actually easy. Too easy. Those Mysra guards had not been prepared to encounter a Knighted Second Lieutenant and her General. We should consider ourselves most fortunate."

Lanico reached down to pull his sword from the dead Mysra. It came out bloodied, with a swirl of steam. The night air outside had quickly grown cool. He wiped his blade on the Mysra's still body. "We'll have to drag them out further into the woods to bury them," Lanico sighed. He glanced at the fear-weary group—"But we'll worry about that later." He paused, "C'mon—you two need to bed now. There's been enough adventure for one evening."

Lanico entered the house last, and then looked out cautiously over the land. There was no movement, for the two Mysra were dead. He felt it safe and leaned the Reluctant Leader next to the pile of miscellaneous weapons inside, near the secured door, then proceeded further into his mother's home. He stood outside the sitting room, the perfect spot to watch the young ones down the length of the passage.

Marin and Anah met in the small hall that separated their rooms, near the bathing room. So much adventure and energy to end the evening—the air was charged with excitement and a newfound passion. They stood facing one another in the hallway.

"Well . . . uh, g'night, Anah," Marin said awkwardly, attempting to make eye contact with her. He looked down at his oversized hands that he had yet to grow into.

Anah smiled. "I'm sorry about your cheek, again."

"Oh, it's nothing. It doesn't bother me." He smiled, too, and the swollen, purple cheek lifted to crinkle his eye with the smile.

Anah lunged forward to plant a small kiss on his bruise, then stepped away and slowly backed up into the women's shared room. Before closing the door, she peeked out at him and smiled with green, sparkling eyes.

Marin held his cheek, in a daze, staring at the now-closed door.

Lanico, watching, cleared his throat to break Marin from the trance.

Marin, surprised, blinked and stiffened, then turned quickly to march into the room he shared with the other males and promptly closed the door behind himself.

Lanico returned to Treva in the siting room, on the chair that had held him a short while ago. She made a small smile, a worried one. "Treva"—he knelt at her side, taking her former place on the floor while she sat. "Treva, what's wrong?" He looked intently at her, trying to read her expression.

She looked at the floor, clenching the armrests. "What if more find us? What about the other slaves?" An overwhelming reality that had intruded on their pleasant escape. Meeting his stare, she asked in panic, "Lan, what are we going to do?"

Lanico focused on her word—we. It lingered in him. Then he regained focus. "Treva . . . we can't worry about that now. Only one thing at a time." He gently placed his hand over hers, trembling on her lap. The surprise visit from the Mysra, had left her shaken, even after her instinctive heroics.

"I cannot—I *will* not be a slave again," she whispered, fighting back tears. "I—I cannot . . . and *Marin*"—she breathed sharply and growled—"I'd *die* before that would happen." She winced and Lanico knew Greta's pain-numbing concoction was wearing off.

Lanico's eyes slightly widened. He sensed pain here, even now, with danger past and the two of them together. Calm, he leaned in slowly and kissed the softness of her cheek. Warm tears trailed down to splash on the rise of her tunic-covered breasts. He knelt upright in front of her and gently pulled her forward out of the chair, to the floor with him. Her body was light, too light.

He enfolded her with his arms and they lowered to lie side by side. He held her tight. She was in a safe haven, in his strong arms.

His lips brushed her ear as he whispered, "Treva, we've found each other, again. I'll never let you go—not again, not *ever*." He cradled her head in the crook of his shoulder and neck. "It was a mistake I made, letting you go. I knew it, the instant I uttered those words to you all those years ago." He sighed, stroking her hair, "Those words, they've betrayed me every day since." He wanted to tell her everything: how he still held deep passion and love for her even while she had been married to Izra. How he had thought of her and dreamt of her every night. How he had fantasized that the baby growing in her womb all those years ago had been planted by himself.

He didn't. That would have been too much.

He paused, feeling her relax, and settle onto him. The timbre of his voice started again, "You'll never be a slave again. *That* I promise you." He was confident in this. She had suffered far too long. Returning to captivity—it was not in the realm of possibility for him.

Treva squeezed him tight in response.

There was something more troubling him.

He slowly ran his hand down the length of her side, over her injury. He gently pulled at her tunic, bringing it up to reveal her perfectly smooth stomach, side, and then, her lower ribs. *There*. There it was. The glaring scar that plagued her. Deep and concave, just under her rib. An archer's mark. He exhaled through the shudder he contained.

Still assessing the injury, his eyes widened in shock, his face twisting, as he understood the severity of her pain. He spotted, almost touching the arrow wound, a thick scar that clawed around her side, leading to her back. *A whip's mark!* He turned her a little, lifting the tunic further, edging toward her back. His stomach dropped. *There are more?*

Sensing his shock, she grabbed his wrist to prevent him from pulling the tunic further up. He met her gaze—there was anger there now, flashing. Though his insides reeled in burning rage, in disgust, he gave a slight, forced smile as if to say he hadn't planned to look further. He needed her to trust him.

She loosened her grip on his wrist. He felt intensity growing with her every breath. She was nervous.

"Tre," he whispered, looking softly into her eyes, the traces of rage concealed, "I need you to trust me."

She paused and considered for a moment, searching his face but softening under his gaze.

"I'm *not* going to hurt you." He spoke slowly. "I just want"—he paused knowing her stoicism to be as firm as his own— "I just want to help you."

She bit her lip and nodded through welling tears. "All right," she said under her ragged breath. "You are my General as well as my Prince."

He sat up further, gently releasing her to lie alone on the floor on her back, the tunic still pulled up above her leggings. His silver hair draped and dragged down her exposed skin as he held her gaze in his. He moved his face down lower, hovering only just above her center. He moved to her bare side and kissed the concave scar gently. His lips only barely brushed the surface of her skin.

She tightened at the thought of pain. Tears slid from her dimly glowing eyes, but his Fray kiss sent a glowing warmth to her wound, a warmth that ran deep.

The warmth melted her from within, he could see as her muscles relaxed.

She breathed. Slow.

The pink warmth was visible, illuminating deeply through her flesh and all the way to the center of her waist where the old arrowhead had once stopped. A bright luminescent pink emanating from within. He held this healing kiss for a moment, allowing the healing power time to seep. He then placed his hand firmly over her side, pressing it hard as if to set the healing. The pink glow slowly diminished.

Treva gasped softly as the pain and warmth quickly reduced. He kept his eyes fixed on hers.

Once finished, he moved slowly up toward her face again, covering her small body with his. She blinked and nervously fumbled to feel the new smoothness of her exposed side.

"No pain! Lanico!" she asked in bewildered surprise, "did you just"—her hands were still searching, grabbing— "did you just heal me?" Her glowing eyes shone even brighter as she held them wide open.

He grinned at her in a silent answer, causing his teeth and gum-line to glint in the sparse light. His hidden Fray gift was now exposed.

Treva sighed slightly. He saw in her eyes what he felt as well— thankfulness, restoration. She was healed from her wretched curse and would have the ease of full mobility again. The physical pain was gone, and they silently agreed that the pain of the battle that had taken Izra, alleviated.

Treva held Lanico close to her. "Thank you," she barely managed, fighting a bursting sob.

He grinned at her happiness but grew serious. "Now your back."

She inhaled sharply and he knew—the warrior, the Knight within her, was embarrassed at the signs of her slavery. She felt herself relinquish and nodded slowly. She rolled carefully to her stomach and he pulled the tunic up. The diagonal slashes, thick and grooved, ran up her back in many lines that showed it was the same whip master for each stripe. The same distance. The same force. Many times.

The more he lifted the tunic, the further up the slashes trailed. Two touched under her shoulder. One, the highest, curved over her right deltoid. Smooth, perfect skin still hidden in between the trails, a reminder of what once was.

His fists coiled. His chest quivered and he breathed deeply. He put into use *all* his years of royal court experience and summoned feigned, unnatural calm that fought his feelings, curbed the desire to upset a nearby table. Inside, he fought the urge to scream. A shuddered breath was all he allowed himself.

He found himself again. Stilled. He gently touched her shoulder and she recoiled just slightly.

Focus.

He needed to remain focused. The past was gone. He could not change what had happened. Feelings of rage and despair aside.

He needed to remain focused.

He breathed calmly, remaining silent. Calm on the outside, for her and for himself. He needed calm, in order to make this work—he *had* to focus. He

167

had not used his power to heal in years, since Marin had stopped falling from trees. Even then, those were minor compared to this—this atrocity.

He eyed the first of many slashes that would receive his healing kiss. A recent one was still pink and healing. Split skin was only just reattaching its edges.

His breathing became ragged. *Odan on High . . . why?* He ran his fingers through his hair.

Inhaling deeply, he started. He hung just over her bare back and began to slowly kiss—every—sickening—wound.

He started with the most recent.

There in the quiet still of late evening, the rain started down in heavy sheets. Thunderclaps echoed nearby and throughout the wood, a sign of his feelings, perhaps. His soft lips touched gashes and warmed her, but . . . there was something else this evening.

Something else was happening.

Overcome by his unfathomable love for her, he placed every bit of his healing energy, every bit of himself, in healing her. It was more, deeper, than he had ever summoned from himself. His healing warmth transmitted his power onto her, into her mind and her heart. Tendrils of his power touched, but just barely. *Can she feel it?* He hadn't *just* healed her. *Does she know just how far reaching these wisps of power have ventured into her?*

When finished, he was drained. His hidden magic absolutely spent. He was satisfied with himself. Never before had he tested his ability at that level. He had healed her—completely! He could rest a little easier now, knowing she was no longer suffering.

He and Treva embraced, basking in the tender care of one another's arms. They lay on the floor together and comforted one another, feeling relief for the first time in years.

He felt growing love, a future, and a hope. Here was someone to share his life with and it was her, it had always been her. Treva.

Odd as it seemed in those moments, she looked into his eyes as if to tell him she knew this, understood this, and agreed.

The dew tea still coursed through their bodies, and the moonlight covered them. Her emerald hair was soft to his touch. The silver outline of her curves exposed perfection beneath.

He wanted more. *Oh damn*, he wanted more, but resisted. He willed himself to merely hold her against himself, harder. Claiming her, protecting her even in his exhaustion.

In safety, love, and comfort, sleep soon found them both. The glow of their eyes blinked out as they closed them. First hers, and then his.

The woods, the rains, were then at peace.

Chapter Thirty-Two

Things were getting back on the right foot again, a start for the betterment of Odana. Greta was at peace in her slumber, and love was radiating from within her softly lit home. She could feel it surging, coursing throughout the place.

Greta and her Fray sisters were the oldest inhabitants of their world, created immortal under the authority of Odan. Their purpose was also to create life and beauty, peace, and love, then act as guardians over their planet.

Long ago, the Fray knew of the rising power and greed of the Mysra, a people created under the influence of the eldest crafted sister, Fray Jaspia. Odan had foreseen that if they were left unchecked, darkness would continue to spread from the Mysra over time. It wasn't Odan's intention that the Mysra have so much power, so he created the WynSprigns to dominate the Odana. Fray Jaspia was embarrassed, ashamed, and angry that he preferred the WynSprigns to her beloved creations, the Mysra being her most prized of her creations. In a torrent of power, she took her seething anger out on empty canvas of the Yellow Vast and near the WynSprign Kingdom, thrusting her arms into the soil in upheaval. Rocks sharply and defiantly broke the surface of the land and jutted into the sky. At that time, it was her only way to vent the anger that burned her insides.

Under the instruction of Odan, the Fray were to intervene to preserve Odana before the Mysra destroyed the Odana Mountains and lands for trillium. They needed a strong and able WynSprign leader to set things right for Odana and all the inhabitants of the land—a WynSprign that would exceed the longevity of others and would have great strength and ties to the land itself. One who could prepare and challenge the spreading disease that the Mysra promised.

The great responsibility was placed on the second created, Fray Greta, favored by Odan for this task. She was to lie with the WynSprign King Oetam and bear a son worthy of ruling Odana. The son would outlive other WynSprigns—he would be mortal but would enjoy a long natural life. He would live long enough to oversee generations of rightful leaders and set the stage for long-term peace and prosperity in the land.

Greta obeyed her father Odan's request as 'the Chosen One'. Like any true Fray, she recognized the moment of conception, and then stayed in the castle only until Lanico was born. It was understood between her and King Oetam that he was to raise their son in the ways of the WynSprign. He was to have wet nurses and nannies. Later there were to be tutors and professors. He would need to be raised full of wisdom and strength. King Oetam agreed.

Greta was committed to the woodlands and needed to remain in the Odana woods for many years, which kept her from raising her son. She visited the castle occasionally to ensure her investment was doing well.

Until this evening, Odan's original plan had been unraveling with the increasing power of the Mysra and the destruction they wreaked across the land. Greta had felt the growing demise of the great purple mountains, ravaged and hollowing daily over the many years.

Tonight, the plan for security and preservation was yet again in motion. Shifting. Her son was renewing a lost love with Treva, his true soul love. Greta approved. Treva had proven to be a strong, wise WynSprign woman, and they all had long known she had great loyalty to the kingdom. Treva had previously been a great addition to the castle military forces, and would be again. Greta smiled a little as she dreamt—two tough, spirited, good-hearted WynSprigns ruling the Odana, protecting her. Yes. Since Jaspia had created her trillium-addicted Mysra and an array of hideous creations, Greta's purpose had been to ensure the safety of all of the Odana. It was Odan's vision for a way of life, and that was now becoming more a reality by the day.

Greta slept well. She would tell the other Fray sisters that their father Odan would be pleased with the progress.

Chapter Thirty-Three

Fenner reached in, pulled out a giant bell from his loose trousers, and offered it to Stoutwyn. They had stolen it from the tavern, the same bell Trayvor had used to alert everyone to the new rules.

They were only a few paces away from Stoutwyn's tree home now. "Okay, here goes," Stoutwyn announced anxiously. He grabbed the bell from Fenner, using a white handkerchief to grasp the handle—it was still warm from lying beside Fenner's . . . parts.

Fenner eyed that in surprise. "Eh, I'm not *that* disgusting!"

Stoutwyn gave him a sour look. The Mysra had already left the area, so they went to work fast.

Stoutwyn cleared his throat as if to speak but—CLING! CLING! CLING! — he rang the bell with zeal. The loud twang reverberated in their ears and around the wooded area.

"Attention! Attention!" Stoutwyn belted out. "We are calling an urgent meeting! Please gather at Lanico Loftre's home for a meeting!"

Heads peeked out from doors and from behind raised curtains.

Someone yelled out in notable annoyance, "Another meeting?!"

"*Yes!*" shouted Fenner with equal tartness. His dark eyes glared accusingly.

The WynSprigns emerged, darting curious glances at one another, interrupting tending to their gardens and chores. With some anxiety from the last meeting, they moved toward Lanico's home to wait for the inconvenience of yet another meeting.

Fenner and Stoutwyn continued throughout the Great Mist ringing the bell, and more gathered at Lanico's. When the two came near the tavern, they rang the bell, but softly—the tavern was not far from Lanico's home and was their last stop. They wanted to avoid alerting Trayvor, who lingered in the back, hidden. But Maybell noticed them—she stood slowly but didn't move from her table.

"Hey, that's *my* bell," she said, furrowing her brow and digging her hands into her waist. "You two better give that back."

Some laugher erupted from onlookers.

Stoutwyn mumbled and nodded as he continued to hobble to Lanico's.

Once there, they found that just about all the WynSprign villagers had gathered. . Overcome with apprehension at the sight of the massive crowd Stoutwyn wrung his hands nervously. The villagers clamored and conversed among themselves.

Fenner stepped up to help sway the crowds focus, because Stoutwyn wasn't up to it, and Joso sure as fire wasn't going to.

"Okay, ah, listen, fellow WynSprigns!" Fenner announced in loud barks he hadn't used since he was a Chief for the Odana Military. His voice was long rusty. "We have some very serious news to share today!" Fenner backed up slightly as everyone looked to him, and he gestured over to Stoutwyn, jostling his arm to urge him to start speaking. Stoutwyn growled and looked smartly at Fenner.

"Yes!" Stoutwyn continued for his friend, "we—Fenner, Joso, and myself—have all seen Mysra!"

Gasps floated from the crowd and the din of conversation stopped.

He continued: "Now please! Please stay calm and listen to me! They were hiding in the woods and looking over the Great Mist!"

Worried gasps and loud murmurs blanketed the crowd, followed by panic-laden questions. In calm authority for their consternation, Fenner and Stoutwyn were honest and careful to explain the discovery of the left-behind WynSprigns use as slaves. They also explained the Mysra intent was to capture more WynSprigns as slaves to toil in the Odana mines for trillium.

"Since the spying Mysra riders left just today, they may have a few days before they reach Odana. Once there, they will notify the Mysra leader, Grude, who will likely assemble an army of Mysra warriors to march here!" Stoutwyn was shouting over the growing clamor of the crowd.

"PLEASE CALM DOWN AND LISTEN, EVERYONE!" Fenner worked to reengage the crowd. "So, we have several days, most likely—"

"What will you have us do?" someone yelled out.

"Now, *I* propose," said Stoutwyn, wincing at his own words, "that every able bodied WynSprign remain here, at Lanico Loftre's house, to begin training for a highly possible . . . battle!"

Fenner's grandsons perked up at this proposal.

"OTHERS"—Stoutwyn continued through more murmurs—"those that are unable of body, or those that have small babes, may leave the Great Mist to find safety. However, there are too many of us to leave across the Yellow Vast, so we suggest the *best* way to remain hidden is to abandon the village and move further back into the thick wooded areas beyond the Great Mist."

"Aye"' Fenner added. "Those that want to stay here to train will train with me!" He looked crossly into the crowd. "If you remain here, we will help you to learn to use Lanico's old practice staffs. For those who are more skilled, we can allow the training with the few swords we have. And . . . and let's not forget that we have the hunters who are well practiced at using their bows and arrows." He looked proudly at the crowd.

"Swords—yeah!" Fenner's hunting grandsons exclaimed from within the crowd.

Fenner rolled his eyes at this outburst. "You boys are best with bows and arrows," he grumbled to himself.

"The others not able to stay"—Stoutwyn interjected—"will meet me at the tavern in the mornin". We will need this time to discuss our plans and the basic supplies we'll need to take on the journey—and more.

"And what about me?!" Trayvor's voice yelled from the back. He started marching toward them, relying greatly on his walking stick. The heavy, patterned approach of his was all too familiar. The crowd parted to reveal him.

Stoutwyn fumed at the sight of Trayvor, and his face glowed red. "Yes! And what *about* you, Trayvor Odmire?!" His voice thundering now. "It was because of *YOUR* communications with the Mysra that this whole circumstance has come to pass!"

The crowd gasped and eyes landed on Trayvor. Stoutwyn continued to blast at him: "I'm surprised to see you here for once and not *hiding* behind poor Maybell's skirts!"

A few laughs came, but others looked around at each other, shocked.

Trayvor glanced around. There was silence. He had no words, and his confidence was—visible to all—beginning to crumble. He caught sight of Fenner, who glared at him.

Trayvor clamped his mouth shut and Fenner nodded as if to say, "Yes, that's your only defense at this point."

Stoutwyn broke the silence: "You, Trayvor Odmire, can stay here and train with the other able-bodied WynSprigns! I'd prefer not to have you join us, but truth be told, we need every able-bodied soul and ya still have one good leg to stand upon!"

Trayvor looked around for his drinking buddies, but they had turned away. He had no supporters and all were looking to Stoutwyn for leadership. He blustered a little but conceded, hanging his head low.

"Okay, everyone! Training at the staffs and swords starts now!" Fenner announced abruptly. "We haven't the luxury of time!"

"Aye! And Stoutlet clan"—Stoutwyn turned to the crowd—"I need the Stoutlet clan to gather together. Begin making staffs . . . now! Until we have more, we'll have to share the few we have." The sturdy Stoutlets strewn throughout the crowd gathered to give one another brief orders and quickly ran off to do Stoutwyn's bidding.

Chapter Thirty-Four

The wood floor creaked slightly under Treva's careful footing. She tiptoed away from the sitting room quickly. Lanico still lay on the floor in deep sleep. His silver hair fanned on the floor, his chiseled features and power-laden body at rest. He was perfect. Completely *perfect*. A demi-Fray, warrior, Prince. Treva smiled to herself and huffed a silent laugh. She took in the slight of him for only a moment before she made her way to the bathing room to start a hot bath for herself. *Yes, I can turn with ease now.*

This new morning, she could not keep from feeling the newfound smoothness of her side, and the freedom of her enhanced mobility. Alone in the room, she stretched and twisted freely with no pain or limit. She ran her fingers over the skin. *Just so smooth.* The scar had been a burden, a painful reminder of everything that taken from her during the battle, and now she was finally free of it. It was all thanks to him. Her Prince.

Her heart melted a bit as she slipped into the hot pool of perfumed water. Her healed back could rest against the sides of the bathing pool without pain. She closed her eyes and sank in delight. Swirls of perfumed steam rose around her, and she lifted her thoughts to Lanico. The closeness of his body last night, his warmth. She felt, somehow, closer to him than before—they had a tie, a connection of sorts.

~

Lanico began to stir. He moved slowly and groaned, feeling achy. *For Odan's sake, why did I fall asleep on the floor?* His acute hearing picked up the sound of slight movements of water emanating from the bathing room and remembered. Treva was there. *That's right.* He sat up beaming. *I love her and she loves me.* He breathed in the warm, golden morning air. The achiness was worth it. She had fallen asleep in his arms.

He strolled to the kitchen, grabbed a cup, and started searching the cupboards and jars for tea. Greta had many glass jars filled with tea, herbs, and spices that he rummaged through. He couldn't see the distinctive red-leaf dew tea anywhere. He paused, remembering something.

That's right—Lanico's thoughts shifted. He remembered that Greta had once explained to him that she used that one rarely, to encourage people to feel . . . romantic. *She gave us dew tea?*

No wonder he had felt so impassioned last night and had to tame himself. Thankfully, both Treva and he were able to maintain their wits, and he was able to master his thoughts and heal her wounds. Her smile at the freedom she felt afterward—that was priceless. That smile. Those lips. He offered to heal the scar on her lip, but she rejected this. He was secretly glad. It was his favorite place, the one that he longed to kiss.

Kissing her—he wasn't so sure what to think about this. He stood still, lowering a jar of herbs. A concern came over him: *Do I really love her, or was it the tea? No, I love Treva and always have . . . Right?* He nodded slightly to himself, but continued to think about this, resuming the search for something appropriate to drink.

~

Treva finished bathing and went to the sitting room. Lanico was gone and the place appeared neat and organized. *Good*, she thought, *no one needs know we stayed here last night.*

In the eating room, Lanico was sitting with bilberry tea and sweet tea bread, waiting for her. His piercing blue eyes glanced up, and a knowing smile curled at the knowledge of what her skin looked like beneath those fresh clothes.

She looked glorious standing in the doorway smiling down at him. She was radiant and happy. Her green hair sat loose on her perfect shoulders, instead of having been obediently tied in the back, the only way he had ever seen her wear it. The wet tendrils twisted, hinting at normally hidden curls.

The air between them was tight.

Yes. Yes, I really do love her. Normally, he never would have acted the way he had last night. He forgot who he was, letting all manners and proper behavior go, healing her in such a sensuous way, and then having her fall asleep in his arms . . . He did not want anyone else to find out. It wasn't like him. *But, fires, she is smoldering!*

She made a small nervous giggle. "Lan, I just wanted to say thank you."—she looked down; biting her lip, then her eyes caught his again. Heat began to flush to her face as she knit her brow as if considered something, then she saw his eyes roving over her form and grinned. "Lan you have—"

"What's there to eat?" Marin asked suddenly from behind Treva and she jerked, startled. Then he walked over sleepily to sit down at the table. The moment between Treva and Lanico had been brief. Blazing fires snuffed. They looked at each other with small smiles. Candle flames.

Gish came in just after Marin, looking most uncomfortable and groggy.

Lanico knew they had a problem: two dead Mysra warriors lay on the dew-covered grass outside. He wasn't sure how Gish would react to this—but knew it was a task best handled quickly.

"Gish, may I have a moment with you in the sitting room?" Lanico asked quickly, before the others began to talk about the events of the night, so he could break the news himself. Without a word, Gish turned from the chair he had been about to take and followed Lanico out into the sitting room, where Lanico sat and motioned for Gish to take another chair, which creaked slightly under his weight.

"Gish, I know that you were the first to bed last night. While you were sleeping, there was an incident that took place I wanted to tell you about . . ." Lanico paused and tried to gauge Gish's mood. He always had the same grim expression, unreadable. There was no noticeable scent of threat, or so Greta had said, reinforcing his own previous assessment. It was both reassuring and odd.

"Two Mysra warriors tried to attack Anah and Marin at the river's edge last night," Lanico continued. "Luckily, Treva and I were able to intervene in time. Well"—Lanico looked uncomfortable—"we killed them. Both of them." Lanico looked up to meet Gish's small blue eyes. The Mysra seemed to be only slightly more agitated, and Lanico longed to read Gish's feelings.

"Look," Gish started in a tart tone, "I joined you and Marin with the intent of freeing the slaves and *not* siding with my father. I have long been unhappy, an outsider to even my own people. I understand well that this decision to side with you will bring the death and destruction of many Mysra. I have the most to lose of anyone." Gish paused and sighed, and then directed a stony glance to Lanico.

Despite the Mysra's tone, Lanico felt a sigh of relief escape him. "Gish, I thank you for telling me about your feelings about this, and for letting me know that you have chosen to side with us for this larger purpose. We are most fortunate to have your sword—or knife—on our side. I didn't mean to insult you. I just wasn't sure how you'd react." His tone was soft and honest.

Gish nodded.

Lanico then made a loud, weary sigh. "Well, now I have the task of disposing of the bodies"—he paused—"and they are too big for me to carry or drag into the woods to bury—"

"Bury?" Gish asked.

"Well, yes. Bury." It was when Gish looked questioningly at Lanico, he remembered the Mysra didn't often bury their dead.

"Oh, right. I forgot you bury the dead," Gish said, nodding in thought. Even though he was stronger, he'd not be able to carry the bodies into the woods, either. "Won't you bury them where they lie?"

"No, they'd be too close to the river, to our water supply. I'll have to"—Lanico paused, thinking of the grotesque work ahead—"I have to cut them up and move them out into the woods in large . . . uh, parts. And then bury them."

Gish gave a low grumble and another hint of agreement.

Lanico blinked and slapped his hands on his seated thighs before he rose to a stand. Gish followed his movements and stood as well. For Lanico, it was time to get to the chores. He loathed wasting time and enough had been said.

"Well, I don't want to keep you from eating breakfast," he announced. Please return to the eating room and eat well . . . we will be training hard today." Lanico gestured to the eating room—he would not ask this Mysra to dismember and dispose of his own kind.

Gish, though not enthusiastic about the prospect of training, accepted this new duty. He appreciated that they were trying to teach him a new skill. It was more than he had experienced under his own Mysra superiors, who just ordered him to jump into a task and learn by trial and error. Even if their tactics resulted in injury, or death. He walked slowly into the eating room to join the others.

Standing there alone, Lanico decided to lure Treva outside In the only way that he knew would work. Then, afterwards, she could train Gish and Marin while he began his unpleasant task of cutting up the dead Mysra. It was an excuse to exercise before his loathsome task.

He grabbed the Reluctant Leader and stepped out into the green dewy world. Outside he carefully placed training weapons in strategic locations that dotted the small clearing before the mystical home and river. The surrounding pines and timber were a comforting guardian, watching in silence.

Once ready, he gripped his sword. The grip of the Reluctant Leader was an extension of his own arm after the many hundreds of years he had wielded it. He had practiced, fought, and sparred with it for countless hours.

Near the mist-covered river Lanico practiced by himself, lunging the long sword and thrusting strikes in the air. His hair spun around him with his fluid movements. He had balance and a graceful posture, unburdened by the breakfast the others were enjoying.

~

Skillful and perfect, Treva thought, peering out at her Prince from the sitting room window, watching in admiration. He was the Odana General and she had once sought to be as good as him. *No, better.* Long ago, she had sought to be a better warrior then him. And now he seen her crying—*again*! That was twice. The last time was when she told him she was . . . And, last night, last night when he healed her.

It was like a dream that she found herself here safe, away from the mines, pain-free, reunited with Greta, with Marin, and with the man she had always loved.

She sighed out, thinking over this.

How would Marin take the news of their love? "Well," she murmured as she finally went through the door, "that conversation will have to take place another time." Training needed to be done and time was limited. She knowingly took Lanico's bait and went to join him near the misty river. The sound of his slashes against the air called to her, sending prickles to her skin. She'd answer.

Lanico caught a glimpse of her from the corner of his eye and smiled. *It worked*. He thought.

No, you didn't lure me, she answered in her thoughts when she saw his twisted smile of contentment. "I just love the sword," she said aloud.

Wait.

They each paused at the shared thought. Both astonishment and delighted unison brightened their faces.

Chapter Thirty-Five

Lanico and Treva practiced their movements on one another without words—the ringing clash of swords was their private language. Over and over again in a timeless dance, back and forth, in the swirling mist. They knew each other's movements, were deft at each other's strikes. It was remarkable. The healing had linked them somehow and created a bond. Their movements were almost synchronized and smooth.

Treva felt free and almost ethereal. With her side healed, she imagined she *felt* part Fray: glowing, glorious, and light. *Did he give me some of his Fray abilities?* She hadn't felt this fabulous in more years than she could remember and they were so in tune with one another. They came quickly to realize that they could almost sense each other's thoughts through a mere glance.

How is that possible?

But there it was.

A shared connection between them extended the limits of verbal understanding. Looking into her eyes, knowing her, he was feeling inspired and more determined than ever. Her spirit ever clearer to him now only served to embolden him.

Every clash of the sword meant another step closer to slaying Grude and ending countless years of misery that she and throngs of others had endured. They had sparred for a long but timeless time when Treva noticed the audience they had accumulated. She slowed and looked at him with a jerk of her head in the onlookers' direction. He nodded with a slight smile of understanding, so she turned to beckon Gish, Marin, and Anah.

"Okay, your turn!" she shouted at them as they stood idly by, and she extended her arm, beckoning them in near. She turned to Lanico—who smiled back at their students' lack of enthusiasm.

She ushered Marin and Gish over first. They each took a sword and started sparring under Treva's close supervision, and Lanico left them to it—Marin knew what to do.

As planned, he went around the corner of the house and began the task of burying the Mysra while first having to endure the horrible job of cutting up the limbs and trunks of the dead bodies. At first the young WynSprigns and Gish were interested in Lanico's gruesome work, but after Treva's barked instructions, Marin and Gish returned to sparring. Anah sat on a river boulder watching, bored.

It wasn't long before Lanico was ready to take the Mysra body parts to their final resting place deep in the woods and far from the house and the river, back in the direction from which they had come. He dragged them as far as he was able, away from the sight of others, and began the task of digging.

Anah joined him to assist in the burial. She was the odd one out, as she didn't have a sparring partner. She started to help carry the massive body parts to the shallow grave, but Lanico would not allow it. Anah, having a temper to match her fiery hair, seemed set to prove her strength and her worth. For Lanico it wasn't about proving worth, or even strength—he knew that she had to have been very strong to have survived in the mines all these years. He just didn't want her to have to labor needlessly over a task he could do himself. He asked her about her history, to keep her occupied while he worked.

Anah had been born into confinement and lived the entirety of her young life as a slave, she explained to him, so she was not used to being idle while others worked. He still refused her offer to help, trying to make a gesture of kindness to her, but she pouted a bit. Lanico paid her no mind—for she was young. He allowed her follow him anyway, to give her something to do.

As they drew close to the shallow pit, Lanico heaved over the final heavy Mysra body parts while Anah sat on the ground and began to push dirt in over them with a big fallen branch she found. She crouched beside the massive pile of dirt and leaned forward to push in as much dirt as she was able to, in big hefty shoves of the branch.

"Lanico"—she sniffed hard and wiped the sweat from her brow with her forearm—"when will I start *my* training?" She straightened herself and looked at him squarely. Dirt covered her legs, hands, and arms.

"Training?" Lanico grunted, quickly throwing in a huge Mysra thigh—roughly the size of Anah's entire body.

"Yes, like Marin and Gish?" She winced up at him in the stray sunlight. He could see she was serious. She expected an answer.

Lanico was cautious here. He hadn't thought about having Anah train. He mirrored Anah's move and wiped his face with his forearm.

Still waiting for his answer, she continued: "If Marin can handle the sword, I'm sure I can." She flexed her arm with pride, showing off a surprisingly impressive bicep and a twinkling smile.

Lanico wasn't sure how to answer this, but maybe it was good for her to learn. The skill of sword fighting was very useful for protection in general. He turned to face her more and she took in a sharp breath. "Well, I think you can begin once we get back. Gish will undoubtedly be looking for some relief." Lanico smiled at her, his face grimy with dirt and smeared Mysra blood.

She laughed at the sight of him.

Lanico smiled back at her and laughed a little, too. He shook his head at her girlish giggles. He didn't know what he had said to make her laugh. What he said about Gish *was* true. He shrugged and joined her, kneeling to help scoop dirt into the grave.

~

Greta had confined herself to her room for the day, for her regular ritual of deep prayer, meditation, and mental communication with her Fray sisters who dotted their world. Odan hadn't been in attendance in their meditative meetings, nor Jaspia, in years. Fray Greta took the charge of these meetings, wielding authority over her younger Fray sisters and giving them the messages from Odan himself. The meetings were usual in times of duress, but even in times of peace, they communicated on the comings and goings of the lands that surrounded them, the lands that were assigned to them to watch over. Fray Greta continued to assure her Fray sisters that Lanico's prospects of reclaiming the Odana had increased and that victory was on their side. For she wasn't the only Fray impacted by their sister Jaspia's horrendous creations. She was also careful to warn her sisters of Fray Jaspia's involvement. Surely, their outcast sister would not be content to allow the overthrow of her creations that were now ruling that land.

~

Outside, near the river, Marin and Gish were still working at their positions and strikes under Treva's supervision.

Treva shouted relentlessly at them both: "Gish! Yes! Much better—no, no, keep your focus, Marin!"

Lanico and Anah, both filthy, emerged from the trees, and Lanico announced, "I've got the next warrior ready for training!" The glint of his teeth shone in the sun.

They all paused and Marin, sweaty and panting, gulped at the sight of Anah. The girl playfully flexed her bicep at them, and with her unkempt flaming red hair and wide smile, she seemed wild and untamable.

Treva walked over to them briskly, swinging to yell back over her shoulder to her students, "You can stop now—take a rest!" She squinted back at a beaming Lanico. "What's on your face?"

"Ah . . . what's on my face?" He glanced down at a grinning and giggling Anah and then felt at the crusting Mysra blood and dirt.

Ah. Right. He grinned a little understanding now, the reason she had been giggling earlier.

~

Marin went into the house for a drink of water and Gish remained outside. Alone, he began to feel the change that had come in his heart. He rested there, without anyone around to watch over him. He was trusted. He felt truly accepted among them.

In that quiet moment, he knelt over the flowing river and pulled out his hidden trillium pouch. He loosened the strings and turned the pouch over, the purple contents sprinkling into the river. He did not want to think at length about what he was doing, for if he did, he might regret it. He understood that he would regret it later anyway. Gish shoved the emptied pouch back into his pocket just as Marin came back from the house. He understood his body would react to the lack of the precious trillium, but he determined it was the only way for him to gain his own personal freedom.

"Here you go"—Marin held out a large cup of water to the kneeling Mysra—who in that pose was about the same height as Marin.

Gish nodded and smiled slightly at him. "Thanks," he said simply, taking what seemed a small cup in his massive hand.

"What do you think about Anah practicing at the sword?" Marin asked, squinting into the sun-brightened river.

"I think she's going to kick your ass," Gish replied without hesitation, looking at his friend with honesty and complete seriousness. There wasn't a hint of a hilarity on his stone face.

185

Marin tensed and gulped his water, hard.

Chapter Thirty-Six

"You found it?" Grude's shrill voice exclaimed. "The WynSprign village?" He jerked forward from the throne to where Neen and Gax knelt; dramatically hanging their heads low, for they knew Grude appreciated this. Green light from the stained glass cast them in an eerie glow.

Neen rose to stand, and Gax followed the unspoken command.

"Yes." Neen saw the gleam from their leader's eyes, and he'd keep it there. "We found it—it was hidden deep in the woods, beyond Horse's Clearing, surprisingly easy to find." Neen paused to grin. "They had tracks everywhere. They have been living in this hidden realm all this time. When we cased the village, we found no guards, no weapons . . . and they walked around freely without concern." Neen's voice deepened "*Easy.*"

The corners of Grude's stone mouth curled, deeply satisfied.

"Neen, Gax, let me thank you both properly by allowing you to absorb Gish's share of titles and responsibilities." At this point, that had been an easy decision. Grude rose to stand.

"He has not returned?" Gax asked feigning concern.

"NO!" Grude thrust his fist down at his side. His son, his only son and heir, had taken his request and shat on it. "That ungrateful wim—" He stopped himself short. "No. He has not returned." He began to walk around them, still speaking. "He has seemingly decided to roam the land, and has neglected his one last task to prove his loyalty to me. He has decided not to act as my dutiful son, as was expected and as he was told." Grude spat as he strutted.

The brothers stood straight at attention. "You two, however, have managed to impress me"—Grude wiped the saliva from his chin—"and have proven your worth."

"We'll have a celebration tonight to recognize your accomplishments," he continued. "And then tomorrow we'll prepare what's necessary to bring the WynSprigns here."

Neen and Gax smiled proudly as they stood tall. Neen would finally get the recognition he deserved, and Gish was as good as dead to them all. It was a dream finally turning into a reality after their years of unflinching loyalty.

Grude glared at them for a brief moment—his smile fading to disgust at their annoying smiles, but caught himself.

"MAKE READY FOR A CELEBRATION!" The heightened tone of Grude's voice echoed through the hall, and the order sent servants running. "This evening you will eat and drink your fill!" Grude slapped Neen on his large, muscled back. "And then, tomorrow, we will prepare. I want all the warriors called to duty for this."

Gax and Neen exchanged glances, and Grude said with a look at them, "I understand that that is a risk, placing all our warriors to the task. We, however, need all of them, and therefore, I will need as many abled-bodied warriors as we have. I mean to keep this a successful mission. Besides," he grinned, "if they are as helpless and innocent as you say—it should be one of the simplest missions yet!" He roared a laugh.

Gax and Neen's faces softened to hint smiles—horrifying smiles.

Chapter Thirty-Seven

"Slow down, Anah!" Treva's voice sounded against the surrounding trees. "You must hold the sword properly and not like your pick-axe."

Anah gave a low growl in return. She was small with the long sword in her grip, but she held it in strength. She swung and practiced back and forth slowly with Marin. "Huh!" she sighed sharply. "I'd prefer my axe!"

Marin's eyebrows raised slightly. Her strikes now were enough to cause his bones to rattle. He could not imagine the damage she'd inflict on an opponent with deft swings of her axe.

"Perhaps another time when we *have* a pick-axe," Treva responded dryly. "Plus, I need you to try something that will challenge you. The sword is a weapon that you have at your disposal at this time and it's most readily available in battle—commonly even taken off of dead enemies' bodies." Treva's falchion would do well in Anah's grasp, but she gave Anah weapons more easily found. Long swords were common enough. Though she didn't like to admit it to herself, she was now sounding a bit like Lanico with this topic.

Marin was more on the defense with Anah's wild swings. He felt a bit intimidated fighting her. Though her strikes were hard against his, he considered, he might hurt her if he countered too hard. He fought to contain his worry and his grip.

"C'mon, Marin!" ordered Anah with frustration. "Give me what you give Gish!"

Marin held the sword weakly and his posture was off, way off.

Treva held up a hand. "Marin, it's okay—take a break for a few minutes."

Marin panted, his forehead beaded with sweat. "Okay," he said as he handed the sword over to his mother, and then turned on his heel to walk to where Gish was resting on the large river bolder drinking. He'd take some water in as well.

Treva stood straight and tall, cool and calm as she turned to Anah. She was very commanding and stoic, even when not in armor. "Anah"—Treva looked down at the sword—"you remind me a lot of myself when I was young. You have strength from years of hard labor, and fight in you. But . . ." Treva paused. She held the grip, the hilt at eye level, to glance down the sword's blade, and lowered it again. "But," she continued, "When one fights from their feelings, they lose." Treva caught Marin's eye as he looked back over his shoulder on his way to the river nearby, then she looked back squarely at Anah. "So *I* will train you."

Anah was elated, "*Really?!*" she squealed, her freckled face brightening.

"Don't be too happy. You and I have been friends for a very long time, but training is not personal, it's not emotional. So when I yell and get tough with you, you cannot spout off angry. I know that fire in you, but you must listen to my instruction and tame it. I want you to be the best."

Marin, from where he rested on the boulder, took in this lesson as well.

Anah nodded, and her mass of red hair shifted about her head. "Okay, I understand . . . I'll control myself." Her green eyes glittered upward to Treva.

"Good," Treva said sharply. They created a small distance between them, and then Treva gave the sword a few swings in the air, testing the weight, the glide. Then, she raised her sword to Anah to make the traditional salute before starting. Her shoulder muscles flexed, showing a vein at the action.

Anah responded in the same way, but somewhat awkwardly as her grip wavered slightly at the long blade's upright weight.

They began slowly with basics, moving back and forth with thrusts and blocks. It wasn't long before Treva nodded at the potential in Anah, and Marin saw it, too. She was quick and could move the sword fluidly.

"It is Marin's destiny, his life legacy, to be a Knight," Treva said, nodding toward her son. "But I can make you a great warrior as well, Anah—perhaps even a Knight. Why not?"

Chapter Thirty-Eight

Training was exasperating but forgotten as the trainees' dinner disappeared into their hungry stomachs only moments after they sat down. It was another delightful dinner concocted with Greta's magical talents. Treva enjoyed watching Anah hum in pure gratification at the exquisite flavors that radiated on her palate. Before, she never would have believed that food could taste amazing. It had only ever been bare sustenance when they were slaves.

Treva noticed Gish's thick hands trembled slightly. It could be from his raw nerves at all that had happened, from the strain of training, or from something else . . . She noted that he was on edge, but he engaged in conversation, determined to help his newfound friends as he and Lanico discussed the riders that were likely pursuing him.

Treva's mind swirled at that. She stood. "Wait-What?!" She asked in alarm hearing men speak – at what they had just said. *Riders? Pursuing?*

Heads swiveled up toward her, and it took but a split second for her to arrive at the horrifying conclusion that the riders might have tracked Gish coming from Horse's Clearing.

"Don't you see?" she cried. "They won't stop looking for Gish and go back defeated. Grude wants more WynSprigns, and just because Gish hasn't returned doesn't mean that he'll stop his efforts." She snapped her fingers, thinking and pacing the floor around them. She paused mid-step. "He'd probably send someone else—higher in command . . . uh, with more to prove."

The hair on Gish's neck raised as they made eye contact. It was as if in confirmation, that he knew just the Mysra Treva had depicted.

A new level of urgency swept over them.

Lanico, so deeply connected to her now, read her fear. Without missing a beat, he responded, "Then, I need to return there sooner than anticipated. I had planned to leave Marin here while I returned to tell them of what I have learned, but this . . . well; this is now a more urgent task." His eyes darted from Treva to Greta. "I'll still leave Marin here. I'll not have him travel with me to warn those in the Great Mist. I need him to be kept safe."

"He is my grandson," Greta added. "He *must* stay here, and Anah and Gish as well." She slid a knowing glance at the weary-eyed Mysra seated in front of her.

Treva was touched at Greta's claiming of Marin as her grandson. Lanico had considered him his own son all these years, so it did make sense.

"I don't think the young ones should fight in this battle, not yet," Greta declared. "They need more time. And Gish"—Greta regarded his miserable expression—"I don't know that Gish should have to face his former counterparts of Odana."

Gish shook his head in consternation, but he did not object. Nor did Anah and Marin, who looked at one another with shy smiles. What Greta said was true. They were not yet skilled enough to face an army of invaders, and Gish couldn't be expected to kill his own countrymen and women—even though he had said he could. His guidance and his understanding of Grude's mindset, was proving most valuable.

It was decided that Lanico would leave soon, to warn or aid the WynSprings of the Great Mist. He would help them prepare them for discovery and hoped it would allow enough time for them to flee to other lands. Treva insisted on going as well. Lanico hadn't voiced his reservations—he preferred she didn't come with him and endanger herself. He was mindful to let his gaze stray from hers during the conversation.

~

After dinner, Gish decided to turn in for the evening. Greta alone had identified the unspoken pain in the Mysra's eyes. She would tend to him as best as she could without drawing too much attention to his ailment. It wasn't likely that he wanted the others to know his body's painful craving for trillium and the further denial of it yet to come. The sight of his silent pride through the pain increased Greta's anger toward her sister all the more. Jaspia had been reckless with the people she created—instilling the craving for the purple mineral, she also created. Greta so hated to see suffering—especially in the Mysra she had growing affection for. The dejected Fray Jaspia had intentionally created the Odana mountains – Fray Greta's protected territory – with the addictive mineral. It was hard to imagine that her intentions were purely coincidental. It was if she wanted those mountains plundered by her Mysra. As if she *wanted* the deterioration of her younger sister.

~

Treva stood at the doorway looking out at Marin and Anah, who were watching the fireflies again under the darkening sky.

A strong voice was suddenly at her ear: "Treva, can I have a word with you?" She didn't turn to look and only nodded a response to him.

His hand grasped hers. She met his gaze as he said, "Follow me outside."

They walked around to the rear of the house, following the river. She didn't want to venture too far, leaving the two young WynSprigns unprotected—especially after learning that Mysra riders were still out tracking. She released his hand as he walked only a small distance.

The area grew darker under tree cover away from the house and their eyes illuminated brightly with the change in light. Lanico led them to the large boulders that sat near the river, a bend mere strides from Marin and Anah if needed, but cloaked in privacy. Once there, he then slowed and leaned casually against the largest boulder at the river's edge. A half smile formed below his lowered brow. Unsure of what this was about, she was reluctant to get closer. She could *feel* the intensity of his thoughts and with that roguish look . . . It was this new connection they alone shared.

He held up his hand, his fingers beckoning her in closer. She smiled and drew toward him—a magnetic attraction.

Lanico looked down at his feet, trying to find words. It was charming to see him in this way. Vulnerable. She loved the General—his strategic mind, his organization, his constant challenge urging her onward, but this—this *Prince* was something different entirely. He was softer, openly kind, a quiet wisdom ruling his mind.

Lanico summoned the General in himself. He knew his position of authority over her—it wasn't an ordinary role they had, like a villager to a lord. Her commitment to him and to the kingdom was oathed for her the remainder of her life, so she would be near him always. Nevertheless, he knew his own heart. Too much time had already passed for them. Every day was more precious than the last. He did not want her to travel with him, to battle.

"Treva, I"—he hesitated. It was so familiar to him. Suddenly, he felt he was back in time, back in the Odana Military armory with her. Suddenly, he was fighting off an urge. Suddenly, he felt his control slipping. And yet, how was he going to say this without hurting her? *Will this be just as it was, before?* He looked into her eyes and felt courage return.

He continued: "There is no secret I want to keep between us, or from Marin, for that matter. I have always had feelings for you." He looked down, feeling embarrassed by the truth he kept hidden, though he sensed she already knew, with their soul connection. Even the sound of his voice betrayed his long-kept secrets. He willed himself to look back at her.

"I have always loved you, Tre—long before Izra . . . I was a coward then." His voice strong and low. "I never acted on those feelings, for *us*, for what could have been—I held back out of my belief in duty." He fidgeted with something in his hands, and she caught a glimpse of white, but looked up to see him looking back at her. "I will not deny my true feelings any longer, Tre."

Her heart thudded in her chest, a caged drum. This was surreal, a dream. She had always loved him. She loved Irza too, but the love for Lanico had never faltered, not once. Her love for him had been there since she was a young farm girl, reading of his battle conquests, had lasted throughout the grueling training he put her through, had endured even while she was with Izra . . . *That was wrong, but true.* She bit her lip. It felt as though the river fireflies were now flittering about in her stomach.

"My hope, Tre, is to be with you one day . . . one day." The part that hurt.

Her heart stilled. *One day?* It was better than *never*—as he had once told her.

"I respect that you and Marin are only just reuniting. I have only dreamt of this before, only imagined *us*, believing you were"—his face shifted down and he closed his eyes, remembering her lifeless body. The arrow. He wouldn't finish that sentence. Instead he continued: "I want this battle to be over, and mostly, I want you two to spend time together, before you and I grow together too quickly. That is . . . that is, if you'll have me." The glow of his cyan eyes shifted back up to her. His voice was almost too quiet to hear against the rushing water behind him.

"Lanico, it's—it's what I've wanted as well." She stepped closer into his space. "As long as we're talking about this, the truth is . . . I still love you"—she breathed out, as if releasing pain—"and I always have . . . have never stopped." She came in even closer now, but felt uncertain how to respond physically to this, to him, to her commanding General. Lanico answered the unspoken question, pulling her in. She felt his heart beating beneath his tunic, the solid wall of warm muscle, the smell of leather in his long hair. He pulled back slightly.

She looked up at him with golden glowing eyes. It was growing darker. "Lan, we will take things slowly. Now that we're all together, there is no need to rush this—this thing that we have together." It was so new, but so familiar.

"I feel the same. I'm not sure how we'll tell Marin, *or if we should . . .* about us." He felt shy about voicing this, in the open space. "About my feelings for you." He had never been in a position to proclaim his love for another before. Raya was arranged to marry him—he had never had to *try* with her.

Treva was pleased he was thinking about Marin, even still, as if he were his own son. "Lanico, I think that Marin should know. I don't want to start off getting to know my son by withholding important truths from him."

"I'm relieved," Lanico answered. "I am not comfortable keeping anything from him, either. We'll let him know our feelings, but that we're taking time to become more than friends, than colleagues—at least for now."

And there was still the battle he'd have to survive and win. Lanico's cool eyes held a kind sincerity.

She nodded. It was perfect. Slow. They could move slowly with each other. It was a safe promise, to move slowly. For she also understood the risks of tomorrow and the promise of battles to come, and if they didn't survive . . . She exhaled.

He leaned forward and gently grabbed her hand. She looked at him thoughtfully as he opened it. He placed something in her palm and closed her fingers around it, sealing it warm inside.

"It is yours. To me, it has been a symbol of hope, and Marin wore it for many years. I found it when I was searching for him in the Yellow Vast. Now—now I regard it as a symbol of waiting, for what will be." The glow of his eyes met hers again. *A bond. A union. Together.*

She melted at the unspoken.

Feeling the slight weight in her hand, she glanced down with a smile and uncurled her fingers to find the tooth necklace. The very sight of it flooded her with emotion, with awakening memories. It had been over one hundred years since she last felt its weight against her chest—since the arrow took her down. "Thank you for this," she only barely managed. It was perfect. The perfect thing he could have given to her.

Lanico's heart leapt as she bit at her full lip. It was pink and inviting. He had made her *happy.*

This shared connection they had allowed them to *feel* the tamed energy radiating off each other and the tension that threatened to surface. They both *wanted* more. The sting of his piercing gaze numbed her knees. *Slow*. They agreed in the unspoken bond, leashing themselves.

He rose from where he leaned against the rock and moved in closer, standing more than a full head taller than she. He took the necklace from her opened hand in his much-larger one, and she turned her back to him to receive the necklace around her neck again.

The curve of her spine was entrancing. Her lower back, the blooming bottom beneath. He fought against the animalistic urge to grab and claim her. *Oh fires—slow*. *Slow*. He steadied his mind and breathed out. Strands of her deep emerald hair responded, breezing forward.

Stoutwyn. He decided to picture Stoutwyn—his solid, comic friend—to still himself. He huffed a silent laugh.

He leaned close to fasten the necklace behind her neck, pulling her hair from underneath it. The tooth bounced down on her chest, its old familiar weight a great comfort against her skin. It was back home, with her. She immediately grabbed the point of the tooth and pressed it into her thumb. *It's back*.

Lanico came around to take a proper look at her. She was breathtaking. He looked down at her face as his hands circled her waist before he pulled her in closer to himself. He could not keep his hands on her waist—no, it was far too tempting to move them lower. An embrace. An embrace was good, respectable.

She had to tame her own thoughts at his slight force of strength. He wrapped his arms around her and they stood in silence. Her face rested in the bend of his warm neck. There, she breathed him in.

If this was the closest they could get for now, it was still better than a dream.

Chapter Thirty-Nine

As night drifted over the Castle of Odana, rising melodic sounds of various musical instruments and singing drifted in the air, delectable wisps that stirred the spirit. Enslaved WynSprigns who had musical talents played for the Mysra in the castle hall, as was the way for all of Grude's celebrations. The slaves adorned bright orange-and-red uniforms designed to convey a sense of merriment, but with frequent usage these years, they had become thin and worn, truly matching the reality, they felt. Grude loved his parties.

Behind the stage the main singer—the most famous in all the lands, was preparing to usher in the nightly concert for the celebrants. Servants were scurrying to make last-second adjustments to her attire, her hair, and her face. Despite the fact that she had aged very little these years, they wanted her to look her best, for her natural look was most homely. A servant patted her cheeks with too much powder.

"Phhfff! Ewww, just stop it!" she scolded with a voice of venom.

"Sorry Mistress Cantata." The slave servant Trilla dropped her gaze low, her golden locks covering her face.

"Let's just hope you didn't ruin me, Trilla!" Cantata waved her delicate hand in annoyance at the plume of powder.

Suddenly the muffled announcement boomed from the stage: "To the Mysra guests, and of course, to the lovely ruler Grude . . . We are thrilled to announce the performance you've all been waiting for—"

"*Move!*" Cantata ordered to the servants bending low to straighten her skirts. She started to storm out. "Outta my way!" she growled and shoved her thin elbows into the servants' sides. "He's 'bout to call me on!" She pushed her way through to the stage.

"Misss . . . CANTATAAA!" the announcer belted. His voice trailed at length—a trick to both bolster the crowd and give her precious seconds of time.

Wild cheers erupted but soon stopped as, suddenly, soft, melodic music began to flute out over the room. The table lanterns were extinguished. It was a purposeful dimming timed to usher in the main performance, and the only lights in the vast room were now on the dimmed stage. Blinking eyes found the tall, familiar glowing silhouette of Cantata—the famous singer.

The Mysra faces brightened in the growing light and they clenched their fists in anxiousness as she struck beautiful throated chords. Her spoken voice was grading and awful, but in singing, she mesmerized her crowds. The enchantment of even just her practice tuning her vocal instrument sent chills through the anticipating audience before her. Then came the first familiar notes of her voice in a wildly popular song. Immediately recognizing it, the Mysra went wild, cheering madly.

Cantata moved and swirled her gorgeous orange skirts enthusiastically to the music. Unusually tall and pale for a WynSprign, she was not visually appealing of her race. She had closely set brown eyes and wiry black hair. But her voice. It by far surpassed any visual beauty another might possess. Many believed her blessed by the shamed Fray Jaspia herself. Only the Fray who ruled over song *and* stone could have granted a voice like that. The pitch could rise and fall at incredible octave ranges that no other had achieved.

She sang out a lofty melody as her musicians directed the beat upward and gave strong strokes and strums. The Mysra responded in the same way, sloshing their ale back and forth to the rhythmic tune. Their own singing was low and thick—making a surprisingly congruous blend with her melody. She shaped her own voice around the rich gruffness of theirs. It was a weaving, a back-and-forth glorious interplay from one song to another that brought true beauty into the rough lives of the Mysra-*her* Mysra.

It was no secret that Cantata loved the Mysra. She danced and sang for them with everything in her being, giving them her all. She was *their* singer. Her own WynSprigns had never embraced her quite as the Mysra did, and she deeply appreciated their love and support.

Cantata grinned widely to approve of their own singing, and she made eye contact with Grude, who grinned at her slyly across the way. Her famed smile revealed the trademark gap between her front teeth. Her dark wiry hair escaped its stern bun with her spirited twists and turns on the stage.

Grude loved putting on a great party, and he loved Cantata for the added popularity that she brought him. He was quite fond of her and paid her well for her performances. She, of course, viewed herself superior to the other WynSprigns. Unlike the vast majority of her people here in the Odana, *she* was not a slave. She was a paid performer, Grude's muse and a celebrity friend to him. And, perhaps to him alone, something more.

Tonight, was a celebration of the discovery of the secret WynSprign village and promise of the future—of another one hundred years of Mysra succession on the Odana throne. It was the plan for more slaves. A plan to mine the southern Odana Mountains for more trillium, for the mountain chain in those parts had been left unspoiled. Cantata naturally had no opinion of this conquest. It wasn't going to impact her role, so to her, it didn't matter.

At the close of her song, and after the dimming of the cheers, Grude called the assembly to order for his speech. He told his beloved Mysra his plans to increase the trillium and to supply them with the new incoming WynSprigns. With this news the crowd erupted in applause—for too long they had worried over the diminished mineral and the strict allotments doled out daily. Grude made toasts with wine from his private collection and announced his plan to honor Neen as next in line for the throne. More cheers and applause rose from the ranks. No one dared to mention Gish's name since Grude hadn't. Neen raised his goblet to answer the toasts of the crowd, but his lips only touched the wine. He was committed to waking early to prepare for the pending invasion.

Through the cheering, the WynSprign slaves all around stood still. They would never applaud but only held far-off gazes, their minds elsewhere. Defeated by years of toil and abuse, free only in their parents' and grandparents' memories, they stood, unmoving, in their tired uniforms.

~

It wasn't until just before sunup that the celebration came to a close, and the castle was mostly silent again. Several slaves met in the castle kitchen to help with the large cleaning tasks that followed such celebrations. The kitchen was in full swing; dishes were still being washed and food still being stored away for later. It had been a celebration of urgent preparation, execution, and clean up. They could not join any celebration; it meant even more of their people in captivity. Once they finished their work, many hurried out from the kitchen, heartsick and tired, to make their way to their hut homes near the castle base. Others stayed behind to finish up.

It was in the contract that Cantata *had* to assist in cleaning up after a grand party. Until now, she hadn't. This time, she complained to Grude when he gave her this demand, but he reminded her that help was scarce, and it was just this once. He would agree to continue to turn his head if she didn't help at other events, because by then, there would be plenty more help. He also reminded her that she was still just a WynSprign—even if she chose not to dwell on that fact. She huffed in frustration, with anger enough to match the tales of the legendary Jaspia.

It was with great disinclination that Cantata and a few remaining slaves, assisted Tunia. She was an ancient, seasoned kitchen WynSprign who had served so long that she had been under King Oetam's charge as a young woman. Others buzzed in and out of the kitchen. Cantata hated this reminder of her slave fellows, *hated* socializing and working next to them. She felt out-of-place amongst them.

No matter: Grude had assured her it was only just this once and, from the looks of things, she'd be done soon enough.

"This is the last of it," Cantata announced hoarsely after she burst through the kitchen door and slid an oversized tray of unused goblets onto the kitchen counter. Annoyance masked her face. Her sequined orange-red costume brightened the dull kitchen but her wafer-thin body slumped slightly, once free from the weight of the tray, and her exhausted voice was giving out.

With a dry tone, Tunia responded, "Thanks, Cantata," and with her thick forearm wiped the beads of coalesced steam and sweat from her brow. Her hands were wrinkled and soapy from hours spent at the kitchen washbasin, for many decades. She pointed a finger toward the royal stemware cabinet that was wide open. "Now then, please just put those clean ones in there . . . and then we'll be all set in here." Tunia tottered on the small wood stool she stood on to reach into the deep basin and scrub away at the last of the seemingly endless supply of dishes. Her thick legs were covered with holey stockings, mostly covered by her tattered blue skirt. Her gray hair was bundled into a large white cap that protected it from all the steam and grease in the castle kitchen.

Cantata groaned at the task, though her height was an advantage here. She had no need for the stool that Tunia had balanced herself on. After a few sets of goblets had been *clinged* into place, Cantata closed the cabinet door and spun around to head out from this—*this greasy . . . dungeon.*

Trilla, personal maid to Cantata and castle-cleaning slave, came in carrying fresh kitchen cloths to replenish the shelves. Like Cantata, she was assigned to assist in the kitchen when her help was needed from time to time. Trilla was pretty, with soft, golden hair. She annoyed those close to her with her smugly cheerful disposition and her turned-up nose. She prided herself on being Cantata's servant and felt it made her superior to the others. Trilla placed the stack of folded cloths onto their shelf, easing them in, then she looked about and her eyes widened when they landed on her woman.

"Oh! Hello, Cantata ma'am!" Trilla's innocent voice suddenly sounded. "Great performance you gave!" She came to life seeing the most popular performer, her own superior, in the kitchen with the rest of the WynSprigns.

Cantata glanced at her and gave a terse nod as thanks. She didn't care about that little vermin, or about any of . . . whatever was taking place in here. She turned to accept further instruction from Tunia.

Before Cantata had said anything, Tunia responded to the young servant girl instead, "Thank you, Trilla, for your help today," Tunia managed, sensing Cantata's annoyance. "You may take your leave now." She glanced over her shoulder at the young slave.

Chagrined, Trilla wrinkled her nose at Tunia and turned from both of them to leave the kitchen. She would see Cantata later anyhow.

"Cantata, you've been most helpful, but your help is no longer needed either. It seems we're done and you've just placed the last goblet." Tunia's voice remained dull and uninterested in the celebrity.

"Good." *This oily steam is not good for this material.* Cantata fingered a loose sequin on her skirt. She then nodded and turned to head to her small private room hidden deep in the castle. As a hired worker under Grude, she didn't live in dusty huts as the others did, though her room in the castle was a mere closet in comparison to the multitude of other rooms. She sighed as her steps echoed in a cascade of sound against the stone corridors outside the kitchen. She was pleased that she had a place within the castle. After all, she *was* a celebrity and *different* from the other WynSprigns. Blessed. Talented. Grude knew this. She was most pleased with his recent attention to her. He had been making frequent visits to her in the instrument room when she finished her daily vocal exercises.

Her slim figure wound away from the hustle she left behind.

~

The fervent activity in the kitchen had quickly died down once the celebrity was gone and the work had, in fact, been completed. The bustle of the other kitchen staff had ceased. Now, in the still of the kitchen and alone, Tunia shook her head in disapproval of Cantata. However disappointed she was in that particular WynSprign, she was pleased with herself. A smirk lifted on the old kitchen slave's face. She had made her plan without detection. It had taken time to execute, much time and patience. And this was the perfect opportunity to complete her plan.

Tunia wrung out her dishtowel and slapped it on the side of the sink with a *THAK* that freckled water droplets everywhere. Then she carefully stepped down from the wobbly stool. Her legs and feet were sore and tired. In the time before the shift changed and other slaves came to replace her, Tunia dragged the heavy wooden stool so she could sit at the thick butcher-block table. Relaxing her stiff muscles, she held a dreamy smile on her face.

Suddenly the door slammed opened, revealing Nizen's horrible face. He was more sour than normal, having been unable to indulge in the feast throughout the night. His rank made him responsible for overseeing slaves while all the other Mysra dined. Tunia was sorry about that. She truly was. She would have preferred he dinned and drank with the others throughout the night.

"Okay, Tunia, the morning reinforcements are here. Return to your hut at once." He held the large door open, his red cape spreading out behind him. His thick biceps shifted as he held the door, behind which other slaves could be seen waiting to enter.

Tunia nodded, grabbed her basket, and then left the kitchen as the reinforcements hurried to the icebox to prepare the kills from the previous afternoon. Waterfowl. Tunia rolled her eyes. She would later have to clean whatever mess they'd make with that kill and she *hated* cleaning the stray feathers that wafted throughout the space.

She left the castle as the sun was rising and took the slope down to the base of the castle, where rows of castle slave huts were arranged. The castle huts' imperfections blurred in the glow of the new day, making them *seem* cozy and warm. After the battle, Grude planned this housing to have quick access for the WynSprigns to serve him in their castle duties, but he moved the miner slave huts close to the mountain base and their work.

Tunia entered her weathered hut, tore off her apron, and kicked off her shoes before collapsing on the bed. A smile crept across her face and blessed sleep came soon. Delicious dreams of justice and grand retaliation fogged her mind. Yes, happiness dwelt there.

Chapter Forty

The tavern had never been so busy. Maybell had been running around trying to help those unable to fight find chairs to rest on. The sounds of crying babes here and there in the large murmuring crowd quickly shushed. Large sacks stuffed with clothes, food, blankets, and kitchenware covered the floor and tables all around-the majority of them really didn't know how to pack for travel.

Stoutwyn stood solemnly, puffing away nervously at his floog. The smoke filled the air around him and caressed his thick braided beard and hair. His brow furrowed with deep thought as he puffed. He believed he was making the right choice, leading them out from here. His mind still questioned his decision. His wife, Murah, supportively sat nearby, looking at him and then at the intimidating crowd he'd face, that he'd lead.

"I think we're all here now, Stout!" yelled someone from the din.

Stoutwyn's focused gaze gave way to blinks, and he abruptly nodded his head, his great gray beard following the movement. "Aye," he muttered as smoke emanated from between his teeth. "Okay, everyone! Thank you for following instructions and for coming with your needed belongings!" He set his floog down carefully on the wooden table. "I hope everyone is all packed up and ready to head out soon." He tried to manage a small, nervous smile. Some in the crowd nodded in agreement.

He was not about to mince words, though. "Look—I know you're nervous about what's to come. I am nervous, too!" He looked at Murah briefly. She smiled at him and nodded to urge him on. "But we have become quite good at hiding over the years, and, well, we will do this again, until we're able to come back here!" *Or go to the Odana*, he thought secretly, his true desire.

"As long as we march far enough," he continued, "we will be safe. Fenner has been working these days at training the able-bodied. And having been a Major, based on what I've seen, I have much confidence in them. They have come a long way and have learned how to use swords and staffs with ease and knowledge—training that the Odana Military of old would have been proud of. And as we all know, those in the hunting group are already well practiced in archery."

He wasn't sure what else to say, but tried, "I know that this is much for you to endure. This is the path to survival. I have every belief that we will have our safety." He glanced at the hopeful faces that gazed upon his. He honestly didn't know much about what lay ahead in those woods, save for the legend of the 'Blue Woman.' It was likely a fable, he had decided. "We must be brave, courageous—for the warriors that stay behind to fight for us."

Once Stoutwyn's semi-rousing speech had concluded, all soon noticed that the silent and weary warrior WynSprigns, the new ones—the young ones, were waiting for them just outside the tavern fencing. When the meeting adjourned, these new warriors greeted their loved ones and accompanied them to the edge of the woods, assisting them with their loads. For such a large group, it was a quiet walk. They soon reached the thick part of the woods on the northernmost side of the Great Mist. There was silence as many emotions drifted among them. It was a somber time—with the exception of the very old, few of them had ever experienced a time like this, but their group of leaders: Lanico, Trayvor, Fenner, and Stoutwyn himself, had long told them tales of earlier days. Somber days.

"Okay!" Stoutwyn called as he stopped abruptly at the edge of the woods. "This is far enough!" He looked over at Murah nervously and then back at the anxious crowd. "We have to stop here, before we go further into the wood." He scratched at his gray head nervously with a wince, as his stomach turned over. "It's . . . ah . . . it's time to say goodbye."

The crowd gave way to soft murmurs and there was crying heard as well. Warriors embraced their family members, small babes, and pregnant wives. Young warriors took leave of their parents who were unable to wield weapons. The time had come that they all dreaded. They had spent their whole lives together. For the first time, the future that lay ahead of them was uncertain, and therefore, filled with dread. Saying goodbye, possibly forever, was unreal to them. Had it really come this? Was this *really* goodbye? Some could actually die. No. *Would* die.

Stoutwyn watched with a heavy heart. He and the other leaders had gone through this themselves, long ago. He had hoped he'd never have to go through it again. Fenner met his sorrowful gaze. The two elders, friends, and fellow former Odana ranking Officers stood at a distance from one another as the other WynSprigns busied themselves with emotional good-byes. Stoutwyn began to approach Fenner.

"Fen, I—" Stoutwyn started.

"No," Fenner said sternly through the lump in his throat. His voice was thick. "We know how this will end, Stout." Fenner tucked in his thin lips, defying the tears he fought to keep back. The truth of their future, the inevitable loss of life. "No. I'll just say that I will see you as Odan himself allows."

Stoutwyn gazed up at Fenner and allowed a few small tears to swell. It was the best that he could manage. He had always been true to his emotions, but now, with the hope of a crowd on his back, he stifled them back though the dam was about to burst. "All right," he managed quietly, giving a nod.

Fenner came close, heartily grabbed Stoutwyn around the head, and quickly placed a kiss on top of it. "Bye, Stout," he said, backing away.

They slapped each other's backs and shoulders heartily. Their friendship had been fastened together in a brief moment long ago, and their goodbye, their end . . . it was echoing the same. Sure, being both involved in the glory days of leading the Odana Military, they knew of one other, but it wasn't until after the siege that they had forged this friendship.

Stoutwyn stiffened. "Right. Yes." He cleared his throat and turned, and through the ache in the pit of his stomach, he pulled his gaze from Fenner. In a thick sorrow-laden voice he belted out, "C'mon, group! Into the forest we go!" The former Odana Military Major in his days was now striding to lead the way into the wilds.

Fenner stood before his group of warriors, looking on. Alone. They all watched their friends and loved ones recede into the unknown part of the woods. Stray sunbeams pulsated at their ambling within the thickening brush. Slowly, their images were engulfed by thick growth of trees and bushes that snapped and crunched under their footing. Each step brought more weight onto the hearts of the warriors.

Fenner, whose heart only seemed more calloused than others' hearts, turned suddenly. "Okay, warriors!" He cleared his throat, scraping away traces of sadness. The Odana Chief that resided somewhere within him had been summoned. "Back to Lanico's!" Fenner knew that the business of training had to be done, and quickly. Sadness would get them nowhere in battle. Standing, he could see his fierce warriors' downtrodden expressions as they turned with slouched shoulders. They placed trudging steps upon the ground.

At that, he stiffened. *No. This is not the way.*

He was not a one for great words, but he searched himself and called out, "My Sprign warriors—Stop! Now, just hold it there! I want you to consider this sadness that you feel now, in this moment."

Confused stares met him.

"Yes—yes! Take this sadness!"—he spoke through clenched teeth—"This sadness will not help you, but it *is* a tool! Yes. Those WynSprigns in there that you care about, yes, those babes—they are the reason you decided to become a warrior! Find the fight in you! Search yourselves and remember what you are fighting for! Grude wants them—Yes! *Them!*"

Eyebrows raised and Fenner pointed to the woods. "Now! It's time for action! Now is the time to tell him and his warriors, NO—NEVER!"

He spotted a young WynSprign warrior whose golden hair was braided with authority, but her flushed face downcast. "Who are you?" he barked, marching closer to examine her.

She jerked in fear at his shout, disturbing the thick braid that ran down the length of her back.

"I—I'm Felena Odmire." She looked down. Her skin, though fair, held a rosy hue—slightly more color than Lanico.

He came in closer and gently pulled her chin up with his calloused fingertips. "I didn't hear you," he said, his words now softer, but his eyes narrowed with impatience.

"I'm Felena Odmire." Her blue eyes now met his.

"No! No. You're a warrior, Felena!" He looked at her with glaring eyes, "Called to protect those babes in there!" He then looked around at them all. He paced among them; his hands held behind his back. It was coming back, the old fuel in his charge.

"Who are *you*?" He eyed the young WynSprign man standing next to Felena. He had seen them together often enough. They were friends, or perhaps more, but right now, he didn't care. The young man hid himself under a large knitted hat, his gaze reluctantly landing on Fenner.

"I—I'm Stefin Stoutlet, Mr. Fenner," he answered meekly and shot a look to Felena.

"No—no. You are a warrior, Stefin." Fenner glared at the group. He stopped circling, and his thin body stood tall. He took a deep breath in. "I'm going to ask you all, ONE MORE TIME! *WHO* are you?!" He yelled with a voice that was larger than his thin body, a voice that reverberated against the trees and raked against his throat. Birds took flight.

He shot a quick glance at Freck, who looked on with a prideful smile. Fenner was about to speak, but the group responded.

"We're warriors," the few answered.

His heart swelled at that. "I didn't hear you well I—I'm a bit soft in the ears." He winced, and his closed fists quivered. "Tell me like you mean it—c'mon, like you believe it!"

"WE'RE WYNSPRIGN WARRIORS!" They shouted in response. They looked a little relieved at the mighty sound of this answer. Some dared to have small, curled smiles.

"YES!" Fenner responded, throwing a fist into the air. "Okay, now tell me! Do warriors stand around looking sad all day? No! No, I can tell you they don't! Sprign warriors love kicking Mysra asses! Yes!"

There was now some laughter, but he needed to keep them going, "Right! So, we're marching to Lanico's house, NOW! MOVE OUT, WARRIORS!"

The newly energized group hastened to their training headquarters in the home of their absent leader.

~

After some time, Fenner could see that his grandsons were doing well with the swords, especially Freck, and many others were doing well with the staffs. Fenner felt a little proud of himself—he would never have imagined that he could have put this together. However, this pride did not allow him to take his guard down. While watching the training, he started thinking of the Mysra and their brute strength. Fray Jaspia originally constructed the Mysra from mountain boulders. Each one was like a carved, muscled giant. Even the smallest of them could break a WynSprign man in half with their great strength.

What other advantages do the Mysra have over us Sprigns? Fenner began a mental list. *They're bigger, stronger, have trillium . . .* As he stood watching over the sparring before him, he realized the prospects were dim. He *had* to think about the advantages of being a WynSprign instead. *How can being a Sprign be better than being a Mysra?* Distant shouting and clashing rang in the background. *Hmmmm . . . We Sprigns can see well enough in the dark, we're pretty quick—we can jump . . .*

"We can jump!" he shouted aloud. A few heads curiously turned toward him.

Fenner looked up at all the trees that surrounded him. "Sprign Warriors of the Great Mist! Stop your training! Yes—just stop for a moment and listen! You are all making a wonderful transition from simple wood folk to warriors of the Great Mist! But now I have a new lesson!"

Their ears perked up.

~

"Yes! That's it!" Marin paused, smiling up at Anah in the branches. "Okay, I want you to try going higher next time!" Her thin legs dangled freely, but she looked terrified. Marin giggled to himself at the sight of her. He found it hilarious that she was so tough and wild but didn't know how to do something as simple as leap into trees. And these trees weren't exceedingly tall, either. He tried to convince her that she was born to do this. Somehow, even through his charm, she didn't believe him.

"Marin! Marin! How do I come down?" she shouted at him while clinging to a limb as if for her life. Her panicked voice was small in the distance.

Marin sighed and smiled at her. He did not want her to be as scared as she was. He decided to go against his own unspoken rule and in one straight, fast move leapt right next to her to assist her. He didn't need to leap and cling from one branch to another. In fact, there weren't many lower branches, anyway. He could jump and land in one move. This particular perch didn't seem *that* high . . .

He landed on the branch with little bounce to himself or to Anah. They sat closely together high above the ground, thigh to thigh—Anah seemed aflame to him in the early morning sun. Marin tried not to lose his focus on her wild charm, but he still had important lessons he wanted to give her.

"Anah, I know that for all these years you haven't had a chance to climb trees or have any fun, but I promise you this is what you and I were designed to do." He looked at her with confidence.

Anah smiled and only nodded in response.

Through the gaze she gave him, Marin wasn't sure she was actually listening to what he was saying. "Okay. Watch this!" At that moment, he swiftly jumped down to the ground far below.

Anah gasped in surprise. "Oh! *MARIN!*"

Landing clean, he grinned up at her. He liked the way she worried for him just then and that for once *he* was able to shock *her*. Perhaps he could be just was as wild as she. That made him feel good.

"See! You can land from a height like that"—he pointed to her—"safely down here." He bent slightly and, in a sprint, leapt back up to the branch, carefully landing to sit next to her again, in the same spot he had been in just a moment before. "But you also want to get comfortable moving in the trees. It's good to walk about the branches, but always hold onto them. Make sure you have a solid grasp before you move from one branch to another."

He paused, considering, "All right, let's jump down." He extended his hand just in front of her.

"No! No, I don't want to do that!" Anah laughed nervously and dug her fingertips into the branch. Even after Marin's demonstration, she was still scared stiff. A kitten.

"C'mon, Anah. We may as well do it together. Hold my hand"—he held his out.

She tried nudging it away.

"Look," he said, "you're going to have to come down eventually—you might as well do it with me." A corner of his mouth turned up, his eyes sparkled. Her worried eyes met his. "Just believe me on this."

She grabbed at his extended hand tightly and looked at him with wide eyes. He tried to ignore the tingles it gave him.

"Okay, we jump on a count to three . . . One . . . Two . . . THREEEE!"

Together. Down they plummeted, holding hands. Marin landed in a slight bend and stood straight up. Anah, still holding hands with Marin, landed but fell slightly. Her footing was lost and she landed forward on her knees with her bottom straight in the air, and her cheek slid against the grass. They found themselves laughing and relieved that she had been able to jump down from that distance. Marin, still holding her hand, helped her upright. She used her other hand to brush her cheek.

For a second, they paused. He was still holding her hand. Both were smiling.

"Okay, Anah. Again," Marin announced after they righted themselves. Anah was reluctant but realized, begrudgingly, she needed to practice.

~

It was a breathtaking sight that only they, were able to share. Several days had passed since Anah's first jump. She became brave enough to glance around. She could see the sleepy expanse of the Odana Mountain range. On the other side was the Kingdom of Odana. She couldn't see the castle spire at this point, but she tried anyway, to squint in that direction.

Marin followed her gaze. "Why are you looking there? What's supposed to be in that direction?"

"Oh, well, I was trying to see if I could spot the spire of the Castle of Odana." She held her squinted gaze, her freckled nose pointed up at the effort.

"The Castle of Odana . . ." Marin held his hand over his eyes, joining Anah and squinting in the same direction. "I've never seen it."

"Really?" Anah turned, remembering. "Oh . . . yeah, that's right. I forgot you were taken away from there when you were only a babe."

Marin took a big breath before continuing: "Anah, honestly . . . I'm nervous about winning this war against the Mysra."

Anah's emerald eyes quickly widened. She opened her mouth to speak, but before she could reply, he continued: "-Well, I want to win, of course, so the WynSprigns can be free, but what happens afterward?"

Anah was silent on this, waiting.

"Well, you know already." He sighed before answering, "I'd have to go to the castle and live there, right?" He paused. "Lanico would take his place on the throne, and I would have to inherit it one day. And I'd have to learn my new roles. Learn about being a—a royal, I guess and take on the responsibilities. And, well . . . I don't know anything about being a King, or a leader . . . or much of anything." His voice trailed as he looked down to fidget with an acorn. It was a bigger part than he had ever played, in anything.

Anah stared with affectionate eyes. She did want to rage at him for not wanting to win, but now that she understood the weight of responsibility that he considered, it seemed understandable—his reluctance. "Well, you don't have to worry about that now." She made a long exhale. "Worry about that tomorrow." She managed a small smile and placed her hand over his. He stopped fidgeting and held her hand instead. "That's what I used to say when I worked in the mines—'Tomorrow's problem is for tomorrow.'"

She looked over at him and smiled slightly. He was telling her many things on his heart. Perhaps, if he *did* become King, she could be his warrior Queen. He sighed at that thought. He would have to have one of those, too—a Queen.

Oh, fires.

He gulped.

Anah was bold: she leaned her head against his, and they remained, together, looking out to the horizon.

Chapter Forty-One

Morning came—and Neen shook his head in disgust. This time they had celebrated right into the next morning. Of all times to have slept in, on this day, it was disastrous. The warrior barracks were crowded with Mysra that had overindulged in yellow berry wine and food. Not only were they fast asleep, but it was a deep sleep, almost as if they were . . . dead. They weren't dead, though. He had slapped them, jerked their heavy limbs, pinched their noses, and even dumped water over them. He yelled a flurry of curse words that echoed wildly against the walls. Nothing. They snored and slumbered without interruption.

His blood boiled at his seeing the heaps of sleeping warriors lying about. *What in the fires happened?* He felt it—this was not normal. Something was very wrong. Something had gone very wrong.

He growled. *What could have caused this—this enchanted sleep? Why didn't it happen to me?*

There was no time to ponder. Neen was determined to start planning this urgent task with or without the others' assistance. He *had* to. Those WynSprign prisoners he and Gax had encountered in the woods—they were probably going to tell the others. His heart drummed. He feared they'd be preparing to leave—or even leaving—by now. He hadn't dared to tell Grude of the imprisoned WynSprigns that had seen them. He reasoned that he would have to move quickly and he wasn't about to allow his Mysra warriors to stand in his way to the throne. Planning by himself was an immense task, but he had to start leading somewhere. He *had* to move. The others would have to join him once they were awake.

He didn't want to walk over to the WynSprign mining encampment and ask Nizen for help, either. No, Nizen would gloat about how he and his mining guards were better prepared and more committed than Neen's riding warriors and how he wasn't willing to supply him with slaves-as if he wanted them anyway. Neen sighed angrily and rubbed his hand down against his face, his eyes bulging in anger under his pulled-down lids. He proceeded with the preparations—his massive arms carried two large woven baskets that contained other baskets within, and he marched to where the weapons were stored and started sorting and organizing equipment, his movements, mechanical and fast.

As he busied himself with the sorting and storing, he began thinking of the other tasks that needed completion. He'd need to have wagons ready, horses shoed and fed, trillium and food supplies accounted for, and of course, the organized Mysra armed and alert. They would wake eventually, and when they did, Neen had plans for them.

"Lazy bastards," he grumbled.

~

It was true though. The WynSprigns *were* preparing.

"HIGHER!" Fenner trembled while belting out commands. His warriors responded and leapt into high tree branches above them. Though he glared at them, his heart was set on protecting them. Every shout was a push to become better, tougher, and stronger. He understood well the ruthlessness of the Mysra—they could easily wipe out these warriors. Though he fought against the thought, Fenner knew that they wouldn't all survive this battle. He gulped, staring up at the leaping, clinging WynSprigns, and denied his mind speculating which of them would succumb to battle.

"I'm starting to feel a bit ridiculous, like that dreamer . . . *Marin*." Freck's voice came from behind Fenner. Freck's brass toned arms crossed in defiance, his muscular shoulders squared.

A glimmer of sadness for the young boy, for Marin, rested at the base of Fenner's stomach. He was not amused and didn't take his grandson's comment light-heartedly. "Marin was smart to do things his Sprign body was made to do," he hissed. "It's about time *we* remembered that we are WynSprigns and use every available advantage." He pointed at the WynSprigns clinging to tree branches high above—"You think the Mysra can do that?"

Freck only looked down and answered with a low voice: "No."

Fenner's teeth flashed, his lips pulled back. "No, indeed!" It pained him. *Soon Freck will understand*, Fenner thought with deep regret. But how? How could he convey the importance of the events that would soon take place? He hadn't prepared them for the atrocities that were yet to come.

But, *how* could he? These WynSprigns had lived all their lives sheltered and without violence. Their eyes had never witnessed the sizable foe. He—and the other elders—should have trained them. Fenner now understood the

213

mistake in this late hour. Lanico had had it right with Marin the whole time. Lanico hadn't allowed Marin to waste time muddling over which useless village skills to have Marin hone. No, he knew this day could have been a real possibility. And, now . . .

With his hands on his waist, watching over the leaping and climbing WynSprign warriors, Fenner sighed, defeated and a little ashamed at what his grandson had just said. He walked away and found Trayvor sitting alone at a wooden table covered by rows of water cups. His cane leaned against the table. Fenner glared at him while taking a cup of water to quench his thirst. He turned to face the practicing WynSprigns and drank.

Trayvor didn't look at Fenner when he approached, but he started talking: "I know that you must be disappointed in me, Fen . . ." His words were leading, searching for comfort.

He didn't find it.

Fenner did not respond. He didn't care to make Trayvor feel better. Instead, Fenner gulped the last of the water and set the heavy cup down with a thud. He sucked through his teeth loudly, wiped his wet mouth on his forearm, and walked back to the station without looking back at his fellow elder.

Trayvor remained seated and hung his head low, becoming a large blue lump at the table. Unlike everyone else's, his cup was filled with ale. All around him various WynSprigns had answered the call of duty—even the striking Bre Brickelbury, on whom he had gazed many times. She awkwardly tried thrusting the long staff she wielded, clumsy in her attempts to lunge.

"She won't last," he muttered to himself with a woeful countenance. He picked up his cup and tossed back more ale.

~

Fenner organized the swordsmen and swordswomen to spar back and forth. A large crew of those that would wield staffs he had practice with large hanging bedding sacks. Besides the house and the weapons, this equipment was also compliments of Lanico and Marin . . . whether they knew it or not. Fenner had to use *something*, and the odds were that Marin and Lanico wouldn't be back before the battle to use their beds anyway.

The staff-wielding warriors swung and attacked the bedding sacks with all their might, and it wasn't long before they tore open and all the wood shavings came snowing down. The WynSprigns all got a mighty laugh from it—

and they'd simply re-stuff a sack, sew, and reuse it. If they were torn beyond repair, no worries, they'd just take someone else's—probably Trayvor's.

Fenner belted out orders as he eyed their movements closely. He was proud of his grandson Freck's skills and watched him with great pleasure. His other grandsons were promising, also, but Freck outshone them. Back in the Odana Kingdom, they'd all be on their way to be soldiers. Fenner gleamed at that thought. It would have been nice to have had them training in his higher ranks.

"Hey! Grandfather!" Freck shouted at him. "We almost done yet?" He stood with a hand on his side, gasping. Stray sunlight beamed on his bronze skin, kissing it golden.

Fenner grumbled from his daydream, thinking, *If only he'd act like a Soldier*. He shouted out, "No! Keep going!"

Freck slumped and sighed with mock rudeness but continued to train with Felena Odmire. She was proving great at wielding the sword, but even she was beginning to get agitated with her immature sparring mate. Her face flushed pink against her golden hair. She moved quickly and deliberately, and then in a fury she countered one of his slack moves and suddenly Freck found himself at the wrong end of her sword.

"Good, Felena!" Fenner suddenly came back to life. He shouted and clapped excitedly for the young woman.

Freck turned red and without a word, he quickly sprang up and walked away for a drink of water. Trayvor was still sitting there, an ignorable fixture at the table. They paid each other no mind.

After the quick water break, Freck walked over to his grandfather. "May I take a break from the sword, Grandfather? I'd like to learn at the staff as well." He said he wanted to challenge himself in other areas, but without saying so, he conveyed that he didn't want to be out-performed again by Felena.

Fenner was pleased at this request. "Yes Freck, that's a fine idea. You're already a natural at sword fighting, it seems. It's a great thing to have additional knowledge with various weapons."

"Well, I am a Brickelbury, after all," Freck stated smartly. Fenner responded with an intent look and excused himself to walk past him and take a staff from a large barrel.

Meanwhile, Felena, looked around to find another sparring mate. She started practicing the sword with Tarn, who was also becoming quite talented.

Felena would do well at sword fighting, with or without practicing with Freck. She was bent on it.

Chapter Forty-Two

Neen grunted, sulking on a stool inside the empty mess hall. He had already gathered all the bed rolls, water skins, and many pieces of leather armor, and still no one came to help. And it had been hours. All the Mysra were lazy and had over-indulged at the party, or at least that was his conclusion, because he sure as fires couldn't determine what else made them sleep so deeply. But all that slumbering was proving detrimental to his long-term plan. He tried to think of his mental list: *wagons, cages, ropes, canteens, and food . . . Yes, we need these gathered as well. Weapons—only minimal. Knives. We don't need many for this mission.* They were only taking defenseless WynSprigns, after all.

He hadn't tried waking them again. Scrambling through the list of priorities, he felt his mind racing. *Should I try waking them again?*

He was starting to get up from the stool as the door creaked open, and he watched to see who he could rail at. A small, gray figure in a purple cloak appeared—it was Grude, who had made the trip to the mess hall.

"Grude! Sire!" Neen quickly stood from the stool and made a small bow. Grude didn't seem to have been impacted by last night's celebration, either. *Why?*

Grude strolled in casually with a sour face, his thin mouth a straight line, his eyes expressionless. "Neen, I see that you have been working in here," Grude said, observing the long tables filled impressively with supplies and body protection.

"Yes, Sire. I have been up for several hours now trying to put this all together for the other Mysra warriors and guards, so we can head out to the Horse's Clearing. No one has come in yet, for they have been sleeping off last night's party. We still need many things for our preparations." Neen didn't want to say that he had tried waking them earlier—numerous times.

Grude's features remained enigmatic. His mouth was a straight line that seemed irresolute. He walked up and down the length of the tables and roamed his gaze over the row of gathered knives.

"Neen, tell me what you think is needed, and I will make it happen," Grude said with a hiss.

Neen breathed out a sigh of defeat.

~

Misty fog blanketed the Odana Kingdom, and while it seemed that all the Mysra were in heavy slumber in the haze, not Neen, nor any other, had considered the slaves.

Due to the Mysra sleeping it off, things were a bit lax at the mine and at the castle. The slaves, some of them, pondered escape. Others were cautious and remained working, afraid that this was a trap or that they'd be caught running or found out in plotting - or meet their end in the trench.

It was these WynSprigns that had the Purple Hall still in production, dutifully picking away. But the Mysra guards were sleeping on the job—no one was belting out orders or glaring at them and threatening them with large knives. The slaves' thoughts roiled over whether to leave, to return to the huts, to escape, or to stay and pick away. The uncertainty, for many, lead to immobility.

The kitchen servants had made breakfast for Grude, but there wasn't much more he demanded by the brief start of Tunia's shift. Even the stables had been stilled and the only sound had been from the horses within snickering and grunting.

Even though she had had only a few hours of sleep, Tunia, wearing her light blue skirts, danced on her way back to the castle for her shift. She tried to contain her delight and not give her guilt away. Even the thought of the fowl feathers that undoubtedly littered her kitchen floor by now couldn't ruffle her happiness. The small early morning crew had likely completed their preparations for the day.

Tunia had been in charge of the yellow berry wine barrels the previous night and had made certain to give the barrels a hefty dose of her sleepheather oil while they were under her care in the kitchen. Only a few drops of the thick gray liquid could knock out the largest of the Mysra, putting them all in a comatose slumber.

Once back at the castle, as she had every day for innumerable years, she stepped on her stool, and it shook under her weight as it pressed on the loose wooden floorboard just underneath. The board jutted up when her weight was not on the stool. It was the perfect place to hide a bottle of sleepheather oil, even for the past hundred years. She had waited—waited for the right moment to unleash its spell.

Understanding the reason for the celebration: That moment was last night.

Of course. Barrels and barrels of wine had been rolled into her kitchen for her oversight. She smiled thinking about how they'd be out for hours more and, therefore, the plans for the day's departure would be much delayed. It wasn't much perhaps, to cause them such sleep, but the miners could escape, perhaps—if they had the cunning. Perhaps the WynSprigns that the Mysra sought could be given more time to flee or prepare. It was enough to cause Tunia great satisfaction.

What *was* regrettable, though, was that Grude and a few others had not had her yellow berry wine from the tainted barrels. Grude had his own private collection from which he drank. Tunia had realized this but wouldn't allow that thought to weigh her down. The slaves could do what they liked with the temporary freedom. She on the other hand, considered the kitchen her home. She never wanted to leave it, even if being there meant having to cater to Grude. She knew her kitchen and was content here. Her duties were about the same as they had always been, even under King Oetam.

She breathed in the morning air. *Still.*

Still more drops of sleepheather oil remained.

And, there was still some time left.

Chapter Forty-Three

Stoutwyn and his group traveled as far as they could into the deep woods, their arms tired from carrying loads, small children, and babes. Their legs were heavy and burning from the walk and they were drained of constantly watching for fallen tree branches on the uneven ground. They were weary of worrying about their safety and the safety of those they loved back in the Great Mist. The sun was beginning to set and the treetops were slowly painted shades of orange and pink, a reminder that nightfall was soon to follow, an invisible flaming pitchfork poking at their rear ends to move forward. But then—

"Here!" Stoutwyn shouted, breaking the silence. "We'll stop here, everyone!" He looked around, beads of sweat glistening on his brow and gathering in his deep wrinkles. It seemed that this stretch of woods was no different from any other—dense with trees and brambles. It made no matter—his group was exhausted, and he needed to let them rest.

The WynSprigns heaved and sighed as they set the babes down in their wrappings. They dropped their heavy things and wrung out their arms and hands, enjoying relief from the physical burdens while their hearts were still heavy. Stoutwyn began delegating tasks that would lead to an appropriate campsite, for this area was not ready—not yet.

"For those able, let's work to clear this area a bit! Let's move some branches and brambles out of our way. We will need to try to make space here for us to rest for the evening, and we will need to set up shelter and try to gather food later. For now, we can rely on the food items that we've brought."

The snapping of twigs and crunching of ground cover sounded at the many moving around him. Stoutwyn began kicking at a few twigs and sticks at his feet before making the great effort to bend over and gather them up. "We'll make a fire late . . . try to gather sticks like these"—he held up a few thin sticks in his plump hand. Nodding heads of compliant small children promised they'd find these.

Stoutwyn then circled the large camp, careful of those sitting about in exhaustion. He didn't feel confident he was making the right choice for all of them and decided to find Murah. She was a safe, sensible soul to discuss these matters with. She was his lifelong love and best friend. As he approached, he could see that she was busy caring for small tottering children, thus giving the pregnant mothers some much-needed rest and time to put their feet up on the gathered bundles. She had her hands full and looked on at the small ones with tender, loving eyes. She was beautiful to him, the very picture of love.

He decided against burdening her with his ramblings and began wandering away from the camp and into the dark woods. "I'll walk just a little way, only to clear my mind" he had said quietly to a preoccupied Murah—who hadn't heard a thing over the bubbling babe sounds she so delighted in.

As he walked, the sounds of conversation and the glow of fire behind him faded. His eyes began to glow brighter at the increasing darkness that soon enveloped him and the world around. He didn't walk too far, or at least that was what he believed.

Soon a light blue, glowing mist surrounded him, and the ground became wet, very wet. His footsteps squelched loudly as the mud pulled at his boots. The fog had begun to grow thick. He decided it would be wise to turn around and head back to prevent becoming lost. He slowly turned, but the fog was so dense he wasn't quite sure he was walking in the right direction now. He felt his heart pulsing. There was a level of sudden alarm. He swirled around, staring blankly into the dense fog that licked against his hot face.

Perhaps if I yell, the others will hear me and come to my aid, he thought, *but no—no, on second thought*—he lifted his feet against the thick sucking and continued to ponder—*that could harm them, too. What if they became lost as well? In truth, I am more able-bodied than the lot of them.*

Succumbing to his real plight, he was about to resort to yelling for help when suddenly the glowing mist gathered into one large mass that hovered over the ground in front of him. United, the glowing mass grew brighter, shifted, and loomed. It was a soft blue, cool, and misty to the touch. Stoutwyn wasn't distressed at this, but rather, intrigued. He leaned a little closer to this misty substance to examine it. As he reached out to touch its cool silk—*BOOM!*

A clap of thunder sounded and the flash of lightning energy sent his plump body flying. He landed on his backside, his legs high in the air and his heart leaping in his throat, then pounding. The flash crackled and reverberated all around. With much effort and grunting, he worked to pull himself upright and flung his long beard over his shoulder to its rightful place. His face showed alarm and his eyes bulged. The muddy ground received his seated weight, but his heart hammered.

A light, breezy voice sounded out from around him, as if . . . as if the mist were talking: "Stoutwyn . . . I have been awaiting your arrival," it breezed.

Stoutwyn, bewildered, fumbled with his chest pocket and produced his faithful spectacles. With trembling fingers, he placed them on the bridge of his nose and peered into the mist. "Y—Y—You've been expecting *me*?" He paid no mind to the cold wetness growing under his bottom. He squinted through the specs at the glowing mass. It had manipulated and formed, and an exceedingly glorious specter drifted before him. A woman, illuminated, blue. Her floating hair was the deep color of indigo berries. *The Blue Woman of the wood!*

"Stoutwyn . . . I have been told of your journey. I'm glad I was able to find and receive you." She paused and her voice was flat: "I felt a disturbance in my woods." She looked pleasant and unangered, but she did not smile.

"Disturb—no, no, Miss. We don't intend to disturb anyone. If fact, we can leave now"—Stoutwyn sprang up.

"Stop!" she said darkly. "Stoutwyn"—her voice became soft again, weighted as if she were learning to communicate in a way that was pleasant to him. "You and your people are welcome in these woods. I was hoping to lead you to a better and safer spot, but I see that your people have already settled in for the night. Tomorrow I will lead you to my chosen place for protection."

Stoutwyn looked at her in amazement. "Who are you?" he asked, his voice small and hoarse.

"I am called Thara. I am the lady of the mist, the Fray over water and mist, and of these woods." She glided around him and he saw she was quite tall, reminiscent of another Fray he knew. "I am the third created Fray daughter of Father Odan." She slowly held an arm out toward his camp. "I have been summoned to aid you and your people."

"By whom?" Stoutwyn asked, still in a state of wonderment.

"By Greta."

"W—Who's Greta?" He was trying to understand all of this and make sure she was in fact safe, and that he wasn't dreaming.

"Stoutwyn . . . you and a few chosen know Lanico Loftre's rare heritage, of his Fray mother, Greta—second created daughter of Father Odan. Fray over light and woodland. Lanico, and Marin, abide with her in the Odana woods this very moment." Her voice was breezy, a blend of misted sounds.

But she was right. Stoutwyn had been one of the rare few who had known about Lanico's half-breed Fray blood. He remembered the unfortunate day when he had tried to hunt in the Odana woods long ago as a young man and learned of its protection by the Fray. Only he, Trayvor, and Fenner knew about Lanico's hidden Fray identity, about Greta. But it was easy to forget, for they never discussed it among themselves—there was no reason to. Since the days of their sworn secrecy, he had encountered Fray Greta at the castle in her usual elder WynSprign disguise, several times over.

"Oh yes! Oh yes," he said, coming back to the present, his eyes blinking quickly. "I'm sorry. I—I didn't mean to question you. I just want to make sure that my people are safe and that I am not compromising that safety. But since you are related to Lanico and his mother, I feel a bit . . . better." He hobbled towards her, now dully aware of the cold mud covering his bottom—but it was only of fleeting concern.

"I'm pleased," she said. "I will walk with you." Legs began to take shape and appeared from the misty form in which she was enrobed and they slowly began to walk, she towering over him. Stoutwyn noticed that she didn't actually use her legs—she glided. But there was no judgment from him. If he could have glided over all these forest obstacles, he would have done so as well.

She emanated her light blue glow, illuminating their way, but after a short distance she stopped abruptly. "Observe, Stoutwyn"—she waved her arm out in front of them. The dense fog cleared at her hand and a lake appeared in the distance, lit by the soft moon.

Stoutwyn squinted through his foggy spectacles, blinked, removed them to wipe them on his shirt, and replaced them. He could see the glowing lake was teeming with fish that leapt under the hanging silver moon and mirrored the silhouetted trees. Off to the side was a clearing—a vast one. There was plenty of room for his large group to settle for the night, or forever, for that matter.

His heart now fluttered. "Wow, that's beau—" Stoutwyn started.

"Tomorrow . . . once the new light of morning appears, prepare your people for this walk. You may stay in this part of my woods, away from the dangers of the approaching Mysra." Her voice was grim at the sound of that last word. It was also further confirmation that the Mysra indeed were on the move.

"Y—Yes, Thara. Thank you so kindly for your hospitality." Stoutwyn turned his gaze from the lake to her. "Your generosity is much appreci—"

And with that, she was gone. It was dark again. Crickets chirped once more. Stoutwyn was alone again in the wood as the last of the glowing mist disappeared. He turned where he stood and started looking around. He could barely see a glow from the campfire a distance away through the trees. Just barely. It was the Fray Thara's mist that had intentionally shrouded it before. So now, now he started off in that direction again, with clarity.

Chapter Forty-Four

It was much later than Neen had originally planned that they were able to rouse the Mysra warriors from their death-like slumber. The Mysra guards would remain in Odana to maintain continued order amongst the castle slaves and miners, gathering those who might have lost discipline in the morning's break of routine. The other Mysra, the warriors and trained riders, would be part of the plan to capture the WynSprigns, as many as they could gather in the Great Mist. With Neen's description of the area, capturing the WynSprigns of the Great Mist would be easy.

To Neen's contentment, the barracks and mess hall were abuzz with hurried Mysra warriors running about preparing for the trip to the Great Mist as they shook off their grogginess. He and Grude had made another attempt to rouse them and were thankful it had worked. Perhaps it was that Grude, their leader, woke and stirred them? Or at least that is what Neen determined. He mentioned this to Grude himself and the leader was pleased at this concept—that he alone had been privileged with the power and authority to wake them for his undertaking. It was all thanks to Fray Jaspia—their mother, their creator—they concluded.

Gax ran into the barracks to find his brother. His panting voice snapped Neen out from that recent recollection.

"I was able to get the cages from the mines." Gax's voice was confident despite his disgrace of oversleeping.

"Good!" Neen replied. "Take them to the mess hall. I want all the supplies there. We will start putting ourselves in order there."

Gax was bent over panting and only nodded before running off again out the door.

"Nice work, Neen," Grude said with a smile as he looked over the activity. "I am pleased. Fray Jaspia on High will be pleased."

Neen only nodded.

While they supervised, a worried Mysra ran towards them but reluctantly. He came to kneel quickly and bent over catching his breath. "Sire, Neen," he said to the pair, his red cape falling neatly around his back.

"Yes, Nizen?" Grude said casually—a mere annoyance, this one. *Even trying to wear a cape like me.*

"Sire"—he panted—"we took daily count at the Purple Hall." He breathed heavily as he continued: "We discovered that there are six WynSprign slaves missing from the mines."

Grude paused—Nizen had his attention now. "What? Did I hear you say *missing*?" There was brief silence. "You are the main charge for the mines. We are on a mission to collect *more* WynSprigns and you're telling me we JUST LOST SIX?!" Grude slammed his hands down at his sides. "Asinine! Outrageous!" His gawking expression read incredulity.

Nizen's eyes widened and he was covered in cold sweat.

Grude's shout sent nearby Mysra to stop their tasks and look at them questioningly. Without removing his glare from Nizen, Grude lifted his hand and pointed to the onlookers: "No one told you to stop and stare at us! RETURN TO WORK!" At this demand, the curious Mysra rushed away.

"Look!' he admonished Nizen. "I don't know how you lost these WynSprigns, but their number loss will be regained after we take over the missing village. If I *EVER* hear of WynSprigns going missing again, I will thrash you myself—or WORSE!" He growled to punctuate this declaration.

Nizen remained with his head bowed but nodded quickly. "Yes, Sire. Yes, Sire. Thank you for your mercy on me. I don't know what came over everyone with the slumber—"

"ENOUGH!" Grude barked. "You're dismissed."

Grude glared at him before slowly turning to Neen. "Okay, let's see those cages and wagons!" In an instant he had changed, taking on a contented tone. Together they walked briskly in the direction of the now-bustling mess hall.

Nizen carefully rose after they left him and sighed loudly while dusting off his knees. He was not in Grude's favor at this moment, and with this thought and in an effort to get his duties back in order, he marched back to the Purple Hall again, sending his red cape flapping behind him with his quick strides. He'd have to determine a way to never have another misstep. His life depended on perfection. But he was still fuming from the verbal thrashing. He was unsettled at the subordinate Mysra eyes that had hovered over him at Grude's berating.

He balled his fists and glowered as he strode toward the slave mine encampment.

Chapter Forty-Five

It had been another long day of training, and the rainbowed fireflies of Odana had returned to the river for their nightly ritual dance.

The group of warriors sat together at Greta's large table, ravenous for her enchanted food. Greta entered the eating room but not with her usual melodic and cheerful demeanor. She glided, loomed over their table. Her expression was indiscernible. Her voice was cool as she focused on her guests.

"I have spent time in communitive meditation with the other Fray," she started.

The group stopped forking up heaps of food and set their gazes on her.

"According to my Fray sister, Thara, Stoutwyn has taken a group of WynSprigns who are unable to fight into the deep wood beyond the Great Mist." She paused and flicked her gaze to Lanico, meeting his eyes. "It seems that the rest remain in the village. They are preparing to fight off Mysra forces that we understand are planning to take them back to the Odana Kingdom."

Lanico's eyes widened at her words and he shot up from his chair, which toppled over behind him. "When? Did Thara say when the Mysra were expected to arrive? No. No, of course not. What about -when was it that Stoutwyn moved the group to the deep woods?" His eyes bore into hers with growing intensity.

She remained calm at his alarm. "Lanico, Thara spoke to Stoutwyn just before this very meal. She will allow them to stay at her shore and will have them take shelter in her lands."

Everyone remained silent and stared up at Lanico, whose fists curled with his agitation. He leaned forward onto them against the table. "I should have been there," he growled. "Why did I leave them to Trayvor?" Lanico paused to focus. The companions remained silent. He continued and his voice escalated: "I knew. I *knew* that I couldn't trust him! How—How could he?"

Realizing his voice had grown to a shout, he stopped short and said quietly, "I should have left here sooner."

Treva stood up and inclined her head toward Lanico. "We should leave soon—tomorrow." She looked to Greta, and her voice was strong: "We have two horses. Lanico and I will leave in the morning. Perhaps we can make it before the Mysra arrive."

Greta gave her a sharp nod of approval. Treva shifted her gaze up toward Lanico. His mind was focused as he looked at his knuckles on the table—purposely avoiding their connecting gaze.

As it was when this topic had surfaced before, he didn't acknowledge her decision, *that* decision.

"After we've found victory for The Great Mist," Treva continued, "perhaps we can bring back recruits to train, for the reclaiming of the kingdom." Her perfect face was serious, carved stone.

Lanico had reservations about allowing Treva to accompany him. This was dangerous. He didn't want to risk both of Marin's parents being taken in battle—he had already lost Izra. Lanico determined he would wake earlier and then leave without her. "Let's prepare for the morning, then," he said finally. His voice was strong and low, without a hint of his ultimate plan.

Chapter Forty-Six

Close to sundown. They hadn't slept and the sun would too-soon rise again, but Grude and Neen were pleased with the results that played out in front of them. They could see plainly now the unfolding of their idea. Additional cages were loaded along with supplies into the wagons just outside the mess hall. Knives and only minimal other weapons were needed. Every Mysra would travel with his or her own.

The warriors wanted more than merely knives—they had many complaints. At this point, the warriors were tired from having been awake so long, but their grumbled concerns failed to rest in Neen's ear; he would see only victory in his path.

It was his great determination to organize the ranks and outline the clear route that they'd follow, the one most familiar to him. He had strategically mapped out their route, thankful that the last of the hags was dead—and by his own blade, of course.

"My plan is to make it there within a matter of days," Neen said. "I'd prefer sooner, but I realize with this many Mysra, three days would be incredibly lucky." He turned his gaze from the map to Gax at his side and grimaced at the thought of adding additional days, but he was attempting to be realistic. Thinking this deliberation was over, he quickly sprinkled a few crumbles of trillium in his mouth. The crunchy grit was most welcome on his teeth. The sweet sprinkles crackled on his tongue and the sting of brass tickled his nose.

It seemed that just about everything was in order. "We're ready," he grumbled to his brother.

Neen looked to Grude, standing at his other side. "Sire, at your command, we move."

Looking out over the gathered mass of Mysra, horses and wagons, Grude's purple cape whipped slightly in the dusty breeze. He eyed Neen solemnly, with pride. "Neen, it seems all is in order, so I give my command."

Grude's straight-line mouth suddenly turned to a rare bright smile directed at Neen, the expression revealing his large, sharp teeth.

Neen cleared his throat and felt secret pride at Grude's command. He stood erect and shouted orders for his warriors to hear, "MARCH! WE MOVE OUT!"

Horns blew low that sounded from the distance, signaling the large departure and opening of the post-battle Odana gates. The gates were high and placed atop the switchback trail that led over the lower-lying mountains and toward the Odana River. Cranking gears and moans of metal, bellowed from the mountain gate. A swift wind came from beyond the opening giving off a different scent.

Whips snapped in the trillium-dusted air, and the horses neighed to lurch forward with the cage-filled wagons. The heave of the Mysra as they started pushing forward through their weariness was slow at first. After a few moments, once momentum had been gained, the ground started to tremble at their heavy regular march.

"Nice work, Neen," Grude said, slapping him hard on the back. "I'll be awaiting my new gifts."

Neen only nodded and hoisted himself onto his brown horse, a young wild mare. Its anxious footing showed it was determined to prance off—a good thing, because they'd ride all night. "Yes, Sire," Neen said, and made a clicking sound to command the horse. The horse eagerly trotted onward, following the massive group through swirling dust clouds.

Grude stood outside the mess hall and watched as the large group of his Mysra warriors started to head out. He held his hand over his eyes, shielding his view from the swirls clouded dirt. The other hand waved at the thick air. Then he slowly turned and walked alone to the castle to take in a dose of trillium.

~

Stoutwyn made an effort to ensure all the WynSprings under his care were accounted for. The early morning air was no different from which they'd been in the Great Mist—misty and cool. The sun hadn't risen yet and the lingering blue haze was laced throughout the trees, as usual. Stoutwyn began to wonder at the sight of this, whether Thara was in fact this blue haze—*Has she lived amongst us all along?*

The multitude of weary heads of the WynSprigns slowly followed on after Stoutwyn. He had let them know the night before that they were not traveling far. Much to the relief of their weary eyes, it was just as Stoutwyn said—not far. And soon, very soon, a thinning of trees could be seen, an expanse promised in the distance beyond. Had they only travelled a little further last night . . .

Their faces brightened as they trudged through the forest leaves and branches. They had been only a brief stroll away! The land ahead provided encouragement to push onward. The mysterious blue haze hung gracefully over a large, still lake that resembled a silver mirror in the pre-dawn sky. Small ripples crested with occasional splashes from jumping fish. The land encircling the lake was large and clear and surrounded by the familiar protection of dense trees. There would be plenty of room to set up camp for them all.

Their heavy hearts lifted a little.

Chapter Forty-Seven

The sun hadn't yet risen and Lanico was ready, ready to leave for the Great Mist. It was earlier than he had planned—and he was thankful for that. He didn't want anyone up yet. Already dressed and prepared, he rose and quickly moved toward the front of the house. He looked through the screened door, and spied Treva near the horses. Despite the long years since she had last ridden, her saddling movements were expert. His stomach pained him. He blinked hard to take the sleep away and correct his vison.

No, his vision was accurate—to his disapproval he could make out the brown leather armor covering her shoulders. Metal would have been too heavy for the travel. The emerald hair.

"Where are you going?" he called out from inside the house; she was saddling one of the horses while the other tied next to it at the river's edge was getting its fill of water.

"I'm going . . . with you!" Treva called back, squinting at Lanico as the sun began to peek between the trees, highlighting her vibrant hair. She had two swords sheathed on her belt, including her falchion. Knowing her, there were likely more weapons hidden on her. "I've already packed!" She bent down and happily held up a bag, showing it to him with a bright smile. The bag she held was almost as large as she, but she could lift it—since her arrival in the enchanted forest, her muscular form had begun to return.

Expressionless, Lanico turned and receded into the shaded house to think.

He was livid.

He had expected to wake up before her and head out. To his dismay, he now realized she had been off to a start long before him.

Noticing his response, Treva's smile diminished. She tightened her lips and regained her focus on saddling the remaining horse, determined.

Petals slowly drifted from one of the many flowering trees, and several landed in her hair. Lanico saw this from inside the house. She waved at them in annoyance and dusted a few off her horse's rump.

Lanico, wordless, stormed back out again and quickly walked toward her carrying his own bags, his silver hair breezing behind him with his fast strides. The screened door slammed close behind him. She sliced a glance to him but without making eye contact he walked past her, a black-and-green blur heading to the other horse. He remained silent and focused on his task.

She stopped fidgeting with the buckles and looked squarely at him. "Lan," she asked, her voice stern, "is something wrong?" She knew exactly what was wrong and he didn't want to meet her gaze. It was a way to avoid their new connection.

He squared himself and looked back at her daringly, and she breathed in at the rush it made. "Treva, in truth"—he let out a short, agitated sigh—"I don't want you to come along. To join me." He then studied his horse's saddle, her work on it already completed. He slumped over the saddle at this little revelation. "I don't think it's safe for you to come along. There are too many Mysra warriors, and I'd prefer if you stayed here . . . with Marin."

Treva's eyes flew wide open, and her jaw gaped. The audacity! She glanced around, her eyes darting, and she angled her head, trying to get him to look at her while schooling her own thoughts. "Lanico, you are my Prince," she began carefully. "I've pledged my oath to you, to your father, your family . . . to—to *our* family"—she pointed towards the house, a reference to Marin—"I would do anything that you command, as I swore to, for my oath is my life. But Lan . . ." She paused as their eyes locked. "I also swore to protect you. The love I have for you is not in question."

He had heard her say it again—*love*.

She blinked. "Understand this," she continued, "I act on duty and on my oath as a pledged Odana Knight . . ." She paused again, glaring at him now because he averted his eyes. Her voice became stern as she said slowly, "Do not mistake yourself and forget *my* place."

He then moved to look straight at her, an answer to what she had demanded, and he studied her steely face. It must have been hard for her to say goodbye to Marin last night. He knew this—felt this from her. Perhaps it was cruel, but he had allowed that goodbye, pretending he did not plan to leave her here. But she had read it on him anyway. Looking at her, and reading her, it became ever clear, a reminder especially now, that she put her duty ahead of herself, *always*. She always had.

He broke the stare, looking to the grassy ground below. She walked slowly toward him.

"Lanico, I swore my oath to protect you. I am doing *your* will in this moment and with this decision." She reached her hand up to tuck a silver section of his hair behind his ear, the way that he had always been tempted to do the same for her. She moved in closer to him, to look up into his eyes.

He sighed pensively. He knew her words made sense, and he hadn't intended to offend or belittle her status as a Knight, a ranked Second Lieutenant. More than anyone ever to have lived, he knew what her duty had meant to her. She lived to be a Knight—in their early life, it had been what she most wanted. She of all people knew the risks this life brought. But he simply couldn't take it if something were to happen to her. He had been broken over and over again all these years with the deaths of Raya, Izra, and Treva. He couldn't take if she died all over again. He'd likely be tempted to end himself, were it not for Marin.

He closed his eyes and heard himself say, "Treva, you may accompany me." His face was now gentle. He placed his hand on the side of her face, cradling it. It was the same place he had put his hand all those years ago before the siege that changed them. His hand was larger than the length of her face. "I don't want any harm to come to you. You mean so much more to me . . ." *Than an oath*—he would have said, but didn't need to. He breathed—"It would kill me if something were to happen to you." The wounds, the horrific scars, they tore at his spirit. The tears she had cried—remembering her years of slavery—haunted him, and his words were truthful. He'd never allow it again.

His eyes flickered from hers. He pulled a petal from her emerald hair, reconnected to her stare, leaned in, and dared to gently kiss his favorite spot on her lip, the pale scar. He could feel her smile against his mouth. Despite the fear in his heart, he found some peace in that moment. They would be all right, she would be all right, even if he died protecting her.

Her eyes opened slightly looking into his. *It won't happen,* her eyes told him.

He huffed a small breathy laugh against her cheek. He remembered that warm breath caressing other places and knew she remembered, too.

The golden sun beamed, bathing them in a soft pink glow as petals continued to gently drift down. Their mouths were still pressed against each other, with softly caressing tongues. Lanico knew he would never forget how she tasted, how she looked that moment, nor would he forget the feeling of pure tranquility and beauty pressed against him. His alpha female, fearless and brazen, was at his side in this battle. The picture of her as she was now, was a treasure he decidedly etched in his mind.

Chapter Forty-Eight

They would stay here a few days, or . . . as long as it would take. Members of the hunting team trekked through the woods to gather at Horse's Clearing this morning. Their task was to monitor any movement from the Yellow Vast grasslands. They were the fastest runners and were well versed in archery, the only form of weapon that, until recently, any of them had ever wielded. If their bows and arrows were needed for self-defense before they reached the Great Mist, they'd have them at the ready. Fenner moved that it would be smart to have this line of alert and defense at the ready, from this point onward. Once Mysra were visible on the horizon, the hunters would sprint toward the Great Mist and alert the warriors to position themselves and prepare for battle.

Though they traveled far within the Great Mist territory to hunt, they had never ventured this far through the dense forests to the border. It was an exciting but an overwhelming and fearful feeling to have this level of responsibility. It was also a test, to be as far as this from the familiarity of the Great Mist.

As the anxious hunters closed in, they noticed the thinning of trees ahead, and the hint of vast land that lay beyond them. An instant promise of more. More land beyond. More to see. Mysra forces—not yet visible, but somewhere, threatened in that stretched land beyond.

They gingerly drew nearer, finding a spot to set up their camp. With great care, they laid their hunting bows and quivers filled with arrows in a pile on the ground. They were brought for their initial intention, hunting small game. The plan was not to attack from here.

They took cautious steps toward the dazzling tree line to begin their watch. Twigs and acorns gave muffled crunches under the weight of their soft, weathered boots. Pushing aside thin, leafy branches made their pulses race. Then, revealed, the immense yellow expanse before them brightened their shadowed faces. They each drew in a breath. *The Yellow Vast*. They saw further than their eyes had ever witnessed distance before. The land spread so far and wide across, it seemed an eternity of yellow, a color they'd seldom seen in such abundance.

The dark shadow of overhead clouds swept along the land, delivering a warm-smelling breeze that licked their cool skin. The experience was awe inspiring, a true reward for their diligence in being the fastest runners in the Great Mist. And to think, Lanico and Marin where somewhere beyond that!

After a few moments of basking in the warm, sweet-smelling breeze, they pulled their attention away from the golden beauty, from her temptation of freedom and adventure beyond.

"Remember," Stefin happily said to Freck as he gathered dead wood from the surrounding brush, "Fenner said no fires at night."

"I *know*, Stefin. I was just getting it ready, is all." Freck carefully placed a few small logs and brambles in a pile and was clearing away debris. His black hair, a wild mane like his grandfather's, swayed with his efforts.

"And I'm just trying to think now," Stefin said, "should we have watches? For example, will one of us always be awake to watch for movement on the horizon?" He paused, and Freck was about to answer when he started again—"Or—or should we all stay awake?" He carefully unpacked a thin blanket from his sack.

"It's not all that different from when we go hunting." Freck was sure to respond quickly, to avoid another set of what he felt were useless questions. "There is always someone to watch if the others need to rest."

Freck moved his sack a bit on the ground and unpacked some carrots to munch on. "You and I"—he motioned between himself and Stefin—"will take this first watch, and then they"—he indicated Tarn and Jain setting up their area just next to them—"they'll take the next while we sleep." Freck crunched loudly with his ambitious bite into the fat carrot. "It's good that there are two of us, in case either of us falls asleep, so we can nudge him awake again." Orange carrot bits mashed around in his open mouth as he spoke.

"Oh, yeah, that makes sense, Freck," Stefin answered, wincing in disgust at the display of carrot mashing before him. "You know, it's amazing to think that Marin is somewhere out there." He jerked his chin toward the horizon. "I wonder what he and Lanico have been encountering out there—at least, I hope they're together." He tore into a large piece of tough jerky. Then he sat down, his legs out in front of him extending past the edge of the blanket.

"Well, you know Marin. He's a dreamer—probably won't survive long, but he *does* have Lanico looking for him. So, it's anyone's guess, I suppose." Freck moved to lie flat on his stomach and held his sharp chin in his hands.

Tarn and Jain settled onto their blankets behind them, wriggling to get comfortable. It was still quite early in the day, but they agreed to let Freck and Stefin take this first watch of the horizon and they'd nap for now.

Stefin and Freck sat and watched over the landscape as the sounds of snoring began erupting from just behind them. Despite this dull noise and a few birds chirping, it was quiet around them. They were used to hunting and used to the quiet that came with waiting for deer, but this was merely sitting and not *trying* to hunt, not *trying* to do anything; it allowed the mind to wander.

"Felena did great at the sword, aye?" Stefin asked as he sighed and smiled, fumbling with the small tip of the deer antler he carried everywhere. He glanced over at Freck.

"Hmm? . . . Oh, she's okay *I guess*," Freck answered begrudgingly, for Stefin was always up for chatter. He tugged at grass roots, still embarrassed by her having out-performed him.

"Yeah"—Stefin paused—"You . . . You think she likes me okay, Freck?" Stefin fumbled with his antler bit in his hands.

Freck, looking out over the land, was confused by this question. He glanced quickly at Stefin—"What . . . what do you care about whether or not Felena likes you?" Just as Freck said this out loud, his eyes widened. There was amusement splashed on his face. A wide crescent-moon smile grew from the corners of his thin mouth. "You mean to say that *you* like Felena?"

Stefin squirmed, obviously regretting having mentioned her.

No, but Freck pursued this. He slapped his hands on his blanket in front of him and laughed at the idea. He looked at his annoyed friend, now wearing a sour expression. Freck's smile decreased slightly. "Oh," he said, "well . . . I mean"—he calmed himself in search of a better response—"well, she is probably stronger than you." He smiled at the thought.

"Well . . . that's just it, Freck," Stefin began. "Felena is beautiful *and* tough. Think of all the fun that would be to have a life mate like that. We could go hunting together, set up camp, climb trees, and spar . . . it's perfect." Stefin smiled dreamily at a large cloud passing slowly overhead.

There was silence as Freck twisted his mind about this. He held a gaze out at the yellow landscape glowing before them. The smirk he had held was now gone. He had certainly never thought of Felena that way, or anyone. It was true that they were approaching an age when they would be expected to choose a life mate . . .

"I'm just thinking, if I choose my life mate, I'd want her to be fun and to like the things I like, too," Stefin continued.

"Yeah, Stefin." Freck sighed his answer. "Yeah, that does makes sense."

His mind turned this over, and over again.

~

Night came quickly and rested on the river, reflecting the light from the stars and a glowing sliver from the moon above.

Once the Mysra had eaten their caught fish, and rummaged through whatever rations they had, they lay about in the open air and slept. The air was cool and fresh, a stark difference from the crowded dank barracks they usually slumbered in. They had all been practiced at this—long stays camped in the open. It was considered a form of training, one of the few types of trainings the Mysra had. Once in control, Grude hadn't felt there was much need for stringent military discipline, and why would he? They had annihilated the best army in all the lands, and trillium supplied all the brute power they needed. No, most training these days focused on the punishment of the slaves, save for the riding instruction that Gish provided and basic hand-to-hand combat, and even then, these were irregular events and without standards.

Neen spotted his brother awake and took long weaving strides around his warriors and toward him. Gax knelt over his weathered satchel to unpack dried jerky, his hulking arms jerking the sack about in frustration.

"You're eating your dried rations now?" Neen asked by means of greeting.

Without looking up at him, Gax focused on the contents of the sack, and he pulled out his purple rag first to get a better look within. "I'd prefer to eat my fill of fish and rations here and not have to eat when we arrive at the brook." He scowled. "The stench from that place still haunts my nose."

"Ha!" Neen smiled at that. "You always had the weaker constitution, brother. Since I killed the last one, all the hags are now dead, and no carcass should leave a stench any longer." He slapped Gax on the back heartily.

"Just knowing how close I was to . . ." Gax shuddered at the memory and Neen, too, thought of those gray teeth. It was luck that he had killed the remaining one just in time.

"Well, don't complain about hunger later," Neen warned, holding a slight happiness about him, for his troops were faring better than he had originally imagined and he—he was ready to claim his reward. He could barely maintain his composure at the thought of gathering those glow-eyed weaklings into a treasure for Grude.

"I won't complain," Gax grumbled in annoyance, taking a big bite of the brown meat jerky.

The large group was not afraid of being spotted by potential enemies—they found safety and security in their numbers and their ample supply of trillium. They also felt secure leaving their campfires to burn. In this cool air, their resting bodies resembled a field of boulders, and the cool evening air blew in and blanketed them all.

At dawn, after a much-welcomed sleep, Neen sprouted up with energy and enthusiasm. "UP! EVERYONE UP! WE MOVE!"

There were audible groans and he grimaced brightly to encourage them all: "NEXT STOP, THE YELLOW VAST BROOK! . . . WITHOUT HAGS!"

Chapter Forty-Nine

Tall yellow grasses swayed in waves as far as her vision could span. Treva sat where they had made camp in the Yellow Vast near a small creek, remembering the moments of a previous night. She had kissed her son on the cheek and embraced him tightly, taking in the feel of him, his sparse stubble, his scent. Feeling his warm embrace was the best—she loved having her son back with her. She had breathed him in as she buried her face in his curls—he smelled of perfumed water and was the image of his late father. She couldn't help but smile at the recent memory.

"Here. Take this," she had said, reaching behind her neck to unclasp the tooth necklace that had been hidden beneath her tunic.

A dreamy smile curled on her lips as she recalled how Marin's eyes widened in surprise of it. "How did *you* get my necklace?"

Treva looked at him curiously. "*Your* necklace?" She known about his wearing it, but wanted to hear him. Hear his voice a little more.

"Yes, I lost it while traveling here, somewhere in the yellow grassland."

Treva looked across the table at Lanico, who only smiled and shrugged back at her. "Well," she said to Marin, "please keep this safe—it's a promise of our return." She had clasped it behind his neck.

Saying goodbye hadn't been easy. Treva had only just met her son, a young man now, and she had fought the deep urge to burst into tears. Tears of happiness, of sadness, perhaps a mixture of both. But that natural urge somehow made her feel weak. It wouldn't be the last time she'd see him, she reminded herself . . . *convinced* herself. She now sat on the worn blanket, her fingers twirling the yellow blades aimlessly. Her tooth necklace was gone almost as soon as she'd gotten it back from Lanico, and was resting once again on Marin, who'd had it all these years. She had given it back to him as a promise. A promise to return.

Lanico set down the waterskin he'd just filled and settled himself a little closer to her, as if he knew what she was thinking. He stretched out legs unused to riding. "You all right, Tre?" His eyes tried to meet hers.

She still gazed up, into the pink, cottony clouds that floated over the orange horizon. "Yeah," she whispered and swallowed hard. Feeling his intense gaze upon her face, she remembered herself, her position, her duty. She straightened in defiance. "Yes," she stated firmly.

He nodded. "I know. It was hard to leave them—mostly Marin." His words were gentle.

She swallowed again against the lump in her throat.

"We leave to make them—*him*—a better future," Lanico said. "I remind myself of this." He inclined his head and slid a glance at her from the corner of his eye.

She met his gaze. Her love had always been for the kingdom, for Lanico, but no . . . "I don't know. I've never felt so"—she searched for the right words—"connected to someone else."

He moved to face her better, to listen, to read the unspoken.

"He's a part of me," she continued, letting her guard down slightly. "I see so much life, potential—hope, even—when I look at him. I never realized what this—what being a mother was like. I never had the chance to—" *Damn these tears threatening to surface!*

She felt her dry lips tremble slightly—a hint he read well. He reached for her fidgeting hand among the blades of grass. Her hand so was small in his, and yet it was a hand that had *killed* countless others, like his own. The air had cooled but the centering smell of the campfire lingered, and its flames licked the chill away. With the setting sun, she knew her eyes were beginning to glow a soft gold, as his were glowing the hue she loved.

It was just the two of them. Welled tears slid down her face.

"Marin, though not mine by blood, *is* my son," Lanico said, taking up her emotion in himself. "I know everything about him. Every nightmare, every tear, every interest. You and he, you'll grow into one another—there's so much about him that reminds me of you. There is a part of him that kept you alive." He looked out over the expanse. "For years I didn't know if I hated . . . or if I loved that." He had loved her though, always. It had always been her. He turned to look into her eyes again. *One hundred years or only a day, it made no matter. You have always been mine.*

But there it was, the mutual understanding that in that moment they shared. Marin was *their* son. They shared that very thought, and they *knew* it. She felt her heart melt a little at this. Since his having healed her, his heightened connection to her now, she also understood Lanico's unspoken feelings about her, the unspoken love . . . and she felt the same.

He leaned in closer to her. Their legs touched. He licked his lips, thinking. Looking at her mouth then flicking his gaze up to hers, wanting, he dared to slowly raise his hand and caress the scar on her lip with his thumb. His fingers, rough against her jaw, cradled the curve of her face. He felt her take a breath.

Her eyes hovered on his fingers and then slowly drifted to his glowing cyan, so intense they bored into her very thoughts. *Oh, Father Odan*, she could lose herself in them forever. A spell. She fluttered her gaze to his mouth and edged in nearer. A slight roguish quirk to the corners of his mouth. Her own lips slightly parted, ready to receive. She took in the scent of him.

No. A voice whispered to her mind. She needed to focus on this mission. *We're to take things slowly. That is what we discussed. For Marin. And, we have time*—If they survived; she avoided sharing.

She blinked back into focus and slowly backed away from his lure.

Lanico had a brief look of confusion and cleared his throat. She broke free from the spellbinding trance that would have had her in the throes of passion in only a few simple calculated movements. She steadied her focus to the vast before them, their future. Different. She was different from the untamed Treva she used to be. The confinement, the long years, the promise of motherhood . . .

Her voice, normal again, broke the spell: "We need to beat them there. I think if we can set out before the sun rises, perhaps we can—"

"Tre—"

She inhaled before turning her face to him, fighting her feelings. In the battle to come, either one of them could die. She couldn't lose him again.

Their gazes connected, and he thought fiercely at her, *Marry me.* A command. A request. And a dream.

She understood this, felt this. It was hard to say yes—to marriage. There wasn't anything she wanted more than to be married to him, her Prince. Her losses, though, they had been too great. The battles would still have to be won. The danger—it had to be distanced this time. She didn't respond to his question—to his demand. No promises.

At that moment, he knew. He decided against talking about his feelings for her, even for their shared future. It truly was too difficult. He breathed, yielding. "Yes, let's move out before the sun rises."

She nodded in an unspoken *Thank you*, the curve of her sharp chin catching the last rays of rosy sun. This was difficult enough, and pondering Marin, or her feelings, proved too much for her warrior's heart.

He glanced back at their fire.

"Lan, we're going to have to kill it soon"—she gestured to the fire—"to avoid being visible tonight."

He glanced at the leftover rabbit meat still sizzling and nodded: "In a bit."

Their bellies were full and they rested, peaceful, for now. The fire crackled as they sat in silence.

Treva suddenly sucked on her teeth for a piece of meat stuck somewhere, and the sound made him blink slowly. He loved her well beyond her uncouth manners. He truly believed she'd become his emerald Queen, but she would be his *warrior* Queen, after all. She'd been a warrior since she was a young girl following her brother's death. Her father raised her as such.

"Someone had to protect the farm from Mysra attacks and raids," she had once told him. Her father had long retired from the Odana Military as a Knight, to take up farming. As soon as she was old enough to join up, she did, and growing up in the Odana Military only served to enhance her . . . lack of manners.

Treva had such dedication to the kingdom, to him. She would make a wonderful Queen. He didn't tell her this. No. Not yet. She didn't want promises. But he felt that now that they had each other again, there would be time for that later. He glanced back at her lovely, fixed face, and sighed. She was now digging at her fingernails with her silver dagger—the one she kept between her breasts, another place he'd like to become familiar with. Her eyes sparkled up to meet his, and a charming smile spread across her face. She was beautiful, and deadly, and honestly . . . a gauche mess. *Charming,* he thought to himself. *A unique Queen, Indeed. Uncouth, but at least she'd be familiar to most everyone.*

As if to draw his thoughts to a close, she tucked the dagger back into its warmed sheath. Lanico exhaled, and that was better than the laugh he actually felt trying to rise from within.

After Lanico *killed* the campfire, as Treva liked to say, the stars seemed so close they were almost within reach. The cool of the night settled, and next to one another, they lay on their backs looking up with glowing eyes. The indigo sky was laced with twinkling diamonds. Treva moved in closer to him, to share the warmth. He didn't mind—she was the only Knight that he'd ever want to snuggle with on the field, though.

Their sides were against one another, and she nuzzled drowsily to lay her head in the crook of his arm, a corded, muscled pillow. She draped her own arm over his chest and her hand curved over his solid pectoral muscle. How nice it would be to grab onto it and claw. "Mmmm," she hummed. *Wait!*

No. Slowly.

Oh, fires . . . But her body *ached* for him, for the feeling of his skin . . . but . . .

They were to come together slowly. *I'll ride him later,* she decided. She nodded slightly to herself in agreement. *If we live, it'll be my reward for winning the battle.*

His scent of leather and lavender wrapped around her with his warmth, the comfort he gave in the settling chill, with the last crackles from the dimming wood.

He placed his hand over hers. It was a bold move, but, given the other night and his healing, he'd been even bolder with her before. They were meant to be together. He believed this and he knew this. She felt the same—he knew this as well—but they had this battle, and if they lived, there was another larger battle yet to come—the battle for the castle, for his kingdom. Was it worth losing love again? He toiled in his thoughts, in his unsettled emotions.

They both lay awake, quiet. There were no words tonight. A battle would be upon them too soon and any words spoken about this, about their feelings for one another, could prove too costly. This was to be the extent of their affections. It was survival as well.

Eventually, sleep fell upon them, and the glow of gold and cyan faded as they closed their eyes. First hers, and then his.

Morning came. Treva remained snuggled against Lanico, and he smiled in his sleep—dreams of sunshine against her tan face. They danced, waltzed, she in an emerald dress—the music was *real.* The song, so familiar to him. A ballroom . . .

A butterfly flittered and landed on his nose. He crinkled it but the butterfly remained, its tiny legs prickling at his skin. His hand rose to slap it away. At the smack to himself, his eyes popped open. Bright sun rays invaded the sleep that had set in. The butterfly managed to escape and fluttered onward.

They'd overslept!

He sat up quickly. Treva slumped from off his chest, her head thudding to the unforgiving ground. He'd forgotten she was there.

"*Hey*, Lan! What the f—it's morning!" She rubbed the side of her head. The brilliant sky blinded her, interrupting the string of curses she was about to launch at him.

"Yes, we overslept!" he grumbled as he rose and brushed his body of unseen dust and offered a hand to help her up. She accepted and, once hoisted, began to gather their things. She moved in a flash, and it didn't take long to pack up and ride out—much like the time when Izra was about to leave her at a tavern so many years ago.

They moved fast.

Too much time had been wasted already.

Treva's years of riding horses on her farm had molded her into a fine equestrienne, and as they rode, she practiced her long-abandoned tricks. Sure, her legs were sore, but oh, she welcomed it. It was a familiar but oddly comfortable pain. After all these years the muscle memory remained, drilled into her very bones and the rhythm of her heart, blended with the strides of the horse.

Lanico marveled at her ability to turn and ride sideways. She could stand, bracing herself against the gallops beneath her feet, the muscles of her legs pronounced through the fabric of her leggings. The food, the concoctions, the healing, the training. Physically, she was almost back to her rightful self. She concentrated as if Lanico weren't even there. Her focus and training were solely on the horse. It was a meditation in the yellow brilliance, the spirit of the animal breathing beneath her   alive and free.

At one point she poised herself to hang from the side of the horse, upside down with crossed arms. She caught Lanico's eye and smiled mischievously, her small frame bouncing against the horse's brown velvet sides.

Okay. She's just showing off now. The seasoned General in him, though determined, loosed a half-smile. He couldn't do that, *any* of that. She hadn't known any amount of fun, for far too long. And despite her shenanigans, they were still making progress across the grassy plains. He supposed it was a fun distraction on the way to their destination, on their way to blood and death. Skilled horse-riding was needed—he didn't mind this sort of . . . *practice*?

If he was honest with himself, he probably would have let her get away with just about anything. Luckily, she was every bit of the warrior he was, perhaps even more, and knew how far to take her fun.

Her loose emerald hair swept the tall yellow grasses she rode swiftly through them.

Closer.

Closer they rode to battle. It would be upon them soon.

Chapter Fifty

Dawn arrived, blanketing the purple peaks of the Odana Mountains with a rosy hue. The WynSprigns submissively gathered alongside the mountain to enter the Purple Hall mine in their expected uniform order. Then, the line that they had formed going up the hill slowed. The WynSprign slaves stood silent, staring off into nothingness, as usual. Their bodies and minds had been beaten and made weary. Emptied shells. But this morning was different. There was a glint of hope after the latest news reached the encampment, and they warily watched their guard.

Nizen anxiously counted down the row of slaves outside the mine. His thick muscled calves thudded at his slow gait and his red cape lay flat against his broad back. It seemed he took great effort in making sure not to upset an already outraged Grude. Such a large mass of Mysra warriors had left for the WynSprign village that there were not enough available to assist in controlling the slave population. He had an air of determination about him that he was prepared to be harder and punish more severely to keep them all under control.

The line was lengthy, and with only Nizen to conduct them, the work took longer. The ends of the line hummed as whispers flitted back and forth, out of his earshot.

"They made it," Lika whispered with a cocked head to her trainee, Trilla, who stood behind her in line. Lika shot a quick glance back, her round face framed by her tight brown bonnet. Trilla was new to the Purple Halls, her former work had been to assist Cantata, cleaning the castle, and helping in the kitchen on occasion. Despite Cantata's grumbling about losing her servant, the rotation was deemed *very necessary* by Grude, under the heavy need for mining. He hadn't spared a soul in his endeavors.

That was likely why they paired the two. Lika worked in the mine, but also had laundering duties, which she preferred—scrubbing away the evils of this place of slavery. When younger, she had also once served in the castle long ago. She had been head laundress and was charged to arrange clothing for their royal highnesses, for both daily and formal attire.

Trilla did not want to end up like Lika, sentenced to a life of mine work. But due to the increased demand for trillium, she was now stationed to work there, and she was most displeased that she now had to do this lowly work. Cantata would not be happy fetching her own linens and food, and Trilla could not imagine what would become of the work of cleaning, for it never ceased. Now, when Trilla returned to her cleaning duties, *if* she returned to them, her work would be daunting, dust having accumulated in her absence.

"Who?" Trilla whispered, continuing the conversation. She looked straight ahead toward Lika.

"The lost slaves," Lika whispered excitedly. "It seems that the Mysra guards cannot find them. They couldn't find Treva or Anah before, either, and *now* it's said that these six others have gone." She quivered slightly with excitement, her bonnet jiggling.

Trilla swiped stray hair from her brow. *What a waste of my air in even asking, but . . .* She held a smart smile on her face and asked, "Where do you think they've gone?"

Lika was about to answer but paused to wait for Nizen to pass them by. Talking wasn't allowed.

"And 73! 74! 75! . . ." Nizen's thick voice counted off, passing them. His small assistant, Grimle, walked next to him with a paper in his hand. Their steps and his counting faded down the line.

"Who knows?" Lika leaned back and continued to whisper: "The point is, they're not here." Her cheeks flushed pink.

"So, what are you suggesting?" whispered Miken, a tall and large-built slave who stood in front of Lika. He was looking over his shoulder at them, holding his body forward as Nizen expected.

"What I'm suggesting"—Lika puffed in some annoyance—"is that since the Mysra are fewer, we'd have a better chance to outsmart or overrun this place. We could probably free ourselves." A smile grew and raised her round cheeks. "They haven't been able to track them down yet."

Miken loosed a hum: "I wouldn't have to haul tons of trillium any longer, or be the one what takes a beatin' from Nizen's tirades." Miken moved to crack his massive back.

Gesturing to Miken's tunic, Lika explained to Trilla, "That one gets the worst of it—it's rare he wears a tunic without bloodstains." She went on to tell that some days he was beaten horribly, that Nizen used him as a mere object upon which to take out his anger. He was the largest WynSprign and could handle the beating and still be forced to work the next day.

Lika breathed deeply and told Trilla, "After Grude rails at Nizen any given day—we hear of it through the grapevine—later that night Nizen beats Miken so violently we have more than once thought he was going to die." Trilla knew from the sufferings of the castle slaves that here, too, the hushed sounds of night were filled with soft whimpers and cries from slaves inside their huts; fearful of the horrible sounds of approaching death. "One whole night we didn't know if he had lived or died," Lika said.

Miken over heard her and whispered back, "I wished that I had died . . ."

"OKAY! EVERYONE IN!" Nizen belted from the mine entrance. The slaves straightened and walked on without delay. Guilt and embarrassment rested on Nizen's shoulders. He might as well have freed the missing slaves himself. He was determined to change the way he handled the guard duties.

"Grimel"—Nizen barked and looked down at his assistant. He then straightened and made sure his red cape lay elegantly on his shoulders. Wicked but always dressed to perfection, Nizen eyed the passing slaves entering the mine. "Tonight, we're to enforce stricter rules." His was voice a low grumble to Grimel to avoid eager ears. "There will be no more Mysra guards hanging round the fire pits at night." He leaned towards Grimel—"I expect they will *actually* patrol, moving forward." His neck muscles pulsed. "I'm not above punishing *them* with thrashes, either."

Grimel leaned his head closer to Nizen to hear, nodded, and scribbled notes hurriedly.

Nizen continued: "If any more go missing, you *and* I will be to blame." He paused, pondering the severity of the punishment. "The last thing I need is for Grude to be even more upset with me. He'd see us both hanged, wriggling like worms on a fisher's line." Nizen's eyes widened as he raised his hand to the base of his throat.

The last of the WynSprigns hurried into the mine. A waiting guard quickly entered behind them. There would be far fewer guards patrolling the mine and the WynSprign slave encampment now, so the guards had to be strategically placed and their movements had to be coordinated carefully. The guards at the tower must be rotated in a timely fashion, the trenches surrounding the outskirts of the encampment, monitored. Orchestrating these measures had created anxiety for Nizen.

Grimel quickly scribed Nizen's thoughts, the inked pen in his hand scratching wildly. They walked down from the hill to the adjacent WynSprign camp, now quiet and empty.

Seeing him still making notes, Nizen rolled his eyes and turned to walk toward the castle. *Must he notate EVERYTHING?* Nizen wondered in agitation. Perhaps his temper was testy because he was famished. He was due for his morning meal at the castle—which normally would have been delivered, but due to the shortage of slaves, he found himself having to walk to fetch it himself. Yet another annoyance.

"We'll discuss this later—I need to eat." He planted a foot to march on. Grimel nodded and turned away in another direction.

But both stopped, mid-step.

A sweet tune carried in the dusty breeze toward them. An old singing WynSprign woman strolled toward the mine, passing them. No. Not WynSprign—only in appearance. Nizen's eyes widened. He recognized her— they both did. Every Mysra knew *her*.

The Holy mother!

That instant, their hearts hammered.

After a hundred years of running a mine with the same WynSprigns, he knew them all and she, that WynSprign, was *not* one of them.

"What's she doing here?" Grimel whispered to no one.

But, Nizen responded as equally quiet, "Whatever she wants."

The old women peered at the Mysra guards. The very look sent prickles to their skin. A slight smile curved on her lips. She moved toward them and began to speak. Their hearts stilled at the sound of her captivating voice—at the depth of her ancient, knowing gaze.

"If you ask me," she said, her voice a breeze that warned that if she was confronted, she promised calamity in her wake. "Cantata should be the one to make you your meal."

The hearts of the two Mysra pounded at her seemingly innocuous sound.

Closer. Closer she ambled. "She's a fine cook, a WynSprign of many talents," she added. Just a handbreadth away, she suddenly ripped her knowing eyes from them, and turned to walk on. Swirling dust obscured her fading WynSprign form.

It was a cryptic message. The head guard gawked at her, still feeling confusion and wonderment.

Blinking at this oddity, this surprise visitation from *her*, and the message to have Cantata make his meal, Nizen returned to the present.

"Hey, back into the mine!" he barked at the stilled Grimel, who jumped at his command.

Nizen knew they needed to be productive—especially in front of *her*. He hoped he had favor in her eyes. Perhaps that's why she wanted Cantata to make him a meal? It was an odd thought.

Nizen glared at his head guard now striding away. "Endless disorganization!" he hissed loud enough for her to hear – or so he hoped.

He turned back toward his destination and refocused his attention on food. *So, Cantata can cook—should cook?* He now walked quickly and murmured, "I guess our Cantata is a WynSprign of many talents. And the slaves in the castle *are* fewer . . ." Nizen smiled—a horrid sight. *She is not a slave, but perhaps Grude can persuade her to assist—to maximize everyone's efforts. Especially if I tell him our Fray Mother Jaspia came here and said so herself . . .*

Chapter Fifty-One

Lanico was still sore as he stretched where they'd stopped to give the horses time to relax. "Oh . . . how I despise sleeping on the ground." He twisted and cracked his aching back, annoyed at the knowledge that his long silver hair was messy, too. He had forgotten a brush. He growled low.

Treva sat up on the ground next to him, looking at him with great amusement. "You're *still* sore from last night?" She had a slightly surprised smile. "It's the afternoon, Lan."

He twisted and grumbled.

Treva couldn't help herself—she openly laughed at his seriousness and messiness. She, however, was most comfortable in her leggings and a small tunic, not the oversized one Greta had lent her for sleeping in. She was glad she had decided against wearing her metal armor and had opted for a lighter leather version. It was far too hot for the metal wear and she feared it would put unnecessary weight on the horses for this long journey.

"Well, Treva, need I remind you I'm many years older than you?" He flashed her a crooked smile and ceased his dramatic stretching routine.

"Well"—Treva turned quickly to take a drink from her canteen—"I happened to enjoy last night, lying under the stars and the moon. Bathing in their glow." She sighed. "Enjoying more of you." Treva looked at Lanico with a playful gaze and a lazy smile.

He smiled dreamily for a moment but then suddenly stiffened and cleared his throat, remembering to stay focused. *Nothing happened, but it's nice to dream. The ballroom, the emerald dress. Oh fires . . . the song.* The dreams of last night still dancing in his mind. He looked out over the horizon.

Treva smiled at this reaction. *He's so proper and fancy . . . Adorable— like a fancy white cat with crystal blue eyes.* Every bit as vicious, but proper, and at times, snuggly.

"It shouldn't be long before we get to Gray Rock. It normally wouldn't take this long, but I wanted to avoid Mysra forces by walking out, further around . . . They've likely passed us by now." He took a drink and gulped hard.

"It's better that we approach them from behind, anyway. We just need to arrive shortly after they do, reinforcements taking up the rear." He took another drink. "It's possible waking up late worked to our benefit."

She nodded in agreement. Her mouth was too full from her own swig of water to answer.

"Because they are likely undertrained—based on your assessment—" he said, "we could easily wipe out at least a dozen, together." His eyes flashed meeting hers.

A gritty smile spread across her lovely hard face. *Together*. She took out their remaining rations from Greta's home: hard cheese, bread, vegetables, and a special gift-meat jerky. Greta didn't favor them eating animals, so this addition had been a pleasant surprise earlier. She handed him his portion. Together they sat eating as the sun crept high in the sky. They'd make it to Gray Rock before nightfall, as long as they avoided lingering for too long.

Lanico wasn't fond of sitting on the ground. He didn't enjoy the feeling of direct sunlight, or the grit of grass and dirt beneath him. Sure, he had been a seasoned General trained for rough living in the wilds, but there were some things of nature that still picked him-even if his mother was Fray Greta and even if he had lived in Great Mist all those years.

He exhaled sharply and squinted over at Treva, who wore a carefree smile as she leaned back with her eyes closed, facing the sun. She was radiant, glowing under the bright light. Feeling his gaze, she opened her eyes slightly and shifted her focus over to him.

"You know Lanico, I can't remember feeling this great under the sun in a very long time." She sat up to take another bite of her rations, chewing and swallowing hard. "I never really got a chance to see the sun while a slave. We'd enter the mines as the sun was coming up, and then leave the mines as the sun was going down. I *love* to feel its golden glow covering me." She inhaled sharply. Her cinnamon voice hummed, "a golden blanket." She leaned back again on her hands and resumed smiling up at the sky.

Lanico hadn't thought much about that, what she'd had to endure as a slave. He felt guilty for grumbling privately about his own discomfort in this moment. Touched by her happiness, he made the decision to enjoy it with her, and not complain.

Once they finished their adequate meal, they mounted the rested horses, and their sheathed swords bounced at their sides as they rode on the uneven grassy ground. Though both she and Lanico were well versed in a large assortment of weaponry, she had pilfered from Greta's weapon trove and had turned herself into a walking armory. But, Treva's long sword sheath was not properly fastened to her belt and it bounced more than Lanico's.

As they reached the summit of one of the several large, grassy hills, they were alerted to the unexpected sight of several Mysra on foot, just ahead where the hill plateaued. They were heading in the same direction as the couple, probably to join the Mysra forces. One, as if smelling them near, whirled his head around and locked his eyes on the pair.

There was no mistaking the discovery, as there was nowhere to hide. Lanico and Treva pulled the reins and heard distant battle shouts erupting from the Mysra. They advanced and came close enough that they could be seen drinking back their trillium crystals and drawing their weapons. Their large bodies looked larger by the second as Treva and Lanico closed the distance between them. In a flash, the pair had unsheathed their swords, glad to be on horseback.

"YAAAAH!" Treva yelled, her strong voice and fierce glare blasting out from her small form.

In a burst, they stormed-off.

The horses bolted to a swift gallop as dust rose high in the air, the leather satchels and bundles slapping against their sides, the animals grunting as they charged. Treva dug her feet into the stirrups and squeezed her thighs tightly around the horse's warm sides. The Mysra's were actually charging toward them, and wielding knives! Trillium made them irrational, foolish.

As they closed in, both Treva and Lanico made flashing low swipes with their swords, taking advantage of the horses' height and magnificent speed. They swung deeply, cutting the two Mysra that ran in between them. The Mysra warriors both cried out, and the remaining Mysra, in the middle, understood his low chances of survival and ran off.

"I'll get him!" Treva breathed, eyes focused.

Lanico leapt off his horse and into battle with the gravely injured warriors.

Treva rode off after the remaining Mysra, her faithful falchion still at the ready, warm blood dripping down from the blade into the palm that grasped the hilt. She raised herself from the saddle to secure her footing on the galloping horse's back and, once near, launched her tiny frame and tackled the running Mysra, the force sending them both to the ground in a rolling tumble, her emerald hair and a sheathed long sword flaring outward—losing it. She was nimble and quickly rebounded to a position crouching on top of the warrior's broad back. Instantly, her hands ran over her side, noting the first missing pummel. So, in a flash, she swiftly held her palmed falchion sword at the base of his neck, the tip of the blade digging into his skin, just barely.

The Mysra panted hard enough to bend the stalks of grass at his face. Treva's own body rose and fell with his breathing and her own.

"Where have you come from?" she asked in a thick growl. The Mysra only gulped. She slid her sword down, against the side of his neck. The Mysra flinched at the sharp cut, and warm blood began trickling, feeding the parched ground.

"O—Odana," he managed, straining his eyes to look at up at her.

"Where are you headed?" she demanded, her expression wild and unpredictable.

The Mysra glanced over to where Lanico was just about to slaughter the remaining fellow warrior. In the space between them, Lanico brandished his long sword and in one mighty swoop pierced the Mysra's chest. Treva's captive moaned in anguish at that sight. Lanico wiped the sword on the trunk of the lifeless body and quickly sheathed his sword.

"SPEAK!" Treva demanded, jolting her captive's attention back to her.

"I—I'm to join the Mysra troops," he replied. His fear was now delightfully palpable to her.

Treva stood, releasing him, her sword still drawn. She knew well that he was no match for her skills, even with his hulking size. She had once been known as "The Mysra Slayer," for Odan's sake. Still holding her sword steady, she dusted herself off as he continued to lie on the ground. She backed away slightly, contemplating whether to allow him to live. Normally, in the past, she hadn't been one to let them live.

After an analyzing breath, she grumbled slowly, "You may go."

He looked dubious but slowly rocked himself to sit up and then, with effort, stood.

Treva rolled her eyes at his feeble attempts. "Pshh, some warrior. Pathetic."

From his full height, the Mysra could just make out his companions' dead bodies lying like boulders in the small distance. He gulped and his shoulders slumped.

With stealth, she freed one of her daggers from her leather vambrace, just in case he made a sudden move toward her. She preferred both hands holding blades. "What do you call yourself, Mysra?" Treva asked with a gaping scowl and razor stare.

"Merkum," he responded quietly.

"Head back to the Odana Kingdom, Merkum!" Treva ordered, pointing her steady falchion at him, looking at him down the length of the blade.

Lanico stood panting nearby, staring somberly at this exchange.

The warrior dusted himself off and dared to glare at both Treva and Lanico.

"GO!" Treva barked, still holding both of her weapons steady. "Trust me, Mysra, it is taking *EVERY* effort for me to not kill you!" Treva trembled as she shouted in a thick voice. It was the truth. She desperately wanted to swipe her blade through his thick neck and drain the warmth from inside it—she trembled at her effort to resist, biting her lower lip.

The Mysra started in surprise, then deliberately turned and walked slowly toward the Odana, keeping his gaze on them. Treva shouted as he walked, "If I see you heading north, I *will* kill you, Merkum! I will know! I will hunt you! And I will kill you!" Her face quivered as she held back the intense desire to kill.

The Mysra ended the stare down. Defeated, he turned and walked due west. Even if he lied and rerouted himself toward the Great Mist, since they were on horseback, they'd still beat him to the battle. He wouldn't be able to alert his comrades in time.

"Consider yourself most lucky, Mysra!" Lanico yelled out, moving toward Treva. He was a bit surprised that she managed to let him live.

Treva looked down at the grass, shaken. There would be plenty of death soon enough. She lowered herself to grab - and this time - properly sheath the long sword that had fallen from her side in the collision. She replaced the dagger she had housed in her vambrace. Lanico watched as the Mysra cautiously passed, still heading west, to Odana.

Once satisfied with the distance, Lanico then stared at Treva and whistled high for the grazing horses. The mounts came bounding back. "C'mon!" he called out to her and he mounted his own horse. Treva nodded and stopped staring at the ground, at last sheathing her falchion. Without looking in his direction, she reached out to her horse just at the moment he pranced up to her, and in that instant, she pulled herself onto him as he continued to gallop. There was no pause for either of them.

Lanico was stunned—another amazing horse-riding trick. But he could see Treva's expression, flat and unimpressed with herself. *She really wanted to kill Merkum.*

Chapter Fifty-Two

Tunia heaved open the heavy wooden door to the castle kitchen and walked gingerly to the washing trough, her feet aware of every memorized dent and dip in the floor. She set her bundle down and began her daily routine alone—there was no Mysra guard to escort her in, not after all these years of service.

It was hot outside, but the cold bare countertops breathed life into her twisted hands as she leaned onto them. Cool relief. She sighed deeply. She had been most fortunate to work in the castle, without the Mysra eyes on her that the mining slaves constantly suffered. Because she had been the head cook, she was a staple in the kitchen. The others that bumbled in and out throughout the day at other odd kitchen jobs, well, they had been scarce. It seemed these days everyone was scarce. Some guards had gone off to fight or the castle slaves to replace the slaves in the mines. The remaining guards were being worked harder.

Perhaps we can take advantage of this situation and allow time enough for more, for ALL slaves to make their escape. She could encourage Nizen to drink yellow-berry wine. *He deserves it.* At this, she stepped on the loose, creaky floor plank beneath her foot, and the familiar spring of it flattened under her weight. She looked quickly to ensure no one was watching, then removed her foot from the plank, which lifted slightly. She bent down and dug her fingertips into the board's raised wooden lip and pulled up. The bones in her hands cracked and the board creaked, the rough wooden edges scraping her nails and fingertips. She grimaced, holding back a growl. Then the board gave suddenly and sent her falling back slightly onto her bottom.

"Ooo," she grumbled, massaging her lower back and forgetting a moment about her arthritic hands.

Her eyes quickly found the prize beneath. There. She could see her precious bottle lying there still—the sleepheather oil, still enough left to deliver a few powerful dosages. It was a beautiful sight indeed. She stared at the glass bottle dreamily. The thick silver-gray liquid was potent and almost tasteless— when combined with other liquids, the color diluted wonderfully.

Suddenly she heard voices, bit her lip, and hastily replaced the floor plank and set her stool on top of it. She stood abruptly and settled on the stool. Under her weight, the plank settled in its rightful place. She needed the right moment and to figure out a way to convince Nizen that he deserved a break, that it was acceptable to end his day with a harmless glass of yellowberry wine. She glanced around the big, empty stone kitchen. A small barrel of wine sat silent, *waiting* to be tampered with. The other larger, barrels had been all used up in the large celebration. She just had to find the right time to empty the contents of her bottle into the barrel.

It had been hours later. Tunia knew merely from the sight of her water-wrinkled hands that her shift would end soon. It would be dinner time and another round of workers would be sent to take her place. She began to put away dish rags and the usual herbs and spices from the latest meal. It had been the same, it seemed, forever. It was lucky that Grude thoroughly enjoyed her meals and had kept her in this kitchen all these years. She cared for it—it was *her* kitchen.

It would be slow for several days with only Grude and a few others to serve. Tunia enjoyed the quiet in this moment. She allowed her mind to wander, to reflect on the days under King Oetam's rule. He would stroke his white-red beard after a carefully prepared feast and delight at his even larger protruding belly.

Tunia smiled to herself at this memory. She had enjoyed serving him. When she prepared a meal for King Oetam, she often considered how that particular meal was nourishing and energizing him to rule over his beloved Odana. There was a sense of pride in a purpose as large as that.

As she began to think of him, she lowered herself from the stool and worked to pry the board from its spot and retrieve the bottle. The cool glass shone in her hands, and the gray sleepheather rolled slowly in its vessel. She stood in thought, remembering the day he had died. It was the siege. The sudden, horrific attack. The look on his face was forever etched in her mind. She watched his eyes and knew the moment his soul left his body.

The King had been seated at the large dining table. It wasn't breakfast, which was still several hours away. Still, he was up. He enjoyed his eggs mixed and cooked in the way only *she* made them.

Tunia felt herself begin to tighten at recalling that day when three castle sentries stormed into the kitchen—her kitchen—with the King. They were looking for a quick place to keep him safe until they could clear out the Mysra invaders. *For who would ever think to look for him in here?* The low horn blew for the first time and the hair on her arms prickled. She had only heard it for rare military trainings before that.

Her fingers pulled the cork free.

It was for his immediate safety, until things were under control, they had explained. The kitchen was close to the dining room, and the enemy wouldn't guess the King would be hidden there.

Then came the loud *SMACK!* from the door banging back against the wall, a sound she still heard every time someone hurried in to her kitchen.

When the guards rushed in, Tunia loosed a loud gasp.

The King was panting at the great strides he had made to get there. He wiped at his brow. The sentries separated; two running outside to guard, and the other to stay in the kitchen as a last form of defense for the King.

Her throat knotted as she remembered his face those final moments. While sitting in absolute silence, they looked at one another with panicked and disoriented gazes. They listened to the sounds of screaming outside, and even from just outside, in the hall. Then, growing in sharpness, the sounds of swords clashing loudly just outside the kitchen. Odana sentries were fighting, spending their very lives to protect the King at every cost.

She poured the gray syrup into the small waiting wine barrel. A few drops had been enough to set all the Mysra slumbering a few nights before.

Suddenly, the remaining sentry had dutifully left the kitchen to go to their aid. But returning to the kitchen moments later, instead . . . was Grude.

Her heart pounded violently, even now, in this moment, she felt it.

The King had leaned slowly from the stool, looking at Grude. *The look on the King's face.* He was done. That look of abandonment. For he knew in that instant, it was over.

With a silver flash, Grude had delivered a smooth strike through the King's heart. Fast. So fast, Tunia didn't know if she was actually *seeing* it. The

King, her beloved King—his lifeless body thudded onto the wooden kitchen floor. His eyes remained on hers. He just crumpled there, his arms and legs giving no response to the fall.

Grude said not a word. He merely gave Tunia a cold smile and stormed out. His vengeance for the King's denial of the trillium he so craved, was now delivered.

Tunia had loosed a piercing scream and rushed over to the King's lifeless body. She threw herself on the cold stone floor and jerked his collar to rouse him. Blood spewed crimson from his shirt, pouring out. But no matter her attempts to revive him; she knew he was gone. His lifeless eyes stared into eternity with unwavering focus. There was no one to come to his aid, and even if there were, he was already gone.

In this moment of quiet memory in the kitchen, Tunia felt rage building. She smacked the bottom of the bottle, an attempt to empty the last of the contents into the waiting barrel. *Damn, it's so thick and slow.*

The door of the kitchen flew to *SMACK!* against the stone wall behind it. The sound made Tunia spill viscid drops of the potion.

Oh fires!

Tunia's eyes flicked up to Nizen as he stormed in.

"I'm hungry, I want"—the guard inhaled and stopped short. His focus was now on her hands where she stood. On the wine barrel. On the hole. On the liquid dribbling out.

Tunia was balancing on her stool, still holding the glass bottle. She looked *guilty*, and it was a look he had never seen her wear.

"*You!*" He stomped closer to her, his steps rattling the hanging pots and pans. "What is that?!" His voice was low. "What *are* you doing to the wine?" His eyes glared red in mounting fury.

Tunia tried to quickly squirrel away the bottle in her skirts.

"No. Give me that!" he growled, grabbing her fleshy arm hard. He squeezed and she winced in pain.

He'll crack my bone! And it wasn't the first time he had hurt her.

He raised her tightly squeezed arm and squinted at the revelation—a glass bottle containing syrupy silver liquid. He grabbed it from her hand, lifting the bottle closer to his squinting eyes for further examination. He refused to wear spectacles and look like a weakling.

"Sleepheather oil," he read from the faded yellowed label. He paused, thinking and then realizing. "*SLEEPHEATHER OIL!*" He railed, turning to the large barrel. Visible traces of the gray liquid oozed around a small opening at the top. His eyes widened at the revelation.

Tunia interjected feebly, "It's—It's medicinal. I—I use this to sleep." Nizen stood looking gravely at her. It was possible he'd slam his fist against her head, but it was more likely he was going to kill her. But she continued. "I—I thought it would be helpful for everyone to get rest since they've all been working so hard." Tunia stumbled over her words.

She could see in his reaction that he didn't believe her. Understanding that she was out of options, understanding she wanted to avoid a public thrashing and hanging like punished mining slaves, she decided to end it. End the years of joylessness, the never-ending moments of despair. She'd reunite with her beloved King and loved ones. Her eyes quickly welled with tears.

She snatched the glass bottle back from Nizen's grip. Throwing her head back, she gulped the dense liquid, but only a few thick droplets left. It was tasteless in her mouth. He grabbed it back. But it was too late. She swallowed hard against the thickness, forcing her throat to squeeze it down. Its power struck. That instant, in a flash, she entered an eternal slumber. Her skirts billowed around her in a soft blur of blue as her body fell from her stepping-stool. She landed on her familiar wood floor with a heavy thud.

Nizen stood still with his hand out, holding the bottle. Anger brewed from within, a blazing furnace in his gut. He wouldn't leash it. No. He squeezed his fingers into rolled fists as a growing heat surged to his face. That moment he realized this dead slave was responsible for the heavy slumber that had plagued his warriors and fellow guards. The heavy slumber had allowed *six* precious slaves to escape. She had been the culprit all along! *That lowly bitch!*

The sleep that caused Grude to degrade and to humiliate me—to put me next on his butchering list! He had to make an example of this—this . . . deceitfulness. She was lucky to have ended herself. He would have skinned her alive in front of everyone. He'd find a way to make her an example, meant to show the slaves what consequences look like. This disobedience would stop. *Now.* Too much had been at risk around here these days.

He had the perfect ammunition to drive home the severity of her betrayal and raise fear about the punishment of such treachery.

He dropped the bottle, which thudded and slid across the floor. The glass remained intact, thick syrup still coating the inside.

His dark red cape brushed the floor as he squatted and scooped up Tunia's stout body with ease. Seething anger pulsed through his veins and blurred his vision even more. He turned from the kitchen and stumbled through the open doorway and into the hall outside. Tunia's lifeless limbs and head hung and swayed at his strides. His heart pounded against her corpse, seemingly weightless in his muscle-wrapped arms.

He walked down and around the spiral mountain slope to the base of the castle. As he approached the castle slave encampment carrying Tunia, gasps and shrieks erupted in their horror. Some ran, and others disappeared into dilapidated huts at the approaching horror.

Nizen held a scowl as his eyes darted around, contemplating where to drop her body. Dizzy from hunger and rage, he tumbled Tunia to the ground. He didn't bother to fix her tangled blue skirts or the awkward position of her body. She was nothing more than a pile of refuse to him—he forgot her that very instant.

He stood erect to yell for anyone within earshot. "THIS!" he pointed, "SEE THIS! THIS IS WHAT HAPPENS WHEN YOU BETRAY!" Thick spit flew at his forced words: "LEARN FROM THIS-THIS CORPSE!" His glare took in several random, paled faces. "I WILL *ALWAYS* FIND OUT IF THERE IS PLOTTING!" He caught the fleeting gaze of a horrified male slave. "YOU . . . take this body to the slave cemetery and"—he threw his arms up—"deal with it." The slave nodded with a gaping mouth.

Nizen grunted. He still needed to eat. He turned from them and paced the incline back to the castle.

He thrust open the kitchen door, smacking it against the wall, and Cantata jumped. She stood in the kitchen holding a hand over her chest. She had hoped to find Tunia in here – anyone one in here. But when she found the kitchen slave absent, she had been sneaking around for something to eat. Trilla *had* been ordered to the mines after all. Her heart now raced at the menacing Nizen. The kitchen grew warmer in an instant as boiling anger radiated from his body.

His eyes widened in recognition. Trying, but not succeeding, to damper his anger, he spoke to her in a slightly lightened growl: "You're Cantata, the singer . . ." His red eyes glared down at her.

Death. His eyes looked like death to her. Her mouth hung open and she gave a silent nod.

"I understand that you also assist in the kitchen," he said. That had been truly only once, but sensing his rage, she gave more silent nodding. "Good!" he breathed. "You're to take Tunia's place in the kitchen—for now." He stared threateningly at her. The next round of kitchen slaves weren't due for a small while yet.

She knew no matter how popular she was, he'd rip her to shreds at a hint of her refusal. Nizen wasn't one to cross. She might have been able to mold Grude a little, but not this hated guard. She again nodded silently, her wiry hair swaying in the air. She'd question the details later, and correct the misapprehension that she was a slave, but that would be at a time when she was not fearful of losing her life. She'd tell Grude—or perhaps show Grude—her dormant culinary skills. *Perhaps I could get paid even more—*

"HERE!"

She jumped again.

He inhaled sharply. "Fix me lunch." He stifled the shouting in the back of his throat with every word the came from his mouth. "I want what Tunia served from yesterday. You can find what's left over, in there." He pointed a commandingly to the icebox in the corner.

"When you're done, I'll be in my tent near the Purple Hall." And without a further word, he turned and marched out. The door smacked open again and his red cape whipped from the draft as he turned the corner.

Cantata stood quivering in silence. Then she collected her breath, patted down the sides of her head, and wiped her hands against her dress. She looked around. *Lunch. Lunch. Lunch.* The icebox, right. Her eyes landed on a forgotten glass bottle. She bent to pick it up. "Sleephea—"*Sleepheather oil!* She inhaled and slapped her hand over her mouth. This was a rare find indeed. A potentially useful poison. She licked her thin lips.

"Mmm . . . where can I put you?" she muttered under her hand. Her dark eyes went to the small wooden barrel that held yellowberry wine, a drizzle of gray liquid running down the side. *Tunia was caught trying to poison the Mysra,* she gathered. *All the more reason to stash this bottle away.* "Never know when I may need you," she whispered, tucking it away in a cupboard behind the royal stemware and crystal. It was invisible so far back and this was the only cupboard she was familiar with, for now.

Nizen had been so overcome with rage, he'd forgotten about this detail, for the time being. She could sweeten up to him a bit, gain his trust. If he asked, she'd simply say that she threw it away. He'd believe *her*. She was Cantata, the most trusted and talented WynSprign.

A sly full smirk curved across her ivory face. She turned on her heel and danced to the icebox to fetch Nizen some lunch.

A song fluted from her lips.

Chapter Fifty-Three

Dust swirled in the air as the Mysra camp stirred. It seemed dawn had arrived in her purple hue a bit too soon, and before long the beautiful shades of purple, pink, and orange would give way to the white-hot, dry Yellow Vast. Neen was determined to get his troops out quickly. He figured they didn't need to be well rested or prepared for the minor task ahead of them, and their rider had probably reached Grude by now to alert him of their location. Taking the WynSprigns would be simple enough. They weren't used to fighting and his warriors were. Plus, he had many small barrels of trillium in tow.

The day before they had safely arrived at the brook. The horses had their share of water, and the Mysra enjoyed more fish. The stench from the dead hags had reduced since his last visit—it seemed all was going as planned. They were rested well enough, fed, and ready for the siege.

Neen raised his arms in the air as he called the charge: "DON'T DELAY! WE WILL BE MOVING OUT IN MOMENTS TO CLAIM OUR NEW SPRIGNS!"

Other Mysra warriors shouted and cheered in great anticipation. They were ready for this. They were determined to make Grude happy and to enjoy their trillium reward and the plunder.

~

The sun was up, and the Yellow Vast was bright in the unfiltered light. The land was stable, as if sleeping—with no hint of disturbance, no birds or other animals stirring about. Freck was starting to wonder if the Mysra were *actually* going to come. He was more than ready to defend his fellow WynSprigns. He was made for this, having famed ancestors whose warrior blood ran thick through his veins. He was ashamed to admit that he almost looked forward to the challenge—learning, testing the extent of his warrior training in the real-life scenario. The downfall, however, was having the others succumb to battle injury, or even death. Ultimately, he didn't want the impending battle.

Thinking over the possible realities of a battle, he looked back at Tarn and Jain. They were relaxing, munching on the wild berries they'd found earlier, peaceful and unaware. He looked over to his other side, where Stefin was lying on his stomach, holding his chin in his hands and staring out into the bright wilderness. Freck was glad to see him quiet for once and not rambling on as he usually did.

Freck returned his hunter's gaze out to the Yellow Vast. Then he spotted something . . .

His now-familiar view had changed. Far off in the distance a thin black line skimmed the horizon, and tan plumes of what he imaged was dust lingered over it. His heart stopped. He focused. Yes. Something was coming, *fast*.

"Hey—HEY! You guys, look!" He whirled to look back at Tarn and Jain, and then over at Stefin. "You see that? there on the horizon"—he pointed to the thin dust cloud in the far-off landscape. His voice held slightly below panic.

The three stood to peer in the direction he pointed and they, too, saw the dust cloud grow over the movement beneath it.

"You see it?!"

A flash of curses erupted behind him. "Yes—YES!" Stefin shouted. "I see it too!" He paused. "You think this is it? Should we leave now?" His previously calm gaze had grown wild.

Freck remained steady. He took a deep breath. He needed to be sure there was a reason for alarm. "Let me see just a bit more," he mumbled, squinting. "I just want to make sure before we go running and getting everyone ready for battle." He focused on the horizon, licking his thin lips. Sweat beaded on his brow.

Stefin narrowed his gaze at Freck, waiting anxiously for his response. He was fidgeting with the antler bit in his pocket—a normal reaction from him.

It had only been seconds when suddenly a long trailing line of riders could just be seen, still far off, but enough to show the line curved over the horizon. A thin, dark line of death. It was hard to tell at this distance, but they looked large and there were many of them—*Oh fires, perhaps a hundred!* Any movement in the Yellow Vast, they knew from their short time there, was rare. This was definite cause for alarm.

"Yes! We must move!" Freck yelled as a pungent kick of reality brought him to the present. "MOVE! MOVE! Leave our things—it won't matter if they see 'em. With our foot traffic, they'd be able to track us into the village anyway! We need our hunting bows and arrows! Take them up!"

In swift movements they responded to his orders. The young hunters turned, grabbing their quivers and bows, and bolted for the Great Mist realm. Adrenaline coursing through them, they ran faster than they ever had before, whizzing past the trees. The sparse boughs slapped their faces as they raced haphazardly through the dense brush, hardly noticing as low-lying brush whipped at their charging legs.

~

The Great Mist warriors had gathered at Fenner's house with their weapons, to train where the trees were loftier. In the midst of morning training, they stopped at the sound of the approaching runners, and at the head of them, Freck wasted no time shouting his announcement: "THEY'VE COME!"

Heads whirled in his direction. The new warriors froze in unfamiliar alarm, their weapons lowered. Staring. Blinking.

"It's time! They've come!" Freck insisted. "We spotted them on the horizon!" He panted, searching for air, trying to stir them to action.

"They're probably much closer by now!" Stefin contributed, panting at Freck's side.

Warriors looked around in disbelief, like stunned deer.

Freck's mouth gaped at them. "Did you hear me? Get going to your posts! *NOW!*"

They scrambled as they awoke to his leadership.

Hearing the shouting, Fenner stumbled out from Lanico's home. "They've come?" he asked, peering through his thick eyebrows and finding Freck.

"Yes. We spotted them on the horizon." Freck swallowed and staggered toward him, grabbing at his aching side. His breathing was ragged.

"Okay." Fenner patted Freck on the shoulder. "Good work, boy," he said quietly. "You make me proud. Your efforts are saving us." All at once he forgave, forgot that Freck had made him go into the cage at Trayvor's charge.

Freck, however, had not forgotten. A stone grew in his throat as he remembered that crime.

Fenner smiled briefly and glanced up at the surrounding organized chaos. He was pleased that Freck had the warriors on the move, grabbing their swords and staffs. Hunters had all readied their bows and arrows.

The old warrior, the Chief grimaced at Freck. "Go to your post, boy." Those might be the last words spoken between them. His experience and wisdom told him that not all would make it through this alive. He pursed his thin lips and pressed on to gather his own weapons. He had promised to protect. He would honor his word, his promise.

The brown plumes of traveling dust swirled high, feathering into the blue noon atmosphere. The large Mysra army traveled hard against the land, kicking-up a dirty curtain that rose many feet. It was a signal, a beacon for searching WynSprign eyes, and it extended for miles. For this reason, it was a blessing that rain hadn't come upon the land in days.

~

The air was cooler the instant Neen crossed the tree line. The feeling was familiar. "Leave the supply wagons here with the horses!" he belted in a booming voice, the dark shade within almost hiding his gray face. "We will carry the cages into the woods. It'll be easier to throw the captured ones in there, closer to the village—less struggling over the walk if they're caged at the go."

He sneered at their prospects. He'd made it. Horse's Clearing was *aching* to be breached and the hidden village . . . easy.

The Mysra warriors on horseback dismounted, and the unfortunate low-ranking grunts slowed their march to a stop just behind them, slumping in exhaustion. Horses were tied to trees before the Mysra entered the mysterious shade of the forest, and they unpacked their knives, strapped on their belts and sheaths, and packed their pouches. In a jagged unison, a tradition kept without command, they tilted back their heads to ingest the purple crystals. The charge of it immediately tingled in their fingertips and send an itching crawl up their limbs as the trillium coursed through their blood. Sweet grit lingered and abraded the tips of their tongues. They couldn't wait to ingest more later.

Feeling the glorious surge, Neen blasted, "WE READY?" Thick purple-tinged saliva bubbled at the corners of his mouth, his red-rimmed eyes glaring savagely. "WE READY TO TAKE BACK OUR SLAVES?"

His troops shouted their own rallying cries and bang their fists against their chests. He began to pace among his troops. He looked at them, eye-to-eye, glaring wildly, and he breathed hard. "REMEMBER! WE ARE TO DENY OURSELVES KILLS! WE NEED THEM ALIVE!"

Heads nodded and stances steadied.

"WE WILL BRING THEM ALL BACK! WE WILL GET OUR REWARD FROM GRUDE, AND TRILLIUM WILL BE OURS FOREVER!"

More shouts erupted. The invigorated Mysra warriors, fiendish, raised their large fists and knives. Their thick shouts were engulfed in the nearby trees, and perched birds flew up and away.

"READY?!"

"YEAH!" Shouts and fisted knives thrust upward, clouded in unison, the quick-pulsing trillium fueling them all.

"LET'S GO!" Neen raised his jagged knife, turning on one foot, and pointed his weapon forward, aiming it toward the Great Mist.

The warriors cried out war shouts as the cages they bore rattled wildly. They stomped into the dense growth, trampling, following Neen's lead. The hunters' abandoned items made it obvious this area had been recently occupied, and the Mysra trampled over the team's bundles and blankets with as much worry as if they were just grasses, they crunched through in the Yellow Vast. It was just as easy as Neen had promised as they followed the tracks to their destination.

Neen continued his trillium-heighted blusters throughout their heavy march, scaring more birds from perched trees.

Chapter Fifty-Four

As the Mysra approached, the WynSprign warriors could hear, at first, faint sounds of shouts. Drawing ever near, every step, every beat, their footsteps sounded, breaking twigs and thudding with intensity. The fast flight of birds above stilled their resolve. The WynSprigns' hearts became thundering war drums, captive in their chests. Sweat glistened on their brows as they swallowed with dry, nervous gulps. Waiting. Their fingers tingled as they grasped weapons and balanced themselves. Their eyes were fixed on the village ground, following Fenner's silent command to remain steady.

Waiting.

Waiting.

Waiting . . .

Suddenly, the first towering Mysra emerged from the dense foliage. The WynSprigns' breath stopped and their hearts skipped at the beings' immense size. The muscled, boulder-like bodies at every movement demonstrated sheer power that quaked the WynSprigns' nimble frames. The large cages they effortlessly carried could easily hold seven to ten WynSprigns each!

More and more of the massive enemy forces piled into the clearing, and more cages appeared. Within moments they had filled up almost the entire open area of the village. They were waiting, panting as they gathered, knives and glares ready to strike fear. Cage doors rattled at their rallying cries, and their eyes darted for any sign of movement from their prey.

But there was no movement.

Then one Mysra came walking through the crowd from the rear, others parting to let him through. He had led them here, but once at the edge of the village had stayed behind to ensure all his warriors were gathered for this mission. He then strode into the village, coldly assessing the surroundings and his troops. He eyed the houses and the empty walkways around them.

"Where are they?" a suspicious Mysra asked, eyes narrowed on him, their leader.

"I don't see any WynSprigns," another piped out, a hint of worry in his voice.

Neen stomped his way to the front of the group. He didn't bother looking at the Mysra who had asked the questions when he replied, "THEY MUST BE *HIDING* INSIDE THEIR CUTE LITTLE COZY HOMES, *AFRAID* TO COME OUT!" He gave a roaring laugh as he pointed with his knife. Others jeered and laughed, joining him. He circled the clearing as he taunted, "COME OUT AND FACE US!"

At the dimming of their raucous voices and chants, silence.

Many sets of glowing eyes watched them from within the thick foliage, hidden. The WynSprign leader was skilled, tactical, his warriors waiting for the right time, for his command. For there were many, so many of the Mysra.

"Well, let's get them to come out," Neen finally said, his smile darkened. "They won't want to roast themselves, *will they*?" He looked at his troops.

Anxious, the Mysra enemies ventured from the tight group and ran to yell, banging on house doors, trying to flush out the WynSprigns. In the waiting group of Mysra, a single torch was lit.

The WynSprigns warriors quieted their fear, their anger. They remained hiding, waiting. The fire of the torch now dancing in their eyes.

Neen grinned at his warriors. "No answer?"

Mysra smiled, shaking their heads, swaying in their wide stances, waiting to be unleashed under his command.

"Well! Torch 'em."

Without further word, the torch-bearer tossed his torch onto the nearest wooden tree home, Fenner's. Several other Mysra approached the growing flame and ignited their own torches. They wanted to turn this place to glowing orange and red, a reflection of their own fury. They'd get the WynSprigns even if this whole forest scorched. They couldn't give a shit about the damage.

Quickly other homes were ignited, and the air grew thick with eye-burning smoke, and the bright glow painted all the dark forest surrounding the village.

Fire flickered in Fenner's narrowed eyes. It was hard for him to watch his house below engulfed in raging flames, but he pursed his lips tighter and inhaled deeply. He was a warrior. *Let them burn our homes*. He made himself shrug at the thought, conveying his bravado to his fellow WynSprigns around him.

"Perhaps they ran off further into the woods!" Gax offered. He wiped away sooty sweat with his purple rag.

"Yes! Highly possible!" Neen turned to face his troop and said, "We'll have to follow them in whatever direction they went!" He then waved for them to gather closer in around him.

Watching his every move, they obediently came closer to surround him and he turned in a circle to address them: "Listen up! Expand out, track them! As we've learned, they take no steps to cover their tracks. They probably ran off and left the village, and went further into the wood." He continued to circle. "Look out for tracks, prints, broken limbs and twigs!"

The Mysra nodded. They would.

"Dismissed!" he yelled. The troops broke from him and began to dash out to the surrounding woods.

No-NO! Fenner did *not* like this. This was the very thing they'd tried to avoid by choosing the front lines. Now the Mysra would find the WynSprigns who were unable to fight, for such a large group would leave unmistakable tracks. He gulped, his heart knocking in his throat.

Fenner quickly met gazes with Freck, positioned near him. That moment they made a connection, sharing the same thought. Freck nodded slowly. Fenner looked down and with a grim face, he erupted: "*NOW!*"

In a flash, WynSprign warriors leapt from the high treetops, landing to surround the group, these 'ground warriors' already swinging swords and staffs. There was no time for the Mysra to react, and they hadn't considered a surprise attack *at all*. The WynSprigns had seconds to make the battle theirs, seconds to kill as many of them as possible. Everything relied on these precious seconds.

A shower of death rained down from above as the remaining perched WynSprigns loosed their arrows onto more Mysra targets below. They fell, swiftly. Towering forms fell to the ground, at once.

From behind the Mysra, guttural shrieks erupted. There was a split-second of confusion for Fenner, for the WynSprign warriors hadn't landed *there*.

In a blinding motion, Treva and Lanico had begun their own assault. They leapt from behind the stunned Mysra and started their own wave of terror. Treva cried out a hoarse yell, swiping her blade across a thick Mysra neck. His neighboring soldiers began to turn toward her, and fast as lightning, Lanico swung his sword low, taking out their legs.

"I had them"—she breathed fast—"they had barely turned toward me."

"I know," he responded. "I was only testing my sword's sharpness." He was already moving toward the next Mysra victims.

She rolled her eyes and scoffed before thrusting into another Mysra. *Yeah, right.* "Taking my kills from me," she muttered with annoyance.

Several Mysra fell to unsuspected death in that instant. The onslaught of attack—from the air, from behind them, from all around—was quick. Before they understood what was going on, their warriors went down by the dozens. Ill prepared.

Staggered shouts arose from various WynSprigns: "It's Lanico!"

"Hail, Prince Lanico!" someone cried out from somewhere. Winning energy spread amongst them. There was a chance. A chance that perhaps they could win this! The favor was already, quickly, with them.

Lanico didn't stop his pursuit to greet them but stayed focused, a signal for them all to do the same. This wasn't one of their damned garden parties.

Treva leapt onto a Mysra warrior's shoulders and jammed her sword down, thrusting the blade through his skull. Thick black Mysra blood splattered her face. In a deft whirl, she leapt onto another Mysra. His slow swings at her caused her to dance, balancing on top of him. He jumped and bent low— anything to get her off.

She jumped off her Mysra perch and engaged him. He fought with only a feeble knife, and she almost felt sorry for him, almost. But, after moments of useless redundant swings, she finally charged, giving a throaty roar. Her white teeth were splashed with inky black. This Mysra ducked and dodged her swings until she became tired of this boring dance. She held her sword like a dagger and thrust it into him, a silver lightning bolt through his chest. *Easy.* She was glad Lanico had given her that idea previously. She quirked a wicked smile until the taste of blood turned it to a frown. *Ew.*

The Reluctant Leader sang its metallic song at Lanico's power. Clashes and clangs came from a more-skilled, mature Mysra who'd stolen a sword from a dead WynSprign and moved swiftly, trying to keep up. The Mysra gaped with a pointed-tooth grin, his mouth so wide Lanico's whole head could fit inside. Lanico sniffed hard and wiped his face with the back of his arm. He could take this one. Another swing was countered by the Mysra's sword. Lanico stepped quickly, and it didn't take long to know that even though this Mysra had some sword skill, he was slow. He might be stronger, larger, but he was much slower.

Rumbling thunder grumbled in the distance. The sky grayed as Lanico felt Reluctant Leader's energy singing into his bones. It had been enchantingly forged for him. He watched with a keen eye after a failed attempt from the Mysra to take his arm. The Mysra lunged again, but Lanico swung, taking him off his center. A repost from the Mysra. Lanico jolted to the side and forcefully pushed him toward where his sword had been headed. Off balance, the Mysra fell but turned over quickly to meet the sharp end of Reluctant Leader, right in his throat. Lanico looked into the Mysra's panicked eyes and made it quick. He thrust the sword in and allowed his massive body to rest on the ground. The Mysra's dead eyes looked up into the eternity of the sky. So far, the General Prince hadn't noticed Grude amongst the enemy horde. No. In disappointment he realized he wouldn't – not yet. Not today.

WynSprign air warriors stayed perched in the trees, aiming and loosing their arrows effortlessly into more unsuspecting Mysra below. Jain and Tarn kept steady in the high trees, quickly firing their arrows to take down one Mysra at a time. Arrows whizzed by in a flash, piercing thick gray Mysra flesh and muscle. Roars of pain and agony rose into the air.

It was not easy to do all this killing, for, aside from animals, the WynSprign never killed, but they pressed on relentlessly shooting, the command obeyed. They would have to contemplate the killing later, a thought for another day. Today they needed to wipe them out, to ensure their own survival.

Tarn's eyes teared up as he shot, swallowing against a lump, quickly wiping the tears away with his pointy shoulders. Accuracy. No suffering—only lethal hits. He was steeled at the thought of his latest nightmare turning into reality . . . these monsters taking his beloved family and turning them into slaves—he wouldn't let that happen. His wife was expecting another—the Mysra wouldn't have her.

Never.

He loosed another arrow. Another arrow, and another. One. After. Another.

Unwavering arrows hit their mark as his tears streamed. Another. Another . . . down.

Much damage had been inflicted when the Mysra spotted the archers, hidden high in the trees. But they couldn't reach them. There'd be no climbing. They moved to set trees ablaze. It was only now that the WynSprigns sorely missed the rain.

Just as the Mysra had hoped, the WynSprign archers leapt quickly from their branches to avoid being taken by the blazes. The fire, though destructive, wasn't enough to kill the fast-jumping WynSprigns. They had practiced well and jumped with ease from limb to limb, tree to tree. What *was* unaccounted for was the towering burning trees that soon tumbled, swiftly taking out warriors on both sides like a mighty, burning hand smashing scrambling ants. The crashing trees and their own leaps quaked their bones and rattled their chests.

The air warriors now had to begin their next level of fighting, sword and staff sighting. A tree Freck had been perched on was set ablaze, and he had been so focused that it wasn't until heat reached his legs that he realized he needed to leap—*now*. He jumped sideways from the burning branch, thrusting his bow aside to nowhere and landing on his haunches on the ground, shaken but all right. He stood, to fight, for he was skilled at the sword as well as the bow.

A Mysra beckoned him closer with a snarl, a purple rag dangled from his side. Freck drew his sword slowly, the metallic whisper sounding against his thigh. He lost himself in the moment, and he was another person. He answered the invitation and paced to the Mysra, swinging with passion and fury at the other looming Mysra warriors in his path, slicing their legs and arms, making deep cuts to the bone. He had to move fast. One mighty swipe from them, and he'd be done. They fell to the ground at their sudden injuries, grabbing at their disabling wounds. Thick blood painted their hands. *The other WynSprigns will claim them*, Freck thought, and smiled.

Freck knew somehow that this Mysra, the one beckoning him with the purple rag, was his target. He continued to walk; eyes locked on his foe. Freck quickly swung and the Mysra, his Mysra, tried dodging the sword. It sliced air as, turning and ducking, the Mysra deflected several crashing blows with his comparatively feeble knife.

This Mysra could move.

Though he had shown his own skill with the sword, Freck knew that he had to fight smarter with this one. Only one wrong move, just one, and the Mysra would end it all with little effort. The small WynSprign frames were no match for the muscled trunks of Mysra bodies.

The Mysra circled the WynSprign slowly as he held his large jagged knife. He smiled a large, open smile, exposing his sharp white teeth and purple-stained tongue. The Mysra was only waiting for his chance to either injure and capture the WynSprign . . . or kill him. No. Freck knew the Mysra meant to take them alive, that they weren't supposed to kill the WynSprigns. But, with bloodlust, this one licked his lips.

The clang and clash of swords all around pierced Freck's ears. Glowing embers and fiery ash drifted through the air, filled with frantic shouts of both WynSprigns and Mysra alike. He shook off the din, holding his sword steady. He couldn't identify who was screaming, injured, or dead in those desperate moments of horror and raw survival. He panted, blinking, finding focus. As he stood still, keeping the Myrsa at bay with his extended sword, he realized his efforts to swing the sword would only be hindered by the Mysra's dodging. The swinging just moments before had taken up energy. Feeling the weight in his arms, he realized he needed to adapt his skill. He wouldn't be able to keep up against the hefty Mysra strikes.

Summoning his nimble WynSprign body, he swiftly swung his leg out, and with the tip of his foot, he kicked the purple rag out from the Mysra's belt. It landed on the damp ground. Simple. It was just enough. At the odd movement, a distracted Mysra looked down. A flash of steel and Freck took one heavy and swift swing that sent the Mysra's head flying as he gazed at the purple rag. The head fell with a muffled *thud* and rolled slightly on the muddied ground. Freck's eyes were wild and crazed as his sword followed through and stuck into the ground.

Another Mysra caught a glimpse of his fallen fellow warrior in that instant and stopped short, frozen in the moment.

"NO!" his hoarse voice bellowed in horror. He pulled his knife from a slain WynSprign. His eyes bulged in disbelief and blind rage, and he swung his knife at anyone in his way, even his own unfortunate Mysra. He focused his blood-red vision on small Freck and stomped toward him, his steps heavy and fast.

Freck felt his heart beating in his throat. He was shaken by the sight of this massive and furious Mysra charging at him, a red rag dangling from his pocket. He knew that the warrior he had just killed—the one with the purple rag—was someone important. He felt his body quiver, his heart racing, and his hand felt numb on the sword's grip. He didn't know if he had energy to continue the fight with this looming monster.

Neen was closing in on Freck when suddenly, as if from nowhere, Fenner came flying between them. His deep glaring eyes and wild hair caught the Mysra's focused attention.

Fenner held his sword out as he stood in front of his grandson Freck, who noticed in that moment that Fenner was bloodied and bruised; he had probably already killed a Mysra. Without a word, Fenner began showcasing his hidden prowess, twirling the sword with ease between his hands, bending his wrists, sending the blade revolving in an endless torrent of sharp steel that sang in the breeze. The Mysra had to jump back twice to avoid the rampant blade, the approaching promised death trap.

Fenner could feel a deep rage exploding in him. The last time he'd taken up his sword had been when his twin brother Frik was killed by the Mysra during the seizure of Odana.

Fenner was smaller than this Mysra, but his charge at the sword was mighty. He was extraordinarily skilled and his mission was to save the life of his grandson. The Mysra had stolen his brother from him, his other half. *They will not steal my grandson, nor any other Sprign, as long as I breathe.*

"YAH!" the Mysra yelled as he leapt forward with precision timing to swing hard at Fenner's sword. He would not easily yield to this WynSprign. The sword and the knife clashed loudly. The Mysra was powerful, but slow at his attempts, and Fenner's thin arms and body accepted the forceful clashes and blows in defense. The anger between them was palpable and the flames of burning trees surrounding them only intensified the engulfing rage.

~

Chaos enveloped everything in the village, where Mysra warriors had wandered further in search of hiding WynSprigns. Despite the unfolding mess of battle, they'd still need to bring back slaves. It was getting out of control.

Two rogue Mysra came across a lone WynSprign seated at an emptied tavern. He had a sword, but it leaned away from him, out of reach. The Mysra easily trampled the small wooden fence of the tavern and approached the still WynSprign, who seemed more interested in the contents of his cup than in the fire and violence taking place so near. The Mysra looked at one another with amusement and stood quietly behind this large old WynSprign.

Trayvor tossed back another big swig of ale. He didn't seem to know that they were directly behind him, or perhaps, he didn't care. He had decided not to engage in the battle. He never meant to in the first place. He decided his strength lay elsewhere and preferred not to anger Grude by engaging.

"Come to claim me, eh, boyss?" he asked unexpectedly without looking at either of them. "I'm old, I'm tired, and . . ." He paused, turning around in his seat to look up at them, trying to focus his eyes on their faces towering high above. "And . . . I'm drunk," he concluded. "I hear the sound of distant thunder. My, my. So, Lanico decided to show up, did he?" Another tug at the mug and a wet sigh: "I'm afraid you boysss won't get much use out of me as a slave—why, I can barely walk. But I *do* have a businesss mind." He gestured to his cane.

The Mysra looked at each other, confused. Did he want them to fetch his cane for him? It was true—what use would they have for this elderly, immobile WynSprign back at the mines? They didn't give a rat's ass for his "business mind." Clearly, he was more a smart ass, if anything.

"Grude and I go way back," Trayvor said. "You see, *I'm* the reason that you are here today, actually." He made a smug face at the two warriors. "I wasss the one that gave Grude the idea to have more WynSprign slaves." Trayvor seemed very proud of himself despite his slurring.

Grude had never mentioned sparing this WynSprign. He never mentioned any WynSprign involvement in his plan, other than turning the lot of them into slaves. This one, this old WynSprign, he was cunning. Trying to get out from his fate. The Mysra warriors knew better.

"You're probably right," one Mysra said, still standing behind Trayvor. He lifted his knife, pulled the old WynSprign back against him—"But we haven't a use for smart asses." In an instant, he dragged his knife across Trayvor's thick neck and the WynSprign's eyes widened in sobriety, in disbelief. He wasn't expecting *that*.

The warm crimson blood flowed from his neck and quickly flooded down his chest to soak his tunic. He choked, starring at the leafy tree branches high above that had shaded so many hours here, at the tavern. Drowning gasps bubbled from his exposed vocal cords. He jerked and convulsed until he fell backward from the seat and onto the blood-muddy ground. His trusty cane tipped and fell on top of his body.

The two Mysra looked at each other in amusement.

Trayvor felt himself become cool as his warm blood flowed out of him. His sight darkened and his heart slowed. His last breath was a fog in the cool air.

The Mysra wiped the blood from his knife on Trayvor's shoulders. They took a few drinks of his remaining ale. They didn't want *that* to go to waste. One stepped over his corpse and reached for his cup. Then, they'd seek out other deserters.

~

Despite the smoldering rage they both felt, the warriors began to tire at the limitations of their bodies. Fenner moved heavily through Neens defensive strikes and a failed thrust through his sternum. He was moving slightly slower than Neen at his final thrust and received a fatal jab in an instant.

Neen, large, powerful, and determined, drove his knife through Fenner's thin flank. The WynSprign took the deep pierce but remained stubborn and unrelenting. He'd see his purpose through. Fenner, never letting on that he was willing to die, used his sword to return the favor as Neen lunged forward at him, delivering a deep stab up into Neen's unguarded chest, so deep that the long sword's tip jutted out from Neen's upper back.

Neen's eyes widened in shock. His mouth hung open and gushed purplish saliva. The heavy Mysra fell hard to his knees and grabbed the hilt of the sword that protruded from his chest. He couldn't believe that this thin old WynSprign had just run him through.

Returning to rage, Neen looked at Fenner eye-to-eye and glared with seething hate. Bloodied saliva was thick now in his gaping mouth: "You bastard Wyn—"

That instant, the glide of metal sang, unforgiving, taking the final words from Neen's filthy mouth as the swipe freed his head from his neck. The head rolled and landed to the ground. Freck loomed from behind the headless form, his stare unflinching.

"I hated the sound of his voice," he commented with a deep look into his grandfather's eyes. The Mysra's body leaned and then toppled. "You finished him grandfather—I only ended the nagging." A quick flash of silver, and Freck sheathed his sword.

Fenner had bested the Mysra, whose decapitated head held a blank face, staring into the void. Fenner huffed slightly and glanced back up to meet the worried gaze of Freck. The old Chief then felt an urgent pain. The deep stab wound radiated agony from his side through his whole body, with much bleeding from within. Fenner quickly crumpled to the ground and hot blood leaked from the wound as he clutched at it. Already, a sizable pool had collected beneath. He was bleeding out.

Freck collapsed next to his grandfather, panicked. He held the old man in his arms and felt his body light, bony. Fenner gazed at him peacefully.

"Freck, you fought well today. I've—I've never been prouder of-of you than I . . . now." His voice had become softer, a mere breath. "This moment . . ."

Freck's eyes welled as blood began to bubble from his grandfather's gaping mouth. His breathing was labored and his lungs gurgled.

It was happening!

It was happening too quickly!

"I love you, Grandfather," Freck whispered. "Please. Don't d-I'm sorry. Sorry I dishonored you."

Fenner's glazed eyes rolled, behind his lids. He sighed and steadied his focus on Freck, in effort. A thin wisp of a voice, "Forgotten, boy . . . it matters not."

Freck tightened his grip on his grandfather. His heart raced, on the verge of exploding.

Fenner continued, almost too quietly, "I love you, my boy. My pride." A long sigh sent his breath floating to the air as a silvery slip, at that moment; his body was emptied of his soul. Fenner—Odana Chief and warrior, grandfather, and trustworthy aid of Lanico—died.

Freck looked down and sobbed with large heaves of groaning. His ebony hair was caked with mud and leaves and his soot-covered face stained with trails of tears. In those final moments, Freck had forgotten the battle happening all around him, and the roars and screams had dulled in his numb ears. His tears reflected the orange glowing flames, and as if he were under protection from Odan, no one seemed to notice the saddened Freck collapsed over his grandfather, in the midst of the battle. And the familiar and comfortable damp of the settling mist began to kiss at his hot skin.

Under Fenner's command, a large number of unprepared Mysra had gone down within the first few seconds. Under his command, an army of the innocent had arisen. The quiet, the humble, the faithful, and determined rose . . .

And won.

Freck would pick up where his grandfather left off. He would live to make him proud.

Chapter Fifty-Five

Nightfall had reached the deep forest, setting crickets chirping and tree frogs croaking. The WynSprigs that had fled, the ones unable to fight in the Great Mist, had found safety among the trees, settling into their tents and eating fish they'd caught in the lake. Stoutwyn was pleased to see the young ones enjoying themselves. They shouldn't have to be burdened with the worry and fear that he and the other adults carried.

When time for bedding down came upon them, campfires were extinguished, candles blown out, and voices quieted. Stoutwyn was thankful for this peace, this quiet. He dismissed the concerns in his head by delegating tasks and providing assistance to others. He peered around at the open space, at the now-empty campsite. *Everyone has turned in, it seems*, he mused.

He directed a glance towards the Great Mist, where he sensed a faint orange glow. *But the sun didn't set in that direction.* An ominous feeling grew. *This isn't right.* The brighter aura lingered over, beyond the tree line – from miles away. He squinted through his spectacles and gasped as his mind caught hold of the truth.

Oh, Odan on High! A fire! A roaring blaze in the Great Mist!

The heavy blanket of worry shrouded him. Panic. His mind raced. *What to do?! What to do?!*

Then he remembered himself. He steadied. *My group—they are safe, bedded, at rest.*

He peered around, making certain that everyone was indeed in their tents, that no one else was out seeing *this*. There'd be no sense in waking others to worry further with him. But he needed to find a way to help. He covered his gaping mouth with his thick hand, then went to his and Murah's tent.

He startled her as she was getting dressed for the night.

"Stout! Why on earth would you startle me so?" She shook her bonneted head. "For goodness sakes!" She held up a nightgown against her chest.

Stoutwyn quickly closed the entrance flap behind him. "Shhh!!!" He waved his hand in the air. "Listen, Murah"—he came close to speak low and quiet, for the tent was merely fabric and his voice would carry if he was not careful—"I think there is something wrong at the Great Mist." He pulled away, holding a serious look.

She met his frightened gaze. "What is it, Stout?" Her tone now matched his. Low. Troubled.

He whispered lower, in a small voice just over his breath: "There is a bright glow over the woods in that direction"—he gestured—"a fire."

She breathed in shakily, an attempt to stifle her panic. "What should we should do?" Her hands trembled, but her voice tried at control.

He paused. His mind raced. There was nothing that *he* could do, but . . . "I'm going to walk toward the Great Mist, and perhaps the Fray—Thara—will meet me again. She is the Fray over water and mist. Perhaps she could—"

Murah stared.

He didn't wait for her response. Fray Thara *was* the only solution. He turned to grab for his robe, which had been flung over several satchels on the freshly cleared ground.

"Oh, do be careful, Stout. I wish you wouldn't"—she sighed and her mouth began to quiver.

What is going on in the village? he wondered. *What is happening to all our friends and loved ones?* He locked eyes with her, her soft gaze meeting his. This moment, Stoutwyn and Murah knew, people they cherished were suffering, were perhaps *dying*.

A sob broke from her. She covered her mouth and sniffed hard to contain the sound.

He leaned in close to embrace her, pressing his lips to her forehead, feeling the warmth of her skin. "I'll be back soon enough, my blossom." He leaned back to meet her tear-laden eyes. "Tell no one I've gone. There is no sense in alerting the others. We need them here, safe."

She nodded another silent reply.

He held onto his own resolve. To do what was needed, he denied his feelings, at least for now, to focus on his mission, his path.

He reached out to pull the ribbon from Murah's tied bonnet, to loosen it. She managed a small smile as she recalled she still had it on. Stoutwyn looked at her, reluctant to go. Then he turned and opened the flap to walk out into the misty night.

The night air was cooler than the trapped air in the tent. The smell of decaying leaves grew as he went deeper into the forest, leaving behind the smell of lake and earth worms. He had been walking toward the Great Mist for some time, trying to follow the same path they had used to make the journey there. It wasn't long before the trees grew dense enough that he determined he was far enough from camp.

"Thara!" he called, his hands around his mouth to further the sound. "Fray Thara of the Great Mist!" His eyes darted about, looking for sign of her. The lingering blue mist intensified. Time was passing, and seconds were precious. He walked closer, moving toward the glow, toward the Great Mist, looking for any signs of her. "Th—Thara! Please! I—I need your assistance!" He believed he could feel the warmth of the fire as he drew a little nearer the glow.

Then the blue mist thinned out all around him and collected in a gathered but shapeless mass. The blue luminescent form shifted slowly, hovering over the ground. It was Thara, the blue lady of the mist. The glowing mass moved several times until she transformed into her beautiful glowing form. Just as before, her light periwinkle skin and rich violet hair pierced his vision.

"Fray Thara!" He held back a cry of relief. "Oh, thank Father Odan you're here!" He didn't delay: "Urgent help is needed. I noticed the orange glow of fire, just ahead"—he pointed—"I'm starting to smell wafts of smoke from beyond the trees."

Her face gave no hint on her thoughts. Just as before, she was beautiful, but expressionless.

"I ask humbly," he said, nervously fidgeting at his buttons, "that you use the power of mist to slow the expansion of the blaze. WynSprigns, my WynSprigns, could be dying." His eyes pleaded at her.

The ethereal being loomed, towering over him. Her purple hair floated in a phantom breeze that he could not feel. Her cool breathy voice emanated out to him: "Stoutwyn, it's true that the Great Mist has fire, from battle." She smiled slightly. "I have already moved on this, and that is the reason for my delay to your call. My mist, the slight rains, will work to slow the spread." She lowered, edging closer to him. "Though my mist will bring success here, you, Stoutwyn, are needed. Please advance—the warriors, your warriors, need you. Now."

Stoutwyn was surprised they *needed* him, but he nodded without question. "Yes. Yes, Fray Thara. I will continue on."

After what seemed to be hours of walking, the smell of smoke was unmistakable. His eyes burned, and his body was covered in sweat. The air that breezed his way was suffocatingly thick. The orange blaze was not as bright has it had been earlier, even from afar. It seemed Thara's mist had indeed slowed and perhaps diminished the fires. A quick flash of relief washed over him, but that was replaced quickly. Something had caused that fire; some*one* had caused that fire. It was from the battle. *What dread will I find? What horrors? . . . Death?*

The village could be seen ahead where trees thinned and gave way to the ground of the clearing. He stayed back for a moment to gauge the scene ahead. He needed to exercise caution. Despite the hammering of his heart, he stayed hidden and silent, fearful of what he would see. *Who* would he see? He squinted his glowing eyes. But there were no screams. No running.

There were large, still lumps on the ground ahead. He caught his breath. *Bodies.*

"Who are they, the fallen?" he mumbled to no one.

Still. A death-covered stillness. The chaos had already come, leaving devastation and death.

His hands began to tremble, and he swallowed against the dryness in his throat. He didn't want to look, but he *had* to.

As the woods thinned, his face responded to the glow and heat of the fire. He could see it was reduced based on some evidence gained with a few glances. He willed himself to stop shaking and pursed his lips. Cautiously he stepped over the brush and gained purchase on the ground beyond the tree line.

He tried to remain silent as he approached the closest dead body, his head swiveling around as he looked for trouble, for Mysra. Once he found no one was near enough to stop him, he closed in and found that the large mass wasn't a WynSprign. No. No, it was much too large. It was the corpse of a Mysra—dangerously close to the forest where the WynSprigns had travelled to safety. He breathed out, finally. He hadn't realized he was holding his breath.

The Mysra, even in his death, held a scowl. Stoutwyn frowned down at him. The Mysra's mission—to track them, perhaps—had been upset.

He caught a movement out of the corner of his eye, and his heart stopped. But he turned his gaze upward from where he crouched to see a tall, thin WynSprign, limping.

Freck! It was Freck was walking slowly, with a lost gaze and a bloodied sword dangling from his hand. Black blood.

"H—H—Hey! Freck!" Stoutwyn blasted. He jogged toward him. "Freck, my boy, I'm so pleased to see you. Tell me now, what's happened!"

Freck blinked hard, waking from his death-filled thoughts, and looked down at Stoutwyn. Tears had once slid down the young WynSprign's soot-covered face, leaving it striped. At the sight of Stoutwyn, Freck slumped to the ground and took in a deep, shuddering breath. His eyes welled and his face crinkled.

Stoutwyn felt a pain in his gut. He hurried to lower himself to sit next to the young warrior.

"Stout"—his mouth opened once or twice; saliva strands glistened from the roof of his mouth—"I-I killed." He breathed deeply and began to sob softly, then uttered a hoarse cry. His back was slouched, his shoulders curved over and heaving at his sobs.

Stoutwyn gulped at the lump returning to its place at the back of his throat. He hadn't had to have this conversation in years. He remembered the first time he had to kill on the battlefield, and he tried his best. He spoke slowly, with a calm tone despite his inward chaos. "Freck, in life we are all given choice. There are times when that choice is taken advantage of." He glanced to the lifeless Mysra, so close to the tree line and continued. "Some—like that Mysra there—choose to put you in the position where it is a choice to end you, or you end him. You won that choice, my boy. Why? To save yourself. To save the lives of those you love."

Stoutwyn met Freck's welling gaze.

"Choosing to take another's life to save your own," Stoutwyn continued, "well that is a terrible place to be, but you didn't choose to be in that place." He paused. His voice remained gentle. "Tell me, what would have happened if you had let him continue?"

"He said he was going to track our people down," Freck answered, "and that there were more WynSprigns hidden. Someone had to—"

"Exactly." He paused considering, "Freck, you prevented him from moving beyond those trees." He pointed to the woods. "Why, you saved even *me*."

Freck nodded silently, and held his downcast face with dried-blood-crusted hands.

"Your grandfather? —"

Freck raised his streaming eyes to Stoutwyn. The young man's full hair shifted as he shook his head slowly.

Stoutwyn's heart ached. He pursed his lips and nodded slowly in answer, managing to fight back the raging cry that rose in his tight throat. His dear friend. "Oh, he would have been proud." He managed to say.

After a few moments of silence, Stoutwyn needed to know the rest and pressed on: "Freck, now my boy, I need you to tell me, what of the Mysra? Where did they go—what happened with them?" His eyes were soft on Freck's.

"Well, we killed them."

Freck's face clouded, and Stoutwyn saw the cogs of his mind *trying* to turn, trying for rational thought. The slow waking movement, from having been stunned.

"I think some got away, but most, almost all, died," Freck managed.

"Were any . . . Were any WynSprigns taken?" Stoutwyn was afraid of the answer.

Freck shook his head—no.

With a sigh of relief, Stoutwyn placed a hand over his chest. "All right, my boy," he breathed, "Right. It's going to be all right."

A rumble of thunder grumbled in the distance. The scent of rain was absent.

Stoutwyn's eyebrows raised. *He's come.*

Chapter Fifty-Six

Mist and smoky haze lingered after the fires died down, and the smoldering heat still crawled over the charred homes and trees. A wisp of white air, blanketed and rolled across blackened roofs and branches. The soil was saturated with blood and gore. There was so much destruction, so much *death*.

But they lived.

Felena, braced against a tree, lurched to vomit, her braid tumbling to the side of her head. Freck spotted her and darted near, his face washed with concern.

She tried to stop the urge to heave by muffling her mouth with the back of her filthy hand. "*Go!*" She ordered the warrior, yet he continued toward her. She hated this. All of it—the smell of blood and ash, death, and Freck's once-proud eyes staring at her with pity – it was mostly that. She hated him looking at her like that. And—and then there was Stefin. *Oh, Father Odan, Stefin*, her heart hurt. It was just too much. She felt her insides roil again.

"I—I heard you. I just"—he started.

She lurched to vomit at the thought of *him*. *Dead*. The thought of what would never be.

"I wanted to see that you were all right," Freck said foolishly.

Of course, I'm not all right. She had just been through battle and was retching at the atrocities she'd witnessed, the killing she'd done, the ache-

"Freck, just *GO!*" She spat out the remnants of vomit, and her blue watery glare on him was filled with anger. *He's infuriating.*

He looked defeated, helpless. It was as if she had slapped him in the face. He tightened his lips and nodded and obediently turned from her. He slowly headed to join the group that had already gathered at Lanico's house, just around the bend.

Felina turned back to the tree she braced her hand against. She felt guilty but mostly embarrassed. Her stomach had been emptied enough, so there was no more twisting. She wiped her forearm over her mouth and sniffed hard. Sighing through the bitter taste in her mouth, she stood straight to regain resolve—she'd have to join the others as well. She knew that forward movement was needed-was all that could be done. She'd go help with the next steps that had to be taken. She was a warrior, and she took that position seriously. She brushed her feelings aside—brushed Stefin aside—and followed Freck's direction, but at a distance.

The large group were covered with blood and mud, their clothing reduced to tattered, soot-covered rags. It seemed that all the survivors had gathered, and she was the only one just trickling in after them.

Everyone's focus was on Lanico and his mysterious warrior friend, Treva. She had green hair. *Green*, like a deep emerald—or what Felena imagined an emerald's shade to be. Treva was a small, muscled warrior who looked as if she'd seen suffering and war before. Her face was like carved stone, somber and beautiful. Felena knew the stories of the first female WynSprign Knight. The Emerald Knight. It seemed she had been forgotten by everyone else here, but *not* by Felena.

Treva's gaze at the crowd was confident, regal almost. She stood proudly next to the General Prince.

"But this is only the beginning," Lanico warned. Our brother and sister WynSprigns are still toiling as slaves. The rumors were true." He looked to Treva next to him and added, "She was there . . . was a slave . . ." His voice broke off. And now she stood stoically at his side. He swallowed emotion away, looked back at the crowd, and continued:

"I propose we head out, regroup and descend upon the castle." No one spoke, no one nodded. Lanico looked around for assent, but the beaten group only stared at him, and some looked down at the ground.

"Lan"—Stoutwyn, next to him, interjected in a soft voice Lanico bent to hear—"I think this group isn't quite yet ready for another battle. These aren't trained soldiers of old, not like—not like us."

Lanico darted his gaze back to the crowd—and Felena knew they looked pitiful. Their eyes were still fixed on the haunting images that they'd witnessed. These weren't hardened warriors, not really. They were villagers who had defended their families, themselves.

Lanico gave a somber nod.

However, he caught the light of a few eyes in the crowd, those of young ones who seemed interested—like Felena.

A spark glinted in his eye.

He continued to speak, but now with confidence and hope rising: "I realize what I suggest is a heavy burden to consider. The reward, taking back the kingdom, would not only ensure that the slavery of our people ends, but also allow for opportunities. Once on the throne, I would be in need of warriors, Knights, a new army." He cleared his throat. "There would be a new place for you in the Odana Kingdom, a new place. A new life."

A generation of would-be warriors, those who had long heard the tales of his adventures, blinked in wonderment. The prospect of leaving the Great Mist realm was terrifying, yet awe-inspiring.

A spark started in Felena, too, and she saw it in Freck—stirring energy at the thought of becoming an actual Odana Knight. A royal Soldier, like his grandfather used to be. *We can do this.* She knew he wanted to wield a sword and protect his people, especially now. Especially since there must be others across the lands that need help—*their* people needed help. There was nothing here, hiding in the Great Mist, that would offer them such a chance. They'd travel, train, and serve a bigger purpose.

She grasped Freck's hand and they looked at Lanico with the same wonder-filled eyes.

Chapter Fifty-Seven

Stoutwyn had returned to the deep woods where the rest of the WynSprigns were staying and met an anxious Murah, who cried at seeing him all soot-covered. He gathered them all and explained to the crowd his findings. Many gasped at the details and trembled with emotion. Some wanted to know who had died. Stoutwyn didn't provide answers, for he didn't yet know who had perished. Guesses or false information would prove helpful to no one. With some brightening, however, he encouraged them that General Prince Lanico himself had come in and assisted in wiping out the Mysra, and that the group that attended the meeting with Lanico was quite large, suggesting that perhaps the death toll was limited.

"Now," he sighed, "we have to travel back home and rebuild. Regain and restore our battered home." That, he understood, that was his new purpose.

No matter how much information he had tried to provide, nothing prepared them for the reality that they'd face at home.

As the they walked into the village, they heard the pummeling sound of digging, and the smell of smoke haunted them. In the village the ground they walked on had been torn up by long wheel ruts, deep holes, and blood-stained puddles in the thick mud. The upheaval of the earth was a sign of the struggle, the fighting, and the dying that had taken place here.

The arriving WynSprigns gasped at their surroundings, at the living warriors. They wept at the news of the dead. The dead warriors they knew, now being prepared for burial.

The village was mostly silent, with little conversation. The warriors were lost in thought and grief as they covered the remaining bodies with the loosened soil, their eyes swollen red from smoke and from weeping. They had worked without end to bury WynSprign and Mysra alike, not far from the dense forest, being careful to place death markers on the WynSprigns' graves.

Shrieks and cries broke the silence as loved ones reunited and shared news of the loved ones that had died. It was a time of mixed emotions. Of happy tears and of tears of sorrow, for the reunited and the departed.

Tarn's wife spotted him before he noticed her. She cried out his name, her voice bearing both desperation and relief. Bewildered at that call he looked desperately for her face, her pregnant belly, and halted in his tracks. The sight of her brought him to his knees. His mouth hung wide open in a silent scream to her. He had killed for her, for them. With uneven strides, she came in closer and knelt on the ground, hovering over his crouched body. Together they wept.

Stoutwyn and Murah walked slowly to their home, in a quiet march away from the smell of smoke. Or could it be the senses were dulled?

Murah held her breath as they came closer to what had been their happy abode, not sure what to expect. Stoutwyn had not checked on it when he was here before—it hadn't been his highest priority at the time.

There was the large tree. And as they rounded it toward the front of the house, she sighed in warm tears and relief. Their home was spared. She heaved a sob of happiness through her balled fist. Stoutwyn took her hand and held it. She turned slowly and embraced him.

"Home at last, my blossom," he whispered.

~

Lanico and Treva set out for Horse's Clearing, Stoutwyn alongside them and recruits Felena and Freck in tow. They didn't have to track their way back to the clearing, for it was an obvious route the heavy Mysra feet had taken. Tame horses had been tied to a row of trees just at the tree line, and there were many, too many for their needs.

They did not bring many belongings. Unbeknownst to Lanico, Freck had previously raided his home for maps and documents about the Odana and secreted these away in his own bags. He determined that Lanico and Treva knew these lands well, but he and Felena didn't. The young warrior had taken time to remember details of the faraway lands. He wanted to ensure a back-up plan in the event there was ever a separation-though he didn't think spending time away with only Felena would be bad either.

It was hard to tell how many Mysra had survived and ridden back to Grude, but there were *many* horses and wagons left behind.

Stoutwyn had seen the group this far and suggested the people of the Great Mist keep a few horses, to allow for travel, and free the rest. They'd once again know the Yellow Vast as their wide homelands. The horses grunted and neighed slightly as their ties were loosed.

The four parted ways with Stoutwyn there. It was a difficult goodbye but only temporary. Stoutwyn would be in charge of the Great Mist now, a lord of the area for the time being. He'd see to the rebuilding and the resettling of the village until Lanico reclaimed his throne. Once that took place, Stoutwyn would return to the Odana Kingdom with any WynSprigns who wanted to follow. By then, he will have fulfilled his purpose. Stoutwyn had never voiced his desire to return, but he confided in Freck that it had been something that had burned within him for many long years.

Lanico and Freck shared one horse and Treva and Felena the other until they traveled the short distance to retrieve Lanico and Treva's two original horses, Aspirim and Criox. These two horses still had been equipped with their belongings. Then, they had four horses between them.

Lanico explained his determination to make it back to his mother's home quickly but reasoned that they'd need to take it slower than he'd like. They had two young warriors, and all of them had been exhausted physically and emotionally from the battle.

After Lanico and Treva shared basic riding instructions with Freck and Felena, Lanico announced his travel plans: "First stop will be the Yellow Vast brook, for watering and rest for both us and the horses." Freck smiled to himself, being somewhat familiar with these locations based on his quick study of the maps he'd pilfered. "Then," Lanico continued, "we'll stay the night at Gray Rock. I'm certain any Mysra warriors will have headed out to the Odana by then. Then we'll head through the remainder of the Yellow Vast and onto Fray Greta's."

"And then," Treva added with a cat's wide grin, "on to the Battle for the Kingdom—for your throne, my Prince."

Freck caught Felena's eye with the excitement they now shared with their Prince—their King.

Lanico loosed a low laugh. "No. For *our* throne . . . my Emerald Queen."

* * *

Acknowledgements

It would have been impossible for me to have made it this far through the writing, editing, self-publishing, and emotional processes without the help support from many others. I was humbled over and over. I am thankful, and most fortunate to find that help came in numerous forms, from: kind words of encouragement, education, and the personal experience of others. I am most grateful to each and every single one of you.

Mrs. Cindy Rinaman Marsch my editor, my educator, my mentor. You took a chance on me. Since day one you remained committed to helping me grow. It has been a humbling process for me, but you always made my ideas feel welcome. You've encouraged me and inspired me in a way that no other was able to. You've dealt with my inconsistencies, my changes, and my seemingly endless questions. You've nudged me forward with this since the beginning and have stayed beside me the whole time. Thank you from the deepest part of me. How could I ever thank you enough? The truth is, I cannot. Thank you. I hope we may continue to work together on other projects.

My husband: My mate, my life partner who puts up with my constant daydreaming and silliness. You urged me, Every. Single. Day. You told me that I cannot go back. I can't stop. I have to keep moving-moving-moving. And, thank you. Thank you for having *that* faith in me – even when I didn't have it for myself, even when I questioned myself – you never gave up on believing I could do it. I love you.

My children, my little sweets: Anasofia who at 11 years old you told me, "Mom, you *HAVE* to do this." Yes, my mini, you helped to make this happen more than you could even understand. To Mateo, my littlest of the littles, you are my viewing buddy who doesn't complain about my countless fantasy and medieval movie choices, watching along-side me wanting to learn more and more about medieval times – you helped keep me up on my knowledge. Thank you to you both my little loves. This is all for you . . . *My* Legacy.

William 'Bill' Fowlkes for being my friend, co-worker, and beta reader. For having devoted hours – yes, many countless hours, to this endeavor of mine.

Your talent in proofreading and beta-reading has proven invaluable. It was not an easy task. Okay, you don't have to say it, but I will: It was not an easy task – so thank you. Your help and feedback were wonderfully candid and precious. What would I have done without your support? I really cannot say.

My other co-workers and friends – I'm so thankful there are so many of you – I have always felt supported from the very beginning and for that I am beyond thankful. Special thanks to: Mark Saffell, Steven Wieckowski, Russ Shumshinov, and Mario Bueno for wonderful guidance on this. Co-workers: Hope C., Ken R. Dan N. and Kim B. - for helpful information, for always wondering about my progress, and encouraging me on. To my teammates at work: Chris Z., Gabe R., Michelle F., Maddie G., Rob E., Leslie B., Anne N., Kayla K., Ed S., Ryan H., Lauren S., and Victor R . . . for your support. Thank you all. You are the best teammates that a person could have.

My parents: I am truly fortunate to have grown up with four amazing parents. I can't imagine my life without you. You carved me, molded me, and helped to make me who I am today. I thank God daily for your wisdom and parenting – even now in my own adultness because I'm still being formed and molded. I still don't know everything. To my dad, Edwin Reyes, for having read my book and telling me "You've got something here – keep going, keep going . . ." Your words were quenching – teaching me always to use my imagination and the power of music. Thank you, from the depths of me. My mom, Elida Reyes, a devoted reader encouraging me to make a difference in the world around me. My dad, Juan Cantu and my mom, Brigida Cantu, for praying over me during this process and telling me that you will not read it until it comes out – YES! You know exactly what drives me – that challenge! I love the blend of the parenting over me. Thank you. My Siblings: Norman Alegre, Jessica and Gregorio Riojas, as well as, Rick and Ewa Malone– for your love and encouragement. For believing in me. Thank you. My plentiful families: I love each of you. Special thanks to: Aunt Pat Mitchel and Uncle Rene Flores for all the prayers.

To the people at Reedsy – The entire process. Seriously. There was wonderful support from the very beginning until the end. I ask so many questions. I imagine you started your meetings with a big problem-solving board that read "Today's topic: Maria- How to Solve???" The education, the tutorials, the professionals – you folks made this happen. I am thankful for all the wonderful things that you do - thankful for your team. Thank you. Thank you. Thank you.

To Dan Van Oss – Talented cover artist and designer: Thank you, not only for your genius and beautiful work, but also for your patience with me throughout this process. You're amazing – I mean, seriously. Hats off to you and to your awesome talent, good sir.

To my teachers. Yes. I am so thankful to have several of you in my life. Thank you for helping me identify this fire that resides in me and for teaching me the basics: the alphabet, sentence formation, spelling. Teachers - educators make the future, guide the future. Thank you: Ms. Lynn Campbell, Mrs. Patty Greenlees, and to Mrs. Kelly (Webster) Rice for my 2nd grade writing assignment that started *all* of this. It was about different ways that seeds can be spread in nature. I wrote of a fluffy dog with seeds stick to his fur. I had that 'A' graded paper on the fridge, forever. That writing project that started all of this - proof that sometimes teacher's 'seeds' take time to sprout. Thank you to my friend Mrs. Melissa R. Stevens for bringing us all together.

To my long-time friend and photographer Mrs. Gerri Milkovie – Thank you for the lovely picture, that eye for detail and the ability to identify beauty found in a mere split second. You are talented my dear friend.

To Amanda Rutter: You assisted me in the beginning stages of the editing process. With your help, I was able to construct a fine manuscript. Thank you for feedback.

To Heather Wallace for your wonderful advice and guidance on my marketing strategy and to Matthew Prodger my web site creator and designer. Thank you for the lovely website. I am so very fortunate to have had your help on that.

To my pastor for helping in the beginning of this process when I wasn't sure if I was focusing where I needed to focus. For helping me understand that this is a talent that I should be working at. Thank you.

To my readers: Thank you. I hope and pray that you were pleased. Your support and time have brought me here to this point. It's humbling. I promise you; I could not have done this without you. Thank you from the depths of me. I promise to write to my full potential for YOU. This is for YOU.

If you're working on your passion – don't you give up. Never give up. You are ageless-but don't wait. You are smart enough-but humble and open yourself to learn. You are tough enough-but don't be hard. Be relentless. Be bold. Be brave. You've got this. You *are* going to make this happen. Keep going!

To my Father – For Jeremiah 29:11-14

Dear Readers,

The first book in a series can be a little rough for the author, and this is because we are creating a new world, culture, places, and likely, unusual names. However, writing this book has been a wonderful learning experience that has allowed me to grow my skills as a writer and it brings me great joy to share this newly crafted world with you.

Now that you've had a chance to join Lanico on his quest, I would love for you to stop-by and provide a review on Amazon.com, to let me know your thoughts. You can follow me on: Instagram and Twitter. In addition, there is always my website: ecantualegre.com, to see the latest on upcoming books and updates.

There are books to follow, including: "Return of The Son" the sequel to this novel and "The Book of Treva: Emerald Knight" a prequel about the first knighted female soldier for Odana. Presently, this is planned to be a series of five novels! The fifth novel is still under construction. The Legacy of Lanico turned out to be a sizable legacy indeed!

From the bottom of my heart

Thank you

E Cantu Alegre

About me

I am a mother of two school-aged children. I work full-time in a fast paced and high demand position for a non-profit. I'm up at 3:50am, four times a week to hit the gym - because I try to stay fit like Treva. I obsess over my dream and my work as a writer, and aspire to be an efficacious author. I've learned that success doesn't happen with eight hours of sleep, or in a state of comfort – sorry, it just doesn't.

Inspiration

I honestly have always been inspired to write. I daydream frequently and during those times, I've usually invented some story in my mind – usually about two daily. The difference was that at some point in college, I started writing down some of these story ideas. They usually turned into short stories. It wasn't until the Legacy of Lanico, that a short story became an epic journey.

Facts

Writing almost daily, this particular novel took me two years <u>exactly</u>, to create. I wrote this to classical symphony music and Celtic/fantasy music. Like Lanico, my favorite color is emerald green – random but true. I have a mostly vegetarian diet.

Made in the USA
Coppell, TX
20 September 2020